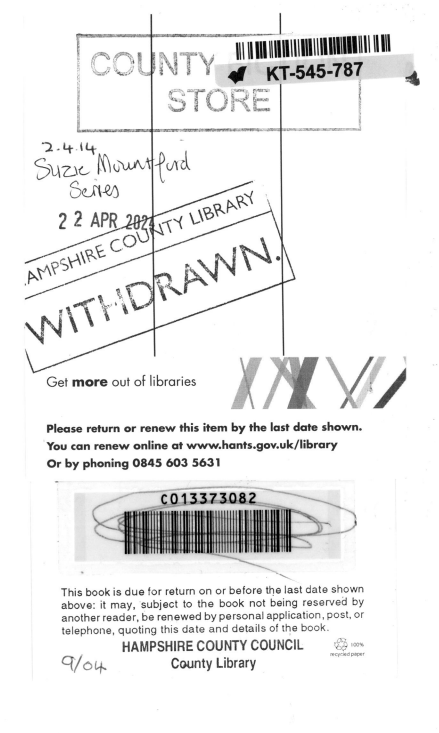

Get **more** out of libraries

Please return or renew this item by the last date shown.
You can renew online at www.hants.gov.uk/library
Or by phoning 0845 603 5631

This book is due for return on or before the last date shown
above: it may, subject to the book not being reserved by
another reader, be renewed by personal application, post, or
telephone, quoting this date and details of the book.

HAMPSHIRE COUNTY COUNCIL
County Library

100% recycled paper

9/04

THE STREETS OF TOWN

OTHER BOOKS BY JOHN GARDNER

James Bond Novels

Licence Renewed
For Special Services
Icebreaker
Role of Honour
Nobody Lives For Ever
No Deals, Mr Bond
Scorpius
Win, Lose or Die
Brokenclaw
The Man from Barbarossa
Death is For Ever
Never Send Flowers
SeaFire
Cold
Licence to Kill (from the screenplay)
Goldeneye (from the screenplay)

Suzie Mountford Books

Bottled Spider

The Boysie Oakes Books

The Liquidator
Understrike
Amber Nine
Madrigal
Founder Member
Traitor's Exit
Air Apparent
A Killer for a Song

Derek Torry Novels

A Complete State of Death
The Cornermen

The Moriarty Journals

The Return of Moriarty
The Revenge of Moriarty

The Kruger Novels

The Nostradamus Traitor
The Garden of Weapons
The Quiet Dogs
Maestro
Confessor

Novels

Golgotha
Flamingo
The Dancing Dodo
The Werewolf Trace
To Run a Little Faster
Every Night's a Bullfight
The Censor
Day of Absolution
Blood of the Fathers (writing as Edmund McCoy)

The Generations Trilogy

The Secret Generations
The Secret Houses
The Secret Families

Autobiography

Spin the Bottle

Collections of Short Stories

The Assassination File
Hideaway

For further details, please visit the author's website:
www.john-gardner.com

The Streets of Town

John Gardner

This first world edition published in Great Britain 2003 by
SEVERN HOUSE PUBLISHERS LTD of
9–15 High Street, Sutton, Surrey SM1 1DF.
This first world edition published in the USA 2003 by
SEVERN HOUSE PUBLISHERS INC of
595 Madison Avenue, New York, N.Y. 10022.

British Library Cataloguing in Publication Data

Gardner, John, 1926-
    The streets of town
    1. Women detectives - England - London - Fiction
    2. Detective and mystery stories
    I. Title
    823. 9'14 [F]

    ISBN 0-7278-5921-8

Typeset by Palimpsest Book Production Ltd.,
Polmont, Stirlingshire, Scotland.
Printed and bound in Great Britain by
MPG Books Ltd., Bodmin, Cornwall.

To my friend Allan Vousden,
with thanks for saving my bacon

Author's Note

I have tried to be accurate regarding the experience and language of those of us who lived through the 1940s during the Second World War. However, now, in this enlightened age, some are all too easily shocked by the callous attitudes of times gone by and seem offended when these views are reflected in a work of fiction set in the historical past. In this case I know that some will be amazed, even offended, not so much by the brutal horrors of war, but by the ideas and opinions of certain characters in this work: particularly regarding race and/or sexual preference.

I must make it clear that all attitudes concerning race, all jokes at the expense of race, and all remarks/jokes concerning sexual preferences of some minorities do not reflect views held by the author, but rather they are an accurate reflection of the general beliefs and mores of the time.

As in *Bottled Spider*, the first book starring Suzie Mountford, Camford is a fictitious area of London. West End Central Police Station does in fact exist. I have no idea who was stationed there during 1941, but those mentioned in this book are all figments of my imagination and are not meant to portray anyone living or dead.

John Gardner

The streets of town were paved with stars.
It was such a romantic affair,
And as we kiss'd and said 'goodnight',
A nightingale sang in Berk'ley Square.

Eric Maschwitz:
'A Nightingale Sang in Berkeley Square'

One

It happened suddenly: no warning. Early in the Blitz: Wednesday of the first week, which made it September 11th 1940. He had been taking a catnap, lying on his bed with no lights on, early evening, and the bombs woke him.

Immediately he knew that he was invulnerable. He could walk the streets and go where the bombs were falling and he couldn't be harmed. He had to go, for there was work for him to do.

He went out and wandered around, bombs falling near him, no fear in his heart or mind. They couldn't hurt him, so out in the fearsome night he discovered why he was there. The sky was dark crimson and the air howled and shrieked with the explosions. Fires threw heat into his face; he could taste the grit in the singed air and smell death and burning in the ruins. His obligation was to the dead. His job, he knew now, was to care for people killed in the bombing.

As he came to this realization, he stood in a circle of dust and wind, with his ears ringing and momentarily deaf from the bomb that fell close at hand, all but destroying two houses nearby. He clambered into the wreckage, smelling gas from the mains, a sandy cloud of debris clogging his nostrils, his eyes streaming. The house had been cut almost in two and the young woman – in her twenties he guessed – was lying among the rubble in what had been the front room. She had dark hair and a slight, trim figure. He took her out and through what had once been her little kitchen. As he went, so a white marker flare hung in the air above, illuminating the ruins in its dazzling glare. One wall leaned inwards above a plywood cupboard, its door swinging open, displaying for a moment a pack of Bisto, a jar of PanYan Pickle, a packet of Mitre

Margarine and a tin of Heinz Chicken Soup. He grabbed at the PanYan Pickle because he liked it; took it with him, still dragging the girl.

He pulled her out and began to move her through the tiny garden at the back, lugging her over the patch of grass, his hands underneath her soft armpits, the air around white with floating waste like snow. At the front of the houses, ARP people were already coming through the debris: he could hear them shouting to one another, then calling into the rubble, asking if there was anybody down there. He hauled her into the lane behind the houses, the flickering vermilion lighting up dustbins, a crabbed tree, a gate and a pram lying on its side. He heaved the girl into the pram and piled things on top of her, his coat and jacket. Her skirt rode up and he could see her underwear dark pink with a pathetic trim of thin lace.

With the flames jumping near at hand, he pushed her back to his place, got her down the cellar, switched on the light and pulled her on to the old mattress and blankets he had prepared. He'd intended to use the cellar as his private shelter but now he knew it would be shelter for her and her friends. As he straightened her on the mattress, lifted her shoulders, she seemed to open her mouth and give him a horrible roar, so that, frightened, he jumped back and stood trembling, watching her, wary of her as though she would rise up and attack him. Then he realized the roar had been air trapped in her stomach, released as he lifted the trunk of her body.

The girl was lovely, not a mark on her until the rigor, then the decomposition, set in. Until it was time to put her into the ground he would sit down there for hours of his free time. He would just look at her; undress her and wash her, then dress her again. He talked to her constantly but she never spoke to him, her friend. He knew he was helping her: doing a lot of good.

Eventually he buried her, there in the cellar; said a prayer, covered her up and knew she was there. Last of all he sang 'There'll always be an England'; seemed the right thing to do.

Every couple of weeks or so the longing came over him and he would walk out among the bombs raining down, the flame from the incendiaries, the terrible noise as the high explosives came whistling and the awful way they exploded and destroyed. He wasn't hurt once during the Blitz. It was obvious that this was good work: it was his bounden duty. So he did it.

He knew exactly where the desire came from. He had left school a few months shy of fourteen and was immediately given a job with the town's undertaker, J. B. Melling: J for Josiah and B for Bertram. The Mellings had been in the undertaking business for five generations and took a pride in always having a young lad working for them. In the old days he would have been the undertaker's mute, the boy who wore black mourning and walked at the head of the procession to the church and then to the grave, silent and with an air of gravitas. The job Oliver Twist had done in the Charles Dickens novel of the same name.

Mr Mellings had thrown him in at the deep end, and the older lads taught him about the habits of corpses, how the nails still grew and the hair as well, and how younger men often died with an erection – come to that, older men also. He had quickly become accustomed to the dead and in due course became attached to young women who had died, or been killed, before their time. He was at ease with them, even in his way loved them. That indeed was why he sought now to be with them when they were plentiful.

After the third one – a young girl, about sixteen – he thought: I'm a Ghoul, that's what I am, and he looked up the word in a dictionary and it told him a Ghoul was an evil spirit; a phantom associated with dead bodies; one who fed on corpses. In his way, he fed on corpses and he always knew there was something evil in his make-up. But he *was* clever.

He was a clever Ghoul.

By the end of 1940 he had taken as many as eight bodies – seven girls and one boy – down into his cellar. Now he had a permit to use his car, so he would drive around during a raid with an ARP sticker on the vehicle. He always got through without being mixed up with the real ARP people – except once when he had helped them move bricks and a beam off an old lady who had died in her house. He didn't tell the others that he had spotted a younger woman in the little garden round

3

the back. He got her later. Took her home. Talked to her and looked after her.

That was his contribution to the war effort.

In the spring of 1941 the bombs stopped falling regularly on London. But still, every two or three weeks the Ghoul would waken and go out, haunting the streets, looking for bodies. He always managed to find one and brought her back to the cellar. Ministered unto her. Sometimes he thought they weren't quite dead when he found them; sometimes they were only dead afterwards.

Summer came and he was forced to move, to live closer to the centre of London, but he kept on the old place and returned there regularly with his girls, and the occasional boy.

By the autumn he had taken twelve young women and two boys in all. By day and night he did his job and knew he was exceptional. It was only when the terrible yearning came over him that he was forced outside to prowl the dark streets in his obsessive search for the dead. They were always there, and he managed to take most of them back to his cellar where he looked after them in their final hours above ground.

The Ghoul was greatly moved by the way they would lie, calm and silent, as he said the prayers and sang 'There'll Always be an England'. Sometimes he was so moved that he wept and the tears ran down his cheeks as he sobbed and couldn't quite get the words out.

Then, by the next day it was over and he wouldn't be a Ghoul anymore; went back to his job with vigour.

Now there was autumn and then winter . . .

Two

Porky Pine shouldered his way up the almost empty pavement of Shaftesbury Avenue. 'Porky' because of his immense girth: people swore his stomach was solid lard, but in fact it was solid well-honed muscle. Porky would joke with the Twins, saying that in order to control people all he had to do was threaten to sit on their hands. In turn, the Twins equated Porky Pine with Porcupine, which translated into several unsavoury jokes using the quills of the animal as springboards to sexual *double entendre*. 'It is hard to kick against the pricks,' they would chant, blasphemously quoting Holy Writ.

It was a cold December Sunday and there was hardly anyone about in Shaftesbury Avenue as Porky charged along past theatreland in his bulldozing, unstoppable manner. There was a purpose to his rolling stride, relentless like that of an unleashed fat accident heading towards a prearranged disaster. The Twins had told him to 'have a serious word with that wop Falconetti', so Porky had gone straight to Falconetti's restaurant, Tosca in Charlotte Street, where an elderly crippled waiter told him that Carlo was 'up the Scout Hut', which he took to mean St Ursula's Scout Hut, the one blocking what had once been an unadopted alley running between Shaftesbury Avenue and Old Compton Street.

This hut, St Ursula's Hut, was the prime cause of the Twins telling Porky to have a serious word with Carlo Falconetti, and it should be remembered that in their parlance 'having a word' did not necessarily mean engaging in dialogue.

That afternoon the Twins had discovered Falconetti was about to open a club in what had been the Scout Hut – 'Got a booze licence and everything,' their informant told them over

5

the telephone, and Charlie Balvak went berserk. 'What you think we effing pay you for?' he shrieked. 'We effing pay you for effing infor-effing-mation. Top-quality effing intelligence. Where would this country be if you worked for effing Winston up effing Downing Street? The country wouldn't be effing nowhere. Action this effing day, that's what effing Winston would say.'

'What effing Winston would say,' echoed Conrad Balvak, the twin who had a tendency to repeat the final words of his brother's sentences. Tommy Livermore had pointed out to Suzie Mountford that this habit did not bode well regarding Connie's psychological stability. Some trick cyclist had told Tommy that repeating the last words of a person's sentences was a condition known as echolalia. 'Very bad,' the trick cyclist said. 'Shows a tendency to rely on the other person; shows inadequacy.' The trick cyclist's name was Colin Champion Chamberlain, so he had problems of his own. It was said that Chamberlain's father would have rather had a horse than a son.

The final straw came when Charlie, still talking to the informant, asked who had done the restoration on the Scout Hut – 'Who?' he cried. 'Who? The Trinity Building Co.? God in heaven. Connie, you hear that? The Eyetalian had our boys doing the place over. We've been subsiding his effing building programme, eff it.'

According to the Twins' way of thinking, this projected club of Falconetti's was going to be slap bang in the middle of their manor and thereby hung the entire configuration of their business. The Balvak Twins owned almost every club, knocking shop, spieler, dive and clip joint in Soho and its environs. One must understand of course that to *own* these places should not be taken literally. Owning didn't really mean that you held the mortgage, paid wages or could use the bricks and mortar as security for a loan. *Owning* usually had something to do with scooping up a large percentage of the weekly takings, or decreeing who could actually work where. This was why the Twins had sent their hard man, Porky Pine, in the direction of the Scout Hut. As they saw it, Falconetti was trying to muscle in on their territory. Incidentally one way or another they also *owned* pretty well every girl on the game in the same location, and this came to a tidy amount of money in used ready oncers. They thought of the girls as a financial speculation, so Porky was there to protect their investment.

They said of Charlie Balvak: Charlie never misses a thing.

Early evening was cobweb time, dusk, the gathering of darkness. Another three minutes or so and Woman Detective Sergeant Suzie Mountford would not have been able to see Porky Pine from the top of her Number 19 bus as it came blustering down from Cambridge Circus as the day turned dark – British Summertime all year round now; Double British Summertime through the Summer.

The windows of the buses were blacked out with paint but they had small elongated diamonds or rectangles scratched out in the centre so you could get a glimpse of the view during daylight. Inside, on the upper deck there would be a pinprick of blue light under which the 'clippie' would find it difficult to distinguish copper from silver.

Hello? Suzie wondered, squinting through the clear rectangle. Where's Porky off to in such a hurry? Porky was a 'face' in the area looked after by the nick they called West End Central and since she'd been moved there from the Reserve Squad she'd got to know all the 'faces' – Porky Pine, Iron-Foot Jack, Nosey, all of them like she'd got to know Two-Faced Golly Goldfinch, who'd caused her such grief last year.

Porky Pine was one of the Balvak Twins' hard men. She knew that as well because she had first come up against the Balvaks when she was posted to Camford nick last year. They were born and bred in Camford, the Twins, and they had ruled the area with rods of iron. They also ruled it with coshes, knuckle-dusters, knives and shooters. Well-feared the Balvak Twins were: a very dodgy couple, and now they had moved up in the world – out of Camford and into other parts of London – they spread their nasty little ways with the fervour of evangelical missionaries let loose in a heathen country.

Suzie was still thinking about Porky Pine when she got off the bus in the Dilly and walked up Regent Street, eventually turning left along New Burlington Street, clicking her way into Savile Row and up the steps of West End Central, which

7

was fully staffed and working overtime now. Last summer, 1940, it wasn't completed until July and people said it was finished just in time to be blown to buggery by Adolf. But it was still there.

Suzie said hello to the desk sergeant, who tipped her the wink about the Chief Super being in the main CID office. The uniformed Chief Super was in command of West End Central. She could hear him now as she approached the office's open door, talking in the basso profundo that was his trademark. 'So there you go, lads. A new officer to swell your ranks and keep you all on the straight and narrow: another pair of hands and another brain.' He had difficulty with his Rs, so 'ranks' came out as 'wanks', 'straight and narrow' was 'stwait and nawow', and 'brain' was 'bwain'. Nobody laughed because that would have been a cheap crack and they rather liked Chief Superintendent Farquar. Behind his back they called him Fawquaw.

Then Suzie heard the new officer's voice.

It was a voice she knew well. The voice said it was nice to be here at West End Central, and he knew they'd all get on like the proverbial flaming dwelling place.

Suzie Mountford stopped breathing for a second; felt her heart thud and her stomach turn over, for the voice belonged to Detective Chief Inspector Tony – Big Toe – Harvey.

He had arrived, just as Dandy Tom had promised her six or seven weeks ago.

Dandy Tom, as the newspapers liked to call him, was Detective Chief Superintendent Tommy Livermore (the Honourable DCS Thomas Livermore if you must, reluctant heir to the Kingscote millions, not to mention a fair slice of land and a large number of buildings in the country, and also here in London, plus the title of course).

Tommy Livermore was the officer in charge of the Reserve Squad, which had its offices on the fourth floor of New Scotland Yard, that elaborate red and white brick building designed by Norman Shaw and erected in 1890 on Victoria Embankment in all its gothic glory of false gables, turrets, crenellations and dormers.

The Reserve Squad hid a multitude of sins: a group of

specialist police officers who were sent out to investigate particular selected crimes as and when they were required. Whenever Fleet Street or Broadcasting House spoke of Scotland Yard being called in on a case, the officers came from Dandy Tom's Reserve Squad, who were sometimes, wrongly, referred to as the Murder Squad. The Reserve Squad was never properly explained either to the press or the general public.

Even more important from some points of view, Tommy Livermore was also Suzie Mountford's first ever lover – her unofficial fiancé because they had yet to announce the engagement. This last was a tiny bone of contention.

When Suzie had returned to work at the beginning of 1941 she had half expected to read the announcement of their engagement in *The Times*, but on reflection she knew this to be a vain hope, for she had yet even to meet his parents, the Earl and Countess of Kingscote. Just as she had yet to visit the ancestral home, Kingscote Grange, as yet to take a peep at the deer in Kingscote Park or the sheep and pigs littered around the Home Farm.

As they got deeper into the year, so the engagement remained under wraps, and in the end she was forced to bring the matter up. She did this one Sunday morning as they lay in bed together in her *pied-à-terre* halfway along Upper St Martin's Lane. The flat really belonged to her mother but she had lived there for so long that she regarded it as her own. In fact Suzie often wondered if her mother had ever told the Galloping Major – as she called her stepfather – about the flat's true provenance, for she suspected her mother had hidden even its existence against a day when she might have to escape from her second husband, Major Ross Gordon hyphen Lowe DSO, the aforesaid Galloping Major.

'Tommy . . . ?' she began, thinking: Lawks, I sound like a gold-digging vamp.

'Ye-es?' Suspicious.

'Tom, when're we going to get the banns read, announce our betrothal and all that?'

His eyes moved, then he hitched himself up on to one elbow so that his face hovered directly above hers. 'Marry you tomorrow, heart, if that's what you really want. You know that.' He was constantly telling her that he loved her; enumerating all the particular parts of her that he especially loved, down to the very last detail.

It was a continual source of wonder to Suzie that out of all the eligible jumpers-pearls-and-sensible-shoes girls on offer, Tommy had chosen her and fallen head over heels (or base over apex as he would have said) in love with her. And she with him.

'Really, Tommy?'

'Really, heart. Truly.' Raising a quizzical eyebrow, running a finger down her cheek, smiling at her: the smile that blew her heart out. 'Haven't mentioned it recently because I thought you wanted to carve out this career in the Met.'

Quite late in the day, Suzie had discovered her temporary rank and appointment to plain-clothes work had really been the result of a scheme in which Detective Chief Superintendent Livermore was more than negligibly involved.

'Yes.' Throaty and breathless.

'Announce it tomorrow, heart, and by Tuesday morning they'll have you out of here. Lands End or John of thing . . .'

'. . . Groats.'

'They just won't let us go on working together. Move us to different ends of the planet.'

'No?' She knew he was right; had known it and gone along with it from the start. Other people in the Reserve Squad might have their suspicions but it was unlikely they'd gossip. Very loyal, the Squad. The only one who really knew anything for certain was Brian, Tommy Livermore's driver, and he had been brought in to the Met especially. 'Almost one of the family, Brian,' Tommy would say.

'If we announce the engagement, they'll shift us.' Now he moved his elbow slightly. 'Split us up. I know. I know what they do to people who want to get married. Not good for discipline they reckon, people in love working in close proximity, not perfect for good order and discipline. Balls, my view of course; but we can't argue.' His mouth relaxed and the smile went like a light going out in his grey green-flecked eyes. 'Heart, I'm absolutely serious about this.'

She knew he was serious and remembered how he had rarely

10

allowed himself to be seen with her out of the office. They didn't exactly skulk around but they were careful. 'I've told you, heart: when you're ready to get married we'll do it. I wouldn't play around with you.'

Of course he wouldn't.

They batted the problem back and forth for around an hour and Suzie couldn't bear the thought of being forced to leave the Squad, which meant being separated from Dandy Tom. Eventually it would have to happen but for now she was so in thrall to him that she couldn't face it.

Eventually on that Sunday morning they made love again, and Tommy like the good lover he was took great care because they didn't want to court disaster with pregnancy. Oh, but she adored it and life went on as usual, except that she was sent off to do the detective course in Regency Street and in the summer she sat the sergeant's exam and passed: so she was no longer a temporary WDS. Through the whole of that period she would return to the flat in Upper St Martin's Lane and nine nights out of ten Tommy would be there or he would arrive later, using a lot of stealth and cunning.

In July a great wedge of the team went north, to Harrogate where there was a double murder. Then about seven weeks before the early cold December Sunday when she saw Porky Pine in Shaftesbury Avenue, Tommy sat her down at her own kitchen table – a Saturday evening this was, when he had scrounged a joint of beef from the Home Farm adjacent to Kingscote Grange and she was cooking it slowly and had the potatoes roasting, carrots and swedes cooking, and parsnips, and some really good horseradish that she'd got from her mum in Newbury.

He cleared his throat in the way he had when something important was about to happen and she immediately focused her attention on him.

At first she thought it was going to be something dreadful: he couldn't marry her after all, or he was leaving the Met to go and fight the war in his father's old regiment. But it was something else entirely.

'Remember the Balvak Twins, heart? Remember them from Camford?'

'Of course.'

Of course she remembered them. She only saw them once in the short time she had been in Camford, but she knew they ran all the crime there and elsewhere, and she'd seen some of the results: Charlie and Connie Balvak: evil flashy little men who could – as she knew from their files and the word around the nick – be very dangerous. Camford's heart of darkness.

When in Camford she'd listened to the stories – 'We own the streets of this town, and don't you forget it, lad,' Charlie Balvak had said to a detective constable who had flouted the unspoken rule and gone down to their public house – the Duke of Wellington – to question them.

She would never forget the one time she had seen them, on the night the Luftwaffe had bombed the railway marshalling yard that was the reason for Camford being where it was. The yard was ablaze, crimson flames dancing against the thick black smoky sky and the two little men, flash in camel-hair coats.

'*Look at all that damage and destruction, Connie.*'

'*All them flames. A lot of people're going to need help after this. Some won't be able to meet their debts.*'

'*The flames, Connie.*'

'*All the colours of the rectum, Charlie.*'

'They've come up in the world, heart, Charlie and Connie,' Tommy said behind the memory spooling like a bit of film in her head. 'Nowadays they run most of the illegal endeavours on our side of the river: certainly everything illegal in Soho and Westminster.'

She had heard rumours, seen scraps of information.

'So, I now hear they're even living in the West End. In the purlieu – if that's the right word – of West End Central.'

She waited, still wondering what was coming next.

'And guess who's been clamouring to be sent to West End Central for over a year now? Guess who's been writing letters saying he really fancied the change; making little phone calls to old friends asking them to put his name forward? None other than an old oppo of yours – Big Toe Harvey.'

'What's an oppo?'

'Opposite number . . . friend . . . mate . . . mucker.'

'Big Toe was never a mate. Come to that he was never an opposite number, nor was he a friend, mate nor mucker.'

How do you make a good cup of tea?

That was the first question Big Toe Harvey ever asked her and almost her entire experience of him was of a man who regarded women as highly inferior beings. The Met, to Big Toe, was wholly male dominated. Women were not welcome and only just tolerated as girls to do the typing, filing, get the tea and coffee and even go out to do the DCI's shopping once in a while. When Suzie had been briefly in charge of a murder investigation – after Harvey had been injured in the Blitz – there had been almost an outcry. National newspapers had castigated the Met for allowing a woman to take over a murder case – which they hadn't. Probing into a particularly unpleasant killing was not appropriate work for a female, who was at her best in the kitchen or pregnant.

Women are unlikely to get permission to drive in this nick. I hold a firm belief that women drivers all have two left arms and three left feet.

Suzie could still hear him saying that when he took her out to see a couple of girls whom the Twins had punished, putting them in hospital.

She really only served under DCI Harvey for a handful of weeks but in that time she formed a definite opinion of him. Suzie remembered clearly that on the first time she was really alone with Tommy Livermore she told *him* exactly what she thought of Tony Harvey.

He could be bent, sir. I shouldn't have said that, Guv. I couldn't prove it in a month of Sundays.

She had regretted saying it, but it was what she felt and by the time she moved up to the Reserve Squad under Dandy Tom's aegis she knew that Big Toe was bent as a butcher's hook – as the saying went. More, he was almost certainly in the pay of the Balvak Twins: their own personal copper.

'You see, heart.' Tommy wasn't looking at her, something dangerous coming up. 'You see, we've granted his wish. Harvey is to be moved to West End Central in a few weeks time; which is why you're going there this coming week. You'll get your chance, Suzie, your going in to nail him and prove his connection to the Balvaks. Going in to do the work of the Rubber Heels.'

She asked what the Rubber Heels were, when they were at home.

'The Rubber Heels, heart, are the police investigation department. The police that police the police. The shepherds who shepherd the shepherds,' and because that sounded good and tripped off his tongue he repeated it. Then, 'Savvy?' he asked. 'Savvy or no savvy?'

'Oh, savvy, Tommy.' Savvy in spades, Dandy Tom, she thought. Then realized that she was not going to see as much of Tommy as she would like.

'Don't worry, heart. I'll be around. When you come home late and weary I'll be here with a square meal on the table, the flat clean as a new penny, the laundry done and ironed.'

'Who else is involved?' like a small frightened girl.

'The two of us, the Commander (Crime) and the Head of A4.' A4 was the Department that dealt with the women police. 'You'll be working under my old friend Detective Chief Superintendent Sammy Battescombe, and we're not telling him anything. Nobody else is going to have the slightest idea why you're suddenly moved out of the Yard and into West End Central. Some might suspect, but nobody's going to know for sure.'

'But how . . . ?' she began.

'We have a public row. The door to my office partly open and we'll spread a bit of unhappiness for a couple of days previous. Know what I mean?'

'And I storm out?'

'No, I chuck you out, then I'll seal up the holes.'

She opened her mouth to protest, but he lifted a hand as though he was stopping traffic. 'As I've said, some of them might have their suspicions but none of them'll know for sure.'

'Except Brian.'

'As you say, heart, except Brian. Leave Brian to me.' There was a long pause before he asked her – belatedly, she thought in retrospect – if she felt up to doing the job. 'Tell me now, heart, because within half an hour it'll be too late.'

'I'm going to West End Central to keep an eye on the Balvak Twins *and* DCI Harvey?'

'And you do whatever Chief Superintendent Battescombe tells you to do, and on top of it all,' the raised quizzical eyebrow, Tommy's comic turn, '– on top of it all, you collude with me in setting up a cast-iron case against Big Toe Harvey and the Twins.'

'And in my spare time I try to single-handedly defeat Adolf Hitler.'

'That would be quite handy, heart, but you may not have much spare time.'

For the rest of that weekend Tommy Livermore coached her in emergency procedures: telephone numbers and one-word codes that would alert him should she get into difficulties or require a crash meeting. Then they started to work up the row they would stage for the consumption of their remaining colleagues.

As Tommy went through all the details – stuff about DCS Sammy Battescombe, the way things worked at West End Central, the fact that she should treat the whole business as though she were going into enemy territory – she realized that for the first time since she had met him, she would really be away from Tommy Livermore. A few days after she first worked for him she had behaved like a wanton, and nervously declared that she loved him. Unbelievably, he had responded and since then there had been times – terrible times of horror, pain and tumult; also times of huge happiness, with her crossing the line into womanhood, and the confidence which came with that and her growing attachment to Tommy. 'Welded at the hip,' he'd said. 'Siamese Twins, joined hip and thigh.'

'Bit difficult, that.' She gave him a cheeky grin. 'Restrict our movements, hip and thigh.'

He had become all the things she'd really needed: lover, friend, the father who'd been missing since he had been killed in the road close to the gates to his house near Newbury. With the job, Tommy had become her life, but it was still a secret life because, as he said, 'Can't tell the troops till I've broken it to the Ma and Pa.'

Now, though he swore he'd always be within reach, and that he'd see her most evenings, she felt scared, afraid about what life on the job of being a policewoman would be like without Dandy Tom to guide her.

Tommy suggested that their set-to should come to fruition after a very small beginning. 'Divorces arrive because of some tiny irritation left to fester.' He also said their row should have a basis in fact.

'But I don't irritate you, Tommy.'

'Oh no?'

'And you don't irritate . . . What?'

'You said you didn't irritate me.'

'Well, I don't . . . Do I?'

'I am well known for my patience, heart. Patience of a saint. Born with it. Noted for it.'

'Do I irritate you?'

'Far be it from me to nag, but . . .'

'But what?'

'I wasn't going to mention it until after the nuptials, heart, but yes there is one tiny thing.'

'Irritates you?'

He nodded. 'Truth is it gets on my Hampton – as they say.'

'What does?' Mildly outraged.

'You fiddle, heart. You fiddle, you faddle, you fart about rearranging things – the objects on the mantle, straightening the pictures, moving things on my desk: putting papers into neat piles, repositioning that little model artillery piece I use as a paperweight and the little guillotine I got at the Paris Exhibition in '37 . . .'

'I think that guillotine is in rather bad taste actually, Tommy.'

'Bad taste my lights and liver. It was the only decent thing at the damned Exhibition. You see it, heart?'

'No.'

'The British exhibit was nothing but huntin', shootin' and fishin'.'

'You really and truly find it irritating if I tidy up after you?'

He gave her both barrels of his most charming smile. Blew

her over with it, made her head reel, all but shot her straight out of her pants, which of course was one of Tommy's tactical objectives when he used *that* smile. 'Well,' he drew the word out making the double-L into a long sustained note. 'Well, no actually, not yet. But give it time, heart and it'll send me dotty. My view.'

'Oh.' For the wings of a dove, she could have added, 'I'm sorry. You were going to tell me though?'

'Eventually. In about a hundred years or so.' He grinned his schoolboy version of the knock-out smile.

'Ah,' she said, then reached forward and kissed him.

Ultimately they got around to rehearsing. Worked out some good lines. 'You should be on the stage,' Dandy Tom told her, and she preened.

They did their big performance on Wednesday afternoon: a matinee around three o'clock. On the Monday and Tuesday they did what Tommy called 'straws in the wind'. Tiny spats, little explosions of bad temper and acts of frustration: 'Oh, Susannah, stop following me around and tidying up. You're like Mary's bloody little lamb.'

Then on the Wednesday everything appeared to come to a head. They stood inside his office, the door part open, and began low key, then went into the dialogue they had worked out rising to anger and finally –

'Susannah, this cannot go on,' he shouted, banging his desk. 'You're constantly interfering and getting in my way. I can't have you working here any longer.'

'But I—'

'But nothing. Susannah, I really think it would be better if you went out there and learned some proper policing in the real world. This is quite ridiculous! Following me about with a dustpan and brush. You're like Mrs Mopp. 'Can I do you now, sir? Out!'

'I suppose you want teacher's pet in here: Molly Abelard. You'll put up with her doing anything.'

'Enough . . . Enough of this.' Punctuating the enoughs with blows from his fist on to the desk top, so hard that Billy Mulligan, his sergeant, standing in the conference room, flinched. He had never heard Tommy so angry.

'Sir, I've never—!'

'Never is right. You don't seem to have grasped the first thing about—'

'I resent that, sir! I resent your attitude regarding—!'

'Well resent away! Far away! Get out! Get out! Go home and stay by your telephone. I'm going to have you moved. You're no longer with the Squad, Susannah. Now go, it's time you learned some real policing in the real world.' He was so good that she felt the singe of his anger and blundered out of his office in tears.

Molly Abelard standing in the conference room with some of the lads, reached out to her as she lurched past, shaking her head and sobbing. But she shook Molly off and lunged for the door.

'Should give you some kind of award, heart,' Tommy told her later when he arrived, by night and stealth, at the flat.

'You were damned convincing.' Snuggling up to him as though trying to persuade herself that it *had* really just been an act.

'It'll be everywhere by now,' he grinned. 'Good girl. Tomorrow the A4 Super's going to telephone you. Sammy Battescombe's agreed to take you at Central.'

'Does he know why?'

'Personality clash. That's what everyone believes. It's happened before, heart.' This time it was a wry smile: almost a rueful shake of the head in shame. She knew that some people found Dandy Tom difficult, and he acknowledged that there were members of the Met's hierarchy he just couldn't work with. 'Not difficult,' he muttered now. 'What you have to do, heart, is go along with what Sammy tells you to do. Do your job, get the lie of the land down at West End Central, keep an eye on the Twins and wait for Big Toe to show up.'

Which is exactly what she did; and now, six weeks or so later – after twenty-five burglaries, ten robberies, seven arrests for importuning, several drunks and fifteen GBHs – Big Toe Harvey was here.

He was now.

She walked on, towards the door, and was almost knocked over by the Chief Super on his way out looking confused to see her – 'Oh, Sarn't Mountford. Old friend of yours, I believe.'

The lads were grouped around DCS Battescombe and there was DCI Harvey, his back to the door.

'Evening, Guv,' she said to his back, and he turned.

'Well, I'm damned,' said Big Toe. 'It's old home week. Suzie Mountford as I live and breath.'

'Hello, Guv.' I've even got the gall to greet him with a smile, she thought. 'How goes it, sir? I haven't seen you since the Blitz of Camford, the night Jerry parted your hair for you.'

The smile on Anthony Harvey's lips flickered, but didn't completely fade. 'Well, it's nice to see you again, Sergeant Mountford. The real thing now, is it? I tried to see you when it all . . .'

'Yes, I know, sir.'

'Mr Livermore wouldn't let me come down.' His eyes stayed on her face. It was like having a burning glass focused on your forehead, she thought.

'No, Mr Livermore's like that sometimes.'

Harvey nodded and there was a kind of relaxation among the lads on duty who'd been paying attention to the new DCI. 'Not working for Mr Livermore anymore then, Susannah?'

Sammy Battescombe, on Harvey's right, coughed and looked down at his feet.

She had told Harvey that was her real name – Susannah – and that her mother only called her by it when she was cross: told him that on her first day at Camford nick. In the short time she'd worked with Big Toe he had continuously used the name to put her on edge.

'Not any more, Guv, no. He said that I should get out into the real world and do some proper policing.'

Big Toe smiled again. Then he nodded. 'Dandy Tom can be a shade rarefied they tell me.'

'Need an oxygen mask most days, Guv'nor.' I'm going to get you, you bastard, she thought, you chauvinist bullyboy, you prosser. She smiled into his face, all chums together.

And when I get you I'm going to cut off your ears and present them to my lovely Dandy Tom, she thought, and smiled.

Big Toe smiled back.

19

Three

C arlo Falconetti was proud to be British. 'They call me a wop, a wog or an Eyetie whenever they like,' he'd say. 'Is water off a duck's back. I'm British and have the paper to prove it.' Privately, he would admit that he was very lucky because he'd got his citizenship just in time – July 1939. 'Water off a duck's back, eh? We British have a saying for all things.'

During the summer of 1940, his native Italy had stood to one side, watching the collapse of Holland, Luxembourg, Belgium and France under the weight of Hitler's leapfrogging armies. Then when they were overrun, and the British had been hurled back to their island fastness like whipped dogs, Mussolini declared war.

Funny what you remember, Carlo thought. The week after Mussolini stabbed Britain in the back, one of the newspapers had an editorial headed 'ENTER THE SECOND MURDERER'.

Sure, once Italy declared war, Carlo, like everyone of foreign birth, was forced to appear before a tribunal, where he was categorized Class C and allowed to carry on his business. But Class C aliens were still restricted: they had to conform to a curfew and were not allowed to own motor cars, bicycles or maps, and they were banned from travelling outside a thirty-mile radius of London. Most of the Class C aliens had lived in the country for twenty years but few had applied for citizenship.

When he received written notice of these constraints Carlo marched straight back to the tribunal and showed them his papers of citizenship. The restrictions were lifted immediately. Uncle Pasquale was right, for it was Uncle Pasquale who had advised Signora Falconetti to start applying for citizenship as soon as they settled in London. 'Lot of people aren't doing this,' Pasquale said, nodding and holding up his right forefinger. 'One day they gonna regret not having papers. The braggart Mussolini, he'll a causa trouble.' And he was right. Musso did causa trouble. Signora Falconetti used to say, 'Your Uncle Pasquale has a wise finger, Carlo.' He never quite worked out what that meant but he knew she was right.

Now he stood just inside the main door of what had been St Ursula's Scout Hut and thought just how fortunate he had been. In spite of the Blitz and deprivations and everything, his restaurant, Tosca, was a going concern, and he had been shrewd to buy the Scout Hut from Father Keogh, the Parish Priest of St Ursula's, who in turn had introduced him to a member of the church council, Bruce Dulcimer, who was on the planning committee of Westminster Council. So Carlo had got permission to convert the hut into the club he was going to call Ursula's Place. Father Keogh didn't mind that either because, as he said, the hut had been more bother than it was worth. Bruce Dulcimer had helped him get the alcohol licence as well, and not a hint of dropsy. Carlo had picked up London slang fast as Whip-it-Quick – the *ITMA* character.

He'd been lucky with the three lads who'd done all the work: Dave, Dick and Derek: they called themselves the Trinity Building Co., yet Carlo had never seen a printed letterhead and their work telephone number kept changing. But they'd done the work, torn out the interior, put in new walls and ceilings, new partitions and doors; laid a splendid new floor suitable for dancing, and a half circle of stage for the band or a cabaret. They'd also fitted up the kitchens, knew how to connect the hobs and ovens; completely rewired the electrics, including the fancy sconce-like brackets for lighting; and finally they had decorated the place to Carlo's specification. Better still, they got the paint and the very high quality wallpaper at cost: money in hand, no questions asked.

Carlo Falconetti had his suspicions about the whole thing but kept them to himself: after all he was taking a big enough risk and they worked all hours and didn't grumble even when the bombs were falling all around them.

He stood now looking at the main room, feeling very proud of himself.

Then he heard the noise coming from the direction of the kitchens and the office they had built right at the back. Damn, must have left the back door unlocked, he thought and took a pace towards the swing doors between the bar and the half-circular stage. As he did so, the doors opened and this big heavily-built man came through.

Smiling.

'Signor Carlo Falconetti?' he asked.

'I thought I'd locked the back door.'

'Oh you did, squire. I have this knack, see. Locks surrender when I look at them.'

'Then I'd better go and lock it again, eh?'

'That would be the right thing for you to do, squire.' He stood to one side and allowed Carlo to walk slowly back through the kitchens and the office, where he not only locked the door but set the dead bolts.

The big man was still waiting patiently in the club when he returned.

'Okay. How can I help you?' Carlo looked straight into the man's eyes and didn't like what he saw.

'Wrong question, chum. How can I help *you*?' He stuck out his hand, holding it in front of his body, palm flat, thumb cocked backwards. Carlo looked at the hand and, finally, reluctantly shook it.

The smile broadened. 'Good. The name's Pine. Friends call me Porky. Porky Pine on account of the weight I carry and the injury I can inflict.'

'I think you better blow while we're still friends, Porky.'

'Wrong again, Charlie. That's your name in the mother tongue innit? Carlo? Charlie?'

Carlo shrugged and began to walk past Porky, moving towards the door.

'How's your insurance, Charlie? Who's covering this place against theft, fire, flood, Act of God, Act of War? Who's your broker?'

This prodded a sensitive nerve in Carlo. He had a general policy on the building, but the flood and fire clauses excluded bomb damage, and there was no cover for an Act of War. Indeed the policy contained a special clause that eliminated anything to do with war. It was near impossible to get insurance to cover the probability of war damage or even death by enemy action. 'Why?' he asked, deadpan. 'You come here to sell me insurance?'

'Right on the bullseye, Charlie. Slap on the target for tonight.'

'You got some kinda policy? You want to show me?'

At Christmas time Carlo had fallen into the British habit of going to a pantomime or Christmas show. The one he liked best was *Peter Pan*. He had always liked *Peter Pan*, especially the part where Captain Hook got attacked and eaten by the crocodile. He'd liked that since he'd first seen it soon after he arrived in England. He found the crocodile very funny. But now he saw that the smile splitting Porky Pine's face was very like the crocodile's grin in *Peter Pan*.

'It's very simple.' Pine spread his hands apart as though he was about to embrace Carlo. 'For a cut of the take in this place the Twins'll guarantee you'll come to no physical harm. On a personal basis, naturally. They'll also guarantee to cover the fabric and contents of the club against any damage, except of course Act of War, like bomb damage. Say twenty-five per cent of the weekly take. Payable on a Saturday evening. How's that sound?'

'The Twins?' Carlo asked. 'Which Twins are these? The Tweedle Twins? Tweedle Dum and Tweedle Dee? The Tweedledum Twins? The Twenty-three Skidoo Twins? Which Twins we talking about, eh?'

Porky Pine's smile reached up to his eyes, and the eyes reflected the compassion of ice. In fact ice probably would have shown a shade more compassion than Porky's eyes. 'You don't know the Balvak Twins, then? You haven't heard of Charlie and Connie Balvak? Charlie being your namesake and all. Shame that. Can hardly believe it that you've never heard of them.'

Of course Carlo had heard of the Balvaks. If the truth was told he had been expecting someone to turn up at Tosca making him some kind of offer. Anyone who owned anything in the area said the same thing – *If Charlie or Connie Balvak come calling give them exactly what they ask for: no more no less. Don't fuck with the Twins. Ever.*

'No, can't say I've heard of them, these, what was it? Balvaks?'

'Well Charlie, I'd say that was possibly your loss – not ever hearing of them.' Pause during which he sucked his teeth and shook his head sadly. 'You see, Charlie, this insurance policy they're offering you . . . well, it's a one-time offer. Unrepeatable. And if you don't take it up they might not be able to help you in any way. I'd be a shade worried by that. Won't you give it some thought?'

'No thought needed.'

'If you have an accident, or this place burns down – not on account of the *Luftwaffe*, mind – I doubt if they could do anything. And if anything happens to you . . . They would have to think their terms over again. Could cost a lot more, Charlie. Cost a great deal more. Goodnight, Charlie.' He nodded, manoeuvring himself towards the door leading into the small closed-off entrance hall: one heavy door in, leading to the double doors at the front of the building. Now he looked Carlo in the eyes, unblinking, still smiling. His hand came out again, palm open, fingers slightly curved, and, without a thought, Carlo Falconetti, glad to see him leave, reached out automatically to shake the proffered hand.

Only much later did Carlo realize what happened. Here and now it was blindingly fast.

Porky's fingers reached higher than the palm, reached for the wrist and locked like a steel bracelet while the other hand came across and grabbed the first two fingers of Carlo's right hand.

It was a kind of gentle tug settling the fingers straight across the jamb of the door. In the same moment Porky Pine's shoulder caught the door itself smashing it closed with great force. One hand came away while the other still tugged on the fingers as the door crushed it against the jamb.

He heard the bones crack in the fingers and felt the jolt of blinding hurt, like an electric shock, sweep from the fingers across his hand, then down again as though the world's pain had settled in his fore and middle fingers.

Carlo heard himself scream as he jerked his hand back, cradling it with his left hand and doubling over with the concentrated agony.

'Carlo! Be careful. You want to watch that. Nothing worse than broken fingers. If it happens to both hands you have real difficulty dressing yourself. And you need embarrassing help to pee. Take care, Charlie. Take care.'

And he was gone as Carlo still howled.

Police Constable 461 Colin Preece passed on the news about Carlo Falconetti to the desk sergeant, 'Darkie' Knight. 'Broken fingers, eh?' Darkie muttered.

'In shock, I reckon.' Preece was a tall thin lad, very grave in all his deliberations. 'I went with him to the Middlesex and they X-rayed his hand – two fingers broken, compound fracture, they said.'

'And you saw Porky Pine just before?'

'Walking up Old Compton Street. Fast almost running, but not quite.'

Sergeant Knight knew that one of Porky Pine's favourite targets was hands and fingers. Suzie had mentioned seeing Porky crunching his way up Shaftesbury Avenue and he reckoned this might be a good lead. 'Go and tell WDS Mountford,' he told PC Preece. 'Then help her any way you can.'

Before this, Suzie had been going through the beat coppers' reports for the Saturday night: an attempted break-in at a chemist in Poland Street; three men causing a disturbance in Great Marlborough Street; three solicitings; a pair of drunk and disorderly; and a lewd behaviour with a flasher thrown in. No good at West End Central if you blushed easily.

'Well, Suzie, how're you doing?' Big Toe Harvey stood in front of her desk. He stood with the light behind him so that his face was in shadow when she looked up.

'Sit down, Guv,' she motioned him into a chair.

'It's good to see you again. How *are* you doing?' he repeated, with emphasis. 'And how are all your friends and

25

colleagues? Dandy Tom still got that girl Abelard trotting around after him?'

'Molly's still with him, yes.'

'And the other girl? The one who was at Camford. Cox?

'Shirley Cox. Yes, she's in the Reserve Squad.'

'What was that all about, Suzie? Out of the blue, Tommy had her switched on to the Squad.' He had settled himself comfortably in the chair, relaxed as though he was going to be there for a while.

'You know Dandy Tom, Guv. Built up his own private army. Name of his game. Takes a fancy to someone's talent, picks them up . . .'

'. . . and drops them. Yes. What particular talents did Shirley Cox have? I never recognized any specific gift in her. A run-of-the-mill WDC. Not very bright. What I thought.'

'Maybe he wanted someone to keep me company, Guv.' Indeed, she had asked Tommy to bring Shirley into the Squad and he did her a favour. They had been together when they first caught sight of Tommy Livermore striding into the ornate hall of a building that housed service flats with his little private army around him.

Orchestra, dancing girls, the lot, she had muttered.

And a male voice choir, Shirley Cox replied, her mouth hanging open.

'And why did he choose you, Susannah? You weren't trained for anything. Just an acting temporary WDS with no training. Tommy's known for picking people with certain skills.'

'You must know why he picked me.'

'Must I? I never knew why they foisted you on me in the first place. Mystery that was. Very leery of you I was. Never figured it out.'

'I think you know why he chose me, Guv. He wanted to use me as bait. I think he had the whole thing worked out. And it went wrong.' She was referring back to the murder of the BBC announcer, Jo Benton. The murder she was investigating when Tommy Livermore came on to the scene. She knew well enough what Dandy Tom's real reason was, just as she knew that Big Toe Harvey was at this moment quietly pumping her,

26

trying to fill in information about the Reserve Squad. Intent on getting her to trust him – which she'd never do: not in a month of Sundays, as her mum would say.

'You know there was a story going round that you and Tommy had more than just a working relationship?' Harvey had a nasty smirk playing around his mouth.

'I hadn't heard that, Guv. But all sorts of stupid stories go around.' She counted to three, slowly in her head. 'Actually we did have more than a normal relationship. Mr Livermore took a special interest in me: he gave me some good on-the-job training, pushed me along to take the Sergeant's Exam; went through a lot of the detective course stuff. He was very good.'

'Until he told you to sling your hook, eh?'

'Tommy's touchy about some things. Maybe I got a bit cheeky; took liberties. He likes you to know who's boss; and likes everyone to know. *Pour encourager les autres.*'

'And you've got that sorted now, have you Susannah?'

'I think so, sir. Yes.'

And that was when Sammy Battescombe came waltzing into the CID office and called to Harvey across the room.

'Ah,' Big Toe lowered his voice. 'Talk to you again soon, Sue. I've got to go on a familiarization jaunt with the boss. Lived in London all my life and I've got to be taken round pubs and cafes and whatnots like someone up from the sticks.'

'Old chums, eh? What?' Sammy Battescombe had come over and started to talk before he reached Suzie's desk. 'Good to have people who've worked together before. One of the Met's strengths, I always think. Like one great big family.' The DCS in charge of the CID at West End Central played the old buffer, not quite up to the job. He had thinning snow-white hair and a red face with a blue-veined nose, like a boozer, Suzie always thought; and a trim little moustache that reminded her of her stepfather: the Galloping Major.

Sammy Battescombe liked playing the role of a dim old senior copper, just past it, harmless and friendly, but it didn't fool Suzie because Tommy had already primed her.

'He's about as dim as a searchlight, harmless as a rattlesnake, and friendly as bear,' he'd told her. 'And he's a bloody good

policeman. Don't you ever forget it. If he rumbles you he'll find a way of letting you know.'

'Over at the Yard on Friday,' Battescombe said, looking directly at Suzie. 'Saw your old boss. Saw Tommy Livermore. Looked very fit and well turned out. Trim, know what I mean?'

'Yes, sir. DCS Livermore keeps himself fit.'

And I knew you'd seen him because he was in my bed when I got home in the wee small hours. I climbed in with him and he woke up and nuzzled me. Nice. Then he said, 'Heart, I saw your boss, old Sammy Batter 'em at the Yard yesterday. He was creeping around like one of the "Funnies" from MI5. Keep your eyes open, will you. Watch him, he can be a canny old thing.'

'Batter 'em' was the DCS's nickname and it was said that the name was rooted in fact, that as a young DI, Sammy Battescombe was not averse to clobbering a suspect.

'Taking Mr Harvey for a trip round the manor, sergeant. Want to come?' Face wreathed in smiles. Like a cat's arsehole, Tommy would have said. Very crude Tommy could be at times. Suzie's mother would be shocked because she thought the sun shone from his – well, she did.

'Too busy, sir, I'm afraid. A lot to do.'

'Pity. Never mind. Mr Livermore didn't ask after you, if you wondered.'

'I wouldn't expect him to, sir.'

Dandy Tom's not that stupid. He's not going to draw attention to me.

'Ah. Right. You fit then, Harvey? Come round the manor with me sometime, Sergeant. Yes?'

'Of course, sir.'

Big Toe Harvey nodded, grinned at Suzie and followed Battescombe across the room.

Suzie sat and wondered if Mr Battescombe had been trying to tell her something. She saw Big Toe's back disappearing through the door and thought what a clever bugger he was as well. Tony Harvey had pulled a very sharp stroke at the Camford nick last Christmas, and she knew all about it: planting weapons on the Balvak Twins and pulling them in on a trumped-up charge he knew would never stick. He even got them in front of Camford Magistrates, who dismissed the whole sorry business. Lack of evidence.

I felt the collars of those two – the Balvak Twins – but they had a clever brief and walked before we could get any real dope on them. But I was the first to put them inside. That would be Big Toe's line.

She looked out across the room. DC 'Sneaky' Williams was talking into the telephone; DC Bates – 'Batty' Bates – bent over his desk studying some papers as though his life depended on them; DC McCocklin putting on his coat prior to leaving the nick on some sleuthing task; and WDC Dottie Dobson – Dinky, as they called her – sat at her desk with her mouth slightly open and eyes glazed over, thinking of something not in the least connected with the Job.

Then PC 461 Colin Preece came through the door looking a shade crumpled in his uniform, about to change Suzie's evening – maybe her whole life – completely.

Somehow Preece reminded Suzie of a long balloon well past its prime, starting to deflate and lose its party spirit. He was by nature a serious and doleful man and looked concerned.

Suzie asked what she could do for him and he started in along the scenic route – 'Sarn't Knight said you'd be interested, Sarge. Man called Carlo Falconetti ring a bell at all? Born Eyetalian got British citizenship, been here for ever, since the Ark, owns a restaurant called Tosca – Charlotte Street. Lives above the shop, nice place he's got, married to a neat little woman, Londoner. Know him at all, Sarge?'

'No, I don't know him, and why should I be interested in someone called Carlo Falconetti?'

'Porky Pine.' it sounded as though she should immediately link Porky with the Italian.

'I might just be interested in Porky Pine, yes. Are the two connected?'

'He's converted that scout hut – Old Compton Street.'

'Porky?'

'No, Falconetti. Opening a club there. Going to call it Ursula's Place, which is a bit of a dead liberty actually, Sarge.'

'Where does Porky come in?' She hoped Preece wouldn't have to give any evidence in court for a long time, and if he did someone would have to drill him into saying the right things in the right order.

'I was proceeding up Old Compton Street and I saw Porky Pine hurrying along in the opposite direction, trying to look casual. The new club – opening next month – had all its blackouts in place but I had the impression that Porky had been up to something in there.'

'He came out of this building?'

'No, but I had the impression that was where he'd been. I crossed over to have a look-see and as I reached the front of the building I heard groans of pain – well, shrieks really. So I tried the door and went in.'

'And you found Mr Falconetti beaten up?'

'No. I found him with two of his fingers broke.'

'By Porky Pine?'

'He – Mr Falconetti – reckoned he had trapped them in the door, accidental but I couldn't really see it.'

Suzie nodded. 'You think Porky smashed them in the door . . . ?'

'Broke them.'

'So what did you do?'

'It was nasty. I mean really bad: there were bits of bone sticking out—'

'Compound fracture.'

'—of the finger. I thought he was going to pass out any minute. I mean he was sitting on a chair just inside the entrance of the club – it's going to be a lovely place; he's had it done up real nice . . . and . . .'

'What did you do, Constable?'

'Took him up the Middlesex. Rang "Darkie" . . . er . . . rang Sergeant Knight from there and he told me to accompany the injured man home if they let him go home . . . Which they did. Eventually.'

'And Falconetti maintained he'd trapped the fingers in the door? Wouldn't admit—'

'I didn't even suggest it, Sarge.'

'When are you off duty?'

30

'03.00 hours, Sarge.'

'Right. Tell Sergeant Knight that I'd like to talk to Falconetti, and would like you to come with me.'

'I get a cuppa first, Sarge? Tea and a wad? I missed me break. "Darkie" said I was to help you any way I could.'

'Good. The Scout Hut's been done up, you say?'

'Very smart job, yes. He's had the old interior ripped out and completely rebuilt the inside. Very classy. Looked like a sprung dance floor. Good woodwork. Beautiful job. Luxurious.'

Suzie grunted. 'Where does he get work like that done with things as they are?'

'Search me, Sarge.'

'I might just do that.' A tight little smile. 'Fifteen minutes at the front desk and I'll talk to Sarn't Knight before we leave. Okay?'

Four

Before Suzie went on her posting to West End Central, Tommy Livermore told her that Jack Knight was a great source of information. 'Sergeant Knight,' he said, 'has been working Soho one way or another since Jesus was fullback for the Jerusalem Artichokes. So if you don't want to ask Sammy Battescombe and you need some local knowledge, go to him.' So here she was, at the front desk, waiting for Constable Preece, chatting up Sarn't Knight – if you could call it chatting up.

'Where do I find Porky Pine when he's not carving people up for the Twins?' she enquired. A year ago she couldn't have even asked questions like that.

'It used to be the Admiral Duncan.' Knight sucked his teeth. 'Old Compton Street. Gone now of course. Direct hit. May.'

'So where does he drink now?'

'Bateman Street. Only lunchtimes though. Never at night. The Dog & Duck. Bateman Street. Often with that Page. Flash Stan Page.' Jack Knight spoke in fragments. It was like reading an ancient letter that had suffered serious water damage, making it only decipherable in patches. Flash Stan Page was an odd job man, in the assault and battery line of business.

'I'll take a look for him tomorrow then. There was something else though. A man by the name of Falconetti? He's got a restaurant?'

'Carlo Falconetti. Yes. Tosca's the restaurant. Charlotte Street. Nice bloke for an Eyetie. Wouldn't know it though. Speaks proper, like a Londoner, been here so long. Just occasionally there's a trace, a hint, that he's got Eyetie connections.'

'He's had St Ursula's Scout Hut converted. Done up. Old Compton Street.' She was falling into 'Darkie's' speech patterns.

'So I believe,' he said. 'Darkie' had reddish hair thinning badly across the whole of his head. Suzie gave it a year. Twelve months, she thought, and he'll be completely bald: a billiard ball; bald as a bandicoot.

'Going to be some kind of club. Very tasteful, Preece tells me.'

'No doubt there'll be women, wine and song.' 'Darkie' shook his head in despair for the ways of the world. 'And the contravention of one act or another.'

'Young Preece says he's had it done up something fierce. Ripped everything out, had it reconstructed. Preece says it's very smart.'

'Taking a risk. No real Blitz since May. But still taking a risk. He won't get insurance. No.' Shaking his head at the folly of it all.

'He certainly won't get insurance. Even iffy insurance.' Suzie laughed. 'But who would he get to do a building job like that?'

'Now you're asking. I really couldn't say. In great demand, builders. Doing a lot of shoring up. Not much actual building but a load of propping up. Lot of make do and mend.' He sucked his teeth again, shook his head. 'Well, I suppose there're some older men, craftsmen still around, knocking about. Builders though?' Shaking his head again. 'There'll be plenty of work for builders when this lot's over. If it's ever over,' which was why they called him 'Darkie', because he could always be counted on to look at the bleakest side of life.

Suzie smiled and at that moment Preece came up the stairs from the canteen chewing a sausage roll.

'Ah, sweet mystery of life,' 'Darkie' mused under his breath in reference to the sausage roll.

On their way to Charlotte Street, Preece told Suzie he was a lay reader at his chapel. 'I get tremendous comfort from my religion,' he said. 'Spurs me on and gives me courage.' He spoke as though reading from a manual. Then

33

he broke into song, pitched low and quiet, as though this
was proof –

'No foe shall stay his might
Though he with giants fight
He will make good his right
To be a pilgrim.'

'You fight with giants then, Preece?'
'I reckon we all do, Skip. Villains are kind of giants,
aren't they?'
'Not in my book, they're not. Shifty little men most of them:
shifty little men and desperate big women.'
They walked to the Tottenham Court Road end of Oxford
Street, navigating by the tiny 'glimmer lights' in the shop
windows, and above signs, then turned left heading for
Charlotte Street.
In the last hundred yards or so Suzie told Preece that she'd
do all the talking when they got to Falconetti's restaurant. 'You
don't speak at all, right? And don't be surprised at anything
I say. Just keep quiet and let me ask the questions.' Tommy
Livermore had taught her a great deal about interrogation.
'Getting at the truth requires the use of guile, heart,' he would
say. 'In other words you have to be adept with the porkies.'
'Your job's to listen,' she now told Preece. 'Listen carefully
and watch Falconetti. Watch him and judge his reactions to
everything I say. Just observe.'
'Right, Sarge.'
'And don't call me Sarge.'
Tosca had a narrow frontage with the name illuminated by
a 'glimmer light' above the door. When they stepped inside,
Suzie saw the interior was really a long room limited by
its width. At the far end there had been a conservatory,
now blacked out with heavy dark-green paint slapped thickly
over the glass. There were fifteen tables, of which only
three were occupied – a couple of middle-aged civilians
ate in a binding silence; an RAF officer with a young dark-
haired WAAF pushed their food around wanting to get on
with more carnal matters; and a Naval sub-lieutenant sat on

his own, near the door, wrapped in thoughts of the hungry sea.

When Suzie and Preece entered Tosca the waiters froze as though caught by a flashbulb. Suzie almost giggled for it reminded her of 'Statues,' the game they used to play at Larksbrook, the family house near Newbury. The waiter close to the door was removing a plate from the sub-lieutenant's table, while his colleague bowed over the two civilians: both the men stopped moving and glanced back into the room looking for orders from a woman seated behind a tall desk at the far end.

Preece bent slightly at the waist and muttered low into Suzie's ear. 'That's Mrs Falconetti at the desk, Sarge. Over there at the receipt of custom.' Trust Lay Reader Preece to translate everything into scriptural terms.

In the back of her head, Suzie's memory caught the scent of incense and a whiff of chalk from long ago, and a nun at St Helen's, Sister Rachel, teaching them what they called Divinity. Learning passages of the Bible – 'And he saw a man named Matthew, sitting at the receipt of custom: and he saith unto him, Follow me. And he arose and followed him.' Suzie was also instantly reminded of the guilt that had swamped her in early adolescence.

Mrs Falconetti was small and neat, with little protruding breasts straining against her thin cream blouse, a nipped-in waist and her light hair carefully rolled, dropping to her shoulders. There was a flash in the blue of her eyes, a hint of anger, and her mouth tightened as Suzie walked towards the desk, taking in everything: the cash drawer half open, the bills spiked in front of her and the diary in which reservations were noted.

'Mrs Falconetti . . . ?' Suzie hesitated. 'Or should it be Signora . . . ?'

'*Mrs* Falconetti. Beryl Falconetti. We're English. My husband's got his citizenship. You're police as well, aren't you?' Accusingly, her eyes going to Preece in his uniform then back to Suzie in her belted trenchcoat and the russet mannish hat with a wide brim at the front and a divide across the crown.

35

Suzie showed her warrant card. 'WDS Mountford,' introducing herself. 'I need to ask Mr Falconetti some questions. I—'

'Why? Why d'you have to bother him again?' Beryl Falconetti was truly angry, the eyes flashing once more, anger showing from the tilt of her head to the movement of her shoulders under the blouse. 'Wasn't it enough sending him home with a copper?' A sneer, she was flushed and her hands moved around, joining and separating, then back again with the fingers twisting: a dancing act of distress. 'I don't understand it.' Shaking her head. 'He hurt himself and now you're behaving as if he's done something wrong. I don't know that he can answer your questions. He could be asleep. They give him some tablets for the pain up the hospital.'

'Mrs Falconetti. I really am sorry, and no he's done nothing wrong but we need to ask him some questions about his new club: Ursula's Place.' She did her best to sound sincere. The situation cannoning around her mind: This is the first chance I've had to get anywhere near the Twins, and I'm not going to throw it away. I'll use anything, even Porky Pine if I have to.

Falconetti's wife moved her head again, twice, quickly as though her hair was soaking and she was trying to shake droplets from it, like a dog. 'I don't know! I don't know!' she said. Then again, 'I don't know. I'll see,' turning on her heel and walking quickly to a door at the far left of the room.

'That's the way up to their flat, Sarge,' Preece muttered and Suzie took a pace forward then stopped, holding out an arm to restrain Preece. 'Wait,' she said quietly, counting in her head, a game she had played as a child: If I get to a hundred, things'll be okay; if not – well. She reached a hundred and twenty-three.

'Mrs F. made a right song and dance when I brought the hubby back from the Middlesex,' Preece murmured almost to himself.

It must have been a trick of the light but Mrs Falconetti's hair, bouncing around her shoulders, seemed to be lighter in colour as she came back down the stairs, but her brow remained a thunderhead. 'I wish you'd leave him alone. He's not feeling at all well, and – like I said – he's groggy from the pills.' But she held the door back for Suzie, giving silent permission for her to go up, glaring at Preece as if to say he was the one who was not welcome.

As she climbed the narrow dark staircase, Suzie heard the Falconetti woman telling one of the waiters to close up as soon as the last table had finished. 'The bills are on my desk,' she added, 'all ready, and switch the glimmer off.'

There was a small landing at the top of the stairs, with a further flight going up to another storey – the bedrooms, Suzie decided as Mrs Falconetti told her to go on through the second of two doors on the landing. There was a mirror between them and Suzie jumped as her dark reflection slammed back at her. Oh God, she thought, stomach rolling. For a couple of seconds she imagined it was the fetch, that legendary doppelgänger sent to conduct you to death.

Inside, the room was heavy with Victorian furniture. A picture of the Sacred Heart hung on one wall and there were others, watercolours of terracotta roofs stuck to the side of slopes running down to water, and there among the roofs a campanile, the sky behind them cloudless and deep blue and, like the water, unruffled. A small statue of the Blessed Virgin stood on a side table and there was a bead curtain separating the room from a small kitchen beyond. The curtain looked out of place, an Italian convention sneaked among the outdated furnishings.

Carlo Falconetti lay back in an easy chair, his face a dirty chalk white, the right arm resting across his chest, the hand bandaged and splinted. Suzie introduced herself and apologized. 'I wouldn't bother you if this wasn't so important,' she said leaning forward to get a look at his face.

He nodded and his trim little wife came up silently and perched on the arm of his chair, running her palm over his forehead, brushing hair from his eyes: being the dedicated, loving wife.

'My fingers are important as well.' His voice was weak – you could almost feel the pain in it. 'I'm sorry,' he said, 'I don' feel so good.'

'My constable here tells me you've done up the old scout hut.'

He gave a tiny nod and a weak smile.

'It's really first class,' she said. 'Very professional. Luxurious, he tells me.'

Falconetti was a short stocky man: not fat but muscular. She thought Porky might have really been out of his class going for someone like Carlo who looked like a man who could handle himself. In her head she saw Italian men working on a building site, stripped to the waist. In 1932 she had been taken to Venice – family holiday – then, after the week in Venice, a journey up through Milan into Switzerland. She could still see those building workers as she'd seen them from the train window, bronzed to the waist with their muscular bodies.

'It's for the long term,' Falconetti said in what she thought of as a dying fall. 'Going to be the breadwinner in our old age.' A visible wince of pain crossed his face and his left hand moved gently down to cover the bandaged right.

'I'm sorry,' Suzie leaned forward. Knowing that she was apologizing too much. But she did sound genuinely distressed on his behalf. A good-looking man, she thought: short curly hair with the white frosting on it, dark intelligent eyes with laughter lines around them. Probably quite something when he was my age: a real man.

She looked away then back at him again, saw his eyes close, longer than a blink, the pushing away of pain. And –

'Who did the work, Mr Falconetti?' she asked.

His eyes opened and he frowned. 'Which work?'

'St Ursula's Scout Hut. Ripping everything out and rebuilding the interior.'

'Oh that. Yes. Oh, a little firm. Trinity Building Co.'

'They from round here?'

'No. No. Just three lads. Three-man firm. Trinity Building Co. It was a joke they had. But they knew the work; knew what they were up to. Very good lads. Experienced. Craftsmen.'

'You got an address for them?'

She saw his eyes shift up wearily towards his wife, then quickly back. 'Beryl probably has something.'

'A telephone number perhaps?'

Beryl Falconetti said yes she had a telephone number, went over to the small bureau in the corner of the room, lowered the flap, riffled through papers, then, 'GERard 3542,' she said.

'They're from around here, then?' Suzie didn't labour the point.

'That's a contact number,' Carlo sounded weaker than ever. She could see that the pain had got worse, his colour had become washy, and it looked as though he was now running a fever: beads of sweat above his upper lip.

'Any names?' Suzie asked.

'He's said there's only three of them,' Beryl seemed to have stepped in, taken over answering the questions. 'And we don't know any of their surnames, do we, Carlo?'

'Dave, Dick and Derek. I think two of them, Dave and Dick, are brothers, the other one, Derek, is probably a Derek Green. But that's all I really know.' His voice was going up the scale, tired, fragmented. 'Just three mates.'

'It's okay,' Suzie calmed him. 'Always looking out for good blokes who can turn their hands to jobs.'

'These're craftsmen.'

'Good. How did the accident happen, Mr Falconetti?'

'My hand?'

'Yes.'

'I told him,' a tiny inclination towards Preece.

'Humour me, Carlo. I'm going in a minute. Just tell me.'

Beryl gave a sharp angry sigh, and moved her shoulders signalling irritation.

'It's okay. I was in the entrance hall. It's kind of boxed in: a double door out on to the street and between it and the club it's like a large cupboard: a little box of a place. Well, the single door into the main room . . .'

'Into the club?'

'Yes. I didn't have the light on. It's pitch dark in there. The inner door closed on me. I put out my hand and pulled the door open then I must have tripped. My fingers curled round the edge. Trapped. I sort of fell. All my weight behind the door. Then I must have blacked out. There was pain and . . . well, that's how it happened.'

'You get some rest. I'll come back and see you again in a

few days. Make sure you're okay.' She nodded towards Beryl Falconetti, 'Thank you,' starting to walk towards the door, Preece crowding behind her.

Then she stopped and turned. 'Oh yes, when you were in the entrance, this little dark box of a place, Mr Falconetti,' pause, count three, then another three. Now go in with your Sunday punch, Suzie. 'When you were there where was Porky Pine?'

'He was nowhere near the door. He was—' He stopped, stabbed by his stupidity. You could almost hear him curse. 'No, it was—'

'It's okay, Mr Falconetti. We know what happened. That's the way Porky does his business.'

'We'll leave him to twist for a couple of days,' she told Preece as they walked back up Oxford Street.

'He's in a lot of pain.'

'Wouldn't have caught him out otherwise.' She half laughed.

'Always take into account a suspect's health and temper, heart,' by which Tommy meant physical and emotional state. 'A man in discomfort, or acute physical pain's likely to cough when he doesn't mean to. Catch him unawares, heart. My watchword.'

The sooty smell of London was comforting, she thought, like some old garment clung to in childhood. As they paced their way back up Oxford Street the years rolled away and she was confronted with her own childhood. There had been a piece of old towelling that she wouldn't be parted from and she was surprised that, at this distance in time, she could remember she called it her 'nummy' – sucked on it, clasped it to her at the close of day when the corridor light cast shadows of evil sprites and hobgoblins across the bedroom wall. Her mum had understood about 'nummies'. A little blue piece of cloth.

Nowadays, as well as the sooty smell in the London streets there was a touch of brick dust and burning wood: a hint of autumn all the year round. Particularly down Fleet Street, running up Ludgate Hill into the City, which had been burned to buggery.

'Heard the news?' Darkie greeted them at the front desk.

'What news?' Suzie said, her mind still back with Falconetti.

'News?' Constable Preece asked.

'The Yanks. The Japs've bombed the Yank fleet at Pearl Harbor. Hawaii. Bombed them out of the water. Took them by surprise. Now perhaps we'll get this show on the road.'

Suzie went down to the CID office and got out their reverse telephone directory. GERard 3542 was a bed and breakfast place deep in the heart of the clubs and clip joints. Marshall Street. She picked up the telephone and started ringing around the private informants she'd acquired in the past few weeks. Eventually she wandered out, walking around the streets and lanes on the east side of Regent Street. Every copper worth his or her name had private sources and she had hooked in several during the few weeks she had been assigned to West End Central.

She checked back in at the nick a couple of hours later. Big Toe Harvey and the Guv'nor were still out.

'You hear the news?' She asked Tommy Livermore as she slid into bed beside him in the Upper St Martin's Lane flat in the small hours of the morning.

'Japs have bombed Pearl Harbor,' he grunted.

'No. I think I've found a way into the Twins' inner circle.'

He was immediately awake. 'Tell me, heart,' he whispered, and after she had told him he said, 'That's my clever girl. Let's be spoons'

'No,' she said. He couldn't see her grin. 'Let's play trains.'

The Ghoul's eyes snapped open and he knew he'd heard the call again. Always late at night, early in the morning he'd wake like this and forget who he was: go out and search the highways and the byways, like the Bible said: compel them to come in.

He was dressed and out into the deep black night and moved quietly, waited for a moment or two, then set out, walking this time towards the river as though he could scent the dead on the night air.

She was coming back after working late in one of the clubs up west. Long way to come this time of night, he told her. Chancy. Dangerous.

'No bombs tonight,' she said. 'I came up here from the

41

West End in the Blitz. Never hurt me. Never once hurt me.'

He took care of her. Sang 'There'll Always be an England' over her grave. She was safe now: safe for ever.

Five

C harlie and Connie Balvak did not like living above the store, even so they kept a flat in the block that housed the On & Off club near Golden Square. This was their most choice place of business but they only stayed in the accommodation when they were pressed for time, or had to be about in the Soho area at dawn's early crack. They owned the On & Off – really owned the bricks and mortar – and they had a small string of real brahma birds to act as hostesses: truly prime material. The drink wasn't watered, and food was cooked on the premises – they employed a chef who had deserted from the French army at Dunkirk, and a head waiter called Maurice who was supposed to be French but came from Harrow and was medically classified 4F – his feet – so would never be called up. The On & Off also had a music licence, so a live band played there five nights a week, and there was a small floor for dancing. You had to be a bona fide member of the club to get in and they seldom accepted passing trade. It was the kind of place to which Carlo Falconetti aspired with what used to be St Ursula's Scout Hut.

The Twins' real home was a five-bedroomed service flat on the west side of South Audley Street right on the brink of Mayfair. Brought up in the insalubrious pubs of Camford Cut, the Twins now enjoyed luxury and the better things of life.

They were not big men but they preferred high ceilings, space and a place where they could look at their reflections: somewhere to pose like the Hollywood gangsters with whom they had spent their childhood years on Saturday afternoons at Camford Pictures: the Odeon. Though Charlie and Connie were not tall they were stocky and had powerful shoulders;

43

these were men who knew they were born to lead: totally confident of their status in life.

Yet there were subtle differences – physical and personal – between them: Charlie was razor sharp, but Connie was slower, dull around the edges, though quick to anger. People said that at times it was difficult to believe they had come out of the same womb in the same hour, in the same day and year. On the surface Charlie was apple-cheeked, turning to fat; Connie was lean, hungry and had more of a ferrety look.

They were in the Mayfair flat tonight: Sunday 7th December, 1941.

At around ten o'clock Little Nell arrived. Little Nell was an inch or two under four feet in height, he had a head that was slightly out of proportion to the rest of his body, his name was Neville Bellman and he was the Twins' accountant and Connie's lover. Connie, as everybody knew, liked something a shade different. Bizarre would be one of the words that sprung to mind.

Charlie's lover of the moment was a brassy young woman by the name of Cleo Sweet. 'My women,' Charlie always claimed, 'have to be blessed with curves, good sense and must know the art of keeping their traps shut.' Cleo had peroxide blonde hair, an elaborate figure like a motor racing track – all chicanes and curves – and a voice that bordered on an air raid siren doing the single note 'All Clear'. Charlie must have decided that one out of three wasn't bad.

All four of them sat round a low glass-topped table on quite unsuitable oxblood-leather buttoned chairs in the aggressively masculine living room – leather-bound books by the yard; imitation seventeenth-century prints of race horses and political satire. Between the two windows that looked down into the street hung a large looking-glass – they called it a mirror – in an elaborate gilt frame; a number of cut glass ashtrays the size of soup plates were placed on side tables. It was like sitting on the set of a B-picture, a second feature straight out of Hollywood. Tasteless and loud.

Little Nell had brought his badge of office: a bulging leather music case that he used as a briefcase. The chair he sat in all but swallowed him, and his feet stuck out, ankles resting on the edge of the seat. The briefcase was open and he was already sorting out papers.

'There are some irregularities.' His voice was paradoxically deep and resonant when you expected it to match his size. Little Nell took his accountancy very seriously – rightly so, because the Twins' main interest in life was the accumulation of cash via their various, mainly nefarious, undertakings. 'Some definite irregularities,' he gazed around, looking at the Twins as though daring them to contradict him.

'Irregularities?' Charlie questioned.

Connie shrugged.

Nell nodded. Slowly.

'Nell, we talking iffy accounting here?' Charlie asked.

'Iffy, Charlie? Yes, you might say iffy accounting. Dodgy accounting also. Iffy, dodgy and downright criminal accounting.'

'Crinimal?' Connie mispronounced. He had always had problems pronouncing 'criminal'.

'What you mean to say, Nell, is that some bastard's been fleecing us?'

'Not one bastard, but several bastards, possibly five.'

'Five people taking advantage of us? That's a dead liberty,' Charlie's voice grated. When he was angry his mouth and throat became dry, producing the voice of a corncrake. He could become angry about even small quantities of money.

'Liberty,' Connie added with feeling.

Little Nell looked around as though he had finally cracked the secret of life. 'Difficult to tell, but I'd say five. Maybe even six.' Nell said, dead serious. 'But you've got to start with one out of a possible three.' He ticked them off on his fingers. 'Greek Rose at the Nightlight; Bankie Blankovitz at the Melody; and Cab Carter at the Bandbox.'

'Not Honest Cab?' For a second Charlie looked stricken. Some years ago he had loaned Carter money to go into the clip joint business. Cab'd been born in Camford and gone to school with the Twins; he'd paid back every penny of the loan and now owned the new place – an outwardly swish drinks club called the Bandbox in Kingly Street. Charlie's stricken look lasted around three seconds, then – 'Can you prove any of this, Nell? I mean honest-to-God proof.'

'I have my sources, Charlie. You know that.'

Both Twins knew that Little Nell had sources for which senior Scotland Yard officers would have given many molars and bicuspids. Nell would have made a tremendous spymaster.

'How much is missing, then – all told?' Charlie had adopted his leaning-forward position, the same one he used when the vicar said, 'Let us pray,' in church. True it was not often that anyone saw Charlie in church, and in Charlie's line of business it usually coincided with the odd funeral and, very occasionally, a wedding.

'Hard to say how long this has been going on. It's not a huge amount. Petty pilfering really, but that's not the point, is it? Point is they're doin' it. You'll have to take steps before the rot sets in. Show them who's boss.'

Charlie was shaking his head in disbelief. 'Greek Rose? I'd never of thought it. And Bankie. Effing hell they're all trusted people.' Then again, 'How much?' Charlie Balvak didn't remain in the incredulous mode for long periods of time.

'Well, three clubs. Maybe a ton each, but that adds up. We're losing more'n three tons a week – maybe four. Often more; sometimes less.'

'A ton each? Three tons a week? Maybe four? And that's not much?' The ton had got Charlie's attention. One hundred pounds a week was not a huge sum, but it was enough in this day and age. Also he reckoned it was their money by rights. Like royalty, the Twins rarely used money or carried it. They were provided with everything a man desired. Those who worked for them clocked up the cash and paid the bills. They were not greedy as long as they could have everything they wanted.

'I reckon it's one of them – the owners – because they're all using the same method.' Little Nell inspected his nails giving the impression that he had everything sussed, right to the most minute detail. 'If you ast me it's being done to order for one of the owners.' For owners read frontmen, or in Greek Rose's case possibly woman. Greek Rose was a bull dyke of magnificent proportions.

46

'How much we take a week out of these places?' Charlie was all business. 'I mean legit.'

'In a good week we get a couple or three ton out of the Nightlight and Melody. A shade less from the Bandbox. That's a good turnover, Charlie; and it only happens when there're plenty of punters around, which is not a regular thing these days. We get paid about twenty-five per cent of the daily take. But it's the take that's being skimmed.'

'How? How's it being done?'

'They slip it out of the membership fee don't they?'

'I'm asking you, Nell. How?'

'Normal membership fee to tourists is a tenner, right?' A *tourist* was anyone who was in London for a short period and wanted to take advantage of the iffy clubs. Once they had a licence, the clubs were quite legal and above board as long as people paid a membership fee.

'They charge the punters a tenner to get in, yes?'

'Right,' said Nell. 'Each of the clubs has got two geezers working the doors, right? Well, usually one geezer and a pusher. Two at each place, and they're smart, they're men and women who know what they're at. Normal punters trolling around the area are looking for one of two things: booze and crumpet. Possibly both.'

'And they want to get in out of the rain as well, Nell,' from Connie with a smile. This was the wit of Oscar Wilde from Connie.

'Well, yes, out of the rain or away from the bombs.' In fact the clubs had done their best business very late on nights that Jerry was over: which was not so often these days. Your actual sustained night Blitz was reckoned to have finished in May 1941. The bombs had usually all fallen by one or two in the morning and the tourists who'd been down the Tube or in the few public shelters (having been caught in London overnight) came up and wanted to celebrate their survival. The pubs were closed tight as a mouse's earhole, and very few girls ventured on the streets at that time in the morning, so the clubs were geared up to take in the joyful tourists. Everybody was a tourist, a mystery, or a punter even if they were in uniform, and most were these days. All of them were either drunk or mugs who thought they were going to get what they were after in the clip joints and spielers in the heart of Soho.

Wrong.

All they'd get was very expensive cheap booze; sometimes a strip show, and later what the girls called a 'lick and a promise', which being interpreted was a very fast and unsatisfying bit of the other. True there were a few enthusiastic amateurs who aimed themselves at the officer classes – dressed and ready for anything at a fiver or a tenner a pop (breakfast included). The Twins and their cohorts were trying hard to get these girls into their stable because there were quite good pickings from officers on leave – and these now included the Free French, Czechs, Poles, the Cannucks and the Anzacs, South Africans and other troops from around the Empire on which the sun still never set.

'So, it's the doorkeepers pulling a stroke?' Charlie's eyes had hardened to the consistency of broken glass.

'More'n likely. They can read the punters you know.' Little Nell nodded. 'They're artful. They can suss out who's got plenty of poppy and if there's someone coming in who'll pay more: a pony, say, no questions asked. They'll mark them quick as kiss yer arse. So, they charge a pony, pop the usual tenner in the till and pocket the rest. The takings are down fifteen quid.'

'So you reckon one of the owners're in on it?'

'Stands to reason. If you were paying off twenty-five per cent of your take as insurance to us you'd make sure the take was substantially reduced.'

'That's a diabolical liberty.' Charlie moved his shoulders around as though trying to locate a target to thump.

'Then what you going to do about it, Charlie?'

'I'm going to frighten them stupid. Going to frighten them into forty fits. Frighten seven shades of shit out of them.'

'I'd better put my boots on then,' Connie grinned happily. He liked nothing better than putting the frighteners on people: it was his favourite thing. 'Give them a good kicking,' he added just to delineate his motives.

'Tomorrow, Con. We'll do it tomorrow night. Bring your bayonet.'

Connie's grin widened. He loved the big old Great War bayonet that hung on the wall above his bed. He could scare all hell out of people with that bayonet. Just taking it out caused heart attacks – and in one case a stroke.

'We can do up the door minders then ask some pertinent questions of Greek Rose, Bankie and Carter. Squeeze 'em till the peas run out of their boots.'

'Lovely,' Little Nell was well pleased with himself, rubbing his tiny hands together with glee. 'Give 'em one for me. All of them – 'cept Sybil helps mind the door at the Nightlight. Sybil is a good girl. Right?'

'If you say so, Nell.' Charlie looked blankly at the little man. 'She stand you on a chair to do it round the back then?' And Nell shot him an evil look. Nell didn't like Connie to know that he swung both ways. Connie could get terribly jealous when roused.

'While we're on the subject, Nell. What time would I find the doorkeepers at, say, the Nightlight? What time do they clock in?'

'At the Nightlight things don't start happening much before ten, maybe eleven.'

'No, what's the earliest they come in?'

'Okay, right, they would usually drop in, have a look round about three in the afternoon. See everything's okay. Then they go away till about nine thirty, ten.'

'Good. Then we'll know when to catch them. Sybil an' all, Nell.'

'An all,' Connie chimed in.

After a few seconds, Nell looked away from Charlie and into Connie's eyes. 'Come on then, Honeypot,' he grinned. 'Let's go and make hay while the sun doesn't shine.' He began to slide his bottom forward down the armchair.

'Whoa, boy!' As though to a horse, Charlie growled from the back of his throat and held up one hand, palm out, flat and facing Nell with fingers spread in a Greek curse. 'We've still got a lot to talk about.'

Little Nell sighed and slumped his shoulders. 'What other business, Charles?'

'A little matter of the redistribution of food, Nell. Or had you forgotten?' Charlie sounded dead antsy and Connie looked as though someone had goosed him with a red-hot poker.

'Oh, yea. No, I hadn't forgotten. Just didn't think we needed to talk about it yet.' Nell was a master of dumb insolence.

'Well, we do need to discuss it. We got a lot on, Nell.' When Charlie became calm and reasonable, people usually covered their testicles or their breasts, depending on gender.

'Lot on, Nell,' mirrored Connie.

On top of the clubs, the girls, a bit of organized crime and protection around the smaller hotels and restaurants of the battered West End – with some straightforward thieving on the side – the Twins had just got a foothold into the lucrative black market in food.

'Oi, Cleo,' Charlie snapped round, clicking his fingers at the peroxide blonde who had been sitting quietly minding her own business, and catching flies with her mouth open.

'Yes, sweetheart' She always called Charlie 'sweetheart' and it grated on Connie something terrible, but he never said anything because it was safer to leave out the things that bothered him about his brother's women. Live and let live was the wisest option when you came to Charlie's birds.

'Cleo, go and find yourself some work. Maybe do the washing-up or make the bed again, eh?'

'Yes, sweetheart,' and she walked off towards the door with her itsy-bitsy, teensy-weensy steps and her backside piggly-wiggling fit to bust with everyone's eyes attached to her rear.

'Young Cleo –' Charlie smiled at his brother and Nell – 'young and lovely Cleo has a very short attention span,' he said by way of explanation. 'Gets bored doing nothing. And she loves washing up, cleaning, polishing, making beds. You know how it is?'

'I'd of never guessed that.' Nell shifted his rump on the leather cushion and began to delve into his music case for papers relating to the Balvaks' latest business ventures. Then he looked from one twin to the other, sucked his teeth and said, 'You're twins, yet you don't really look like two peas in a pod. Funny, innit, this business of what you inherit: the genes?'

'Funny peculiar or funny ha-ha, Nell?' Connie asked with feeling.

'It's just funny. See, my brother's a good eighteen months older than me yet we could be well mistaken for each other. Same lack of height, same quirky nonsense. The eighth dwarf: not Doc, Sneezy or Dopey, but Nasty. People used to mistake us for one another on the dog. Voices match. Very similar.'

'What'd they call your brother then? Little Titch?'

'As a matter of fact, no. His name's Bartholemew, so they called him Little Bo Peep. You want to talk about the latest investment?'

At the end of 1940 they had *bought* three farms in East Anglia in order to bypass the food restrictions that were growing faster than the food itself. The farms themselves would be subject to all the new laws relating to foodstuffs and rationing, but a large percentage of their output was safely hidden from view, siphoned off and moved by stealth to London where it was distributed to selected hotels and restaurants which bought at top prices. You could, as the Twins put it, 'Pad out the income in a sizeable way by dealing with the yokels.'

The first season had gone well and the Twins now waited for the figures that Little Nell was supposed to have prepared. 'I think of it,' Charlie had told his small accountant, 'like the days of prohibition in the USA. Instead of booze coming in we're supplying food off the ration. Consider it a service to the community.' The Twins both enjoyed the gangster films of the thirties: couldn't get enough of the big old cars and the tommy guns.

Certainly Charlie, the brains behind the business, had chosen wisely. In the spring and summer of 1941 they had done a roaring trade in fresh young lamb, nice prime beefsteak, new potatoes, baby carrots, tomatoes, peas, beans and asparagus – 'sparrow's grass' to the initiated. Now through harvest time and on the cusp of winter, hotels were stocking up on vegetables that could be laid down, while they were placing regular orders for choice cuts of meat.

For an hour or so they talked about the safety of bringing goods into London from the country: how transport had become more difficult with the tightening of petrol rationing and similar restrictions. Then they went on to the way money was collected and changed hands: the Twins had always been careful about hard cash, making certain they got their proper share. Charlie quizzed Nell closely while Connie became more involved, throwing odd questions at Nell counterpointing his brother's inquisition. After a short time it became obvious that Little Nell did not like being questioned this closely.

It was getting late, but they next discussed their latest moves: the purchase and sale of game, a more legal operation and a prized one because farmers and landowners already had their own customers, and had supplied traditional purchasers for generations. Nell began to explain these problems, but the Twins had little time for what they called 'pussyfooting around with the hayseeds'.

'Just get it sorted, Nell or we'll go down and lean on 'em,' Charlie told him.

They were also entering a new market: fish. Only a month ago Charlie had accompanied Little Nell to Scotland – they went in Nell's van, painted a whitish-grey over the old scarlet and the GPO sign – where they had *bought* a smokehouse, a fishing boat and crew. They had also paid over the top for a small but well-stocked lake. Tomorrow the first fruits of this investment would arrive: a lorry load of smoked salmon was already on its way to London. Smoked salmon was at a premium.

'You'll see I get a couple of sides for myself, Nell?' Charlie was very keen on smoked salmon.

'Charlie, it's already ordered and the hotels're wetting themselves to get their hands on the stuff. We've got a huge mark-up and so have they.'

So it was on the following afternoon, Monday, around one forty-five, that Charlie was seated at his reproduction Georgian dining table eating his favourite meal – scrambled eggs and smoked salmon prepared for him by Cleo, who, he had discovered, could actually cook simple meals and did a credible scrambled eggs and smoked salmon and was proud of it.

Little Nell had personally been down to see about the distribution and brought a couple of sides back to the flat.

'You want to try some of this, Con. Really good. Has a nice bite to it.' Charlie grinned at his brother.

'No, I'm happy wiv my poached egg on toast.' Connie had never been very adventurous when it came to food and had once complained loudly in a famous restaurant that his steak tartare was almost raw. Charlie had been mortified and vowed to stop trying to educate his brother in the delights of sophisticated cuisine.

Charlie had wolfed down half his plateful of scrambled eggs and smoked salmon, pronouncing it better than excellent, when the telephone rang.

'We might have a problem,' Porky Pine said into Charlie's ear after he had picked up.

'What kind of trouble?'

'The Falconetti business.' Porky was not backward in coming forward. Over the years he had learned that with the Twins it paid to be up front and honest. If the news was bad, the rule was to tell them sooner rather than later.

'Oh, yeah, what happened about the Eyetie? You were talking to him, right?'

'I talked to him. Then the fool went and fell down. Trapped his hand in the door. Broke a couple of fingers.'

'Painful.' Charlie took another forkful of scrambled eggs. 'He ought to watch that.

'Just what I told him, but he was a bit lippy,' Porky growled. 'Out of line.'

'Understandable him catching his fingers in the door then,' Charlie said, chewing with relish.

'Who's caught his fingers in the door?' Connie asked.

'That Eyetie, Carlo. St Ursula's Hut Carlo. Falconetti.'

'Oh, only the Eyetie then.'

'So what's the trouble?' Charlie asked.

'Better come and tell you.'

Half an hour later, Porky arrived and had to try the smoked salmon and was given a small whisky by Connie, who was dealing in spirits at the moment – a case here, a case there, funnelled into London and offloaded to several places: mainly clubs *owned* by the Twins, who were branching out in all manner of directions.

After the usual courtesies, Porky leaned back and told his story.

He had gone for his usual heart-starter in the Dog & Duck around noon. Flash Stan had yet to arrive and Porky did not see the young woman in a duffel coat moving into position just behind him as he stood at the bar.

'Porky,' she said, 'we need to talk.' He turned around and she was smiling at him. Her eyes said, 'I'm trouble,' and her lips were parted in what Dandy Tom called her tattered smile.

'I was a bit startled. Not expecting her and that,' Porky now told Charlie Balvak.

'Who was it then?'

'That Woman Detective Sergeant tart out of West End Central filth. The young one: slim, good gams on her; good tits an' all; dyed hair, pageboy.'

'That sexy one?'

'Well, Charlie, I wouldn't climb over her to get to you, know what I mean?'

'So, what she want?'

'Comes straight out with it. "You seen Italian Carlo lately? Falconetti?" Asks it straight out: no messing. Naturally I say, "Carlo who?" and she gets stroppy, "Come on, Porky, I saw you steaming up Shaftesbury Avenue last night with your brains on fire. Then one of my officers saw you coming out of what's going to be Carlo's new club, Ursula's Place."'

'You was seen, Porky? You effing pratt!'

'No, hold hard Charlie. I don't think I *was* seen. I think she was trying it on because if she'd of had something hard on me she'd have pulled me: felt me collar sharpish.'

'And you'd of had sunink hard on her, Pork, right?' Connie sniggered.

'See, she went on about me being seen coming out of the Scout Hut, yet I couldn't of been.'

'Why not?'

'There *was* a copper. I seen him, but he was right up the other end of Old Compton. He'd have to've had a bloody long neck to have eyeballed me coming out of the Scout Hut. Anyhow, the tart filth as good as told me that Falconetti wouldn't drop me in it. She said he maintained he'd had an accident, broke his fingers.'

'Then what's the problem, Porky?' This from Connie.

'She's a nosy cow, that one. Gets her teeth in and doesn't let go. I'm worried that she's even got an idea I beat him up because she'll not leave it out until Carlo coughs and gives me to her on a plate.'

'Well, you did give his hand a going over, Porky.'

'True, Charlie, true. I done it for you though, 'cos you asked me. I just don't want her ferreting around.'

'And after all you were only asking for a reasonable donation: am I right?'

'Course you are, Charlie.'

'And he refused?'

'Didn't fully understand the risks of not taking out insurance with us.'

'A bit ungrateful when you consider how much we've already assisted him in getting this new business off the ground. If it wasn't for us he'd not have stood a cat's chance of getting the basic work done, I hear. You remind him of that, Porkie?'

'Not as such, but he'll gradually come to the truth. As I say, I just don't want the girl sticking her smart little nostrils in our private and personal affairs.'

'Well, listen to me. I had to hear from outside about those three builders doing the work for Falconetti. So would you remind them that I rule the roost: let them know they work for us first and last. Now I know what you mean about that policewoman and I'll fix things. Don't worry about it.' Charlie picked up the telephone and asked for a number that meant nothing to Porky.

'Yes, Jacko,' he said quietly when someone at the distant end answered. 'You know who this is? . . . Good. Has our old chum arrived? . . . He has . . . Fine. Tell him to give me a bell on the dog as soon as he can. I've a little task for him . . . Yes, right. Goodbye Jacko.' He cradled the earpiece and looked across at Porky Pine. 'That's the first step in a long journey, but if all goes well the girl'll be pulled off you within an hour or two.'

'You're a marvel, Charles.'

'Yes. I know that girl. Saw her once when we got bombed down the Cut: down Camford Cut. She'd got a dirty face.'

'Yeah, I was with him,' Connie joined in. 'And Charlie's right. She had a dirty face.'

'Okay, Porky.' Charlie looked very serious. 'I got another little job for you. We're all going off to have a word with some people who've been a bit naughty. Going to straighten them out. So I need you and Flash Stan here about three o'clock, and we'll go on after I've fully explained the situation. Don't want to say no more for now.'

Connie's face underwent a transformation. People who knew the Twins intimately always spoke of 'Connie doing a gargoyle'. He was at it now: the gargoyle. Connie had the ability to contract his facial muscles, pulling the skin tight so that his features appeared to harden; eyes set in his face like chips of flint and the texture of his skin changing to hard granite. 'I'm going to put my boots on and I'll have me bayonet with me,' Connie said with an evil smile.

Later, the telephone rang and Charlie had a long talk with his friend who'd got the message from Jacko.

Six

On that Monday lunchtime, after she had put the wind up Porky Pine in the Dog & Duck, Suzie Mountford paid a few just-happened-to-be-passing calls in the general area. Sammy Battescombe was a good boss who drew your attention to what had to be followed up, what cases were your personal priority, and which you had to work on with other members of CID. He also allowed his staff to fashion their hours to the job in hand, and conducted a weekly meeting with each of the officers working under him.

Because Suzie was officially covering the night shift it was going to be a long day before she got back to her flat and, with luck, into the arms of Dandy Tom Livermore. Not that she'd be at a loose end: she had plenty to do, and her cases included a serious GBH on a young waiter from an Italian restaurant called Café Romana in Brewer Street. It was not unusual nowadays to find squaddies, Erks or Matelots on leave getting kalied and having a go at people who worked in Italian restaurants and delicatessens, many of which now sported signs telling people they were being run entirely by British nationals. People shook their heads and concluded that some parts of H. M. Forces didn't have enough to do. Soldiers needed either to parade in glittering uniforms or fight. There were no in-between measures.

Suzie was also investigating a petrol racket and a possible ring that was producing forged papers ranging from ration books to medical certificates. And in the background of her current workload there were several missing-persons cases – men and women who appeared to have just vanished into thin air. As like as not they had been swallowed up by the Blitz and disappeared into fragments, but some of these cases had the mark of more serious crimes including murder and kidnap. So Suzie could produce reasons for being out of the nick for a dozen different causes on any one night. Her current investigations, however, had nothing to do with any cases earmarked for her attention. Now, she was more concerned with Carlo Falconetti's builders: the three men known as the Trinity Building Company – Dave, Dick and Derek. Suzie had been digging into the backgrounds of these young men for some weeks, so it was an added bonus when they turned up unbidden last night in connection with Falconetti's Ursula's Place. She had already discovered that they had only been on the scene in this part of London since June of 1940; and found out they were not easy to contact – the telephone number supplied by the Falconettis had been the number of a small private hotel – a euphemism for a superior rooming house for transients – and the trio were not there. This was a disappointment because Suzie saw these three men as a possible entrée into the world of the Balvak Twins, and their dealings with Detective Chief Inspector Anthony – Big Toe – Harvey.

Dave, Dick and Derek, she knew, did a great deal of work on properties owned by the Balvak Twins. She was also certain that Dave and Dick were known as the Bishop brothers, while their other partner called himself Derek Green. As well as these names, Suzie was aware that in reality they were three other fellows altogether. Oddly she was prepared to overlook this last fact.

The Trinity Building Co. had a very good reputation in the area. 'They really worked for the Twins a lot of the time,' an informant told her. 'Other people wanted them for jobs because they were very good at what they did,' said another. 'Very skilful,' added a third.

Around three in the afternoon she began to make her way back towards West End Central nick, but stopped to call at a newsagent's shop in Beak Street. She bought ten Players cigarettes and was given them in spite of the notice near the till that said, 'No Cigs. Sorry'. Then she fiddled with her change and handbag until two other customers had been served. When they had left the shop she quietly asked, 'What's going on?'

'I've got news,' the newsagent almost whispered, bending low over the counter so that his face was only a few inches from Suzie's. 'They're living at the Regent Palace this week. Don't know the room numbers, but they've got two of them. They're working nights, and using the names you give me. If you want to catch them in, I should call round about seven in the morning. Between seven and eight. They have a spot of breakfast when they get in, before they go to Bo-Peep.' He laid a forefinger alongside his nose and tapped it twice.

Suzie slid a couple of pound notes across the counter and the newsagent's hand clawed it in like an alligator's jaw. Now you see it, now you don't.

She nodded thanks to the man and left the shop, walked slowly up to Regent Street, turned left and strolled down towards Piccadilly Circus, under the arches that were all that remained of John Nash's eighteenth-century dream of the Quadrant – arches and a balustrade that was to surround the Circus. She crossed the road, veering left and went on through the revolving doors and into the Regent Palace, where an elderly commissionaire touched his hat as she entered.

'Ma'am.' He thrust his chest out, so that the row of medals on his green uniform coat danced and tinkled.

'Brenda on duty, Jim?' she asked.

'I seen her come in this afternoon, ma'am, so I think she's still in. You'd best ask at Reception.'

She nodded, went through the thick glass doors and down the long hall into the big open area with its reception counters. She thought how shabby-looking the carpet was for a hotel that, as a child, she had thought of as being the lap of luxury with its 1,069 guest rooms, its bars and restaurants and public salons. She remembered Brenda Marks telling her they even had a special chute for dead bodies: people moved into hotels like this to die but the staff dared not let the other guests spot the corpse being moved.

Brenda Marks was a tall, dark girl with big hips: an undermanager working in Reception. Brenda's father had been caught receiving dodgy tom, a pile of diamonds and rubies that had been prised out of their original settings. Suzie had caught him but didn't have a real case to hold him, there being nobody willing to cough to ownership of the tom. In the end she leaned heavily on Bernie Marks and he led her to his daughter, Brenda, who promised to cooperate with Suzie should she ever need assistance with the hotel trade. In return Suzie let the father go. It wasn't much of a deal because she'd have had to let him go anyway. But Suzie would come in and see Brenda every couple of weeks, top her up so to speak, drink a coffee with her, chat about this and that, hear what the word was in the hotel business or on the street. This was the first time she had come to actually ask a specific fact from Brenda.

Brenda was talking to another girl in Reception, so Suzie touched her right ear, holding her hand in place until the undermanager saw her, nodded and came over looking very neat and smart in her claret-coloured business suit. There was a little white oblong pinned on to her lapel. 'Miss Marks', it said, helpfully.

'I'm sorry, Suzie.' Brenda looked concerned and tired, with heavy black smudges under her eyes. 'We haven't been able to do anything about them yet. But I'm aware of it.'

'Aware of what?'

'The two girls working the downstairs bars. We just haven't got enough male staff these days.'

'You've got some brass picking up men in the hotel?'

'Yes, I thought that's what you'd . . .' She made a small grimace of irritation with herself.'

Suzie told her not to worry. 'I'll go down and take a look. Chase 'em off if you like. I understand. You can't be everywhere at once.'

'No, we can't but it gives the hotel a bad name. Even drives some customers away.'

'Yeah, and makes some of them a bit frisky, I'll bet.'

'Probably.' She sounded prim.

How I used to be, Suzie thought. How I used to be till relatively recently. 'Don't worry about it now,' she told Brenda. 'There's something more important,' nudging the girl away towards one of the long leather benches against the wall. 'I think you've got some jokers staying with you that I'd like a word with. Nothing heavy, I won't be coming in mob-handed, breaking doors down, ruining people's beauty sleep.'

'What then?'

'I need the room numbers of three blokes, and I want access to them about half seven, eight o'clock in the morning. There'll be no trouble, I promise.' For an instant Suzie caught the tone and drift of her voice swooping from her ear to the depths of her mind. Christ, she thought, I sound like some trollop wangling my way into another's confidence.

'I'll see what I can do.' Brenda was looking past her, gazing down the long tunnel towards the entrance doors. 'You got names?'

'Two brothers, David and Richard Bishop. The third bloke should be booked in under the name of Green. Derek Green.'

Brenda nodded and went back to Reception, vanishing into her office, reappearing again ten minutes later. 'The brothers are in 375,' she told Suzie. 'The man Green's next door, 373.' Her look said, 'That good enough for you?' 'A friend of mine – Susan Wood – is duty manager from nine tonight until nine in the morning. I'll have a word with her. If you want to get into those rooms it's up to her, and it's possible that she'll insist on being with you, might even insist on a warrant. It's the best I can do.'

It was not the most ideal situation but it was obviously the best deal Suzie was going to get, so she thanked Brenda and went down to the bar and public rooms on the lower floor, ordered a coffee from a floating and disenchanted waiter with long hair dyed an iron grey.

'You a resident?' he snapped.

'I'm the Met,' she flashed her warrant card and mentioned that Brenda Marks knew she was around. The waiter gave her a malign look but didn't argue. He returned ten minutes later with the coffee and tended the tray with an obsequiousness that jarred like fingernails being scraped down a blackboard. It was late afternoon, and the bars had been opened and were filling up with people: drummers on the road, middle-aged men pondering mischief, people in for a quick one before heading away from London as fast as the GWR, LMS or LNER could carry them.

She finished the coffee, saw no girls looking as though they were on the game, so she went into the bar and had a look round. There was one possibility but she was slightly up-market for this area and Suzie didn't want to make a costly mistake, so she left the hotel and walked back to West End Central thinking about her proposed visit to Falconetti later in the day.

As she walked, she thought that a great deal had happened since last December. This time last year – this time in December 1940 – she had spoken to Tommy Livermore on the telephone but was only on the brink of meeting him. She had put him down as a plump avuncular senior officer on the edge of retirement: glasses, a paunch, worn suits, occasionally a Harris Tweed sports coat and flannels. She recalled how thrown she was when they were forced to meet at the service flats in Marylebone: Derbyshire Mansions with its rather chi-chi pink glass and the huge faux impressionist painting in the foyer.

One look at Tommy and she was lost for ever, though it took a few weeks for her to realize what had happened. Eventually Dandy Tom had, literally, swept her off her feet and made a woman out of her. Thank you very much, heart, she thought to herself. Heaven knew how long it would have taken for her to get fully into the grown-up world if it hadn't been for Tommy.

And so much more had been going on during the present year. The direct hit on the Café de Paris in the late winter; the renewed German attacks on Coventry, Plymouth and Liverpool; the end of the sustained Blitz on London; Crete; the sinking of the *Bismark*; the Nazi's treacherous invasion of Russia that Tommy had said could tie up the German military machine for years. Then, in the past few weeks, the sudden sinking of the carrier *Ark Royal*, and now the Japanese attack on Pearl Harbor. In the back of her mind she heard the opening bars of Beethoven's Fifth Symphony. Beethoven's Fifth was very big now towards the end of the year, for those opening bars repeated the Dah-Dah-Dah-Dum of the Morse Code sound for the letter V. V for Victory, everyone recognized, together with Churchill's finger salute.

Darkie Knight maintained that they had been forced to point out to Winnie that he had to turn his hand round the other way because he was really giving the up-you sign beloved of the lewd and licentious soldiery. That was a bit naughty and they'd all had a giggle over it.

Big Toe Harvey was waiting for her in the CID room. 'Susannah, a word in your shell-like,' he murmured with what looked suspiciously like a leer, putting a hand on her shoulder and steering her towards his office. There were only two private offices – apart from the interview rooms – in the Criminal Investigation Department: Big Toe had one and the other was occupied by DI Sutcliffe, a dour Scot with an encyclopaedic knowledge of Victorian crime and a special zest for the crimes of Jack the Ripper. DI Sutcliffe was writing a book about Jolly Jack and talked about the case non-stop if he once got going.

'Suzie,' Big Toe closed the door. 'You went to see that Carlo Falconetti I hear.'

'Yes, Guv. It's an interesting bit of business.'

'I've no doubt, but I've been asked to tell you not to get too interested.'

She looked up sharply at him. 'Oh? Why's that then, Guv?'

'Ours not to reason why, Suzie. Ours just to get on with it.'

'I'm serious, Guv. I picked up this Falconetti business when it was only half-baked last night, and got on with it. So why're you warning me off now?'

'I'm not warning you, Susannah, I'm telling you.'

'But who's telling *you*, Guv?'

'I wouldn't be surprised if it turned out to be your old boss.'

Bloody hell, she thought, he's bought that story. If he had any inkling that she still saw Dandy Tom, or that the explosion between them was all an act he would never have used the unspoken name. 'Don't want to hear about surprises. I want the truth, Guv. Give me the full strength.'

'Alright. It's the funnies in Baker Street if you really want to know. But you didn't hear that from me, understand?' Big

Toe's face was set in a hangman's smile. Baker Street meant the relatively new organization, SOE, set up by Winston Churchill to 'set Europe ablaze'. Special Operations Executive, the new mailed fist of the Secret Intelligence Service.

'Good luck to them.' Suzie laughed. The very idea of Carlo Falconetti being sent back to his native Italy to bring confusion to Mussolini's military seemed about as likely as putting the BBC's star comedian, Tommy Handley, in charge of Bomber Command. Especially the RAF's Bomber Command, which was now on the edge of being reequipped with four-engined Stirling, Halifax and Lancaster aircraft and redoubling its attacks on Germany itself.

'See that you leave it alone, then, Susannah.' Anthony Big Toe Harvey's humourless smile sent a shadow across her face. When they had first met, in Camford a year plus ago, she had confided in him.

Susannah. That's my real name. But my mum only called me that when she was cross with me.

She remembered it was like giving away a part of her soul telling him.

Oh Susannah, don't you cry for me.

And he had remembered it well.

'All right, Susannah?'

'Whatever you say, Guv.'

'Good, write up your report on last night for me, please. Let me have it tonight before you go off.'

'Guv,' she acknowledged.

Desperately, she wanted to get out of there and talk to Tommy. Find out what was really making things tick. But she headed for the canteen, where she had a late afternoon meal. Beef and vegetable stew was on the menu and was palatable if you added enough salt and pepper. There were carrots, potatoes, turnips, beans and swedes in it with Bovril-flavoured gravy. Suzie liked to mop up the gravy with dry bread. She'd always liked to do that since she'd been little. She ate so much that her dad said she had hollow legs. Tonight she also had a piece of fruit cake – light on the fruit – and a cup of coffee, though it didn't have the flavour of any coffee she'd ever tasted.

Back in the CID office she dealt with some routine paperwork, then wrote the report on the events of last night into which she injected her suspicions regarding Carlo Falconetti's injuries. After reading it through twice, she got up and began to walk towards Big Toe's office.

But before she could get there she heard his 'phone ring and at the same time a police cadet stuck his head round the main door. 'The Chief Super sends his compliments. Says would Mr Harvey take a team to the Nightlight up Warwick Street. Been a fight and there's a body on the floor. There's two uniforms there and they want some CID and back-up.'

Big Toe catapulted out of his office, having already been summoned by the telephone. Suzie automatically glanced at her watch. It was three minutes past eight exactly.

The Nightlight was one of the Balvaks' places, Suzie knew. Luck of the draw, she thought. 'Luck of a pox doctor's clerk,' Dandy Tom told her later.

'With me, Suzie Anna,' Harvey growled. 'Who else's in the building?'

'Cheesy Fowles and Bob Paine're in the canteen, Guv.' The detective constables had looked into the office to tell her where they were going less than ten minutes before.

'Get 'em out of the canteen and into my car. Tell 'em we've got to see a corpse about a grave charge.'

Ten minutes later they were in Harvey's car riding the rampage towards Warwick Street with the bell going full pelt: Harvey up front, Suzie sandwiched between Fowles and Paine in the back. Bob Paine had the camera bag at his feet; Fowles had crammed in the murder bag. Suzie thought how lucky she had been. In Dandy Tom's Reserve Squad they had specialists to do the evidence collection and photography. Ron Worral, she thought: Ron had done nothing but photographs, had his own dark room and everything up on the fourth floor at the Yard, where the Reserve Squad lived, moved and had its being.

'Anyone,' Harvey shouted at the roof from his seat beside the driver, 'what d'you know about the Nightlight?'

'Up-market clip joint with revolving hostesses of the nubile variety, known for their attractive *à la carte* menus.' This supplied by Cheesy Fowles, who had salt-and-pepper hair and a baby face, smooth jowls, and pink cheeks that made him look about ten years old.

'You shouldn't know about such things,' Harvey told him. 'Owner?'

'Run by Rosie Antonakis. Greek Rose,' said Paine.

'What, that big girl? Ten feet tall and shoulders like a rhinoceros on heat?'

'The same. She minds the place but the word is that it's one of the Twins' properties.'

'She really ten feet tall?' Suzie asked.

'No, about six two, but she has muscles on her like Joe Louis.'

'Proud of them and all. Suits her personality.' Cheesy chuckled.

'Her personality?' Suzie queried.

Big Toe softened his voice a shade. 'Greek Rose,' he said, quietly. 'Greek Rose is a bull dyke of astonishing talent. They tell me she eats her bar girls. Literally.'

They pulled up at the small entrance to the Nightlight on the corner of Warwick and Brewer Streets. The entrance was down the area steps of what had been a Victorian town house. A uniformed constable stood guard over the steps, an ambulance pulled up just behind them, and it started to rain as DCI Harvey led them down to the neat little club. There was a body lying on the linoleum floor just in front of the elaborate bar; it had a pool of blood where the face had been, and it lay on its stomach in an uncomfortable claw-like rigid attitude: as though it was trying to climb across the floor.

In spite of having seen quite a few bodies in her life, Suzie never got used to it, especially the freshly dead. This man had walked and talked only a short time ago. Now he was gone. No use to anyone. Only a memory to those who knew him. She could see that he had been stocky and built like a fighter, a street brawler, with wide shoulders and, probably, well-muscled arms.

Where are your jabs now?

Along the wall to the side of the bar stood a ragged group of men and women with closed faces, wary eyes. One of the women was in tears. From this little group Greek Rose stepped like the leading actor in some provincial amateur dramatics. Tall to the point of absurdity – for she wore very high heels with lifts in the soles – Rose looked what she was, Greek and mannish with a good touch of the gypsy thrown in. She had dark features and wore her soft jet hair girlish, hanging to her shoulders, the ends curled up in a style she had long grown out of. She had black eyes set in the swarthy face with its hawk nose, like a small sharp bill, and her clothes spoke of dusty Greek campfires, tents and the odd caravan. The clothes she wore were brown from head to foot, a golden brown shirt made of some material that glistened in the light, and an earth-brown skirt, full and falling to a point just below the knees.

She fixed Harvey with a questioning eye. 'Who are you, darling?' she asked firmly.

'Met. Detective Chief Inspector Harvey.' A pause while the ambulance men came down followed by the doctor who had been summoned by the nick. 'And you are Greek Rose, yes?'

'Is what they call me, yes,' she rounded out the yes, let it tumble along, drawn out with the *e* becoming an elongated *a*.

'And who's this dead on your floor then?'

'Is Buller.'

'Buller?'

'Buller Belcher. Buller like bulldog. One he had. Called him Winston, like Prime Minister.'

'He work here, then, Buller?'

'He mind the door for me. Come. Sit,' her right arm swept out towards one of the little tables that dotted the room, with its tin ashtray and raffia-coated, candle-topped bottle. Suzie thought how awful, cheap, tawdry and greasy it all seemed under the glaring overhead lighting. It would take more than a few drinks and subdued candlelight to make her imagine this was a place to be enjoyed: in which you were wooed and won to the accompaniment of over-priced cheap champagne. But, then Suzie seldom drank and never to excess. She put herself on the left of Greek Rose, who had started to talk before she had even pinched at her skirt as she prepared to take her seat.

The girl still cried, quick little bursts, head down, face

hidden by a handkerchief. 'Who's doing the sob act?' Harvey asked.

'Sob act?' Rose didn't follow.

'Who's crying?' Suzie supplied.

'Is Sybil.'

'She his wife or something?'

'Helped mind door with him. Good girl.'

'So what happened, Rose?'

'Stupid.' Greek Rose took a deep breath. 'We wasn't open. None of the girl here. Nothing. Then these army appear.'

'Whose army, Rose?'

'No. Army men. Six, maybe seven. Possibly eight. I don' know. Buller was at his table just there, other side of door. Bottom of steps. These Army come down. Buller says, "No, not open yet." Nice. Quiet. You know. Delicate. They start shout. Want drink, they say. Can't do it. I hear this from office. This happen with Navy men: sailors up the road las' week, maybe two week back. Anyhow, Army men insist, we wanta drink now. Buller say, "Look. Not even girls here yet. No drink; no food; no girl even. Come back later when we open." Then these peoples, army men, they push forward. They push. Batter at Buller. Waiters come help, no good. Buller tries defend 'imself. Suddenly – crash-bang. Buller go down. Lie still. One man say omygod. You kill 'im. Jesus he dead, you kill him dead. They all turn backsides and run off. Go away up steps. Waiters chase then come back. Is no fucking good. Loose them and Buller 'ee really dead. Stone on floor. We ring policemans.'

'You rang for the police. You rang the nick?' Harvey asked.

'No. Wrong,' shaking her head violently. 'Police come. Waiters bring police from street. Police ring Police Station. Sorry.'

Suzie thought, she's learned this by heart. She's apologizing because she got her words wrong.

'Awright, awright,' Harvey held up a hand. 'Awright. Suzie, please shut Sybil up, she's getting on my wick.'

Suzie went over and pulled Sybil from the little knot of men and women. She was a tall girl, a bit skinny with red hair and wearing a red dress that clashed with her hair. Another girl detached herself from the crowd. 'I'll take her back in Rose's office. She knows me. She's in a state.' This girl was tarty with a lot of make-up and a plethora of eyeshadow that made her look like a giant panda. 'Come on, Sybil,' she said, putting an arm around the other girl's shoulders. 'What you need is a nice cuppa tea,' which sounded odd coming from the tart because she was obviously more used to saying, 'Nice drop of champagne, darling, eh? Do you good.' She led Sybil off behind the bar.

Cheesy was in among the other men and women, throwing questions at them, making notes, confirming times. All seemed to agree with Greek Rose's version. Bob Payne was dancing around with the camera, taking pictures of the corpse, while Big Toe continued to question Greek Rose.

Suzie went over to the uniformed constable by the door from the bottom of the steps. 'What time did you send for the Guv'nor?' she asked him.

'Eight o'clock,' he said. 'We got here about ten to and saw pretty fast that there was nothing we could do for chummy here,' head nodded in the direction of the body.

'You got pulled in from the street?'

'One of those waiters came roaring up Brewer Street, shouting himself hoarse: shouting bloody murder as it happens. We followed him down here. Three or four minutes later I used the phone to call the nick. Took you about ten minutes to arrive.'

Like Greek Rose, everyone was saying the killing had only just happened. The thing they didn't agree about was the number of squaddies who had come into the club. Some said six, others seven, one of the waiters, like Rose, said maybe eight, 'Don't know, didn't really stop to count them.'

Big Toe came over as the doctor stood up. 'Can the lads take the body, Mr Harvey?'

Suzie had looked down, then quickly looked away again. She could take sudden death, but she didn't like to dwell on it for too long. From this side of the body you could see where the face had been caved in.

'Chalk it,' Big Toe told Paine, who fumbled around for the

stick of chalk which was in the murder bag. 'Soon as he's chalked it they can take the body. What's the story?'

'Well, there's a broken neck,' the doctor shrugged. 'Maybe the odd rib. They knocked him down and stamped all over him by the look of it. Doubt if his mother'd recognize him now. Someone took a boot to his face several times but I suspect the neck did the trick.'

'Got a time of death?'

'He's been down there three or four hours, I reckon. Certainly not less than three.'

'That all fits then,' Big Toe Harvey said.

Suzie told herself to keep quiet, and at that moment Big Toe turned his head and looked straight into Suzie's eyes, then straight through them and out the other side. 'You want to go and talk to Sybil, Suzie? Sybil and that other tart. Just check them out, would you?'

She said nothing: just gave him the look that, in her schooldays, had been called 'the evil eye'. Behind the bar a gaudy curtain hung from a lintel hiding the jambs of what had once been a door into another area of the lower ground floor. Suzie went through the curtain and found herself in a short corridor leading to a door at the far end. About halfway up on the right there was another door, which stood half open and from behind which came the sound of voices.

'Why should I keep quiet, Danny?' asked one with a slight catch in her throat, undeniably the voice of Sybil.

'Because Rose'd have your liver for breakfast if you talked, and she'd give you some Gorbals kisses into the bargain.' There was a strong Scottish flavour about the other girl's voice. 'Canna you see, Sybil? If Rose didn'ee have you, the Twins would; and I wouldn'ee give a penny for your chances if one of them little buggers came looking for ye. Or their wee friends either. That Porky Pine frightens the living daylights outa me, and the fella Page could give ye a hard time, hen.'

'I know, but I don't like to be at anyone's mercy. Jesus we all saw what happened.'

'Aye, we did an' a' hen, which is just why you should had your wisht. As they say doon here, keep shtum.'

70

Suzie kicked the door open. 'Keep shtum about what?' she asked.

Sybil lay on a sofa, her head resting on two pillows, her bruised eyes still wet with tears. The girl with panda eyes and streaky hair sat beside the bed, though she had now swivelled round to see Suzie in the doorway.

'Keep shtum about what?' she repeated.

'I was trying to stop her greetin'.' The Scottish girl didn't quite meet her eyes and Suzie had to think for a moment before translating 'greetin' as 'crying', though the sobs had started again; not as severe but Sybil was certainly distressed.

'Why's she taking on so?' Suzie asked the girl. 'She was close to him? To, what's 'is name? Buller?'

'I worked with him,' Sybil supplied. 'Worked with him minding the door. He was a good mate. Now he's . . . he's . . .'

'Deed,' the Scottish girl said.

This brought a further wail.

'And you are?' Suzie asked.

'Danny. Short for Danielle. Me mother thought it sounded a wee bit French.'

'It sounds absolutely French. Tell me what happened, Danny?'

'To Buller?'

'Of course to Buller.'

'He got rushed by the drunken sodjers.'

'Army, yes?'

'I dinna na any other kinda sodjers. There's sodjas, sailors and airmen aren't there? These were sodjers. They're what the sailors call brown jobs.'

'And they just rushed Buller, knocked him over? Started kicking him?'

'More or less. Maybe a wee bit more than less. They'd a had Sybil as well only she skipped oota the way.'

'How many of them?'

'Six. Seven. I didn'a stop to count. They were making a guy bit noise.'

'And Buller didn't give them any cause.'

'He told them we weren't open. He said they should come

71

back when we were open and the girls were here. That kina aggravated them. They were sorta angry: like kids wanting to play now. Couldn'ee wait. Know what I mean?'

'More or less. And Sybil, you tell me about it.'

'It was like Danny said. They suddenly went out of control. Squaddies, that's what they were. Didn't give him a chance.'

'You never open in the afternoon?'

'Only when there's the trade.'

'But these fellows were trade.'

'It was much too early.'

'What's too early, Danielle?'

Danny opened her mouth then closed it quickly. 'We don't get going till around ten or even eleven at night.'

'Never in the afternoon?'

'Sometimes. Not today.'

'What time was it?'

'You know what time it was.'

'I'd like to hear it from you. From you and Sybil.'

'After it happened,' Danny began, 'I dinna watch the clock. Steve and Nicko, the waiters, went up when they knew he was deed. Went inna street to sairch for the police.' She pronounced it in the Glasgow manner, 'polliss'.

'Sybil?'

Sybil sniffed, swallowed and said, 'It was like Danny says. Soldiers. Squaddies.'

'Go on through and tell my guv'nor I've talked to you,' she signalled to Danny with her head and the girl obeyed, so Suzie stepped back into the room, holding out one hand. 'Sybil,' she said softly. It meant: 'Sybil, stay where you are.' And Sybil, who had half risen from the sofa, sank back as Suzie drew out her pocketbook and scribbled on a spare piece of paper. 'Keep this. Don't share it with anyone.' She looked Sybil full in the eyes. 'It's my name – WDS Mountford – and the CID number at West End Central nick, and my home number. If you want to speak to me, ring me, and ask for me. Don't speak to anyone else, and don't say who you are. If someone else answers, or says I'm not in, just put the phone down. Talk to me only. Understand?'

Sybil nodded and tucked the paper away, out of sight, down her bra probably.

'Right, let me take you upstairs.'

I could take both of them down in about an hour, she thought. She had watched Tommy do that: bring people down with no hard evidence, throwing in trick questions, tripping people up, making outrageous suggestions just to get a reaction. If she was able to keep pounding away she would break them in a short time. But Suzie wasn't sure that she wanted to break them. She already had enough to report to Dandy Tom. The time of death discrepancy. Where had three hours gone? she wondered. She also thought that Sybil wanted to talk to her: that she had something to say, which was why she left her the means to do it. It was intuition, nothing clever, nothing scientific. 'Follow your intuition,' Tommy Livermore taught her. 'If you feel something, don't try to rationalize it. Just follow like you'd follow the merry, merry pipes of Pan, heart, or join in the Cornish fucking Floral Dance.' Tommy, Suzie accepted, often used language inappropriate to the vocabulary of a future earl, but she knew she must put up with it even though her mother has probably never heard the words. She had once caused her mum and her stepfather – the Galloping Major – great offence by saying that Tommy called an arsehole an arsehole. They were scandalized.

Upstairs they were getting ready to move the body and Big Toe was itching to get back to the nick. As they walked to the car, Harvey looked back at Suzie. 'Spot the deliberate mistake, Susannah?' A saw-tooth edge to his voice.

There used to be a radio show called *Monday Night at Eight* and a segment of that was 'Inspector Hornleigh Investigates': a little playlet – a murder or big robbery – and you were told that Inspector Hornleigh believed every criminal makes a mistake that gives him away. The audience had to pit their wits against Inspector Hornleigh. Big Toe was now asking Suzie if she had spotted the deliberate mistake for Buller's murder. 'Of course, Guv,' she said with a cheeky smile.

'Good. Someone's telling porkies, aren't they?' Harvey replied, grinning, but Suzie knew that the three-hour delay would be glossed over, the record would be altered, the

73

report quietly erased, degutted. Whatever happened to Buller Belcher happened sometime much earlier, around four or five she reckoned, and it wasn't done by a group of half-sloshed, belligerent soldiers. She was pretty sure that the violence came from the Balvak Twins or their cohorts.

Seven

Porky and Flash had arrived at the Twins' flat on the dot of three o'clock and were given large whiskies to see them through Charlie's briefing. The Twins always gave out large whiskies when there was dirty work to be done. Connie wore his heavy boots with metal toecaps and heels; he also carried his Great War bayonet that was brightly polished.

'Going ta teach someone a little lesson,' Connie said, slapping the bayonet against his thigh.

A couple of years ago Porky had been to a pantomime: *Cinderella* it was, and the girl who played Prince Charming had legs right up to her arm pits, and shapely tits that were shown off nicely by the costumes she wore. He remembered at the time they reminded him of jelly moulds, pert and upturned. Not a bad tight little bum either, Porky recalled now with a sigh. She had made the same move, but with a little sword decorated with glitter. She slapped her thigh with it and said, 'Dandini, send out the invitations to my ball.' Which had made Porky snigger. It was a signal for the girls and boys of the chorus to come in and start singing about how wonderful the ball was going to be, and they sang another number about the music going round and round oh-oh-oh-oh-oh-oh and comes out here. Porky had liked that bit – the slapping of the thigh – and if the truth be known he would prefer to be back in the theatre watching Prince Charming than sitting here watching Conrad Balvak slapping his leg with the bayonet. He knew from long experience that when Connie had his kicking boots on and was wafting the bayonet around someone was going to get unpleasantly hurt. Not that there was anything intrinsically wrong with that. Some people, Porky would preach, ought to be hurt regular. Step out of line and

75

there would be retribution in the shape of a good spanking. In Porkyspeak a good spanking meant a severe roughing up. Possibly with blood and bruises. Moonlight and bruises, he thought to himself. Make a good song that would.

'Some of our employees have had their fingers in the till.' Charlie began looking at each of them in turn as though they were guilty. 'And we've got to make an exhibition of one of them. The particular trouble spots are three of the clubs. The Nightlight, Bandbox and the Melody. The people who've got sticky fingers are the doorkeepers.' He shook his head as though in great sadness. 'I think we only need to cause one of them a little pain; leave a few scars; maybe put him in plaster for a month or three. Nothing serious, but what they're doing is small-minded, they're pinching pocket change. Once we've made a little example, everyone'll catch on. Right?'

'Right Charlie,' Porky agreed.

'That'll do the trick,' said Flash Stan.

'Just the one?' Connie sounded a shade mournful.

'Just the one, Connie. We'll go and have a look at Greek Rose's place, the Nightlight. Maybe administer some punishment. Descend on that bulldog bugger, Buller Belcher. Do him over.'

'Learn him a lesson,' grinned Connie.

They left around quarter to four and returned at around five thirty.

'He squealed, didn't he? Squealed like a stuck pig, didn't he?' Connie was capering about with glee; doing a bizarre little dance, singing.

'Yes. Squealed 'till he went quiet, Con.' Charlie was not altogether happy with his brother.

Connie had become uncontrollable.

'Slammed him in the face with my boot, didn't I?' Connie laughed.

'You did indeed, Connie,' Porky agreed. Stan remained silent. He didn't really like sudden death. You could be done as an accessory before and after the fact, and for that you could get yourself one of those nine o'clock appointments with Mr Albert Pierpoint, the public hangman: get yourself topped, get your neck stretched, go up the dancers and do the Tyburn jig.

76

To tell the truth, Flash Stan felt a bit sick. There had been no stopping Connie. He hadn't even taken his camel-hair overcoat off.

'Buller, you've been a bit of a naughty boy, haven't you?' Charlie had said. The door was closed, two of the girls were there, so were the waiters, Nicko, Steve and Spiro; the bartender Busty Kate Thomas stood behind the bar, tending it; and Greek Rose was outside her little office, her little caboose as she incorrectly called it.

'I done nothing,' Buller denied. 'Ask Sybil. She's with me most of the time when we're here. What I done, Charlie?'

'You've got a bit sticky, Buller, that's what you've done. Developed sticky fingers.'

Buller Belcher's face had lost its usual colour and he was gradually assuming a defensive stance, knees bent, fists clenched, arms up and in front of his body.

Porky Pine looked across at Flash Stan, nodded and they both moved in to grasp Buller by the arms. It was a practised manoeuvre and Buller struggled trying to get himself out of the line of fire, desperate to move out of Connie's reach. But Connie was fast. His right foot thrashed forward, thumping hard into the apex of the man's thighs. Connie stepped sideways as Buller gave a strangled cry, an odd noise that seemed to come from deep within him, half a howl, half a dreadful groan of agony.

As Connie stepped to one side, so Porky and Flash let go of Buller's arms, intuitively getting out of the way as the unfortunate man clutched at his groin and retched as he bent double with pain. Now Connie's right arm was raised and he brought the flat of the bayonet down on the back of Buller's neck.

There followed another low moan, a gasp of pain, as if all the air was being expelled from his lungs, and a groan combined with a harsh little crackle like the breaking of dry sticks under foot. Buller pitched on to his face and his fall sounded like a wet dishcloth being flung against a tiled floor.

What followed took less that fifty seconds, but Charlie and the two minders, together with the mixed bag of employees of the Nightlight were unable to move in their stupefied horror.

Connie Balvak leaped upon Buller Belcher with his feet a blur as he danced in and delivered kick after kick around the face, neck and head: a concentrated choreography of violence. By the time Charlie pulled himself together it was far too late. But it had been too late some minutes ago.

'Conrad! Enough! Enough, Connie!' By this time he had caught his brother's arms and physically pulled him away, with Connie grumbling like a child deprived of some activity that he imagined was his right. By the time he had steadied up, he was breathing hard in an almost trance-like state. The Welsh have a word for it – *hwyl* – which is the moment when the spirit takes the preacher and gives him the golden words, the poetic power and the emotive force to carry his congregation with him. For Connie this was the *hwyl* turned upside down and plunged into dark iniquity. His mind and body were taken over by some terrible demonic spiritual force, so that he stood shaking and staring at the work he had done.

By this time Porky Pine was on his knees, knowing that things had gone too far. He bent his head and put an ear near Belcher's mouth, the fingers of one hand feeling for a pulse, the ear trying to detect breathing. But he couldn't hear a thing or feel a blip, so Pine moved his head and in so doing got a streak of blood across his light-grey silk tie – the one Charlie had given him for his birthday. He looked up at Charlie now and shook his head, like he'd seen it done in those American films when somebody is hurt really badly. The shake of the head was always accompanied by a pained and serious expression. A hint of religious gravitas. Let us pray.

'It's gone too far,' Charlie said, and they all heard him. 'Shouldn't have gone this far, Connie.' And Connie reacted like a child about to be ticked off, or worse, for doing something he knew he shouldn't have done. He gave out a thin, tormented wail.

'See to his boots,' Charlie ordered, looking at Porky. 'Get that tie off and see to Con's boots.' Then he flicked his hand in the direction of Greek Rose, and noticed the faces of the other staff, shrunk back and stricken. One crying noiselessly. 'Rose –' for a moment he sounded like some over zealous town clerk – 'Rose, I think there are some matters arising.'

And he signals her to join him at the end furthest away from the scene of the action.

Porky Pine, who knows his job when something unusual occurs, cleans the speckles of blood off Connie Balvak's boots, pulls at the knot in his bloodstained tie and removes it over his head. He mutters something at Flash Stan who goes over and looks outside to check that nobody's lurking around in the street; he then locks the doors and puts the bolts on. Flash looks much like Porky, eyes flat and dull, lips thin and face set solemn, as if in stone. Porky knows that these are all the outward signs of shock, and that they will pass quickly because they are all used to the trauma and have been since last year when death came nightly out of the burbling skies.

Charlie and Rose at the far end of the room are talking, urgently and quietly. They do not smile, maintaining serious faces. Charlie has this terrible knowledge writhing inside him, he knows what has occurred is long past due, been expecting it for years. He even suspects that maybe it has happened before, for he is not his brother's 24-hour keeper. Connie's violence is awful, terrible to see, frighteningly close to a demonstration of madness. Now Charlie must keep calm, but he's also aware that when Connie has settled down, and started to glory in what he's done, he'll demand that his brother should do the same. Since childhood there has been sharp competition. Sometimes Charlie wonders how far Connie has grown out of childhood.

Now the whole distasteful thing will become a dare.

And while Charlie could do it, riding a bicycle with one hand tied behind his back, he doesn't really want to be in this contest at all. He turns back to Rose and together they draw up the right story.

Porky has cleaned Buller's spattered blood from the steel caps of Connie's boots with a piece of rag. He has folded his bloodstained tie in the same rag and now he waits quietly for the next scene in the unpleasant drama.

Charlie and Greek Rose split up and come back to the lifeless pile that was Buller Belcher who looked after the membership of the Nightlight but wouldn't ever see the Nightlight again. Nor daylight.

79

Then Charlie starts talking to the few assembled employees. 'Listen to me, and listen well. None of you's seen me here tonight. You never seen me here or my brother or my friends. Never laid eyes on us. Never heard us speak. Didn't see what happened. Right? You're the only ones who witnessed this sad accident – 'cos that's what it was – and if there's the smallest hint that we were here we'll know who grassed us up and I promise you you'll wish you was never born. Got that?' His eyes roamed over the scared white faces, then he shouted, 'Got that?' again, and they mumbled their various affirmatives.

'We're off and Rose is going to tell you what you actually saw here.' For a second or two Charlie appears tongue-tied. Then, 'She's going to tell you, then she's going to ask questions: make sure you know the truth. It's like something that happened up the street a couple of weeks back. Group of matelots, pissed as a boiled owl, the lot, fought to get to the bar and they had to take two people to hospital. The same as the several pissed squaddies that forced themselves in here tonight, when sadly poor old Buller got topped doing his job. Should be proud of him. Give him a medal, 'cos he died on active service, didn't he?' He looked around the faces, eyes steady and voice convincing. 'There was either six, seven or eight men, drunk as a rolling fart, feeling no pain but inflicting a lot. Rosie, you carry on, make sure they're word perfect, and give us plenty of time to get home. Three-quarters of an hour: an hour even. Make sure it sticks tight as a nun's fanny or you'll be hearing from us.' Rosie nodded seriously and watched as Nicko argued and held back two new girls emerging from the curtain hanging behind the bar, but keeping them in check, not letting them see the broken and pelted body of Buller.

It was a dramatic exit with Greek Rose letting them through the door and fastening it immediately. Charlie let Flash Stan up the steps first, to 'make sure there're no rozzers in the frog' – *frog and toad: road*. Then he followed with Porky wet-nursing Connie in the rear. The car was round the corner and the driver had seen nothing of what had gone on, so during the drive back when Connie tried to say something about Buller Belcher, Porky shut him up sharpish, but not unkindly.

Back in the club, Greek Rose turned to the assembled staff.

'Right. So how many soldier come in here, Nicko?' she asked, and began the question and answer routine that went on for a long while.

Almost before the Twins got through the door of the flat, Connie had started to talk rapidly. 'He squealed, didn't he? Squealed like a stuck pig, didn't he?'

Charlie looked hard at Connie, who was putting distance between himself, Porky and Flash.

'Squealed like a pig; squealed like a pig, like a pig,' Connie sang, grinning and doing a little caper around the hall.

When Charlie had had enough: 'Connie, shut the fuck up,' lifting a hand as though to strike him. He hadn't done anything like this since they were children, but then he had an idea about what Connie was going to do next. He was going to say, 'There I've done it, Charlie. Now you do it. I dare you.' They had both seen plenty of death, but this time it was Connie's doing and Charlie hadn't been quick enough to stop him, so Charlie was angry with himself. Connie had always been the wilful one, the one who pulled wings off flies, who hit that little bit harder, the real chancer and the one – Charlie now knew – who having killed once would find he had enjoyed it, so would do it again and make it into a contest.

Porky kicked the front door closed, anxious to be of help.

'Charlie?' Connie stepped back. 'I did well, Charlie. He squealed.'

'Until he went quiet, Con. Until he died, Connie. You killed him.'

'Learn him a lesson then. He wasn't anyone useful, so there's no need to be cross.'

'Conrad,' Charlie sighed. 'That man had probably done us down, yes. We went there to teach him a lesson . . .'

'I did. I learned him a lesson.'

'It was also a lesson for anyone else who might be thinking of taking a liberty, Con.'

'Well?'

'It can't be a lesson any more. Beating the shit out of him's one thing. Killing is another. We can't go round saying look what happened to Buller Belcher, because if we did we'd end up doing a dangler wouldn't we? Do you not see, Connie?'

'Not us, Charlie. No chance. We're Balvaks. Nobody'd dare to do it to us. We've got everyone in our pockets.'

Charlie looked across at Porky Pine and shrugged; so Porky asked what he should do with the bloodstained rag and his tie.

'Shove it in the bin on your way out, Porky. The bin men come in the morning.' Charlie of course hadn't had the benefit of Dandy Tom Livermore's instruction. 'When your out and about in your manor,' Tommy had told Suzie Mountford, 'when you're out collecting your grasses, make sure you've one or two who'll dig and delve into the dustbins for you. You'll have to tell them which dustbins they've got to tickle, mind you, but you'll be surprised at what dustbins will yield: paper, letters, billets-doux, weapons, the way to a man's heart.' Then he grinned, 'Cigarette that bears lipstick traces. Airline ticket to romantic places. Just a tip, heart, tip to pass on.'

Here, in the hall of the flat almost on the edge of South Audley Street, Porky Pine asked what he should do. 'You won't want me to go round the Bandbox and Melody now will you?'

'Keep well clear, Porky. Sling your hook and take Flash with you. Then, if you take my advice, I'd make certain you've been somewhere else all afternoon and have at least two unbreakable witnesses.'

Porky got to the door before Charlie spoke again. 'Oh, Porky? Flash? Tomorrow. Afternoon, late afternoon, four, five, I'd like to see that girl worked with the Buller up the Nightlight. Worked on the door.'

'Sybil,' Porky said, flatly.

'That's the one. Treat her really nice. Tell her there's no drama. Give her a good lunch. A drink. Take her to the On-Off,' which was how Charlie always spoke of their place, the On and Off club near Golden Square. 'Keep her warm. I ain't going to hurt her and Connie ain't going to be there. Just want a little talk.'

'Right, Charlie,' 'Okay, Charlie,' Porky and Flash said.

Charlie never misses a thing.

As they were going out of the door, Charlie picked up the

phone to call his girl Cleo. 'I want you round here, Clo,' he rapped out. 'Over here with your sister, quick as kiss me. Speed of knots, Clo, and I don't care what Denise says, she's to come with you. I want you both here. Now. Right?' At the other end of the telephone Cleo said, 'Right Charlie,' put down the phone and called to her sister, 'Denise, get some clothes on, we got to go out. Come on.'

In the service flat, Charlie went into the living room, where Connie sat silent and sulking staring at his boots.

Suzie roughed out her report on the events at the Nightlight and completed her work on the Falconetti notes, which Big Toe had insisted on seeing.

'You going out?' He eyed her suspiciously when she went into his office.

'I've got to go to the Café Romana. Promised them I'd look in. Have another word with the lad who got his face smashed up the other night. I may have a lead. Want to come, Guv?' Taking the chance. No way did she want him with her, but if you don't offer . . .

He shook his head crossly. 'Nah. Nah, I've got to go out with Mr Battescombe, wants me to meet a pair of grasses he keeps on a tight leash.' He raised his eyes to heaven as though going out with Sammy Battescombe was the last thing he wanted to do. Word was that Sammy frequented a quiet little drinking club in Romilly Street where he got smashed late and regular most evenings. Big Toe liked a drop as well and wasn't averse to sitting on licensed premises till all hours.

Suzie was going to the Café Romana in Brewer Street, but only to pick up some Italian magazines – a couple of years old admittedly – from the owner's wife who came from Turin but now sported a British nationality. She thought the magazines would keep Carlo Falconetti happy during his convalescence. If Big Toe was holed up with the Super on the other side of Soho he wasn't likely to be cruising round Charlotte Street: though she'd keep her eyes open. It wouldn't do to get spotted by him or one of the DCs he was beginning to cultivate. She had noticed Cheesy Fowles had started to try and please him every chance he could; there was another bloke called Nick Carter, big fellow with a voice to match who was sucking up to Big Toe.

In the streets it was dark tonight, low cloud and a bit of rain as she wound her way slowly towards Brewer Street. On the way she bumped into Tatty Macintosh, named by locals, first after a character in the radio show *ITMA* and second because she wore what had once been a 1914–18 officer's trench coat, now stained, spewed on and covered in seven different kinds of gloop. Among other marks of the beggar's trade she was a scavenger, and one of Suzie's grasses.

'Tatty?' she asked. 'You ever get up by South Audley Street?'

'Yea. 'Bout every other day. It's good over there, they have real coffee and they throw it in their bins after only one pass of water. A frugal person can use it five times. Sometimes even six.'

Suzie gave her the Balvak Twins' address. 'Take a look in their bins, would you, Tatt?'

The crone, at least she looked like a crone, dirty with blackened teeth and the filthy trench coat, bitten and broken fingernails and a smell you wouldn't believe but said she was only thirty-eight, snatched the proffered half-crown from Suzie's hand and went off muttering the Balvak's address. Suzie knew she wouldn't be able to use anything filched by Tatty as evidence, but it was worth a shot: more like eighty-three, Tatty was; thirty-eight long gone.

At the Café Romana they were starting to clear up and call it a night. The last clients were just leaving, scurrying off in the direction of Great Windmill Street and Piccadilly Circus, looking for the odd bus to take them home. Funny, Suzie thought, nobody ever called it *Great* Windmill Street these days, only called it Windmill Street.

She talked to the waiter who had been attacked – his name was Martin Gibbs – asked how he was doing, had the cuts healed? Had they taken the stitches out? No, they weren't any nearer catching anyone; he would have to face up to the fact that they may never get anyone. Never arrest anyone at all.

='This so often happens nowadays,' she said. 'What with so many military personnel on the move.'

Then she went up to speak with the owner's wife, Angela, who gave her ten magazines dating back to January and February 1940. She took the periodicals away, and walked to Charlotte Street, going by the back doubles, stopping every few minutes to make certain she was not being followed. Once at Tosca she was allowed ten minutes with Carlo and found him appreciative of the magazines, and a little less stiff and formal, though he was still getting a fair bit of pain: you could see his eyes twitch with it. 'They give me tablets for the pain but they don't do much.'

'It might be less of a bother if we got the real culprit,' she told him.

'What real culprit? I don't understand you, Sergeant Mountford.'

'Carlo, I've told you already. We know who did it. You might as well tell me.'

'If that was true, Sergeant, I certainly wouldn't tell you. Particularly tonight.'

'Why tonight?'

'Because there's a story doing the rounds. They say that one of the door keepers at a club in Warwick Street was kicked to death this evening.'

'I know about that.'

'Then you'll know who did it.'

She looked him full in the face and gave the official position, though she would fight and go through hell to change it. 'As far as I know it was a nasty accident. Group of drunken soldiers got a bit boisterous.'

'Then you believe anything.' He gave a humourless laugh. 'The word is that Conrad Balvak did it all by himself. That's all the help I can give you and I won't own to it a second time: but that's the word.'

She looked up at him and, for the first time, saw that his eyes smiled. 'Thank you, Carlo,' she said. 'Thank you very much.'

'It's a pleasure.'

Suzie took the Tube from Tottenham Court Road to Piccadilly

Circus just so that she could use the public telephones in the concourse, where she rang her own flat. She let it ring twice then held down the receiver rests and dialled again – the code all adulterers use. This time Tommy Livermore picked up and said, 'Peacock, I hope that's Gadfly.'

'You've got a nice clear night, sweetheart,' she told him. 'You could even go home. I've got a job on at around eight in the morning, so I'll not be back till about ten. Maybe later.'

'Busy little Gadfly, heart. What's on the menu?'

'The works. We've had a nasty evening of it.'

'So I've heard. The Nightlight got blown out.'

'Yes, and our friend Big Toe's pulling a little stroke on behalf of his friends, or I'm a Dutchman.'

'So, Johannes Vermeer, what're you up to?'

'Darling, I've run the Trinity to earth. They're staying at Prinny's Palace, so I'm going to go in and have a private talk with them in the morning. Might even take their early morning coffee up to them.'

'Who's going with you?'

'I'm flying solo, Tommy.' They only used the code words for a bit of a laugh if she spoke to him in the flat, though it was a different matter when she called him at the Yard, where she had to go through a switchboard. 'Can never tell who's listening to who when you're on the blower to the Yard,' Tommy said. 'That lot would listen to the waves in a sea shell and swear it was a couple of mermaids talking about blagging Neptune's Crown Jewels'.

'You sure that's wise, heart? Going by yourself?'

'Probably not, but I'll give you the room numbers in case I go under a train.' She told him they were in 373 and 375.

'By the by, someone's been calling you here all evening,' he said. 'About eleven rings before they close the line. You got a new lover, heart?'

'No, Tommy.' A mite fast, she thought. She hadn't expected Sybil to react so quickly, but that was the only person it could be.

'You want to tell me any more now? For the record.'

'You know their names don't you: the Trinity?'

'Real and assumed both, heart. Watch yourself. There'll always be a lamp in the window for my wandering girl.'

Back at the nick few people were around but there was always some paperwork. Then, around one forty-five in the morning, Cheesy Fowles and Nick Carter brought in one of the men they had been looking for in connection with forged ration books – 'Hairy' MacRoberts, a graphic artist with a bad limp, the left leg from a motorcycle accident in thirty-eight. DI Sutcliffe would not be in until the morning and he was the only other officer with knowledge of the case. He would be delighted when he saw they had got 'Hairy'. She wasn't to know that Cheesy had gone straight off and telephoned him to come in and see what was what.

Suzie had a working knowledge of the whole thing and was aware that they were after bigger game than 'Hairy'. The forgeries were not just ration books: there were petrol coupons, which were gold dust, medical certificates and classification papers that would prove you were exempt from military service. It was also possible that this ring had been forging bank notes, and Suzie was well aware that one of the most difficult things about forgery was getting the right paper. When she sat down with Hairy, a big red-headed bloke with ink-stained fingers and a parchment pale face, she was quite prepared to lead him up the garden path by showing him how conversant she was with the printing trade.

So she drew him in. Talked about point sizes, being on the stone, locking forms in the chase and the number of ems you'd need to put between printed questions on – for instance – an application for a firearms licence. She chatted away for about an hour before she even mentioned the name of the mill from which most government paper was obtained, and, after that, the names of two possible associates – 'Legless' Diamond and Tom Lamborn, known unaccountably as 'Old English Tom'. Once these were out in the open, MacRoberts shook his head and asked Suzie exactly why she wanted to talk to him. 'I haven't seen either Legless or Old English Tom for years, have no desire to see them, have no reason to see them, Miss Mountford, so you can get off that line of probing right away.' He then made some remarks about the two men and added that if Suzie was trying to do a guilty by association she was barking up the wrong tree.

It was about this time that the door to the interview room opened and DI Sutcliffe came in looking like a deeply depressed bloodhound. He switched his lugubrious smile on and off. 'A word, WDS Mountford, please.' A twitch of the nose as though an unpleasant smell drifted below his nostrils.

She thought his eyes were going to swivel right round, like a chameleon checking the twig, measuring up the distance over which it had to shoot its tongue for a direct hit.

At the door, Sutcliffe turned his head and gave his flash of a smile to Hairy MacRoberts, and Suzie saw that the man was undoubtedly put off by the new arrival. If anything, he had gone paler than he was already.

'Young Fowles thought I should know you'd pulled MacRoberts,' the DI said once they'd got into the passage.

'I didn't feel his collar, Guv.'

'No?'

'No, sir. Fowles and Carter brought him in. I know enough about the case so . . .'

'Yes, how far did you get?'

'Nowhere as yet, Guv. He swears that he doesn't associate with Legless or Old English Tom anymore, and he knows nothing about paper.'

'Yes, well he would tell you that, wouldn't he? Eh?'

'I suppose he would, Guv.'

Sutcliffe had flat eyes, blank with not a hint of compassion in them. 'Tell you what,' he even managed a twist of a smile, '– go and get yourself a nice cup of tea, Sarn't Mountford, and I'll take over.'

She went up to the canteen – saw Big Toe in his overcoat on his way out of the building – and took a mug of what passed for coffee down to the office. Nobody was in. It was, she thought, as jolly as a cemetery at three in the morning. Possibly slightly less jolly.

Then the telephone rang.

Her direct line.

'West End Central CID, Sarn't Mountford.'

'I need help,' the girl said. 'I need to get away and hide.'

Suzie would have known the voice anywhere. It was Sybil and she sounded terrified.

Eight

This was a bonus. Suzie had planned to manipulate the building boys at the Regent Palace in only a few hours time. The aim was to penetrate the closed circle around the Balvak Twins, and until now the Trinity Building Co. had been her only hope. She had never expected the Sybil thing to pay off as quickly as this. She had been uncertain if it *would* pay off at all. Now it had turned up, possibly outstripping the other option. Crickey, she thought. It had only been a faint smell of intuition that wafted to her in that little room behind the bar of the Nightlight. A hint, a whiff, a shadow. In any case, she was not about to share her thoughts with anyone else except Dandy Tom Livermore. He was the only police officer who would take her seriously. Most of the others considered that women in the Met were good only for making the tea, taking dictation, dealing with other women, looking after lost kids and doing the senior officers' shopping of a Saturday afternoon.

'What're you afraid of?' she asked Sybil.

'The Twins.' Perhaps it was the effect of the tinny microphone in the public telephone receiver, but in those two words Sybil conjured up all the horrors of the night; the fears of the oppressed; the despair of one who will get caught, and suffer agonies because of it. 'Their people're coming for me.' Her voice trembled.

'Where are you now?'

'I'm in Piccadilly Underground: that main circular part, where they do the tickets, before you get to the moving staircases.'

'The concourse?'

'Yeah. Yeah, I think that's what they call it, goes right round the Circus, but underground. I'm in the Regent Palace end. But

I'll go up to the news cinema in the Dilly.' Suzie could hear the trepidation in the girl's voice. Throat dry, she thought. Throat dry and palms sweaty against the black instrument. 'I can't stay out here for much longer.' Sybil was heading towards breaking point: as though a pack of hounds was baying towards her as she spoke.

News cinemas offered one hour of entertainment round the clock: a couple of newsreels, a ten-minute short – sometimes a comedy, sometimes a Ministry of Information subject – and two cartoons. A bob for an hour in the dark and an up-to-date film taking you into the heart of the war. She remembered being in a news cinema at the time of Dunkirk: she had an hour to kill before catching her train to Newbury. They showed the grainy real film of the men lining up in the water to get into the boats; some shivered wrapped in blankets; men in civilian clothes and in the Naval 'square rig' helped half-conscious men into boats. And suddenly within the darkness of the cinema a woman's voice, plaintive, rising – 'That's my Bert! It's Bert! Dear God, Bert!' And the thump of the tip-up seats going up like mortar bombs along the row: the woman blundering out, helped by an usherette through the minefield out to whatever horror she'd seen on the screen.

Suzie brought her mind back to the frightened girl. 'Of course you can't stay there for long.' Agreeing with her and willing her to be calm. 'But hang on, Sybil. I'll get to you as quickly as I can. I may just walk past you, understand? Maybe slow down and tell you what to do. If that *is* how I play it, you're to do exactly as I say. Alright?'

'Anything – but get me out, please.'

'I'll be with you in ten minutes or so. Are there many people around?'

'Hardly anyone. Please hurry, Miss Mountford. If they catch up with me I'm done for.'

'What you wearing?'

'Got me leopard-skin coat on.'

'Shoes? Can you walk?'

'Well, I'm wearing heels, but . . .'

Shit, the girl shouldn't be allowed out on her own.

'Never mind, I'll be with you as quickly as I can.'

Suzie closed the line, grabbed her hat, coat, gasmask and handbag and left the office almost tripping over her feet to get out.

'I'll be back,' she told Darkie Knight at the front desk. 'Off to see the wizard. Right?'

'Follow the Yellow Brick Road, Suzie,' he called after her.

It took her the better part of ten minutes to get to Swann & Edgar, duck down into the Tube concourse, along the tunnel of gleaming tiles, over to the further side and into one of the phone booths, dialling her own St Martin's Lane number.

'Tommy?' She kept her voice down when he answered. 'Just listen to me.'

'Go ahead, heart.' Not a hint of bleariness as he came out of sleep. Tommy was wonderful at waking up, like a swimmer bursting from the water, fresh and clear-headed.

She wondered if this was the booth that Sybil had used. She could see past the ticket counters to the great painted proscenium which straddled the walls and ceiling above the banks of escalators reaching down into the maw of the underground railway. The picture was a huge panorama of corn, stooked and ready to be stripped and winnowed, and above all there was this glowing and wondrous country lady, skirts lapping around her, bearing a basket with great sheaves of the same golden corn and brown-speckled eggs. When she had first seen that panorama, as a very young child, Suzie had been convinced the woman was God. Only later her mother told her it was the Ovaltine lady displaying the raw product and the health she brought with it. And for a second she heard children's voices piping sweetly: We are the Ovaltineys, little girls and boys.

'Where's the squad car?' she asked, knowing that Tommy's Reserve Squad kept a car and an officer on standby day and night, brushing the cobwebbed memories out of her head.

'Wherever you want it to be, heart. But Molly's on duty tonight and we can't use it. Smash our charade.'

Molly Abelard, fancied herself as Tommy Livermore's personal bodyguard, a leading light in the Reserve Squad. Wouldn't do at all. 'What about Brian?' she asked and Tommy said it may take him ten minutes longer, but Brian would be fine.

Brian was Tommy's driver and it was said that he only joined the Met when Tommy was made a DCS and put in charge of the squad. Before that, the story went, Brian was a driver on the Livermore family estate at Kingscote. Some even went so far as to say that he had known Tommy since he was knee-high to a grasshopper. Whatever the truth, Brian was the three wise monkeys rolled into one: blind, deaf and dumb. Never dropped a hint or raised an eyebrow about what Dandy Tom did, or where he went.

'How long to get Brian doing a circuit, then? Shaftesbury Avenue, Charing Cross Road, then back the other way?'

'He'll be out there in around ten minutes. Fifteen at the most. What's he looking for?'

'I'll walk slowly up Shaftesbury Avenue, then up Charing Cross Road, reversing it at Leicester Square. If he watches for me he'll see – either ahead of me or, more probably, behind me – a young tarty-looking girl in a fake leopard-skin coat, and probably tottering in six-foot heels.'

'Know the type,' muttered Dandy Tom.

'Her name's Sybil, and I want Brian to lift her off the street, drive around a bit with her down on the floor. Then, when he's sure it's all clear I want the girl dropped off with you, Tommy. She's frightened. The Balvaks are after her and she has the combination to a lot of things locked away in their organization. Be kind to her, Tom. Feed her. Tuck her up in the spare room and lie across her door till I get home. First though, tell Brian to be careful because I really don't want him to be snagged or spotted by the Balvaks or others not entitled.'

'Good as done, heart. Proud of you.' Tommy was away.

Suzie went along the white-tiled tunnel, past the Gentlemen's Lavatory reeking of urine, then up the steps emerging under the arches at the bottom of Regent Street. She remembered a joke that Tommy had told her – Man arrives at the VD Clinic and says, 'Good morning, I've come in answer to your advertisement in the Piccadilly Underground Gents' Lavatory.'

She walked as briskly as she dared in the blackout. It was

not a completely pitch dark night, and as she came abreast of the little entrance to the news cinema she glimpsed Sybil huddled against the stone facing just inside the entrance.

There was a soft blue light behind the glass of the box office, and the shadow of an elderly grey-haired woman seeing to the tickets.

Suzie examined her left shoe, fiddling with the heel. 'Follow me, Sybil,' she muttered and as they set off she told her where they were going and what she expected to happen. Then she told the girl to lag behind. 'You'll see me signal the car,' she said.

They headed up Shaftesbury Avenue, Suzie dawdling, aware of the girl tottering along relatively slowly at her heels, taking teensy-weensy steps. She'll topple into the gutter, Suzie thought, and, as they reached Cambridge Circus, she set off across the street, heading into the Charing Cross Road.

'Overtake me,' she told Sybil, and slowed to a snail's pace to let her go past. Then, just as they were drawing abreast of Foyles book shop, on the opposite side of the road, she saw the grey Wolseley belonging to the Reserve Squad, with its down-pointing slits of headlights, looming up through the night and, as it swept by, so she could just make out Brian with his short back and sides as he turned his pugnacious head to acknowledge Suzie.

There was nobody else near them on the pavement. 'You're on your own,' Suzie said, just loud enough for Sybil to hear. 'Car'll pick you up in a minute.' She went through a pantomime of looking at her watch, lifting her wrist to squint at it; hesitating; realizing she was supposed to be somewhere else; turning, taking a few paces in the opposite direction, then turning to look both ways before she crossed the road.

Should've been an actor, heart.

And as she did this last thing, the grey Wolseley came growling out of the darkness as Brian changed down and passed her, slowing and drawing in to the side of the road, calling gravel-voiced to Sybil to get in.

Then the car hustled off to be joined with the night, swallowing Sybil and Brian into darkness as if they had never been. So Suzie crossed the road and picked up the pace, returning to West End Central via Piccadilly Circus and was greeted by Jack Knight – 'You see him?'

'Who?'

'Bloody Wizard of Oz, Suzie.'

'Oh, him. No. Not even a Munchkin or a Lollypop Kid.'

'Not even a Tin Man?'

'Not a Hollow Man,' she said remembering T. S. Eliot. 'Blasted grasshoppers,' she mouthed. 'Typical of men, they get you all excited and then let you down with a whimper instead of a bang.'

'You should be so lucky, Suzie,' he laughed, and she knew he'd be telling his mates in the canteen 'That sergeant bint, Suzie. Must know a thing or two. Talked about not getting banged. My word. Laugh?'

As she went down to the CID Office she heard, in the back of her head, the Ink Spots singing their popular record 'Whispering Grass':

> *Why do you whisper, green grass?*
> *Why tell the trees what ain't so? . . .*
> *Whispering grass, don't tell the trees*
> *'Cause the trees don't need to know.*

And she grinned to herself at the irony of it all. In her mind's eye she saw the black faces of the popular Ink Spots. She who had never in all her life as yet seen a man with a black face, except at the pictures or in a photograph – like the picture of the Ink Spots on the sheet music which you could buy at Alphonse Carey's shop in Northbrook Street, Newbury, along with the records, the harmonicas, ocarinas and Jews' harps.

The CID room was still empty, so she sat down and made some rough notes about how to approach the Trinity Building Co., but Sybil kept coming into her head and she knew that she would rather go home and face Sybil's problems than the builders, so she destroyed the notes and put the pieces in her bag. And she was worried all the time. Wondered if she'd missed anything; if someone had been watching, so that even as she sat there, the Balvaks already knew where Sybil had got to and who had spirited her off the street; and knew exactly

95

what Suzie would be up to at the Regent Palace around seven thirty, eight o'clock.

Charlie never misses a thing.

Suzie walked through the doors of the Regent Palace Hotel a little before a quarter to eight in the morning, having made her way tired and anxious through the drab, anodyne streets. Part-way down towards Reception, she saw a man in RAF uniform talking nineteen to the dozen to a civilian and she thought, I know him, but couldn't remember from where.

At Reception, people were trying to pay their bills and get out of the hotel, catch their trains, get to their meetings, dash from their lovers for it was the morning after the uneasy night before.

Finally she had the attention of one of the young women. 'I believe Susan Wood's expecting me. Miss Mountford.'

'I'll see if she's free.' Half turn, double take and, 'What is it in relation to?'

'It's a personal matter. I spoke to Miss Marks yesterday.'

The girl looked daggers at her and swanned off, pretending to be searching for her superior. She returned in a couple of minutes and invited Suzie to come round to the door that gave her entrance to the Reception area.

'Miss Mountford,' she announced a few seconds later showing Suzie into a small office which had 'Duty Manager' neatly stencilled on the door.

Susan Wood rose from behind her desk, a tall elaborate woman in her early thirties with assisted blonde hair.

'Miss Mountford, I'm sorry I wasn't expecting you. I thought . . .'

'Didn't Brenda Marks . . . ?'

'Oh, yes. But they paid their accounts and left. The Bishop brothers and Mr Green. The gentlemen you wanted to speak with.'

'They left?' A slap in the face. It stung, it hurt, rocked her back on her heels. Since the business of Sybil, she had wanted to bypass the lads who were the Trinity Building Co. Now, suddenly being prevented from seeing them left her almost desolate. She'd had a lot riding on this, had searched for them over several weeks, and in a second she'd lost it all. Worse was to come. 'But, when . . . ?' she stammered.

'Most unusual,' Susan Wood was offering a chair, asking if she would like coffee? Tea? She would and the girl who had ushered her in was sent to get coffee. Did she take milk? No. Sugar? Two lumps.

'They were booked in for another week,' Susan Wood said. 'Then, shortly after I came on duty last night – around nine, just after nine actually . . .' She had one of those Wimbledon or New Malden accents, a thick veneer of what would be called Oxford English, but with the odd slurred vowel and the occasional over-emphasis that gave her away – if you were into the Professor Higgins stuff that is. 'They'd been out – I know because there were messages for them: well, someone had been trying to get them all evening; I happened to be on the counter when they came back. Shortly after nine. Asked for their bills. Said they had to go to a job up North. Mr Green spent a while looking at the train timetables while the others went up and packed. We strung out putting their bills together. Made it last. I personally tried to get you on the phone. Three times, Miss Mountford. They said you were out of the office. But I spoke to your senior officer. He didn't think there was much of a problem. Said he'd tell you when you came back.'

'You remember who it was?' Suzie actually crossed her fingers behind her back.

'Oh yes,' said Susan Wood consulting a message pad by the phone on her desk. 'Yes, it was a Detective Chief Inspector. A Mr Harvey. Anthony Harvey. Sounded nice.'

'Oh, shit!' said Suzie, but not aloud.

'He said he'd tell you. He obviously didn't.'

'No,' Suzie shook her head, confused and alarmed, her tummy turning over. 'No. I'll talk to him tomorrow.' Unless he comes looking for me today, she thought. It should be her day off today. As she walked back through the entrance hall of the hotel she began to count in her head, trying to work out the number of people who knew she wanted to make contact with the trio of young men who made up the Trinity Building Co. She thought of five people who were searching

97

with her, unseen informers. Then there was Brenda Marks. She wondered. Said another four-letter word in her head. Out on the street it was raining and she hadn't brought her umbrella. She thought, Charlie never misses a thing. They all said so.

They had a great deal riding on the Bishop brothers and Derek Green. Tommy Livermore had been trawling for them since before he sent Suzie into Balvak country. They were ninety-nine point nine per cent certain that the three men had absconded from the Army – AWOL, as it is referred to. Absent Without Leave. Serious.

It had happened during the chaos that was Dunkirk: and the reorganization once the armies pulled themselves together and sorted themselves out on English soil – most of them minus their weapons and equipment.

One of the first things the Military Police, in their various incarnations, were faced with, was to discover who had returned safely to the United Kingdom, who had died – which in many cases meant disappeared – who was wounded and taken prisoner, and who was simply a prisoner. Long lists of names fell into the Missing Believed Killed category, and much time was spent sifting the lists, visiting next of kin, and interviewing men who claimed to have last seen certain individuals somewhere in France.

Among those who had disappeared without trace were Richard Bernard Banks, David Michael Banks and the Bankses' cousin Derek John Grimshaw. All three men had been in what used to be described as the PBI – the Poor Bloody Infantry – much to their irritation, for they were all three experienced builders, having worked for Richard Banks senior, much respected in the trade around the Guildford area.

After members of the Trinity Building Co. were first spotted doing odd jobs for the Balvaks, Tommy Livermore had moved in and made a short recce. He pronounced that the builders would be useful, but they needed to have the three of them contained, preferably in a hotel, if they were going to do any good by them. So he started working backwards to make certain the Bishop brothers, and their cousin Derek Green, were in reality the Banks brothers and Derek Grimshaw.

Eventually, making forays among his people in the Military

Police, Tommy tracked down the last known movements of the Bishops and Green. They had made the coast before the main retreat in the direction of Dunkirk. Some four days before the little ships started lifting the troops from the beaches, the Banks brothers and cousin Green hitched a fishing boat out of Boulogne and eventually landed near Folkestone. Their paybooks were checked by an officer in the Pay Corps, they were interviewed by a Military Intelligence Officer, then issued with one or two small lost items of clothing and sent on leave.

A week later, Richard Banks senior was in a right old state having been informed of the death of both his sons; while Hazel Grimshaw (née Banks) had an unconvincing fit of the vapours over the news that her only son, Derek, was reported killed outside Boulogne, stone dead, at his feet a grass green turf, at his head a stone. Then, wonder of wonders, the Grimshaws were spotted by a business rival having a knees up in a pub in the next county.

After that it was easy to reach the conclusion that the Bishops and Green were identical to the Bankses and Grimshaw. Also that they were known to the Balvaks and all who rode with them, and for reasons of their own Charlie and Connie Balvak had thrown a *cordon sanitaire* around them.

'But, heart,' Tommy said to Suzie when they really got down to cases, 'my suspicion is that they're working for the money and not for the criminality. If we approach them in the right manner they'll be as clay in our hands. And if we promise to keep the crushers off them they'll grass-up their protectors quick as kiss your backside – which is what we want. So if we threaten to pee on them from a great height, I reckon they'll be our chums for life.'

At that particular point he actually had them contained. Teams from the Reserve Squad stuck to the trio of builders as close as – to use Tommy's colourful expression – snot to a sheet, and there were many amusing tales that appeared in the surveillance reports. Derek Green, in particular, had a fund of stories from his time in the Army, which he held in great contempt, and he was overheard telling many of these in the pubs he frequented. There was the heart-warming yarn about the corporal who had marched the squad into a Nissen hut containing rows of iron bedsteads – privates, soldiers, sleeping for the use of – and instructed them, 'I want you to dismantle these beds. And when you've done that you can mantle them up again.'

Tommy had the three lads in his sights, then, what with one thing and another going on, somebody took their eye off the ball and the Trinity Building Co. went missing. Actually what happened was that they began to change the place where they stayed about three times a week. They also started to work nights and stopped putting their heads above the parapet. The work was a long old job at St Ursula's Hut. So, when Suzie arrived at West End Central, Tommy told her the Bishop brothers needed finding, as did Derek Green, so she put them on her list – the one she passed on to informers as she recruited them.

'We need those builders,' Tommy told her. 'We should get them and put them in the bank, but Derek'll probably be scared that we'll send him back to mantle up those beds.' And he chuckled his delightful upper-class chuckle. It was the kind you heard at the Oxford and Cambridge Rugby, she thought; and at the Polo, of course.

Nine

When she got into the flat Dandy Tom was sitting at her kitchen table in his shirtsleeves. You didn't expect to encounter Tommy Livermore in his shirtsleeves – he was usually so correct: shirt, tie, suit and polished shoes. But Suzie Mountford had seen him in less than his shirtsleeves, so it did not trouble her. Then she realized there was a purpose in him not being fully dressed. Clever old devil, she thought. He's waiting for the girl, Sybil, to rise from the scallop shell of slumber and he's discarded tie and jacket to meet her. She could see that also, around his waist, he wore an elasticized belt in his school colours with one of those S-shaped snake clasps. She'd bet he had gym shoes on his feet. She'd also wager that when he was at prep school he wore one of those strange English floppy-brimmed grey felt hats. Like Christopher Robin.

This was Tommy in casual dress for the interrogation.

'Coffee, heart?' he asked with one of his best smiles.

She dropped into a chair. 'I feel like I'm shedding my skin. How's our guest?'

'Fed her a big cup of milky Horlicks, heart. Stave off the dreaded night starvation.' Night starvation being the dubious ailment Ovaline used in its advertisements. 'Not a peep out of her since I bedded her down.'

'Since you did what?'

'Perhaps I should rephrase that.' He chuckled and she leaned over to kiss his cheek.

'Nobody spotted her coming in?'

'Dead of night. Not a drum was heard, not a funeral thing. You look buggered, heart, to coin a phrase. My view.'

So she told him all about Sybil: about the killing of Buller

101

Belcher; about Greek Rose and the three hours that had gone missing. Lastly she talked about Big Toe; then her strange instinct concerning Sybil, and how the girl had telephoned frightened out of her wits.

'Always said you were a natural, heart. No doubt about it.' He asked a few questions indicating he would like to do the initial grilling. Then, as he was winding down, she broke the bad news.

'Problem, Tommy. Big Toe Harvey knows I'm after the builders: Dick, Dave and Derek. Someone talked and they scarpered from the Regent Palace. Took off in the middle of the night.'

Tommy received the news stoically. She felt more than saw him wince and ride with the punches, though his mouth moved. 'Shit!' he was saying.

She told him what the undermanager – Susan Wood – had said about Derek talking of going to do a job up North.

'Well, better take a sounding,' he said, and wandered off into the master bedroom, where he had, covertly, installed a telephone with his private number so he could still be available to the Spear Carriers – as he called the specialists of the Reserve Squad – even though he was virtually living here, full time with Suzie, at the top of St Martin's Lane. She wondered what her mother would say if she knew. To tell the truth, she lived in fear of her mum dropping in unannounced on some quick visit from Newbury. Maybe with the Galloping Major, as she called her stepfather. She still didn't quite approve of the Galloping Major, though she'd partly made her peace with him last Christmas.

She bent over her coffee and sipped. It was very good and she knew that Tommy had a special source for coffee, as he did for most things. Tommy Livermore would've made a damned good villain if he hadn't been a peeler. She could hear him in the bedroom now chatting away on the telephone: charming snakes, as he called it. He knows people, and he's doing what he does best, she thought. He's reaching out, trying to get into the builders' minds. Find out where they've gone. What they'd be like on the witness stand.

When Tommy returned he was smiling. 'Looks as though

they're heading up to Geordie land. King's Cross–Newcastle-upon-Tyne late last night – the sleeper, even though you mainly sleep sitting up these days and it'll be running about seven hours late. Serve 'em right. Shouldn't have joined.' Which was about as far as you got in the way of sympathy from Tommy.

Train journeys were really only bearable for civilians over modest distances. The trains that made incursions into the north and beyond, over the border into Scotland, were horrifically difficult. When the Luftwaffe came over, trains stayed in stations or crawled at 25 miles an hour. As the posters told everyone – with see-saw drawings – before the war 75% of trains were for passengers and 25% for freight; now 60% were for freight and 40% for passengers. The entire rail network was overstretched, and a lengthy journey could last twice as long as its scheduled time, was always backbreaking and sometimes heartbreaking. Already the rolling stock was taking the strain, people stood crushed together in the corridors and if you did get a seat you could bet on someone else's elbow in your ribs, or a desperately fatigued head slumped on your shoulder. When soldiers travelled they often did so in full marching order with a rifle and kitbag to lug along as well. And –

'*Is Your Journey Really Necessary?*' the posters blared.

'We'll see,' Tommy mused, and at that moment the door to the spare bedroom across the hall opened, tentatively, and Sybil appeared dressed only in a black bra and a matching lace-trimmed half-petticoat. She wore stockings as well, so was almost certainly wearing the more intimate apparel so beloved of smart girls – the suspender belt and frilled pants – but the slip's colour blacked out further viewing.

Suzie, being who she was, hurried across the hall and propelled the girl back into the bedroom, then operated a shuttle service to take her a spare dressing gown – a blue woollen affair with frogging, an elaborate embroidered badge of rank on the cuffs and a silk rope in a lighter blue with tasselled ends to knot about the waist. It had belonged to Suzie's brother, James, who would doubtless, at sixteen, be delighted to have a half-naked woman covered by it.

Sybil looked suitably tousled, her flaming hair tangled and

103

the bruises beneath her eyes gave the illusion that her eyes were half-buried in her forehead. Like a frightened fox cub, she blinked at each of them in turn.

'You've met Arthur,' Suzie smiled vaguely.

'Last night,' Sybil's voice half caught in the back of her throat.

'Yes,' Suzie gave her the full-blown grin. '*He's* not supposed to be here either.'

'Coffee?' Tommy asked her and she nodded a yes.

Tommy was always Arthur in front of strangers or people who didn't need to know. Such a wag, Arthur, she would say when she wanted to irritate him. He hated being described as a wag.

They got Sybil seated comfortably and Tommy chatted to her, putting her at ease while Suzie fried some of her lover's aristocratic dad's bacon for them.

'You sure you've got enough? You given me three rashers?' Sybil looked amazed that her plate was so full.

'Yes we've got enough,' Suzie grinned at her. 'Arthur's uncle's got a farm. Want a fried egg and fried bread as well?'

Sybil couldn't believe her luck, tucking in like there was no tomorrow, while Tommy volleyed questions at her – about where she lived. She had a room in Paddington. Not on the station, he hoped, and what about her parents? They had a semi on the outskirts of Peckham. Nice, any brothers or sisters? One brother in the Navy and a sister still at school though she was no better than she ought to be at fifteen.

'What were you so frightened of last night, Sybil?'

She had just been lifting her fork to her mouth, a nice piece of lean bacon speared on the tines and the bacon dripping with egg yolk where she'd just dipped it and given it a little twirl. She took the mouthful, chewed and got lipstick on her teeth – she'd remembered to put on warpaint – then before she swallowed the whole lot she said one word: 'Frightened.'

'Yes, that's what I asked you, Sybil. Why?'

She looked at Suzie as if seeking her permission to talk to this man, Arthur. It was as if it was their secret – hers and Suzie's.

'You can talk to him quite safely. In fact he's a very important police officer. Much more important than I'll ever be,' and Tommy made a self-effacing gesture, muttering something about flattery.

'So, what really frightened you?' he asked again.

Sybil opened her mouth to speak, then stopped, nodding towards Suzie. 'She knows.'

'Who's she, the cat's mother?' Tommy asked in a voice that Suzie thought was possibly a passable imitation of his nanny. It was certainly, she guessed, the kind of comment his nanny would have made.

'Miss Mountford,' she said, *sotto voce.*

'I certainly do *not* know, Sybil.' Suzie contrived to sound outraged.

'You must of known. If you didn't know, why'd you tell me to ring you?'

'You seemed unnecessarily troubled.'

'Well, so I should be. They killed Buller and he was my mate.'

'Who killed Buller?'

'The Twins. Well one of them . . . I don't know which one because I was behind the curtain at the back of the bar . . . Then they got up that story about a crowd of Army blokes knocking him down . . . Got it up between them as old Buller lay out stiff on the floor . . . But one of them kicked him to death and that Porky Pine and his friend Flash're coming round to talk to me today . . . Porky rang Greek Rose last night and she told me they was coming round today dinnertime, and I had to be there twelve o'clock sharp because they wanted to talk to me . . . so did Charlie Balvak, and I reckoned that meant only one thing.'

'And Buller wasn't your boyfriend?' Suzie asked.

'No. Buller had a girl who worked up the Melody.'

'You got a boyfriend, Sybil?' Dandy Tom asked, with extraordinary prescience as it happened.

'Little Nell.' Sybil looked away, then back at Suzie, and from Suzie back to Dandy Tom Livermore. 'I know it sounds odd. You know who Little Nell is?'

'I know who Little Nell is.' Tommy said. 'I know full well

who Neville Bellman is. Cartload of monkeys, that's what Little Nell Bellman is.'

'And that's another reason why I'm frightened . . . I mean, well, Little Nell and I, well we're not going to get married or anything . . . I don't fancy him, not really, but it's difficult to refuse someone like Nell . . . And, well Charlie Balvak accused Buller of stealing from the club . . . He's wrong. He should look closer to home.' She paused as though on the brink of taking a leap into the unknown. Then – 'It's Little Nell who's doing the thieving.'

Suzie reckoned that was probably an exceptionally interesting piece of information. Little Nell was another 'face' on the manor, except with Nell it was more a case of his small body being the known commodity.

Tommy Livermore looked across at Suzie and thought – not for the first time – that she was a natural. A marvel, he said to himself. She was one of those girls who had been born with instinct and didn't even know she possessed it. She could look at a painting and know immediately what the artist intended, just as she could look at a crime scene, or read the details of an investigation and have the various possibilities there, like a bunch of markers in her hand. More, she'd know where each would lead. And, ah sweet mystery of life, she had no idea of the extent of the talents that inhabited her senses.

Tommy had been charged with recruiting her for special work, and his early reports on her all said that the instruction she required should lead her towards comprehending the way her own mind worked. Later he had revised his opinion. She should, he wrote after he had fallen in love with her, be left to discover her own methods of disentangling the various knots of jumbled clues; to try to teach her could possibly bring about a self-consciousness that may totally ruin a natural talent. At the same time he could not himself divine the true way her natural intuition worked. She played by ear, he reckoned. Didn't need to read the music. And she really didn't know how she managed it.

'. . . it's Little Nell who's doing the thieving.'

True to everything she had ever been told, Suzie went still. No reaction. Even an attitude of deep indifference. Sybil's information regarding Little Nell seemed to have passed over her head.

Good girl, Tommy thought, then he yawned and asked if they had seen those new posters that had appeared on the underground – 'Careless Talk Costs Lives' by Fougasse the clever cartoonist. Everyday situations, couple of girls on a bus chattering away and, underneath, the warning 'You never know *who's* listening!' And true enough, behind them are seated the Führer and his fat friend Reichmarschal Göring in his full fancy dress with medals and in his hand the Field Marshal's baton. There were three other posters in a similar vein: a telephone kiosk with a plethora of Hitlers peeping from its rear, two women gossips, and a pair of blokes in a gentlemen's club, with a full-wigged Hitler looking down from a Caroline painting. Very amusing.

Tommy was good at languid. Yawned again. 'Very droll that Fougasse,' he laughed lazily then asked, 'So old Little Nell Bellman's dipping into the Twins' pockets, is he? How'd he go about that, Sybil? How does it work?'

She told them in simple words. 'Skimmed the cash off the top. Ten, fifteen per cent of cash paid at the door. Nobody bothered to match up the entrance fees with the number of people who signed up – except Nell of course. You know how money and the clubs go hand in hand.'

They knew how it worked. If it was a private club lots of things became legal. To turn it into a private club they made you a one-time member. You gave money they gave you a little card with your name – or the name you chose – on it. 'You know the rest,' Sybil didn't smile. 'It's amazing how many people lose those membership cards. Mind you they don't always want to come back, but when they do, nine times out of ten they've lost their cards. Like taking sherbet from a sprog. In a good week we'd pocket a ton, clear.'

'And you hand it over to Nell?'

'He comes in twice a week. Buller used to say he didn't need Eno's Fruit Salts, the money kept him regular. We slipped him the cash and he give us a tenner when he remembered.'

'And you reckon he did this over all the Twins' clubs.'

'It's what Buller said he was doing. Had a grand plan,

Buller reckoned. Little Nell was going to take over the world. Dead crafty.'

'And you know what function Little Nell plays in the Twins' organization?'

'He's their accountant. Stashes the cash, pays the taxes, knows all the fiddles, tucks the folding stuff under the mattress, keeps them happy.'

'You wouldn't think he was that clever to look at him, would you?' Tommy winked at Suzie. He genuinely hadn't known what Nell did until now. 'Sybil, a difficult question: treading on a sensitive area. I had been told that Nell . . . Well . . .'

'Was AC/DC?' She grinned and Tommy nodded. 'Well, he is,' Sybil continued. 'You wouldn't know when he's at it, but you can tell when you're in mixed company. One night, down the Nightlight there was this really lovely bloke came in and Nell couldn't keep his eyes off him. Young Naval Petty Officer he was. I said to Nell that I thought he was dead smashing and Nell said, "I'll fight you for him." Very quick, Nell.'

'Like the old greased lightning, yes.' Tommy didn't even smile.

'Oh yes, he's clever all right, and nasty with it as well,' she said.

'I'll bet,' Suzie winked back at Tommy, but he still didn't smile. He was off somewhere else, trying to solve a puzzle that had yet to be set.

So they talked away the morning and part of the afternoon. The conversation must have seemed rambling and inconsequential to Sybil, but to both Tommy and Suzie it filled in gaps in their knowledge, and made bridges over the attitudes of the Balvak Twins and their henchmen. Tommy said later that it was the most comprehensive tutorial they could ever have attended on the subject of the Twins and their world.

They ate a scratch lunch of cold boiled ham, potatoes and runner beans cooked straight from the Kilner jar where they had been sealed between layers of salt the previous summer: the meal spiced up with some of the Countess of Kingscote's green tomato chutney. By this time they permanently kept the front door locked in case Sybil decided that she'd like to leg it back to where she came from. But Tommy was worried. 'She can't stay here for ever, and we need someone to watch over her full time. Any ideas?'

They were in the master bedroom and aware that somewhere else in the flat Sybil was pacing, unsettled and jumpy. After a dull, leaden day the winter sun had finally emerged, albeit weakly, and was fingering its way through the west-facing windows. Suzie had taken a late afternoon bath and was dressing while Dandy Tom lay sprawled on the bed paying an undisguised interest.

'So what're we going to do about her?'

'I rather care for those flimsy Jane-like things, heart . . . Yes, indeed, what are we to do?' Pause while he ogled her standing before the mirror in her diaphanous pink frillies. Then –

'Rod for our own backs, that's what she is.' Tommy stated for the third or fourth time.

'We can't return to sender.'

'No, but perhaps we can use her to our own advantage. You think your mum and the Gallant Major would take her?'

'Yes, of course they would. They'd take anyone, but you'd have to provide a bodyguard and that might prove difficult. After all you need to keep Brian in London and he's the only—'

'What about Molly? I think we could trust Molly if we explained it properly.'

'You *think*, darling Tom? You only *think*? If you told Molly to go up in an aeroplane and leap out with a parachute she'd do it immediately.'

'Oh, heart, yes: she's already done *that*.'

It was Tommy Livermore's driver, Brian, who picked up WDS Molly Abelard as she was leaving New Scotland Yard that evening. Molly lived alone in the Earl's Court Road – the Kensington High Street end – but Brian ferried her to Notting Hill Gate, about a hundred yards from the fish and chip shop where she was told to meet Tommy. There was little fish these days, but they managed to do good portions of chips. When Molly arrived she had done exactly as Brian told her and drawn a revolver, on the Detective Chief Super's instructions. It was a standard Smith & Wesson .38 and she

109

wore it under her woollen jacket, in a canvas holster next to the roll-necked dark jumper, and felt dangerous as a result. But Molly always felt dangerous. As Tommy said of her, 'she's the most lethal person in the Reserve Squad.' He also claimed she was sent away periodically to train Combined Ops people in methods of silent killing and, in Suzie Mountford's early days under Tommy's command, it was Molly Abelard who taught her some of the secrets of the deadly black arts.

'Molly, heart,' Dandy Tom said in his languorous upper-class voice, a chip held between the forefinger and thumb of his right hand, as if he were conducting some bizarre orchestra. 'Molly, heart, this is not to be passed on to anyone else. Life and death matter and all that. Quiet as the jolly cold grave. Strictly *entre nous*. Understand?'

'You know me, Chief. Dead confidential.'

'Good. You'll remember Suzie Mountford and I had a short sharp spat some time ago, that ended with Suzie leaving the Squad.' She hesitated, then nodded, and he was off telling her just enough – that the spat had been a simulation (his word); giving her the right instructions, passing on everything including the route she would be taking to Newbury in the car with Brian, Suzie and the girl Sybil. 'I'll be driving myself. Cross country. Unmarked vehicle. See you there. Suzie says there's some spare clobber of hers down there, so you needn't pack a weekend bag.'

'How long will I be there, Chief?'

'Hard to say. Week. Ten days. I'll put it about that you're in hospital. Anyone we should notify?'

'It'll be fine, Chief.' Most of the squad called him Chief, but Molly was the most punctilious.

'Good. Get cracking.' He sprinkled a little more salt on his chips and continued to eat.

Before leaving, Molly leaned over and squeezed his lower left arm. 'I'm so glad, Chief. So glad that Suzie's okay. And you're . . . you know.'

'Don't breathe a word of it. Not to a soul.'

'Not even to an earwig,' which was Molly Abelard's idea of a joke.

And she was gone.

Fifteen minutes later, Dandy Tom went outside, stood for five minutes letting his eyes adjust to the night. Then he walked the half-mile or so up the road where his own dark-blue private Vauxhall saloon was parked.

They drove roughly west into Berkshire, skirting Bracknell and going south of Reading, then cutting across country towards Newbury. Brian drove with Molly Abelard sitting on his left, her body very still and alert. Suzie was seated in the back with Sybil, who was like a child constantly asking where they were taking her, and how long it would be before they arrived.

'Best you don't know, love,' Molly told her: a voice as dark as the night.

They were cocooned in blackness and Brian seemed to be driving on instinct alone. He had come up to the flat, parking the car a mile away, and Suzie found him sprawled on the floor with Tommy, half-inch-to-the-mile Ordnance Survey Maps laid out before them, going through the route.

Suzie had left the flat, going to a telephone box to call her mother: Tommy had insisted on it. 'Just to be safe,' he said, though heaven knew the GPO were pretty hopeless if they ever asked them to listen in on a telephone conversation, so how Tommy thought the Balvak twins could have rigged something up in her flat was a mystery. When she asked the operator for the number she was told to insert one shilling and realized that every few minutes the operator would be coming on the line and telling her that time was up unless she'd insert more money, which was less secure than phoning from the flat.

When her mother answered, she told her she was in a phone box with no money and would reverse the charges. Her mother, Helen, wasn't too quick on the uptake and wanted to know everything – how she was, how Tommy was, when was she coming down? 'Tonight, Mum,' she yelled and closed the line, dialling the operator again and asking for the charges to be reversed.

There was a down-at-heel coach house and cottage beside the gates to Larksbrook, the big late eighteenth-century house and grounds in which Suzie had spent her childhood. It was the one thing Daddy had done properly, and from a rare windfall investment he had bought the place outright. Later, in the mid-thirties, he'd had the Coach House done up. His own mum and dad would be living with them some day, he'd thought. The resultant accommodation was nice: two bedrooms, a pleasant sitting room, kitchen and bathroom: completely self-contained. This was where Molly Abelard would keep Sybil safe, hidden away from the Twins.

Lord, Suzie thought, my smashing middle-class childhood. She hadn't realized how wonderful it was until too late: two rooms all her own, and the books, the tennis, the long lawn on a warm summer evening, the wonderful freedom, the greenhouse, fresh vegetables, the coppice, her pony, the eternal parties and hols abroad. She thought it would never end, yet nowadays, since the advent of the Galloping Major, she had reservations about going back to Larksbrook.

There had been Daddy's death, within thirty yards of his own gates – an idiot driving a van in the middle of the road on the last bend before the little stretch of straight tree-lined road, with the walled garden on the left, then the gates and the drive.

She had been sixteen then and the first to get to the car, locked to the van in an embrace of metal: blood everywhere and her father dead. The hurt doubled, quadrupled, when Helen, her mother, announced less than two years after the loss of her father that she was going to marry again. Worse, marry the strutting little Ross Gordon-Lowe – the Galloping Major.

True the terrible events of last Christmas had buried some of the animosity between Suzie and the Major, but still, deep inside there were things that rankled. Damn it, he should've taken her mother away, not insinuated himself into Suzie's happy memories down all the years of growing up.

After her father's death every time she had returned to Larksbrook, she felt the pain, the nausea of the soul, and tonight was no different. They entered the tunnel of trees, dragging the darkness closer around them and her stomach flipped over as she felt the car swing to the left, 'Slow Brian, watch for the gates.'

'Gates?' Brian croaked. 'What gates?' and she remembered her mother had told her that the ornamental iron gates and railings had been removed for salvage like most throughout the country. Then she heard and felt the solid crunch of gravel under the wheels and knew they were up the drive and on to the turning circle.

When we arrive, she had told her mother, don't come out. Don't worry, dear, don't worry and she knew then that her mother wasn't listening to her. I'll see to the sheets, the beds'll be made up. Just take care, Mum, and don't come out.

So what happened? The moment the car came to a halt and she could see they were slap bang in front of the iron-bound oak front door, the door opened, spilling light like liquid on to the grey-fawn gravel, and there was her mother, hurrying out, lifting on her toes and, in the background, the Galloping Major peering round her.

Suzie, furious, slid from the car and ran towards the figures, almost pushing her mother back into the hall with its polished mahogany table, the painting of St Michael's Mount and the scent of beeswax polish: the welcoming smells and the warmth and safety of home.

'No, Mum, get back! Back!' She kicked the door closed behind her, heard far away her little niece and nephew upstairs, out of sight: Ben crowing and Lucy singing excitedly in a high, piping voice.

'Please, Mum, stay away from the door.'

'But Suzie I was only trying to—'

'Your mother was trying to help, Susannah,' from the Galloping Major, pulled up to his full height of five foot two.

'If you want to help, stay indoors,' and, like a sheep dog, she herded them into the drawing room and glimpsed through the dining-room door the table dressed overall for a full dinner party with the silver shining, crystal glasses sparkling and the napery white as a winter scene Christmas card.

'Suzie dear, is Tommy with you? I've prepared a little dinner.' It was now nine forty-five.

'Mum, sit down.'

'But I—'

'Mum, this is a matter of life and death. Literally. Please understand this. Where are the keys to the Coach House? Is it ready? And—'

'The keys are in the locks. I've put clean sheets and blankets on the beds. The blackouts are up as well, and I'm having another pint of milk delivered in the morning, and if there's anything else—'

'Mummy, *please*.' She shouted the 'please' and finally got her mother's attention though the Galloping Major was bristling a little: she still shuddered when she thought of her mother kissing that moustache. 'Tommy's not here yet,' as calmly as she could, 'but he will be, and he'll want to talk to you. I don't know how long we'll need the Coach House but, as I said on the phone, this is a very serious matter. I'll let Tommy explain. Now, could you give me the telephone number over there: I just can't remember it.'

Her mother went through a little routine of the 'is it eight-oh-five or five-oh-eight' variety, then settled on the correct number. Suzie, serious, read them the riot act. No prying; no dropping over there to see them; no calling attention to their guests; no loose talk. There were no immediate neighbours to Larksbrook so that wouldn't pose a problem, but any friends calling and noting people in residence should be shut up like clams. She kept repeating the magic words: 'This is more serious than you can ever know. There are people who'd kill to know who you've got over there in the Coach House.'

And when she finally left them, she found Tommy had arrived and was full of practical instructions. He had also sent Brian back to London with the car and tucked his own dark-blue Vauxhall in among the trees that ran along the wall adjacent to the Coach House. His car, she realized, would be hidden from the road.

She had forgotten what a wonderful hiding place the Coach House had been when she was exploding through adolescence. The smell of polished pine, the undercurrent of sawdust and the memories of lying on one of the beds in winter, reading, for the very first time, books like *Treasure Island*, *Swiss Family Robinson*, *The Coral Island*, *Robin Hood*, *The Wind in the Willows*, *Robinson Crusoe* and *What Katy Did* – her mother's old copy, which sat beside the other titles in the little bookcase built into one of the sitting-room walls.

'It's very lovely,' Sybil seemed almost awestruck. They were

114

upstairs, like schoolgirls staying overnight in an unfamiliar house, and investigating – a treat.

'Everything okay, Molly?' Suzie asked.

'Fine. Don't know if I'll get any sleep without the noise of the Earl's Court Road.'

'I'm sure you'll manage.'

The two bedrooms had not changed in years and they smelled fresh and sweet from her mother's ministrations. In one there was a framed print of some poster they had brought back from a Swiss holiday. In the other a large watercolour of a herbaceous border in front of a red brick wall, a slash of colour and in the distance above the wall, the west end of a cathedral, Salisbury, she'd always thought, with the spire a great stone lance against a pewter sky. Both rooms were spotless. Somehow Suzie wondered if she would ever become as accustomed to housework as her mother appeared to have done.

She asked what the Chief was up to.

'He's just realized that we need an extra body here,' Molly raised her eyebrows. 'I can't leave the girl on her own and we've got to eat.' She made a comic face: as though she was a starving chimpanzee. 'Don't know how I'm going to keep her occupied if this goes on more than a couple of days.'

Tommy had come halfway up the stairs and called for Molly to come down. 'Suzie,' he ordered, 'would you stay up there with Sybil? Someone is coming in for a few minutes.'

Suzie went through and sat in the bedroom Sybil had chosen.

'Why does he want us to stay up here?' Sybil asked.

'He'll have a reason. Our's not to reason why. Our's but to do.'

'Our's but to do what?'

'It's a play on a poem, Sybil. "The Charge of the Light Brigade".'

'Oh.' Total disinterest.

'"Their's not to reason why. Their's but to do and die." Don't you know that poem?'

'Don't think so. Didn't have much time for poetry.'

'I bet you know "All or Nothing at All".'

'That's a song. That's Frank Sinatra. He's really good, very attractive.'

'He's very thin, and it's still a poem,' Suzie started to quote:

'All or nothing at all,
Half love never appealed to me.'

'That's different. It's a nice song.'

She was getting nowhere and thought for a moment that for Molly Abelard the policewoman's life would not be a happy one. Poor Molly, our great quick-shooting city commando.

Outside, a car drew up and Suzie, motioning to the redheaded Sybil to stay in the room, moved into the doorway so she could see down the stairs from the shadow of the landing where the light had been switched off. Sybil giggled, thinking Suzie was being funny and daring: going to watch when she'd been told to keep out of the way. Below, Tommy opened the door, so that for a second a gleam fell on a large figure, tall, red-faced and bulkily built, wearing tweeds and one of those floppy plaid hats that Suzie always associated with fishing. He greeted the newcomer and words floated up from the living room below.

'Wilson? Good to see you. This is Margaret.' Hands clasped for a moment: Wilson, whoever he was, pumping Tommy's arm.

'Hello,' Molly said, cutting in, her name disguised as Margaret. Then they moved away from the staircase and the conversation settled into an inaudible buzz.

Later, as they were walking across to the house, Tommy said, 'The fellow who dropped in was one Wilson Sharp. I know a local superintendent, silent as a tombstone, he recommended Sharp. A farmer, but with experience in police matters – a special constable and totally reliable, my friend says. He's coming over every day with food: the staples, bread that his wife bakes, butter, eggs, cheese from his farm, veg and meat as well. I reckon it's all against the law.' His familiar chuckle, really amused at the situation. Then – 'How much did you tell your mother and the Galloping Major?'

She told him about the problem she'd had trying to keep

116

her mum out of it. 'Trouble is she loves fussing over guests. I think you'll have to put the fear of God into them.'

Tommy grunted and as they reached the door he strode ahead. To give him his due, Tommy did give them hell, telling them they were to stay away and draw no attention to their guests, not once but three times. 'Really Helen and Ross, you don't know how dangerous this is.' He said in his firm voice. He also accepted Helen's invitation to a meal.

'I'm so glad,' she laughed like a young girl and the Major huffed and puffed while Suzie went upstairs to see her sister's children, who were still living at Larksbrook, and were awake, excited at their aunt being there.

Once more she experienced the dreadful ache she always felt on seeing little Ben, born with cerebral palsy, unable to walk properly, profoundly deaf and not able to speak – a deaf mute. Yet he showed his delight at seeing Suzie and clung to her, arms round her neck. She soothed him and stroked his head until he dropped off to sleep.

Lucy, also tired out and fighting sleep, began to be boisterous. 'You staying long, Aunty Suzie? Please, please, please.'

'No, Lucy, I'll be gone again when you wake up, but I'll be back soon for Christmas.'

'Oh, Christmas,' a smile wreathing her little face. 'Yes-yes-yes. At school we're doing a Cativity play and I'm a sheep. I say "Baa" and I gambol – that's a kind of dance the sheep do.'

The child laughed and clung to her Teddy Bear – the one Suzie had given her last Christmas; the one she inexplicably called Mr Gherkin.

Eventually Suzie got the child to cuddle down and embrace sleep. She was tired out and Suzie felt drained, like she often felt after spending time with her nephew and niece. It was difficult to forget.

Helen had got hold of some lamb chops and they had them grilled with potatoes and runner beans. The most unlikely people were storing and preserving vegetables now, and, as she helped her mother in the kitchen, Suzie was shown all kinds of things including eggs in isinglass and lots of Kilner jars, and a whole cupboard full of chutneys and pickles. Her

117

mother never used to preserve or do homemade chutney but the war had changed everyone.

Tommy was relaxed over dinner in spite of the Galloping Major, who, as ever, fawned and flattered: he loved the idea of being close to aristocracy, which was, of course, what Tommy hated most of all. He knew that the Major thought the fact that he was the Honourable Tommy Livermore really amounted to something and did his best to steer him off the track.

Late in the meal the GM said something about Tommy's brother, 'Paul Livermore, who served with me on the Somme. Your brother.'

'Ross,' Tommy said quietly, 'that wasn't my brother – it was, possibly, a distant cousin, as I've told you several times.' Then he turned to Suzie's mother. 'Helen, these really are awfully good lamb chops. How on earth did you get hold of them?'

She did the girlish giggles again and said she really shouldn't tell him – 'You being a policeman.'

'Go, on, Helen. I won't tell.'

'Got them from a local farmer. He's very good. Helps us out quite often. I really got these for the weekend, but it's lovely to see you enjoying them.'

Tommy nodded and again said they were excellent. And so passed on to another subject. Then, just as they were leaving he asked the name of the farmer.

'Which farmer?' Helen seemed puzzled.

'The one who sold you those delicious lamb chops. Wouldn't mind getting hold of some myself.'

Suzie was on the verge of saying that he didn't need a tame farmer because they got everything they could wish from Tommy's father.

'Oh yes, the chops.' Helen was excruciatingly girlish now. 'Cotrell,' she said. 'Clive Cotrell. Got a farm out towards Wantage,' and Suzie saw Dandy Tom visibly relax: though she knew she'd be the only one to notice.

'Your mum gave me a turn tonight.' Tommy was driving carefully through the blackness back to London. 'For a horrible moment I thought her tame farmer might be Wilson Sharp. I'd hate to get her further mixed up with Sybil.'

118

Then, later he began to talk in some detail about Sybil and what he wanted Suzie to do. 'They'll have missed her by now, and the news'll get around pretty sharpish to your unpleasant Mr Harvey. Here's what you do tomorrow,' and he gave her the entire speech, almost word for word.

'I'll bet you a week's pay that within half an hour of you telling him Harvey'll be out into a telephone box. Eh?'

'Won't that put Little Nell in real danger?' she asked, and felt Dandy Tom smile in the darkness.

'Serve him right,' he said. 'Shouldn't have stepped out of line. Shouldn't have joined.'

He dropped her off just short of Trafalgar Square and she walked home while Tommy went off to garage his car and walk back to her through the glimmering streets of town.

As she waited for Tommy she wondered if Sybil would make use of any of the books in the Coach House, and decided it was unlikely. When she had mentioned *Treasure Island* the girl had said, 'Oh, we had to do that at school, it was boring.'

It was then, out of the blue, that Sybil suddenly confided that her real boyfriend was one of the waiters at the Nightlight: Nicko. 'Got lovely hands he has, and of course he's a lot taller than Nell.' As if size mattered.

Ten

M uch earlier that evening, Porky Pine and Flash Stan Page had come to the Twins' flat on the west side of South Audley Street. Charlie told Connie to make himself scarce, go to his bedroom and not come out until the girl Sybil had gone. 'I don't want her frightened by you, Con. Understand? Porky and Flash're bringing her here.'

He went to the door, arranged his welcoming smile and took off the three bolts and the long metal bar, before snapping up the lock and turning the Chubb, so opening the door.

The smile faded when he saw Porky and Flash standing there on their own. No Sybil.

'Where is she?' he asked, anger sneaking sideways into his voice.

'Charlie, we have to talk.' Couldn't quite meet Charlie's eye, spreading his hands wide in a gesture of hopelessness.

'Where is she?'

'She's gone, Charlie.' Porky advanced into the hall with Flash trailing dejectedly behind him.

'Gone where?'

'I dunno. Just gone.'

'Why would she just go? The girl Sybil, why?'

'Charlie, I don't know,' enunciated carefully this time. 'She left the Nightlight last night. About eleven, half-past. No need to stay last night. There wasn't much doing. Then she didn't come in this morning. We looked all over, Charlie, everywhere, her drum, every nook and cranny – she hasn't been home. We even went to her mother and father out near Peckham. That's quite a trip over to Peckham. They haven't seen her either, not for a couple of weeks, her mum and dad.'

'Why would she do a flit, Porky?' There was an iciness about Charlie that made Porky uncomfortable.

'Well, could be I've made a slight error of judgement.' He pulled a face: his grovelling expression.

'You made a slight error of judgement? A *slight* error, Porky? How much of a slight error?'

Porky told him about telephoning Greek Rose the previous night. 'I thought she should know, so she could tip Sybil to come to work dressed proper, that's all.'

'So you think Greek Rose told her?' It was when Charlie spoke softly, almost whispering, that you knew to take care: that his temper was about to blow.

'I *know* Greek Rose told her. I think she frightened her off. Overdid it. Exaggerated.'

'You silly bloody idiot,' Charlie began to punctuate his words with blows, heavy cuffs to each side of his head, though that wasn't easy: Porky Pine was a tall man and Charlie Balvak was under medium height, which meant that he had to reach up on tiptoe to hit him –

'You bloody cretin,' right-left-right, 'Have you no sense at all?' Right-left-right-left-right-right, the blows getting harder and the scene stranger, for Porky seemed to bend his knees slightly to accommodate Charlie's shorter stature and reach. 'I wanted to be nice to her, you twat!' The blows knocking his head from side to side, so that Porky had to take the impact of each hit, trying to ride with each wallop, his head like a punch bag being flicked side to side. He thought he could feel his brains sloshing around inside his cranium. It hurt something terrible and his neck was cricked badly.

'I have to chastise you, Porky,' said Charlie breathing heavily, his anger as bad as the rage he felt long ago, in 1935, when his father, Carl Balvak, collapsed and died at half-past six on a lovely August evening in the Duke of Wellington, the largest pub in what was known as the Cut in the Borough of Camford, London. Charlie still missed his father, who had trained both his boys to leadership and whose ambition was to see them running the pub, and the local association of villains.

'Crazy as an effing loon,' dum-dum-dum-da-dum-dum-dum. 'Shit 'n' abortion you great nerk, you schlemiel. Porky,

121

you and Flash you've got one job now. One, and one only till it's done. Forget about the Eyetie, Falconetti. Forget about the builders, gorrit? Go and find her. Find that Sybil. Take your friend Page and don't come back till you've got the bitch. Go!' The last word accompanied by a straight right to the face with much steam behind it, bringing tears to Porky's eyes and blood to his nostrils. When younger, Charlie Balvak was a good middleweight boxer. He could, as they say, handle himself.

'And . . .' Charlie shouted bringing the unhappy Porky and Flash Stan to a reluctant halt halfway to the door. 'And,' not quite as loud, 'when you find her, bring her back quietly. Get her somewhere nearby without a fuss; without anyone else being involved. Bring her without people knowing, so as I can talk to her.' Pause for a count of six. 'Or maybe get someone else to talk to her. Understand?'

'Yes, Charlie,' said Porky.

'Right you are, boss,' muttered Flash Stan.

As he was helped back up the street by Flash Stan, Porky carried on a lengthy monologue. 'Course I coulda wiped the floor with hib if I'd had a bind, Flash. You know that don't you? You know I coulda put hib out for the count?'

'Course I know it, course I do, Porky.'

'I bean it wouldn't have been fair though. Bit of give and take – and sometimes you got to take, for the sake of peace and quiet.'

'Course you have, Pork.'

'I bean stands to reason I had to treat hib soft: he pays by wages, Charlie does. He's entitled to act a bit rough now and again.'

'Course he does – watch where that blood's dripping out of your nose, Porky, or you'll get it on your suit.'

'Right, Flash, right. I bight not be so soft with him next time, bind.'

'I'd definitely think about that, Porky. Definitely.'

'I think we'll start tracking Sybil down in the borning, Flash. Right?'

'Whatever you say, Pork.'

*　　*　　*

Suzie Walked into the CID office at West End Central just before eight thirty the next morning. She hadn't managed a great deal of sleep because Dandy Tom wanted them to stay awake when they got back to St Martin's Lane. Suzie had no desire to leave him unfulfilled and frustrated so-to-speak. She didn't want to leave herself frustrated either.

DCI Harvey sat in his office engrossed in a pile of papers and showed no sign of having seen her come in. She was immediately conscious of him and recalled what Tommy had said to her.

Pass Nell on to Harvey, and Harvey will pass him on to the Twins and we can all watch the fur fly.

She sat at her desk and began to go through the few messages left for her. One from Colin Preece – she had to think for a moment who Preece was: the constable who had taken Falconetti to hospital and who had gone with her to Tosca on Sunday night. One from Cheesy Fowles, who had been with them when they'd gone to the Nightlight. And one from her old friend Shirley Cox who had been a WDC at Camford, where she'd been before joining the Reserve Squad. All three wanted her to bell them and she was flicking through the loose-leaf Metropolitan Police telephone book to look up the Reserve Squad number when she felt, rather than saw, Big Toe Harvey standing behind her.

She didn't even look round. 'Morning, Guv'nor.'

'Susannah, a word if you don't mind. In my office, if you don't mind. Now, if you don't mind.'

She followed him through his door and he stood and closed it, nodding her to sit down.

'Suzie. The girl, Sybil, at the club the other night? At the Nightlight. The crying redhead. You recall the one? You went to shut her up.'

'Yes, Guv. What's she done, robbed a bank?'

'She's gone missing. I've just had Greek Rose on the blower making a song and dance about it.'

'And you want me . . . ?'

'I want you for your brain and your powers of deduction. Your memory, Suzie. Any ideas? She say anything to you?'

'I know her parents live somewhere out Peckham way, that

she has a fifteen-year-old sister, who's no better than she ought to be, and a brother in the Navy.' And I didn't learn that in the little caboose behind the bar in the club, she thought, but wouldn't tell Toe that. I learned it elsewhere: in my own kitchen with Tommy fielding the catches in the slips while I cooked bacon.

'I got all that from Rose this morning.' Harvey gave a thin smile. 'Also, I know Sybil has a room in Paddington. A bed-sitter, somewhere along Praed Street: use of kitchen and bathroom. Not the most salubrious neighbourhood.'

'You want me to go over and take a look, Guv?'

'Young Fowles is doing that even as we speak. Just wondered if you had any other ideas. She say anything in particular?'

'No ideas, Guv. A piece of information though. Should have mentioned it before I suppose.'

Give it to him as though it's an afterthought.

'Oh?'

'I thought she was a bit distraught and was spinning a load of old bunny. But I had a bit of a think later on, and . . . well, for what its worth . . .'

'For what what's worth?'

'She told me that she reckoned – no, she told me she *knew* – that Little Nell, the Twins' so-called accountant, was skimming money off the top from three clubs they virtually own.'

'The Nightlight being one of them?'

'Yes, Guv. The Nightlight, Bandbox, and the Melody. They also own the On & Off near Golden Square, and she also says there were no pongos in the Nightlight last night, no brown jobs, no khaki military. Reckoned that Buller didn't get pushed to the ground and trampled on. Said he got kicked to death by someone with the Twins. Maybe by one of the Twins themselves. Said they were in there last night.'

'You believe her?'

Suzie pretended to reflect for a minute. 'Not really, Guv'nor. I thought she'd got a bee in her bonnet; thought she was bearing some kind of grudge. I mean you'd got it pretty well sewn up with Greek Rose. Rose seemed absolutely clear, didn't she? Jonnick?'

'Yes. Yes, she did. Very clear, but how did Sybil Harris sound? Convincing?'

Harvey moved a fraction closer to her and she caught the strong whiff of peppermint. Someone, a sergeant at Camford, sergeant Osterley she thought, had once said that she should never trust a man smelling of peppermint on his breath, particularly in the morning, trying to disguise the smell of alcohol.

'Convincing?' he asked again.

'More convinced than convincing. But she probably wants revenge, Guv – you know what it's like.' *I didn't know her name was Harris, Suzie thought. I bet Tommy's got her name. Tommy would have locked up all her particulars long before I got home. He was probably only waiting for me to suggest we take her off and hide her at Larksbrook.*

'And you're not convinced, Suzie?'

'I'm far from convinced.'

Give it to him as though it's an afterthought. Throw it away. This was not the first time that she'd detected a streak of ruthlessness in Tommy Livermore.

'Tommy, what'll they do . . . ? What'll the Twins do if we feed this to them through Big Toe?' She had asked that in bed last night, and he had replied that if the Twins had any gumption they'd reward Big Toe and do Little Nell to death.

'Then won't we be partly guilty of Nell's murder?'

Tommy had laughed and said it was all in a day's work. If Little Nell turned up in a concrete overcoat and boots, or with his gizzard slit through, they'd know they were right about DCI Anthony Harvey. She felt that any minute he would say that you couldn't make an omelette without breaking eggs, but he said something considerably worse.

'Suzie, my darling, you'll never win a battle without taking casualties. It's just some of the casualties don't particularly matter. I wouldn't have thought Neville Bellman would matter all that much, because he's rubbish, isn't he?'

It must be something to do with the aristocracy. All those military leaders, like the Duke of Wellington who referred to his army as the scum of the earth. In the dark, in those few moments of speech, Dandy Tom suddenly lost some of his sparkle.

Now in the CID Office Big Toe Harvey nodded grimly. 'Have a root around, Suzie, and unplug your lugholes. See if you come up with something about the girl. About Sybil Harris. Where she's hiding, stuff like that.'

She thought of Molly guarding Sybil Harris, and Sybil bored out of her trolley, and not wanting to read any of Suzie's youthful library. Or maybe not capable of reading them. She couldn't conceive of a time when she didn't have a book on the go.

Ten minutes later she saw Harvey heading out, wearing his smartly cut overcoat, the collar turned up. I wonder? she wondered.

Within half an hour of you telling him the tale, Harvey'll be out into a telephone box.

Last night they had been at the On & Off near Golden Square having gone there after Charlie had told Porky not to come back until he'd found the girl. They needed cheering up so they had eaten a good dinner – the On & Off received a fair share of the food, fish and meat they brought into London to sell to selected restaurants – and then they'd had a pleasant time with a couple of the girls. Connie would possibly have preferred the new pretty young waiter, but he had to make do with Dolly, a bottle blonde with muscular thighs, whose nickname was *casse-noisette*. Charlie had not wanted to stay the night even though the girl, a young woman called Hazel, tried to tempt him. As they left, Connie sang, 'Goodbye, Dolly, we must leave you,' and laughed his unnatural, high-pitched laugh. Connie could be quite a card when he put his mind to it.

They had returned to South Audley Street at almost three in the morning. Now Charlie was in a black and livid mood because he had been wakened by a telephone call just after nine. The news he had received had been, to say the least, unpleasant and he didn't know how to tell Conrad. He suspected that Connie would not believe it to start with, then the iron would enter into his soul and he'd want vengeance. Charlie had a tendency to think in biblical terms like this and he supposed that it was the accumulated images of years spent at the Alma Road C of E school in Camford. They had been very hot on the Bible and the Prayer Book at Alma Road and in spite of the criminal life he had chosen, Charlie thought, wrongly, that he was rooted in an Anglican tradition.

The Ghoul woke in the early hours and knew the spirit was upon him again. Time to go out and find another one. It had been a while. This time he knew who he would find. He'd get him sooner or later and there would be no return journey back to his other place out to the north of where he was, here in the centre of the city. There was no hurry though. He lay in the dark and thought how the corpse would be found, and he saw the man's face looking at him while he sang 'There'll Always be an England' and while he performed the other last rites. Later, he got up and went down into that other world where he looked for corpses, and he made a telephone call, asking this corpse to meet him. And it all happened, just as he planned. Now he could hide for a time.

Charlie Balvak sat, brooding and drinking black coffee, wondering what he should do; coming to the decision that to start with he should do nothing. Then the front door buzzer growled.

It was Little Nell himself who swept in carrying a huge white box almost as tall as himself. It was also heavy and he plonked it down with a metallic thud on the mahogany table with the long drawer and tiger face handles. Later Charlie found that the surface of the table was dented. Yet now, face to face with Nell for the first time since being told of his perfidy, he felt a deep hatred for the small man. He also noticed other imperfections that had scarcely registered before: the odd permanent crick in the neck that made him carry his head on one side; the warped curl of his lip on the right side, a persistent sneer; and the partially closed right eye, a constant wink. What a nasty little fellow he was, and his foulness seemed to wash over Charlie, making him shudder.

'Wait till you see what I've got for you,' Nell grinned, and to give Charlie his due he didn't show a flicker of anger. Mind you, he didn't show much pleasure either, but considering the news he'd received concerning Little Nell Bellman, this was no surprise.

Like a conjurer revealing the surprise ending of a trick, Nell slipped the thick string from the sturdy box and lifted the lid. There, lying packed in newspaper (he noted the headlines on a recent *Daily Express* – 'Ark Royal Went Down Like A Gentleman' – that inadvertently changed the ship's sex) was a Thompson sub-machine gun with one circular drum of ammunition and four flat magazines.

'How about that, Charlie?' Nell did a little gawky dance, part war dance, part *joie de vivre*.

'Where you get that, Nell?'

'Fell off the back of a three-ton truck with a couple of others. Bound for the Home Guard, but as they didn't know they was going to get them in the first place, they're never going to miss them, eh?'

'And where's the other two?'

'Safe.'

'I asked where?' *arsed where?* and there was more than a tincture of menace in his tone.

'In my gaff.' Nell lived in a narrow, four-storey house in Lexington Street.

'Where in your gaff, Nell?'

Nell looked shifty, then told him the other brace of Tommy guns were hidden in an old military chest in his bedroom. 'It's covered with a lion skin that used to be worn by the bass drummer in the band of the Coldstream Guards.'

That would be one way, Charlie thought to himself. I could grass to West End Central and they'd lift Nell on charges of dealing in stolen arms. Yes, that would put him away for a while. Get him off our chests.

And I wouldn't have to tell Connie.

'Well, you want this beauty?' Nell asked.

'Course I want it. This could be just the 'ammer, Nell.'

'Yeah, I know. It could turn out very handy. I mean you could take out all three of them builders in one go. One quick burst and they'd be no more. You seen one of them fired, Charlie?

The .45 bullet doesn't make a nice little hole, it bores in and tears a bloody great gash.'

Of course, Charlie thought, of course, Nell knows about the Trinity Building Co. Now, if he was lifted by West End Central, if a certain friend felt his collar, would he start singing arias to the Old Bill? No, he decided. No, Nell was dead untrustworthy but he wasn't the sort to peach. Nell liked to settle his own bits of bother.

'Right, Nell,' he smiled as though the small man was his closest friend in the whole wide world. 'You've done a good one here. Keep the others safe, hide 'em away, 'cos we could probably do with them. Okay?'

'Good, Charlie. Shall we say a ton for this one then? And fifty for the magazines and ammo? Cheap at twice the price.' Like many men whom God has made in his own image, yet foreshortened from the norm by twelve or eighteen inches in height, Little Nell overcompensated by taking cocksure risks that were bound to catch up with him. He worked solely for the Balvak Twins, who paid him a handsome sum in remuneration, so there was no need for deals on the side, like the one he proposed now.

But Charlie remained calm, showing no outward sign of the anger that boiled furiously inside. Indeed, this was against his nature, for Charlie had what some called a short temper. He was a man whose actions spoke louder than words, and who showed his dislikes with petrifying physical vigour.

Yet now he nodded in a benevolent manner, beckoning Nell to follow him through to the sitting room where he made no display of secrecy by going straight to a small gilt-framed eighteenth-century painting of a racehorse after Stubbs: a long way after. Taking hold of the lower right corner of the picture, Charlie Balvak pulled it away from the wall, revealing that the left side was hinged and the whole painting fitted flush over a safe. The Balvaks had partially learned their trade from Hollywood films, including methods of hiding safes. They had learned well through the thirties from B-movies and actors like George Raft, Edward G. Robinson, and even James Cagney.

Charlie operated the dial with accomplished elan, spinning it three clockwise and two anticlockwise. The locking mechanism clicked and he opened the safe door, moving his body to block Little Nell's view of the interior from which he took out one hundred and fifty pounds in various denominations – mainly big crisp white fivers.

'There you go, Nell. One hundred and fifty nicker.' It was said with a smile that changed as he spoke, becoming gritty and even fearsome. 'Now, Little Nell, effing get out of here before I get effing angry.'

Nell heard the rasp in Charlie's voice and took the hint. He could be foolish at times but he wasn't stupid, so he left – quickly and without another word. Charlie closed the safe door, flicking the dial to reset the lock. Then he let out a roar like some caged beast, picked up one of the heavy glass ashtrays and flung it across the room so that it crashed into the centre of the gilt-framed looking-glass, smashing it so that a hundred broken lines shot out from where the ashtray impacted, and three long shards of glass, like daggers, broke from the frame and fell to the carpet, their points aimed towards Charlie.

'Charlie? What you done, Charlie?' Connie stood in the doorway still in his pyjamas. 'Charlie, you've done it now. That's seven years bad luck.'

'No, Con, it's someone else's bad luck. Go and get dressed.' He was thinking about Nell. Should he drop a word in their tame copper's ear? Let nature take its course? If the bogies copped Nell with two Tommy guns and a boatload of ammunition he could get sent to the Moor on a five stretch, and Nell wouldn't like the Moor. It was a bleak, terrible place, the Moor, with back-breaking work in the quarries, rigid discipline, the barbarous punishment of the cat o' nine tails still enforced, and solitary confinement that meant solitary, and the year-round chill of the stone-walled cells. He would have to think it over. In the meantime he should make certain that he had everything in place. The last thing he needed was an angry Little Nell on the loose.

He went out to the hall and dialled O for the operator, then he put a trunk call through to Newcastle-on-Tyne.

'Matt?' he asked when he was connected. 'Yes, listen a minute Matt . . . No, it's okay . . . No, Matt, leave off them three builders . . . We can deal with them later . . . Look Matt,

I might have something for you down here . . . Not quite sure yet, but I'd be happier with you in London . . . Yeah, as quick as you can . . . Get down quick as you can, eh?'

Matt was Matthew Brown. So hard that he made Porky Pine look like 'the Nipper', who was a cute baby in a cartoon they ran in the *Daily Mail*. They said of Matt Brown that he had kept his mother in terror as a child and his father down the pit until he came out feet first. It was also said that the Twins had done him some huge favour and had dealt with a South London gang who would have killed him for a misdemeanour involving a branding iron, an electric probe and three girls who had raised all hell while on a visit to Matt Brown's territory around the Newcastle docks. Brown was a man with pure evil on his back and in his brain, and they said of him that he was his own man except when it concerned the Balvak Twins. Somewhat obviously, Matt Brown was generally known as Newcastle Brown.

'Is he staying here?' Connie asked coming back into the hall.

'No, I think he should stay in a good hotel. Nothing's too good for Matt.'

'Why aye.' This is Connie's little joke, so Charlie gave a hollow laugh. Humourless and empty. 'Why you sending for Matt?' Conrad asked, having heard one side of the conversation from his bedroom.

'In case,' Charlie said with a slight shake in his voice.

The *Evening News* had headlines about the *Prince of Wales* and the *Repulse* being sunk off Singapore, so Suzie bought a paper as she went down into the Tube to take a train back to Charing Cross. The loss of two capital ships was a terrible blow and she couldn't drag her mind off the hundreds of sailors who must have gone down with the vessels. It was a huge defeat.

She felt anxious as she came up into the fumbling night and badly wanted a cigarette: but ladies don't smoke in the street, even in the fog-dark streets of the blackout. When she arrived back in the flat, she found Tommy Livermore packing an overnight case. He looked as serious as a surgeon with no arms, which was one of his own favourite meaningless expressions.

131

'Heart, I've got to go down to your mum's, the Coach House.' He stopped what he was doing and came over to her, resting his hands on her shoulders. 'I can't do this on the phone. It's Molly's mother, she's been taken ill. Dying, I think. I've got to break it to her, then look after Sybil for a couple of days while Moll does what daughters have to do when their mums're dying.' He paused, turned his eyes away from Suzie, smiled and said, 'Funny you know. One doesn't associate Molly Abelard with having a mother. But she does, lives out the other side of Dulwich, over near Tulse Hill.'

'Tommy, I'm sorry.' It was then she realized she had no other words for him. She also saw that he was frightened and she'd never seen Dandy Tom frightened before.

'I absolutely hate giving people news of death or impending death. Loathe it, detest it,' he told her, but she knew that wasn't why he was frightened. It was something else. Something he wasn't telling her.

'We'd better have codes for Molly and Sybil,' he suggested as he was about to leave. Mrs Héloïse for Molly, cheeky but it'll serve. And Mrs Tweed for Sybil, Okay?'

'Got it, Chief.' Héloïse, the girl the priest Abelard had an affair with in twelfth-century France and got his balls chopped off for his pains; and Harris Tweed she thought was a bit cheeky as well. She kissed him, lovingly, and he held her tightly for a moment by the open door, then he slipped away without another word.

After he'd gone, walking down to Trafalgar Square, where Brian was to pick him up on the hoof, Suzie wandered around the flat. She hated being there on her own and became fearsome: twitchy and frightened, going from room to room and testing the locks on the doors and windows.

Finally, dropping into sleep she suffered the anxiety of bad dreams. She dreamed of her father and Charlotte rising from their graves, next to one another in Newbury. She was used to her dead father, for he appeared often in dreams and made jokes about being kept busy in eternal rest, but Charlotte was another matter: she wore a shroud dirtied by soil as though she had forced her way up from the coffin and burst drearily

132

into the night. She then moaned and pushed her rotting features into Suzie's face, and screamed, but the scream turned into the clamour of the alarm clock pulling Suzie from sleep into the anxious morning.

Eleven

Someone once told him he had a face like a Halloween lantern, and for the man's pains Matt Brown, also known as Newcastle Brown, broke his jaw in two places, unseated five teeth, cracked a cheekbone, broke an arm and four ribs, putting him in hospital for over five weeks. The irony was that Newcastle Brown did have a face like a Halloween lantern. You could see it now as he made his stately way from Platform 7 of King's Cross Station.

Some big men shamble; Newcastle Brown had elegance, all six foot four of him. In his walk he somehow showed exactly what he was, or if not quite what he was, certainly what he was capable of.

The hair was close cropped, and even crammed into the grey suit you could sense the powerfulness of his body. The set of his muscular shoulders, the wariness in his grey-blue eyes, and the hint of cruel humour in that lantern face were all enough to tell any intelligent adversary to beware. Matt Brown's face was, in some ways, his fortune, for the wide smile clashed with everything else about him. In fact the smile sent out rays and creases of humour that covered the face but, if you looked hard, never quite reached his eyes.

He passed the big 4-6-2 locomotive in its LNER livery and grinned even wider than before as he came off the platform and on to the station's main concourse, heading straight for the longest bank of telephones, squeezing his large body into the kiosk, searching his change for the three pennies, dropping them into the slot and dialling the Balvak's telephone number, pressing button A when Charlie picked up.

'Ah'm here,' he announced. Then – 'Why aye, I'll come straight over, man . . . Oh, you want me to do that first?

134

Right Ah will, pet . . . That's the best way . . . Ah'll see you when Ah've done it, man . . . ah-way.' And with his face still wreathed in smiles, Newcastle Brown went on his way to do the Balvak's bidding.

'A little bird has told me,' Big Toe Harvey said with the leer of a seaside comedian, 'there are some illegal arms stashed away in a house in Lexington Street: not a hundred miles from where we are sitting.' He looked round the assembled team, beaming. Suzie sat between Cheesy Fowles and Billy Hobbes, there were four uniformed lads directly behind them, and Chief Superintendent Sammy Battescombe stood in the doorway.

'I'd better tell you that the person who owns the house is Little Nell Bellman who is a well-known face around here, and I for one will be pleased to nick him. He can be a difficult little bugger, so we're taking two pairs of uniforms with us,' he continued.

Suzie took in what the DCI said as he talked about being extra careful going into the house, that the uniforms would be issued with revolvers because Little Nell was suspected of having firearms; and he was specific about the known weapons – Thompson submachine guns, two of them and plenty of ammunition and magazines. She took it all in, but Suzie was thinking about what had happened on her way to work that morning.

As she reached the bottom of St Martin's Lane where it joined with Duncannon Street – on her way to catch a bus up to the Dilly – a familiar figure came out of nowhere and fell into step beside her –

'Whatcher, Skip,' Tommy's driver greeted her, without looking in her direction, and without moving his lips.

'Brian,' she acknowledged.

'The Guv'nor wants you to give him a bell. From a public dog.'

Dog and Bone: phone.

'How soon, Brian?'

'Yesterday, Skip,' and he disappeared into the hurrying crowd.

Suzie went down Duncannon Street, crossed the Strand and

entered Charing Cross station. In CID you always tried to carry enough change to deal with telephone emergencies. Suzie kept a special purse in her handbag containing shillings, sixpences, pennies and threepenny bits. So, she made her way to the first bank of public phones and put through a trunk call to the Coach House in Newbury.

'Insert one shilling please, caller.'

'Dirty Dick's British Restaurant,' Tommy answered. She pressed button A and was immediately connected.

'What can I do for you, Chief?'

'I don't know really. I'm a shade uncertain about Mrs Héloïse.'

Mrs Héloïse for Molly, cheeky but it'll serve.

'I was brilliant,' Tommy in self-mocking mode. 'Sat her down, took a little brandy with me, broke it gently, very gently. She was angry, heart, angry with her mother for choosing this moment to knock on the pearly gates. Said she had been there before, several times. Nothing sounded right, so I think it might be an idea for you to try and talk to her.'

'It'll have to be much later today, chief. Our mutual friend rang me at the crack of dawn. Wants me in for something important. Called it a special assignment.'

'I should keep downwind of him, my advice.'

'So what's really troubling you?'

'I'm just a shade antsy, heart. Can't put my digit on it but there was something not right about the lady. We all know she's tough as an alligator skin, but somehow she didn't convince me. Take a look at her, would you?'

'As soon as I have the time.'

'Got the address and telephone number, eh?'

'Of course. Where did they phone from? About her Mum?'

'Dulwich Hospital. Off East Dulwich Grove. Give it a whirl, heart.'

In the present, Big Toe was telling them that they should really go in at the crack of dawn. 'First light's the best time to do this, but I'm concerned about leaving it until tomorrow. Arms and ammunition are dodgy, things can go missing very quickly, so we're going in now: as soon as we get things together.' He raised his eyes towards Sammy Battescombe. 'If you would authorize the weapons, sir.'

'Course, Chief Inspector. Would you like me to come along? Moral support? That sort of thing? Anything?'

'I think we'll manage, sir. Good of you though.'

Suzie had already decided that Chief Superintendent Battescombe was a lost cause. He sat in on briefings; dealt with minor matters of discipline and paperwork; drank a lot and weaved his way home, waiting for his pension.

They gave Cheesy the axe in case the door had to be broken down. He posed for his mate Billy Hobbes, who had a Box Brownie camera and photographed Cheesy standing in front of the car with the axe at the high port.

Porky Pine and Flash Stan Page went out to Peckham intent on a little chat with Sybil's mum and dad, who had a two-up-two-down off the High Street. Porky and Flash still hadn't heard anything from Sybil. Neither had her parents. Mrs Harris, a small woman who had that faded beauty which reminded Porky of crimson roses that have just lost their bloom, kept shaking her head, and murmuring that she didn't know where they had gone wrong with Sybil. 'We've never been involved with the police in this family,' was part of her litany.

Porky and Flash had presented themselves as plain-clothes police officers, having first cleared this in a telephone conversation with Charlie, who had said, 'Who's going to know?'

So Porky took the lead, popping off little questions about Sybil. Did they think she was happy in her job? What ever her job was, the mother said. Didn't talk about her work at home, the father added with meaning. 'We even thought the worst at times,' Mr Harris tacked on.

'So what would be the worst, Mr Harris?' As if they didn't know.

'You know. You're a copper. We worried in case she was on the game. Which, at times, we still think she is.' He was angry at the very concept, and Mrs Harris didn't know where to look, and said so.

'No,' Porky said somewhat pompously. 'Not far as we know,

137

she's not on the batter.' He stopped and corrected himself. 'Not on the game. Not as far as we know.'

Mrs Harris declared herself glad about that because she'd never live it down if they found our Sybil was on the game.

Did she ever talk about work? Her friends in particular?

No. They knew she had friends because she occasionally said things like, 'I went out with me friends on me day off.' But she never amplified that statement.

'She was a bit secretive, was she?' Flash Stan asked.

'Yes, that and all.' Mr Harris said in a puzzled way.

'So she didn't mention anyone by name?'

'Only that Buller, the one she worked with.'

'The one you say got killed.' Mrs Harris hedged her bets on everything.

'What about her sister, Sally?'

'Oh, she was friends with her sister, yes.'

'I meant would she talk about her friends to her sister?'

'Probably.' Mrs Harris did not sound happy about this either.

'Thick as thieves,' the father seemed proud about that.

So the Harrises, *mère et père,* were under the impression that Sybil had gone missing after some row with her employers. They now waited for young Sally, the fifteen-year-old who was no better than she ought to be, but still at school and coming home for lunch as she did every school day.

'She's the clever one,' pronounced Mr Harris (who was on nights). 'Staying on to take Higher School Cert. Likes the book learning a lot more'n her sister did. Though she still manages to take part in a lot of out-of-school activities. There's something on every night of the week. I don't hold with it myself, but, well there's a war on and I suppose we're all lucky to be alive really.'

'Indeed we are,' Porky agreed. 'And some of us are more lucky than others,' with a long knowing look towards Flash Stan.

'Yes, you must meet all kinds in your line of work,' Mr Harris (Eric, as his wife calls him) comments, and with that Sally arrives home for lunch – a cheese sandwich they note, privately wondering if the Harris family has some contact with a black market cheese magnate.

As soon as Sally walks in, Porky and Flash – who are men of the world and will tell you so – know immediately why she is, as her sister maintains, no better than she ought to be. She is remarkably developed for a fifteen-year-old: a tall girl wearing a school uniform that appears to be one size too small for her.

The grey pleated skirt stops an inch above the knees, and rides higher when she goes about certain actions in her daily life. The stockings on her long silken legs demand red-blooded males to ask how she keeps them up; her cerise blazer has the school crest on the breast pocket: a quartered shield with an eagle in each quarter and the motto below – the hackneyed and Victorian 'Mens sana in corpore sano', which went right over Porky's and Flash's heads. The corpore was certainly sano, and the blazer was undeniably a shade too small, for it gaped open leaving the tight white shirt straining almost to breaking point outlining the swell and thrust of the young flesh. She has unknotted the school tie, green diagonal stripes against a soft silver grey, and undone the top two buttons of the shirt, so that 'teaser' is one of the words that immediately comes into Porky's mind. He takes the initiative, asking Mr and Mrs Harris if they can interview Sally in private.

'Young people often talk more openly to us when they're on their own: not speaking in front of their family, if you follow me,' he explains, then takes the plunge, hoping he has got the word right. 'They're less unhibited . . .'

'Inhibited,' Flash corrects him.

'Yes, that,' says Porky and it is obvious that the parents understand this only too well. In spite of their comprehension they agree, and squeeze themselves into the tiny kitchen at the back of the house, leaving Porky and Flash Stan with the girl, who shows not the slightest anxiety in the face of police questioning.

'Right,' Porky clears his throat and pulls his eyes away from Sally's knees and a strip of thigh laid bare to the right stocking top as she sits back and crosses her legs.

'Sally,' he eventually continues. 'No need to be afraid of us. Just a few simple questions about Sybil.'

'I'm not afraid.' She holds Porky's eyes in hers. 'Why should I be afraid? I've been done over by the filth before.'

'Really?' says Flash Stan, who has used those very words in his personal dealings with the Met.

'Yes, really,' the girl agrees.

Bloody little teaser, thinks Porky not taking his eyes from the rising hem of her skirt.

Little Miss Hornbeam, thinks Flash Stan, getting a crick in his neck from trying to sneak a look up her skirt.

'Now, Sally,' Porky begins, but his voice catches in his throat and he has to cough, then start again. 'Now, Sally, do you get on well with your sister?'

'Course.' She gives a proper-little-madam toss of the head, so that they can see she has the kind of hair that full-grown women hate. The blonde cap lifts and falls back perfectly, not a follicle out of place.

'Did she talk to you about her job?'

'Yeah.'

'What we need to find out from you is did she talk about any particular friends at work?'

'Yea, I knew about all of them. And some of the details an' all.' She giggled.

'Who in particular?'

'Well, there's this one girl from Wales – Gwyneth.' She began to giggle almost uncontrollably.

'What's so funny about Gwyneth?' Flash asks, though both men already know. Gwyneth is chapel and most of the Balvaks' friends who patronize the Nightlight know about Gwyneth.

'Well,' Sally can hardly get it out. 'Well, Gwyneth is religious but only up to a point . . .'

'Yes?'

'Gwyneth won't do it on a Sunday. She said to Greek Rose – that's the club owner – that she won't fornicate on the Sabbath.'

'What about your sister?'

'My sister what?'

'Does she fornicate on the Sabbath?'

'She's not on the game.'

'That wasn't the question.'

There's a lengthy pause, then Sally says all right you didn't have to be on the game to fornicate on the Sabbath. 'Yes, Sybil's got a boyfriend, one of the waiters. Nicko. Yes, she's done it. She told me: said it's uncomfortable the first time but if you really throw yourself into it it's great. Says that Nicko's very good and they do it regular now.' Then she looks Porky straight in the eyes, grins and says she can't wait to be old enough.

Porky swallows hard. 'Other friends?' he asks. 'Sybil's other friends?'

Most appeared to be confined to the club. They were also mainly girls. 'Caro – that's short for Caroline – and there's Nicola, Lavinia (I've met her and she's a stuck up cow) and Danny – that's short for Danielle. And she's quite friendly with one or two of the street girls an' all. Barbara, Tony – that's Antonia really – Patricia and Anna. They're the ones she talks about anyhow, and they work in Wardour Street or down near the Regent Palace. That's a good pitch, down near the Regent Palace. A lot of trade down there: Glasshouse Street, places like that.'

Porky asks her to repeat the last four names because he is a slow writer.

'Kids today,' Flash said as they walked away, looking for a bus to get them back to the West End and Soho.

'Not like it was when we were young.' Porky plunged his hands in his pockets.

'What would you do if you had kids?' Flash Stan asked.

'I really don't know, Flash, and that's the truth.'

'She's at it already, isn't she?'

'That's how I read it, Porky.'

'Disgusting, innit?'

'Dis-bloody-graceful, Flash.'

'All put away?' asks Charlie.

'Settled?' Connie queries, and Newcastle Brown nods his lantern head, smiles his Halloween smile and says, 'Why aye. Al put awa'.'

141

First, Charlie's eyes, then Conrad's come to rest on Matthew Brown's huge hands that lay like garden forks on his saddle knees. Matt is indeed made on a large scale. 'Man,' he says now. 'Tell us why Ah'm here.'

'We have a couple of problems, as you'll have gathered,' Charlie begins.

'. . . gathered,' Connie joins in the echoing duet.

'Men in our position,' Charlie sounds like the Chairman addressing the board, 'can be at the mercy of people with loose mouths: people who think they know a lot about our business dealings and need to be curbed.'

'Why aye, man. Only sense.'

'As our good friend French Claude says – him what manages the Versailles Tea Rooms and Bar in Dean Street – near that Chink restaurant, Choy's . . .' Charlie squints down at a piece of paper resting on the arm of his chair, 'we should make an example of a couple of people poor encourajay les oats,' he read self-consciously. 'This means to warn off any stupid bleeders who think they can steal a march on us.'

Matt nods again. Deeply. 'Common sense, hinny,' he burbles. 'Ah presume you mean them three builder lads Ah'm keepin' an aye on up north.'

'I think they're some of the oats really. The oats what French Claude says we have to warn off by example. See?'

'See?' Connie reflects.

'Why aye, man,' Matt grins and nods.

'I am most concerned about a young woman who's gone missing. Worked as one of our cashiers on the door at one of the places we look after. Called the Nightlight, the club is. The girl's name is Sybil Harris and we've got a couple of the lads looking for her.' He gave a satisfied smirk. 'We have been rather clever over this one, Matt. I've asked to see her in a spirit of friendship: to put her mind at ease. I wanted to reassure her that she was a favoured employee. After that was established we were going to ask you to take care of the matter.' Heaven knew where Charlie got his turn of phrase. Maybe the Alma Street C of E School was better than people gave it credit for.

'Why aye,' Matt repeated. 'Who else?'

142

'Well, the one you know about and possibly a club owner of Italian extraction. Name of Falconetti.'

'It'll be a pleasure bonny lad.'

'Now,' Charlie spread his arms wide, 'let's get down to how much you're going to charge us, Matt. We don't want you to be out of pocket.'

Matt Brown gave both the twins his big smile. The lantern appeared to be lit. He laughed. 'Ah divana na you cared,' he said in his broad Geordie accent.

The first thing Suzie noticed as they piled out of the car in front of the house in Lexington Street was that the curtains seemed to be drawn, the blackout in place. She felt very alert, as though she was seeing things clearly through some kind of magnifying lens. Already, as they came up Rupert Street and turned left towards Lexington, she had experienced that slow roll and agitated butterfly flutter in her stomach. She was remembering last year, thinking of the infamous, hideous, Golly Goldfinch, now locked away in a hospital for the criminally insane at His Majesty's Pleasure. He used to live round here, near Rupert Street. The memory was like a huge ice-cold nudge to her nervous system, and for a second she thought she would vomit.

Two of the uniformed officers had been sent round the back, into the open space between Westminster College and the back of Lexington Street. 'If the little sod tries to run for it from the rear of the building you'll nail him, and don't be afraid to use the shooters,' Big Toe Harvey had said back at the station.

The front door was straight off the pavement and nothing stirred when Big Toe hammered on it using his truncheon.

'Little Nell ought to be afraid,' Billy Hobbes said, and Cheesy Fowles, remembering the tag line of a smutty story, said, 'He would be if he could see what the DCI was hammering on the door with.'

And at that moment Harvey called Fowles up to smash in the door – which he did in three blows of the axe and a lot of splintered wood. The lock was shattered and dropped off, the splintered door swung inwards and they crowded into the

143

house. For Suzie at the back it was like plunging into a tunnel. All six of them were consumed by the dark.

'Lights,' Harvey yelled and Suzie felt to her right, sliding her hand down the wall, then up again, hitting the brass dome switch, feeling for the little lever and activating it downwards. Still only darkness. She flicked the switch up and down rapidly, then shouted, 'No juice, Guv.'

Someone else yelled, 'Get the bloody blackout down,' and she moved to the right, through the door into the front room, fumbling for any catches holding a blackout frame in place. It was as she felt for the blackout that the smell came thundering into her nostrils. Metal? Iron? No. But she knew what the smell conveyed. Someone pushed past her and called out for the others to be careful – 'The floor's wet,' it was Cheesy Fowles shouting, followed by a gasp. The smell, Suzie knew, was blood.

She found the bottom toggle holding the blackout frame in place and slid her hand up towards the top, turning the wooden catch so that the frame began to part company with the window.

'Oh bloody hell,' Cheesy called out. 'What the blazes is that?'

Light began to filter into the room, and as it did so, Suzie turned and saw the strange lump on an old easy chair near the fireplace. Then the blackout frame fell flat on to the floor and she saw that the lump was a human body criss-crossed with dark red slashes.

'Jesus!' Billy Hobbes called out and one of the uniforms backed away and threw up in the hall.

'If you can't cope, get out,' Harvey shouted, and there was the sound of one pair of feet retreating. Then Billy spluttered that it was too much for him. Moving towards the hall and the stairs.

It's a child, Suzie thought, a naked child: she could see the body clearly and realized they were standing on a carpet steeped in blood. The body was stretched backwards, enveloped by the easy chair and covered in deep gashes across the upper torso and the neck, which gaped open like an obscene smile. Certainly the jugular and the carotid were breached, the arterial gore had fountained in a thick jet towards the tall window. It all looked oddly unreal, like some kind of a model, a tableau in the Chamber of Horrors at Madame Tussaud's. The whole room seemed drenched and sprayed with blood as Suzie registered that the body was not that of a child. It had belonged to Little Nell Bellman.

He was their accountant. Stashed the cash, paid the taxes, knew all the fiddles.

Suzie took a step forward to look at Little Nell's face.

There was no face, only the stump of severed neck and an axe lying on the floor drowned in gore – big double-headed thing, the axe: curved blades, looked Japanese, but what did she know.

'Sod me,' Harvey half whispered. 'Someone wanted to make sure of him.'

Suzie dragged her eyes from the corpse and surveyed the rest of the room: the other easy chair; a table pushed back against the far wall; a picture of Highland Cattle drinking from a stream on high ground with mountains in the background; an African shield of, it looked like zebra hide, and crossed spears – only when she looked again there was only one spear and the one that was left had a polished and obviously sharp knife-like head: an assegai.

'Oh my God, Guv, look up here,' Billy shouted from the hall.

Suzie moved sideways and was nearly pushed over by Big Toe obviously eager to get out of the room.

Suzie followed the DCI up the stairs, amazed by the fact that she had been able to deal with the surfeit of blood downstairs. Billy stood in the doorway of the bathroom. 'Look at this, Guv,' he said with a guttural rasp in his voice. 'The bugger had a bath before he left.'

The bathroom was a shambles, there were traces of blood around the bath plug and smears of it on the side of the bath itself – a long and deep Victorian affair on clawed metal feet. There were two large towels – her mother would have called them beach towels – sopping wet and with streaks of blood on them, but the unnerving sight was the missing spear from Nell's living room. It was stuck hard into the floor in front of the handbasin. The iron tip was just visible and, even viewed from the doorway, was obviously razor sharp, like the one left on the wall downstairs.

Rammed on to the top of the haft was Little Nell's head, slightly cocked with the eyes wide open, blank, looking into eternity while his lips seemed to be folded back, bearing his unlovely teeth.

'Did for Little Nell, then took his time with his ablutions. Cool as a bloody cucumber.' Harvey breathed. 'Jesus,' he sounded truly shaken. Then, 'Let not poor Nelly starve. Well he won't, will he? You alright, Bill? Never seen so much claret. You'd never think so much claret could come out of one bloke.'

'No. I'm not really a well man.' Hobbes bent double and pushed past Harvey and Suzie, heading for the street.

Uncalled for, a garbled line of Shakespeare came into Suzie's head, last heard in the classroom at St Helen's with Sister Martha Mary teaching English Lit, relishing the violence. It was something about who'd have thought he had so much blood in him, but she couldn't remember which play or what the circumstance.

Twelve

E arly that evening – around eight fifteen – the warning siren howled. It was the kind of thing they called a nuisance raid: five or six aircraft coming in high and dropping HE and incendiary bombs more or less indiscriminately. A couple of HEs exploded quite close to the Earl's Court Road as Suzie headed in that direction by taxi. Oh hell, she thought. It's that man again!

Even at this time in the evening she was still shaken by the events of that morning, and had what she thought of as 'the horrors'. The whole team had been in a state of nerves, trying to get over the shock of finding Little Nell's headless body. The stench of blood clung to the nostrils and the sight of Nell's familiar face daubed with blood riding on top of the spear's haft would be hard to expunge from the memory.

Of the supposed Thompson submachine guns there was no sign, and Big Toe Harvey was not telling anyone where he had got the tip-off.

If the Twins had any gumption they'd reward Big Toe and do Little Nell to death, as Dandy Tom had said. He also said, in a cruder moment, 'Molly's as tough as a jockey's arse.'

Such a nice turn of phrase, Tommy. Sometimes she was put off by that part of Tommy that was indecent and earthy. Her father had never said anything worse than damnation in front of her, and Suzy held up every man to the mirror of her father.

On the other hand she knew of Molly's hardness because it had been Molly who had taught her much in the way of unarmed combat.

She was off to check up on Molly now, just as Tommy had suggested, and she thought about her now: remembering that in the early 1930s, Molly had worked for Peninsula & Orient, the great maritime company. She was learning the business from the bottom up, and on a round-the-world cruise she was put into the dining rooms as a waitress, work her way up. Eventually, when she had learned all the jobs open to a woman, from cabin stewardess to executive officer, she would, herself, become an officer, but on this trip her hopes were destroyed when the ship stopped for three days in Hong Kong.

She had the second evening off and went to the Peninsular Hotel on Kowloonside, sitting in the big ornate foyer where they serve you at little tables while the orchestra played numbers like 'Alexander's Ragtime Band' and 'Lullaby of Broadway'. Then she had a few drinks with one of the bar stewards from the ship, left him at the Peninsular and went off to take an ill-considered walk up Nathan Road and down a badly lit side street.

She knew there were five of them and she thought they were Spanish. In truth there were six and they were a mixture of Chinese sailors and Laskars, drunk, belligerent and looking for a white woman. Molly was just right for them, dressed as she was in a thin cotton pleated skirt and shirt. The skirt was a shade short – to the knee anyway – and the shirt a little tight; her dirty gold hair was sleek and bobbed and to tell the truth, Molly Abelard was a tiny bit drunk herself.

She experienced slight alarm when they crowded around her and got angry when one of them reached over and took most of her right breast in his hand. Then she pushed and started to shout at them.

It was the last she remembered until she woke up from a bad dream in a hospital, swamped with pain and unable to move. She knew then that the dream wasn't a dream at all.

All her ribs were broken on one side; her right cheekbone had been shattered; there were two fractures in her right arm; her left hip was cracked and the left shoulder dislocated. Just to finish it off she had been gang-raped by ten men. Later it was said that the original attackers had called four friends in to help in the rape, and they only knew that from an account wrung from a Chinese dockworker by the Hong Kong police. She was badly damaged down there and it was said at the time that she would never be able to have sex again, though this turned out to be untrue. They had also given her syphilis, the treatment of which was far from easy.

There had been severe blows to her head and for two days she floated between life and death, coming round on the third day, but not making much sense. The P&O office in Hong Kong made themselves responsible for her treatment and welfare, in spite of a spat between one of the insurance managers claiming the whole thing was Miss Abelard's fault. 'You can't expect anything else if a little totty wanders down into dockland dressed as provocatively as that,' the man actually said, but was promptly ruled out of order by a Peninsular & Orient director who happened to be on the cruise and was slightly more enlightened than most people of his class and standing.

They brought Molly back to the United Kingdom on one of their smaller cruise liners: brought her back first class – posh: port out starboard home. Molly had started to exercise by then and spent much of her time trotting around the deck and working on her muscles in the ship's gymnasium. The rest of the time she spent reading.

P&O had promised they would take her back into one of their training courses again when she was fully recovered, and they also flung her a few thousand pounds in compensation. Molly told them thanks but no thanks, took the cash and started to rebuild her life. She wanted to get very fit, learn to defend herself, take on skills that few women had mastered. At the same time she started a course of reading designed to educate herself to a standard well above her lower middle-class background.

She learned Ju jitsu and Kara te, the empty hand form of fighting, together with a couple of even more frightening oriental systems of unarmed combat. She went to one of the best fencing masters in London and also joined a gun club, learning to shoot both rifle and pistol. She maintained her fitness and went on training her mind. After two years she felt confident to spend a little time learning to box at a gym in the East End. It was there that she met a plain-clothes police sergeant called Billy Mulligan, a big, tough, taciturn officer who hinted that he worked for some special force within the Metropolitan Police.

A couple of months later Molly met Detective Chief Superintendent Tommy Livermore, known to the Press as Dandy Tom, and to those within Scotland Yard as the officer in command of the Reserve Squad. Molly expressed an interest in the kind of work in which they were engaged, and before she knew it she was whisked through a specific training course, made into a Woman Detective Constable and posted to the Reserve Squad, where she had stayed from that day on, appointing herself personal assistant and first bodyguard to DCS Livermore.

The taxi turned into the Earl's Court Road from Cromwell Road, heading in the direction of Kensington High Street. Just short of Pembroke Square the cabby slowed down and turned left into the tiny place that is one of London's great secrets. Even in the darkness the white walls of the charming narrow houses reflected a little light into the area and Suzie thought, Molly how much did P&O give you? Did you really have enough to buy one of these?

In the centre of the square, a beech tree stretched up from the concrete, safely guarded on four sides by stone slabs.

'Which house, miss?' the cabby asked, and at the same moment Suzie looked up and saw a car drawn up diagonally opposite her own cab.

'Just pull up on the right here and switch off your engine,' she ordered. Then, 'I'm a police officer and I want to observe that house for a moment or two.'

'Gee, lady . . .' the cabby began in an attempt to be humorous by using the tired dialogue of a thousand American B-movies. But he glanced round and there was just enough light for him to catch Suzie's expression and see that she was serious. She even slid down in the back of the cab so as not to be seen by the people emerging from the house that she knew belonged to Molly Abelard.

The car in front of Molly's house was the Reserve Squad's grey Wolseley, and the people silhouetted for a second when the front door was opened were Molly and Brian, Tommy's faithful driver. In the few seconds the light inside the house

150

remained on, Suzie saw the two bodies come together and Molly wrap herself around Brian like a python, then bearing her mouth on his as though she would eat him alive.

For several seconds they swayed together, Molly's right knee bending her leg back at an alarming angle, locked in a kiss so passionate that in the darkness Suzie Mountford almost blushed, and pushed herself even lower in the seat.

I never imagined Molly was that kind of girl, she thought and heard an invisible Dandy Tom whisper, 'Most girls are that kind of girl. Deep down they are, heart.'

He was frying a couple of mysteries, sausages, the Ghoul. For his supper, with some cold potato from last night and some PanYan Pickle. Two bombs came down close at hand and he heard the bombs, knocked him on the side of his head. He turned off the gas and put the frying pan to one side, off the ring; felt the tug of his special job and went out, locking the door behind him. Then he walked to the lock-up where he parked the car and he took it out, heading towards where he last heard the bombs.

He found her. A girl of around nineteen or twenty. They were loading her into an ambulance, but he said it was his sister. 'I want to take my sister,' he told them, putting on a big act.

'They'll look after her at the hospital, mate. It's for the best,' said an ambulance man.

'No, I'll take her. I'm her flesh and blood. Put her in my car.'

So one of the ARP men said there would be no harm in it and they loaded her into the Ghoul's car, so he drove straight to his old place; down the cellar. He had a quiet word with her, soothing her; told her to wait there for him; he'd be back.

He went home and finished frying the mysteries and the potato. Ate his supper, had a little sleep. When he woke up he was better: wasn't a Ghoul anymore.

They picked up Nicko – Sybil Harris's boyfriend – on his way in to work: Porky on one side, Flash Stan on the other, linking arms with him and hustling him protesting along Warwick Street and into one of the tart's parlours that lined it once the sun had gone down. Inside, they thrust Nicko into a chair and started being aggressive. 'Nicko? Nicko? Nicko?' Porky chanted, winding his right arm around Nicko's neck and slapping him firmly with the left hand.

'Nicko? Nicko? Nicko? What's your real name, Nicko?'

'People call me Nicko.'

'Yes, Nicko, but that's not your real name. Like Spiro, the other waiter, isn't Spiro's real name.' Porky's tone was long-suffering, as you would patiently address a fractious four-year-old.

'No, Spiro's real name's Sidney,' Nicko agreed thinking his bowels were going to start playing up any minute. 'Sidney Fontwell. We were at school together. Lancing.'

Flash Stan looked puzzled. 'Like lancing a boil? I hate that.'

'No, Flash.' Porky looked at him hard to see if he was joking, then turned back to the younger man. 'Nicko, real name when you were at school, okay?'

'Nigel. Nigel Whithers.'

'Horsey name, Nick. But why call yourselves by aliases, a-k-as?'

'What's an a-k-as?' Flash asked.

'Also-known-as.' Porky sounded disdainful, as though Flash was ill-educated on purpose. 'So why the aliases?' he asked Nicko.

'Rose,' Nicko said with a little tremble in his voice because he was definitely afraid. He knew Porky's reputation. 'When we got the job, Rose told us to go away and get more exotic names, like Nicko and Spiro.'

'So you called yourselves Nicko and Spiro.'

'That's what we called ourselves, yes,' Nigel Whithers said, not looking him in the eye.

'So, Nicko, a simple question. Where's Sybil?'

Nick was starting to sweat and there was a twitch in his fundament. 'I don't know.'

'She's your girlfriend, ain't she?'

'Well . . .'

'Ain't she, Nicko?'

'Well, yes, I suppose that's what you'd call her.'

'Nick, you're taking horizontal refreshment with her, ain'tcher?'

'Well, yes . . .'

'Then she's your girlfriend. So where is she?'

'I really don't know, Porky.'

'It's *Mister* Pine to you.'

'Then I don't know Mr Pine.'

'When you last see her?'

'Two nights ago. Rose told her the Twins wanted to see her, so she should look smart next morning.'

'Then she left?'

'Yes.'

'What time would this be, Nick?'

'Early. Before ten. There was nothing doing at the club. The night Buller Belcher got put away.'

'You speak to her before she left?' Charlie was pushing his face close to Nicko, and leering at him with a great toothy grin.

'Not really.'

'You either spoke to her or you didn't speak to her. There's no "not really" about it. Now, did you speak to her?'

'Well, yes. A bit.'

'What'd she say?'

'She said goodnight, Nicko.'

'Oh, bloody marvellous. Good effing night effing Nicko. Nicko, you want me to break your hands for you?'

'No, Por . . . Mr Pine.' He looked really frightened now because he knew breaking people's fingers and hands was Porky's best thing.

'If you don't want to have your hands in splints and lose all your teeth, Nick, you'll tell me what you said to each other.'

Nicko could see that Porky was serious and as much as he cared for Sybil he knew he had to give Porky Pine something. 'All right,' he said breathless with fear. 'She kind of whispered to me that she may be going away for a few days.'

153

'Really?' This was as far as Porky's gift for sarcasm went. 'So where was she going?'

'Honestly, she didn't say.'

'All right. This is your last chance. If you don't come up with some reasonable answer, I'll get Flash to take your teeth out – one punch at a time.' To show that he meant business, Porky gave Nicko a light punch on the side of his jaw while Flash dipped into his coat pocket and pulled out his punching gloves. These were gauntlet gloves into which he had sewn pennies: give you a nasty knock the gauntlets would.

'Now listen to my question, Nick. What's your best guess at where Sybil's gone? Your best guess.'

'Your most intelligent guess,' said Flash and Porky looked at him sideways because he'd never heard Flash talk about intelligence before.

Nicko thought, Oh shit, it'll have to be good. 'That police-woman. Plain-clothes. The sergeant,' he said.

'The one that was down there, in the Nightlight when the rozzers came and found Buller?' This sounded promising.

'The brunette? Dark hair, works with that Detective Chief Inspector?' Flash asked.

'Harvey,' said Porky. 'DCI Harvey.'

'That one,' Nicko confirmed, nodding his head.

'Bitch,' said Porky. 'That bitch came asking questions of me down the Dog & Duck. Arsked questions about that Eyetie, Falcon-effing-etti, that's what Charlie Balvak called the Eyetie. I told the Twins about the girl copper. Why?'

'Why what?' Nicko asked.

'Why would she be with the woman sergeant?'

'Because that night, when Buller got done over, the female dick spent some time alone with Sybil and Scotch Danny. In Rose's little caboose out the back. Then Danny came out into the bar again, but Sybil was there alone with the WDS. Alone, talking to her.' Nicko leaned back relieved that he'd keep his teeth.

'Good boy.' Porky patted him lightly on the cheek. 'We'll go and search for the girl copper then, won't we. Flash, his teeth,' and Flash began to hit Nicko on his jaw, eventually rendering him unconscious but not before several teeth had been loosened.

'They'll come right out next time, Nicko,' Flash told him. 'Don't you forget.'

They let Nicko go on his way to work and Greek Rose gave him a roasting for being late.

Porky telephoned Charlie Balvak from a call box and as soon as Charlie heard Porky's voice he said, 'You got my message?'

'No, Charlie. You left me a message?'

'At the Nightlight, yes. Then you've got the girl, Porky? You've got Sybil? You've treated her well? Not harmed her?'

'We've got something. Not the girl. Not yet.'

'I told you not to come back without her, Porky. Don't say you've let me down.'

'We think we know where she may be. What was your message?'

'Wanted you to come back and see us.'

'Well then. We think we know how to get at the girl.'

Charlie didn't speak, so Porky continued, 'They could know where she is. The nick could know.'

'I don't think so. You wasting my time again, Pork?'

'It's possible she's been talking to that woman detective sergeant. The one works with Harvey.'

'Mountford? WDS Mountford. Used to be with the Reserve Squad? With Dandy Tom Livermore?'

'We think so. Wanted to know how to find her. I mean. Charlie, you're the one with contacts in the nick.'

'We've had a pile of them round here cross-examining us as if we were guilty as hell. You heard the news, Porky?'

'What news?'

'Somebody died.'

'Who?'

'Some bugger's topped Little Nell.'

'Bloody Hell!'

'You'd better come round, even though you haven't found the girl.' Charlie put the phone down.

*   *   *

155

As ever she loathed coming back to an empty flat. She could hardly believe that it was less than a year since Tommy had invited himself in and began to live with her for most of the time. You get used to having him around. Didn't like it when he had to be away, even just for the odd night.

She went in and didn't slide the bolts or turn the key on the front door until she had done the rounds: looked into every room. When she was completely certain the bogey man wasn't hiding behind the curtains or under one of the beds, she locked the front door. Knew she wouldn't have to make a dash for it before the spectre could catch her.

Tonight she worried. Eventually Tommy would be back and she wondered if she should tell him about Brian and Molly Abelard. It was possible that he already knew and she'd look a fool. On the other hand should she make certain and tell him, or was that sneaking on friends?

She made a cauliflower cheese, mainly to use up a block of Cheddar from the Home Farm, and ate half of it wondering when she'd hear from Tommy again and thinking he could well return any time and surprise her.

Wandering around the flat, she finally settled by the telephone, got the Dulwich Hospital number from enquiries and telephoned to ask after Mrs Abelard. There was a chase around the wards and finally she was told that no Mrs Abelard could be found. So she asked when Mrs Abelard had been released. Eventually they told her that no Mrs Abelard had been admitted in the past three months.

She put the receiver down and the instrument rang immediately.

'I'm on my way home, heart,' Tommy said from the Coach House at Larksbrook.

'Tommy . . .' She was a shade shrill: could hear it in her voice, up there with the birds.

'Leaving now, heart,' and he closed the connection.

Thank heaven, she thought, he'll be back in a couple of hours, so Suzie ran a bath and lay soaking herself for the best part of an hour. As she luxuriated, occasionally topping up the hot water, she thought of Tommy and how it could be when he returned. Escaping into this dream fantasy world of loved and lover, Suzie Mountford almost forgot about the horror of the house in Lexington Street, the blood, the dwarf's head on the assegai and the double-headed axe.

Charlie came to the door himself and made a backwards motion with his head indicating that they should come in. He didn't speak. Simply led them down the hall into the sumptuous living room where Connie sat at the far end looking miserable and doing a gargoyle.

The room hadn't been tidied. Even the broken mirror was still on the wall with the shards of glass lying on the carpet. *Family tiff*, Porky thought. Out loud, he asked if he could clear up the mess.

'Leave it be,' Charlie Balvak told him. 'It'll get done presently.'

Neither Porky nor Flash felt really comfortable sitting around among the fine furniture and fittings of the drawing room. Not their style and it showed.

'So, what's happened?' Porky asked, feeling the tension, unpleasant, around them.

'Someone's topped Little Nell,' Charlie told them. 'The tiny sod was up to some nasty tricks and someone got at him before we did.'

'Before we did,' Connie muttered, looked up, saw Porky and Flash with their eyes on him and cried out, 'Don't look at me. I didn't do it,' his voice thrashing about, his head moving from side to side as though he was trying to escape from restraints.

'You've no idea who squished him?' Porky's eyebrows raised and questioning.

'No, neither've the busies. We've had Detective Chief Superintendent Sammy effing Batter 'em here all bloody afternoon. Him and an army of detectives. Wanted to know what we were wearing last night and again this morning. Effing search warrant to toss this gaffe an' all. Went through our clothes like the Sally Ann looking for jumble.'

'Wanted to know the far end of a fart.' Connie grinned.

'Why your clothes?'

'Apparently there was a lot of blood. Very nasty, I'm told. They didn't find the tommy gun though.'

157

'What tommy gun?'

'The tommy gun Little Nell brought along. He had two more in his gaffe. Hidden, but the law hasn't found them either.'

'The Chief Super tell you that?'

'In a round about way, yes, Pork.'

'Yes, Pork.' Connie was still awake and it was quite dark outside now.

'Then how did Little Nell cop it?'

'It would appear . . . You ever been to Little Nell's drum in Lexington Street?'

'Yeah, when he had that party back in the summer.'

'I remember that. Well, you'll recall he had some swords – cutlasses – and some of them assegais on his wall, and a big Japanese axe, two blades.'

'Assegais?' Flash looked bemused.

'Big long sharp spears. Assegais. Had two pairs, crossed on his living-room wall. Crossed with a couple of shields. African. Covered with zebra skin. Nasty African weapons, assegais. He had four of those, three cutlasses, the big axe and a painting of the Sacred Heart.'

'Yeah, I recall them,' Porky nodded. 'They run him through with them spears?'

'No. No, it was more barbarous'n that. He was stabbed to death, then had his head separated from his body.'

'His body.' Connie musing.

'Cut off with that bloody great axe. Then someone carried his head all the way upstairs. Shoved it on the end of one of them assegais. They stuck an assegai in the floor upstairs then shoved the head on top. Blood everywhere. In the bathroom.'

'Shit,' Porky said. 'No wonder they were looking for bloodstained clothes.'

Charlie nodded. A sage nod as though he knew all about blood getting on clothes.

'They didn't find none, did they?' Flash Stan asked, immediately looking very foolish.

'No, Flash,' Charlie was icy again. 'They didn't find any because it had nothing to do with us.'

'With us.'

There was a long pause during which Porky looked at the

ceiling. Then Charlie said, 'If whoever killed him hadn't of killed him, I'd have done it meself.'

'Meself.' Connie concluded.

After a while Porky asked, 'Little Nell, what was his game then?'

'He was taking a cut from the clubs. From what I hear Little Nell wanted to take over. Prince of Soho he wanted to be.' Charlie clicked his teeth. 'Had big plans, Little Nell.'

'Foolish little man.' Porky looked over at Connie, wondering how he felt about killing Buller who had turned out not to be the villain after all.

'Okay,' Charlie stepped in, 'what's happened to Sybil?'

Porky told him that they thought she was probably under police protection: told Nicko's story about the talk Sybil had alone with the WDC. 'Then she disappeared. Need to know about the copper, the WDS.'

Connie sat up and giggled again. 'She's thick that policewoman sergeant. So thick she thinks Fucking's up the road from Shanghai.'

'Her name's Mountford, Susannah Mountford. They call her Suzie.' Charlie didn't even smile at Connie's remark. 'Stay here, I'll go and check where she lives. See if my contact knows any more.' He got up, went off bustling into the hall to use the extension there. No way was he letting them hear who he was talking to.

Connie, Flash and Porky sat not making eye contact with one another. Flash started to whistle: dead aggravating. Irritated Porky no end so he started singing quietly. 'We three,' he sang, a familiar piece from the radio show *Happidrome*.

'We threee, in Happidrome, Just a set of twerps may be: Ramsbottom, and Enoch and me.'

'That from *Happidrome*, isn't it?' Connie seemed to join them for a second.

'You've got it, Con.'

'Charlie and I listen to *Happidrome*, Sunday nights. Before the news and that J. B. Priestley. What do they call that J. B. Priestley thing after the news Sunday nights?'

'*Postscript.*'

'Yea, *Postscript*. I don't see what he's getting at half the time. He's got a very north country voice, hasn't he?'

'Probably 'cos he's a northerner: speaks his mind,' Porky said, still thinking about *Happidrome*. It was quite a funny programme. Not as funny as *ITMA – It's That Man Again –* with Tommy Handley. In *Happidrome* the jokes were more obvious. Enoch, the thick one, would run in and say, 'Mr Ramsbottom, Mr Ramsbottom, there's a man outside wi' a funny face.' And Ramsbottom would say, 'Tell him you've got one.' Plain easy humour.

Charlie came back and told them he had the name of the woman detective sergeant right. 'She used to be with the Reserve Squad under that Dandy Tom – the Honourable Thomas Livermore, fwaa-fwaa. They arrested Golly Goldfinch last year. Do a lot of the big cases. She looks a stuck-up tart to me. Daft cat.'

Charlie gave them the address where Sergeant Mountford lived, and the flat number. 'She got fired from the Reserve Squad this year, before she come here. Had a big blow-up with Tommy Livermore, and no, they don't know nothing about Sybil being given police protection or the WDS having anything to do with her.'

Charlie suggested that Porky and Flash should head off to Upper St Martin's Lane and find somewhere they could hide out and watch the door to the flats where Sergeant Mountford lived. Might see Sybil, who knows. He also added his personal opinion which was that 'Sergeant Mountford can be a pain in the arse.'

'Somewhere we can keep obbo, yes, right Charlie.' Then Porky pricked up his ears. 'Hello!' Hearing the sound of the front door of the flat being opened and closed, then footsteps coming up the hall and the door opening. Porky and Flash half rose and Charlie said it was okay. 'It's only . . .'

By that time the door had opened. Later Porky couldn't make up his mind because it was as if Newcastle Brown's big lantern smile came in before he poked his head round the door.

'Away the lads,' Matt Brown sounded happy with his cry

160

that was the usual hunting call of the Newcastle United fans. 'Away the lads, if it isn't me auld friend Porky Pine.'

'Newcastle!' said Porky with great pleasure, embracing the big Geordie. 'Nobody told me you were here.' Porky had been the go-between who assisted during the unpleasantness a few years ago concerning the branding iron, the electric probe and the three girls from South London. This had all taken place when the Twins were still living in Camford: before they'd became lords of creation in the West End.

'Typical. They didn'a want you to know, man.'

'That's possible,' Charlie unsmiling and serious. 'You'd best be off to do your obbo, Porky.'

'Yeah. Right.' He checked he had the address correct and that they had to ring Charlie or Connie direct if they spotted anything untoward. 'We'll be going up the On & Off for a bite later,' Charlie said. 'So that's where we'll be if we don't answer the blower here, Pork.'

'We'll see you around then, Newcastle.' Porky raised another big smile.

'Why-aye, Ah'll be here a while yet.'

The Twins exchanged uncomfortable glances.

Left alone with the Twins, Matt Brown grinned his lantern grin, first at Charlie, then at his brother, Connie.

'You done it?' Charlie asked.

'Nah bonny lad. Nah. Too many people around. Had a nice meal though. This Falconetti does a good meal. He was there in the restaurant and I told him it was a good meal, some Eyetalian dish, chicken and that with tomatoes on spaghetti. He's still got his hand bandaged up, mind. But his wife does the cooking and there was quite a few in there tonight. In Falconetti's restaurant, I mean.'

'So when *will* you do it, Matt? We need him outa the way.'

'Oh, Sat'day morning. That's when his wife gans off out to get the food in. Early Sat'day. Ah'll gan up there and get it all put awa' early Sat'day.'

'You see that you do, Matt.'

'Did Ah hear something about Little Nell?'

There was a pause. Count of around ten.

'Well, it's like this . . .' Charlie began.

'He's gone to the Happy Hunting Grounds.' Connie had always liked the cowboy and Indian pictures up the Odeon.

'The truth is,' – *troof is* – Charlie tried to be dignified. 'The truth is he's been divorced from his life, Little Nell.'

'By person or persons unknown.' Connie moved his head and played with his tie like Oliver Hardy.

Matt Brown smiled and pursed his lips. 'Then we won't be seein' much of him in the Royal Enclosure at Ascot, man.'

'You're right there, we've had bloody Sammy Battescombe here all afternoon.'

'Putting us to the third degree,' Connie added. As well as the cowboy and indian flicks, Connie liked the New York cop films where they took suspects down to headquarters and gave them the third degree with the help of bright lights and lengths of hosepipe. The kind of thing they said the Gestapo was doing on the other side of the channel now.

Charlie shifted in his oxblood leather-buttoned chair, so that it squeaked and Connie giggled because the squeak sounded like a fart. Charlie gave him a vile look: daggers. 'Matt,' he was using his dead serious voice and letting his eyes glitter like little chips of glass, 'Matt, you'd better do Falconetti on Sat'day . . .'

'Ah told you, man, Ah'll do it. I'll skelp the bugger.'

'Then get back up to Newcastle.'

'Aye.'

'See the three builders and tell them if they come back here straightaway and see us at the On & Off we'll give them some work, provided they stay good and don't do work for anyone else.'

'You don't want me to give 'em a smack?'

'Well, you can give em a little smack, Matt, but make it so they can walk and use their arms.'

'O' course, Charlie. Whatever you say, man. You ganin' to give them work then?'

'Oh, and when you deal with the Eyetie, make sure you get the keys to his new club: Ursula's. 'Cos we'll be taking over that place. Now, you want to come and have a bite at the On & Off, Matt?'

Matt Brown shook his head. 'Na, I don't think so, Charlie.' *I doant think so.* 'I had me dinner at Carlo's caff, and I dropped into the On & Off on the way back. Ah think Ah'll turn in.' *Torn in.*

'Up to you, Matt. You coming, Connie?'

'Course Charlie.'

'Morrie says he's got a new girl working. Girl called Wanda. Wanda Lee Fook. Chinese from Hong Kong, the lads call her Wanda the Anaconda on account of her agile ways.' Maurice was headwaiter and manager at the On & Off. The Frenchman from Harrow. Maurice Benoit who's real name was Maurice Baldwin. Not a trace of French blood in his veins.

'Why, man, I'll catch her later in the year.' Matt Brown was smiling quietly to himself as though he knew something that nobody else did. He knew all right because he had been introduced to Wanda that very evening, and his smile was one of great satisfaction.

Suzie's friend, Shirley Cox, who was a newly promoted WDS with the Reserve Squad, had once told her that men preferred women to be almost naked but not quite. 'They love the undies,' Shirley said and she had introduced Suzie to French knickers in gorgeous colours with lots of lace and bows and stuff. 'They like all that,' Shirl said and Suzie found it was true as a big white five pound note. Tommy adored it. He liked black and red best: called it underwear not for wearing but for taking off.

So, after her bath she put on the new set she had treated herself to from a shop at the top of Praed Street. It was dark blue and had lace panels in it. Tommy hadn't seen them yet, but she knew they would set him off. She wrapped herself in her best dressing gown – the silky one she had bought in the spring, just when she was getting better. Bought it at Derry & Toms in Kensington. Dead swish it was.

Then she made herself some cocoa and stretched out on the bed, waiting for Tommy to get back from the country. She hadn't yet made up her mind about Brian and Molly.

She put the problem of Molly and Brian out of her head and

started to think about the ways in which the Balvak Twins made their money:

The clubs; the strip joints, the clip joints and the ones that just served booze. They were, she knew, putting their hands on more and more clubs to cater for the influx of more members from HM Forces who were starting to spend time around Soho. Then there was the extortion, the irregular insurance money on businesses, bars and spielers: if the place didn't pay insurance it would inevitably suffer some unpleasant fate, like fires or bombs not dropped by Hitler's *Luftwaffe*. Then there were the whores and brothels; there were the dirty books and magazines sold under the counter in otherwise respectable-looking shops; there were the sneak thieves and pickpockets who couldn't work the West End unless a large portion of their take went to the Twins.

Some said there were drugs, but Sammy Battescombe had told her the truth. 'No money in it,' he'd said. 'Occasionally you get people want to smoke Indian Hemp. Very occasionally there's cocaine or heroin; then there's opium, mainly among the Chinese. It's more of a problem over in Dockland, where people bring it in: try to get others to sell it, though the Chinks kept it to themselves. But no money in it, Sergeant Mountford. There's more money in stolen baccy these days. Don't worry your pretty head. England's not the right country for it. Never will be. Mind you, they *did* have a bit of trouble in the twenties, nineteen hundred and twenty-two I believe, cocaine.'

Lastly, there was also the percentage from crime itself: some set up by the Twins, others operating from bases within the Twins' turf. A tidy little sum: a good weekly earner.

She stretched out in the big old Edwardian bath, closed her eyes and started to sing –

> '*Cocaine Bill and morphine Sue*
> *Were walking up the avenue*
> *Singing, "Honey have a sniff, have a sniff on me*
> *Honey have a sniff on me."*'

She dozed off, then woke again just after midnight when

Tommy arrived home all smiles. 'You miss me, heart?' he asked, taking off his old school tie.

Suzie grinned and turned on to her back, letting the dressing gown fall open.

Thirteen

They walked across to Golden Square, Charlie and Connie Balvak, accompanied by two of the boys, Jacky and Cresswell – Jacky Russell and Cresswell Smith. Porky had been training those two for stardom and they wore identical grey suits: double-breasted with wide lapels, light-blue shirts with pearl grey ties; black shoes with metal toe and heel caps. They carried short lengths of inner tube in their back trousers pockets. The inner tubes were filled with sand and small foreign coins, sealed up at both ends. Good coshes for dishing out pain or unconsciousness to victims or enemies. Charlie had helped Porky get both lads into reserved occupations – with a little assistance from a doctor who performed a number of iffy services for the Twins.

The glimmer lighting of the blackout usually offered a dim guide to walking the streets: tonight it was less effective than usual and they could detect the chill of the damp mist rising between the buildings. There was the scent of charcoal everywhere, drifting up from the City: the smell of burned wood and the scent of fireworks that had come on December 29th last year when the fleets of German bombers turned the City's whole square mile into a sea of fire. You could still smell it up as far as Mayfair when there was a thick mist, or in the wake of heavy rain.

Tonight it was going to be a thick, choking fog.

'We're going to go home like elephants,' Charlie said. 'Tied trunk to tail.' In his head he had a vision of those pictures you saw of men who had been gassed in the Great War, blinded, shuffling along each one with his right hand on the back of the other's trousers as they shambled along in single file like elephants, trunk to tail.

'I get the car, Mr Charles?' Cresswell offered.

'Shit 'n abortion,' choked Charlie. 'What we pay you, Cresswell? Pay you in Dolly Mixtures do we?'

'Only trying to be helpful.'

'Stroll effing on, Cresswell!' Charlie came to a standstill in the middle of the pavement. 'Use your loaf will you. The fog's thickening, and by going-home time we probably won't be able to see a hand's turn in front of our faces let alone drive. We'll possibly have to stay over in the club. A situation that does have an interesting side – well, for us it does: I don't know about you.'

As they reached the entrance of the On & Off two figures loomed up in front of them.

'Sir,' the larger of the figures spoke. 'Sir, can you tell us if we can eat in this place or is it a private club? We're kinda hungry, sir, and it looks like London's all set to have a pea souper; or what do you call it? A London Particular? I read that in one of your wonderful Sherlock Holmes tales.'

Both Charlie and Connie leaned forward to get a closer look at the two men whose accents they had only heard in cinemas. Jacky and Cresswell also moved forward to flank their employers.

'You're Yanks, aren't you?' Connie asked.

'Yank servicemen if I'm not mistaken?' Charlie straightened up. 'Are you the vanguard of your mighty army come to help in the fight against the Nazi horde?' He surprised himself by the flowery speech and wondered where it came from – certainly not from anything he read. His reading was confined to *The Adventure*, *The Wizard*, *The Champion* or *Hotspur*, each priced 2^d a week, all of them had full-length stories you had to read, not like *Beano*, which was all strip cartoons, 'Big Eggo' always on the front page. He looked at *Beano* most weeks and particularly liked 'Musso the Wop (He's a big-a-da Flop)' and saw that for what it was, jokes at the expense of the Eyetalian dictator Mussolini, who, with his fancy uniforms and posturing, was an easy target.

'You have a good turn of phrase, sir. We surely are in the vanguard. US Army Air Corps and this is our first visit to your little old country. Only been here a few hours in fact.'

'You have to be a member here to eat food,' Connie, a shade belligerent.

'But we'd be delighted if you'd come as our guests,' Charlie felt he was apologizing for his brother. There was a slight pause, then Jacky and Cresswell guided the strangers into the club behind the Twins, who were immediately confronted by Maurice Benoit – also known as Morrie Baldwin from Harrow – their head waiter and manager.

'Good evening, sair. And you also, sair, a very good evening to you. It is naice to see you 'ere again, gentlemen.' Morrie was fussing and bowing over the Twins as though they were royalty, oozing obsequiousness and wringing his hands as if in competition with Uriah Heep.

Charlie smiled, tight-lipped, bent forward, trying to signal Morrie to ease up on the soft soap, while Connie muttered, 'Cut the crawling, Morrie, we got guests.'

Charlie turned towards the two Yanks – as he immediately thought of them – his hand making an expansive gesture. 'This is . . . ?'

The Americans had lurched in, momentarily dazed by the glare of lights, one short and tubby, the other tall, slender and good-looking. Charlie pictured Laurel and Hardy, then erased the image from his mind. These men were much too grave for the comedy couple; these men were self-contained, clear-eyed with dark smooth suntans associated with clear skies, palm trees and lithe women in skimpy bathing suits. Standing there in their long, drab-coloured trenchcoats, peaked caps set at an angle, they looked like men slightly out of their depth, happier among their own, more comfortable doing the job they were trained for.

The chubby one stretched out his hand to Charlie. 'Major Hiram Potts, sir, at your service, and this is Major Cannon, Pete Cannon. This surely is kind of you, sir. We really appreciate this, don't we, Pete?'

'A most bodacious gesture, sure.'

Behind Major Potts, Morrie had whistled up the hat check girl, Cynthia, tall in a minuscule skirt and black fishnet stockings, high heels, a red satin blouse that Connie had thought dead tasteful. 'I take your coat, sir,' she asked in a come-hither voice, allowing her right breast to touch Hiram Pott's upper left arm. She had one of those husky voices, like Jean Arthur in *Mr Smith Goes to Washington*. The Americans seemed to be awakened by Cynthia and began divesting themselves of trenchcoats and caps.

Those uniforms aren't *schmutter*, Charlie thought, looking at the officers' tailored dark-brown jackets, with the lighter stone-coloured, nicely cut trousers, his eyes drifting to each of their left breasts and the silver wings they wore pinned to the jacket, metallic bright.

'You're Air Force, then?'

'That we surely are, sir.'

Charlie nodded in a grave, comprehending sort of way, and introduced himself, then his brother to the American aviators. 'People call me Charlie, and this is my brother, Conrad – Connie.'

When they'd shaken hands all round, Major Potts turned towards Cresswell, stretching out his hand, so that Charlie had to reluctantly introduce Cresswell and then Jacky.

'Not important,' he murmured, 'what you'd call the hired help,' and Maurice, with an oily bow, gesturing right arm like a railway signal, led them through to the main room with its small dance floor and the dining area around it: clean, bright with starched napery and glittering silverware totally at odds with the other clubs in the Soho area, all of which had a more lived-in, downmarket ambience. A trio – piano, bass and drums – were playing in one corner and three couples waltzed mathematically round the floor.

There was the usual jostling for positions around the table, Charlie eyeing the rest of the room, pleased that it was almost full, quite notable for a weekday evening. He also clocked the new girl, Wanda, at the bar with a couple of the other girls who were fixtures at the club. By the looks of things, Wanda Lee Fook was an asset; Morrie had done well. All the girls looked high-class material, expensively dressed, sparklers at their throats that could be real ice. They sat on the barstools like proper ladies, two of them smoking through long black cigarette holders, sipping cocktails, and talking sensibly to one another, no silly giggling like you had to put up with from some of the girls.

Morrie handed out the large menus and said, 'If you cannot find anything you fancy, just ask. We can often provide things not on the me and you – sorry, the menu,' pronouncing it *Mun-You*.

'Gee,' Major Cannon looked startled. 'Certainly a good menu.'

Charlie gave him the cold eye. 'So, you've come to bomb the shit out of Hitler, eh? How long have you been here?'

'We arrived Monday,' Hiram Potts explained. 'Well, not here exactly. We flew into Ireland, came on here this afternoon.'

'I should explain,' Major Cannon said. 'We've flown in with an advance party. Two generals, a couple of chicken colonels and a gang of specialists. They're being taken round to check up on sites for airfields. Ready for the 8th United States Army Air Force coming early in the New Year. They're the ones that'll bomb the shit out of Hitler.'

Connie looked dubious. 'Careless talk costs lives,' he said.

'The food was pretty good over in Ireland,' Major Potts smiled, 'but we tried a place a little earlier, near your Paddington train station. Frankly I wouldn't offer what they gave us to my dog.' *Ma dawg*.

Charlie told him you had to know where to eat. 'We been at war for over a year, you know. Been through a defeat an' all. Dunkirk. Food's not easy to come by, what with rationing and that. You really do have to know the right places. I give you some advice. You'll see places marked "British Restaurant": don't even think about it. Cheap and cheerful may be, but not the places for the discriminating palate, sophisticated people, like yourselves. We know bettr'n most. We seen it all at the pictures. I bet you're in and out of the Stork Club and DelMonicos all the time when you're back in New York.' They were, after all, the places where Fred Astaire or James Cagney seemed to go when the Twins visited Camford's Odeon Cinema.

'Never been to New York,' Major Potts said, in his slow drawl. 'You'all been to New York, Petey?'

'Ma Grandpaw used to visit an old friend there. I only been there the once, a couple of years back. I guess those places're in Manhattan, we only visited in Queens.'

Momentarily that shut Charlie's mouth because he couldn't conceive of an American who had only been to New York once in his life and another who'd never ever been there. He buried his head in the menu and ordered the fillet steak and chips. He'd like the soup as well.

'Whatcher got on tonight, Morrie?' Connie asked, and Charlie looked down at his menu again and screwed his eyes shut. He thought he'd trained Connie for the On & Off, but you could never tell. Connie seemed to have become a little bolshie this evening.

'It's the Brown Windsor tonight, Mr Conrad,' Morrie told him with a Gallic shake of his shoulders. *Browen Win-sor.*

'What is that exactly then, Morrie?'

'It's like thin gravy, Con. You don't like it,' Charlie snapped.

'Anything else you might want, Mr Conrad. I always try to 'elp.'

'I'll just have the steak then.'

'Certainly, sair. The fillet, sair?'

'Course the fillet. Whatever else do I have when it's steak?'

'And that will be with the fried potatoes, sair, and the steak well done?'

'Of course well effin' done, Morrie. I can't abide stuff not properly cooked.'

Maurice turned to their new friend Hiram Potts. 'Sair?' Maurice was chubby and he was also tall, so could be intimidating.

'I'll have the steak as well. Rare.'

'And chips, sair?'

'What are chips?'

'What are chips?' echoed Connie.

There was an embarrassed silence.

'Chips,' Charlie said quietly, 'chips are potatoes fried in very hot dripping. Come out all golden brown and succulent. Beautiful with a drop of salt and vinegar.'

'I guess that's what we call fries?'

'Of course, sair, whatever you want.'

171

Pete Cannon would have the same, but the steak well done.

'I take it that this is what you British call a gentleman's club?' Hiram Potts asked.

'It's what we call a gentlemen's club.' Connie cocked his head to one side. Unlike his brother, he had not really taken to the Americans.

'You're members, then, obviously.'

'Oh, we're members alright. Yes, don't you worry about that. We only own the bloody place, don't we?'

Hiram and Petey looked suitably discomforted and Connie asked them what they actually did on this trip to little old England.

'See, we're here with this group of specialists. They're sizing up ground for airfields, for when the 8th Army Air Force arrives. I thought I told you that already.'

Pete Cannon smiled and said they were big-shot army builders, planners, 'guys with the theodolites, surveyors, guys who know about building runways, stuff like that.'

'Careless talk costs lives,' Connie muttered again. Then, 'Airfields? Would that be the same as aerodromes, what we call them?'

'I guess so,' Potts smiled benignly.

'Then what is your actual function in all this: laying out the airfields?'

'We fly the airplane.'

'The air-plane? Do you mean the aer-o-plane?' Connie thought Hiram Potts was trying to sound superior.

'I guess that's what you call it. We fly it to bring these highly specialized officers over here.'

'But if you fly the thing why aren't you there helping them choose the sites? I mean who'd know best: some generals, colonels and people, or you, the men who fly the planes?'

It was difficult to tell whether Connie was just being awkward or difficult and taking the Mick, or if he was just thick as glue.

'Put a sock in it, Connie. You're getting boring.' Charlie had decided that his twin was just having a go.

'Well, I'm just interested,' Connie snarled.

'Tell you what,' Charlie brightened up. 'Let's have a beer. You want a beer, Hiram? And you, Pete?'

'Well, yes. Why not.'

'What you fancy, then? Fancy a light ale? That's a fizzy beer.'

'Yeah, that would be very nice, Charlie.'

Charlie signalled Maurice over again. 'Morrie we want four light ales, and polish the bubbles in them. Right?' He guffawed with laughter and slapped the table to show what a good convivial fellow he was. Then he said it was great to be here in London with our new allies. 'We should drink a toast.'

When the light ales arrived Connie seemed to have cheered up a little and the Twins insisted on the toast to the ultimate overthrow of Hitler and 'all of his ilk', as Charlie put it. They drank and you couldn't miss the fact that Hiram Potts and Pete Cannon did not really enjoy the beer.

'What's up?' Charlie asked.

'Nothing,' Hiram pulled a sour face.

'Come on, what's up?' repeated Connie.

'Nothing's up.' Pete Cannon looked like he had sucked a lemon.

'Come on, don't be shy. You didn't like the light ale.'

'Well, Charlie, I'm sorry. I guess we all have our likes and dislikes.'

'Blimey, Hiram, what is there to dislike about a bottle of light ale?'

'It's warm,' Hiram said softly.

'Tepid,' Pete responded.

'Warm? Shit, yes, it'll be usual room temperature.'

Pete asked if they didn't have ice. 'Ale like that should be refrigerated. Served chilled.'

Charlie and Connie exchanged perplexed looks. 'Chilled?'

'You're saying we should put ice in the beer?' Charlie asked.

'No-no-no. Not put ice in the beer, but like keep it on ice. Refrigerate it. Make sure it's cold.

Charlie sucked in air through his teeth. 'Refrigeration? That'd be a bit of an outlay on the bars. I don't see it meself.'

'In the States it's kinda the way we do things. Down in Florida and along the Gulf Coast anyway. Mind you, it gets awful hot where we come from.'

'And you're all fucking millionaires an' all,' Connie grumbled.

The pianist led the trio faultlessly into 'J'Attendrai', a fourth couple joined those already on the dance floor and they all began to glide around slowly, smooching close to one another. As a young Naval officer, partnered by a WRNS officer slid by, Charlie said, 'You couldn't slide a blank cheque between those two, could you?'

'Moulded to each other,' Connie grinned, and the food arrived,

'You got any of that A1-Steak Sauce, please?' Pete Cannon asked and Morrie looked aghast.

'Steak sauce, sir?'

'Yea, it's a nice tangy brown sauce that gives a steak that extra zip.'

Morrie lifted his nose slightly. 'A brown sauce, sair?' Shaking his head and looking troubled. 'A brown sauce with steak? No, the only sauces with steak are the sauce Béarnaise or the horseradish.'

'Yea, that horseradish, I've had that,' Hiram began to chew on his steak, pronouncing it very tasty. 'A nice piece of steak this. That horseradish, I had in a kinda snooty eatery in Idaho once. They served it this place up in the mountains. Steak with the baked potato, that was good. But that horseradish, brings tears to your eyes.' He laughed.

Pete nodded enthusiastically. 'Sure, I've had the horseradish. Not a patch on the A1-Steak Sauce. That A1's the real good sauce with steak. Made for it. Tell you what, when we're posted over here properly I'll get you plenty of A1-Steak Sauce. We'll be bringing it over by the boatload. All over the States guys're mopping up that A1-Steak Sauce with their gravy.'

Charlie and his brother exchanged glances. These two pilots could turn out to be good contacts and Pete was right – if this brown sauce was what the Yanks ate with their steak then they would have to get hold of it, and other things besides.

'These fries're real good as well.' Potts looked happy.

Charlie leaned over, 'You see anything at the bar you like?' he dropped his voice.

Hiram glanced over and Wanda smiled across at him. 'Gee, fellas that's a nice piece of quayle. You mean it's for sale?'

'Of course,' Charlie smiled his most sincere smile. 'In fact you guys could have your pick on the house if you'll promise to send your friends over to the On & Off Club when they arrive. You fancy that?'

'Gee!' said Hiram Potts.

'Lordy!' said Pete Cannon.

'If you can spare the time between bombing the shit out of Hitler,' grunted Connic.

'You a married man at all, Hiram?' Charlie asked.

'No,' shaking his head. 'I never fancied that close combat, why I joined the Air Force.'

They were just finishing the steaks and chips when Morrie oiled over and whispered in Charlie's ear. 'I've got Porky on the telephone for you, Charlie. In the office. He sounds – 'ow you say it? – concerned.'

So Charlie made his excuses and went through to the office that was down a little passage running along beside the kitchen. It was a small room with a desk, a couple of chairs and a framed photograph of the Prime Minister, Winston Churchill. Out in the club they had a big photograph of King George VI and Queen Elizabeth with the two Princesses. The Balvaks were great fans of Churchill and even greater fans of the Royal Family.

'Yes, Porky, what's happening? Where are you?'

Porky was at the top of Upper St Martin's Lane, in a telephone box.

'Can't see a hand's turn in front of you for the fog, I'll bet,' Charlie said.

'No, I can see right across the road, and hear as well. You'll never guess who we've just seen.'

'Someone interesting?'

'Very. We've been across the road from where that WDS lives, keeping obbo on the door to her building. We're well hidden in a doorway almost directly opposite.'

175

'So?'

'So, about ten minutes ago a bloody great grey Wolseley comes sweeping up and stops directly outside of her door. The door opens and who comes out of the car?'

'Surprise me, Porky.'

'None other than that copper with the title, the Honourable DCS Tommy Livermore: Dandy Tom the papers calls him.'

'Jesus!' Charlie nearly choked.

'And the driver has his window down and calls to him, "You want to go back to Newbury tomorrow, Guv'nor?" he asks and Dandy Tom calls back to him, "I'll have to see how Molly's getting on with Sybil. Give me a bell in the morning, okay." Hears it plain as a bird singing.'

'Bloody 'ell,' Charlie's heart was in his mouth. So they've got Sybil somewhere near Newbury. Well, that's a turnup for the book, he thinks. How can we find out exactly where they've got her stashed away? 'Porky?' he asks. 'Can you stay up there a while? Just till I sort a couple of things out. Shouldn't be long.'

'No bother,' says Porky, and Charlie thinks for a moment, then, an afterthought – 'How're you fixed if Dandy Tom leaves suddenly – unexpected like?'

'I can get the GPO van up here in ten, fifteen minutes,' says Porky, so Charlie is confident. Porky, he knows, is exceptionally good at the surveillance on foot or in a car.

'Get it up there now. Send Flash down for it.'

'Okay, I'll do it now, boss.'

'Keep in touch and don't bugger it up.' Charlie cradled the handset and went slowly to the door, then started along the passage back to the main room and paused. Christ, he thinks, this has really blown him away.

There was a cupboard to his left, just this side of the door leading back to the club. The cupboard was crammed full of all kinds of rubbish: builders trash, old rags, bottles of cleaning liquid, white spirit, that kind of stuff. There was also something alien in the cupboard – a large biscuit tin left over from last Christmas. The biscuit tin contained several items that, if connected to one another, made up a powerful bomb – an incendiary device with a timer. The thing was connected and there was a timing device. A small travelling clock. The device was set to go off at exactly ten o'clock.

It was three minutes to ten as Charlie re-entered the club.

The trio was playing 'I'll Get Along Without You Very Well'.

Fourteen

The biscuit tin was colourful, a big cube of a box, a seasonal special from Christmas 1940 by one of the big biscuit people – Peak Frean or Huntley & Palmer. It had this picture all the way round the sides, and on the top: women in the time of George IV trolling along the street in front of shops with bottle glass windows, holly and mistletoe above the doors, snow on the roofs and some on the streets, a passing carriage and the odd Hussar plodding along in his scarlet uniform looking all big and handsome, just the thing the ladies would like in their stockings come Christmas morning.

This year there would be no tins of biscuits because metal was in short supply, and goods didn't come in tins anymore. They were cutting away park railings and gates, even those metal rails with spikes in front of houses, and hauling them off to make tanks and guns – much good did it do them because you couldn't do anything with that kind of metal. It all ended up on the rubbish tip, but people thought they had contributed and felt better about things, even gave away their saucepans: didn't know you couldn't make Spitfires out of kitchen pans.

It looked as though the biscuit tin had been thrown into the cupboard and, perhaps, partly covered with old rags and stuff, cleaning liquids and the like. The lid was sealed down with insulating tape from Woolworths. Inside was a slice of hell. A smaller Oxo tin was soldered to the bottom. The Oxo tin contained a brick of guncotton, chalk white with a bunghole in the centre. Around it, filling the larger tin, was a mixture of magnesium, powdered aluminium and iron oxide, a lot of it packed tightly. Eventually the mixture would explode and burn to buggery, sending energy shooting out with force.

Out of sight, in the middle of the Oxo tin was a gun-cotton primer shaped like a cork inserted into the bunghole. There was a small drilled aperture through the centre of the primer where a detonator just fitted. A pair of wires, ends stripped and wound together, were crimped into the detonator. The wires went through the magnesium, aluminium and iron oxide, emerging from the mass of chemicals to a flat battery – an Eveready 996 with little metal tongues as positive and negative connectors. One wire went directly to the negative tongue, and the one leading from the positive had been cut in two, both pieces going into a little travelling clock. The glass had been removed from the clock, as had the minute hand. The wire was soldered to the hour hand. The other part of the wire was wound round a drawing pin inserted into the clock face so that when the metal hour hand touched the pin, at exactly ten o'clock, the circuit would be completed, the detonator'd make a little explosion. The resulting spark would ignite the guncotton and whoomph, the tin would rip itself apart.

The explosion would be powerful and the ignited chemicals would produce a violent flame. This was a lethal homemade device calculated to cause serious damage, severe injury and death. You didn't have to be blessed with much brain to know that whoever made and placed the bomb didn't really care for the Twins.

It went off on the dot of ten, the explosion sending tongues of flame charging down the passage, licking into the dining room: it also rolled across the passage, blowing out the wall and sending flame right into the deep fat fryer in the kitchen. The result was horrible. Great clouds of fire ripping through the dining room. One of the couples on the dance floor was enveloped in a moving ball of fire, devoured immediately, the oxygen in their bodies eaten up by the flame.

Charlie Balvak had just returned to his seat when it blew. 'Bloody hell!' he said.

'Shit 'n abortion,' said his brother.

'My God,' shouted Hiram Potts.

'What the . . .' yelled Pete Cannon, never completing the oath.

Jacky Russell and Cresswell Smith said, 'Jesus' and 'Christ'

179

respectively, and Morrie shouted, *'Mon Dieu!'* staying in character.

Jacky and Cresswell did what they were paid to do, they got Charlie and Connie out and into Golden Square in record time. Then they went in again and made sure the Americans were safe, by which time there was a roaring fire going and several people, mainly kitchen staff and those on the dance floor, were burned to a crisp or had dashed screaming through the flames to roll in the street outside to put themselves out.

The girls had got out in double quick time and were flapping and tweeting shrilly, manoeuvring as close as they could to the Twins.

There was a terrible roaring as the flames caught hold and the fire built, consuming everything in its path: the glow and heat appearing to force its way through the fog, which, while thick, wasn't quite as bad as Charlie had expected.

The police, Auxiliary Fire Service and a couple of ambulances were there within seven minutes – good for a foggy night – and across the street, people were turning out and heading towards the shelters, thinking that the *Luftwaffe* was up to its old tricks.

'What the heck's going on?' Major Potts asked Charlie. 'That one of those unexploded bombs just went off?'

'Nah,' Charlie shook his head like an animal that had accidentally got soaked. 'Nah. Nah. This is a different kind of war.'

Connie said he thought they'd better make themselves scarce. 'The law'll be here in force before we know it. We could take the girls with us, and maybe that new young waiter. Play with them in the flat.'

Charlie was baffled. 'Who's done it Connie? We keep people happy. This is some bloody stupid vengeance thing.'

'Charlie,' Hiram Potts was apologetic. 'We're gonna have to get back. The plane's at Northolt. An airfield at Northolt. We're surely are appreciative of your kindness.' His voice told Charlie that this wasn't a question of being late reporting back for duty. This was a man who could fly the Atlantic, could think of being ten thousand feet over Germany, dropping bombs and being shot at, but who drew the line at hanging around with people who had been bombed by someone on the ground. The Americans needed to get back into their own environment. But that was okay because where Hiram and Pete had come armies would follow.

Charlie looked over his shoulder at Cresswell. 'Show them, Cress. Put 'em in a cab to Northolt. Give 'em a pony a piece. If the cabs 'en't running, show 'em how to get the Tube. And give them our number.' Back to Potts and Cannon, 'Call us without fail next time you're in town. I'm sorry about this. Makes us look idiots. I'm sorry.'

Then he went back to raging about what had happened. 'You know what they say about me, Con? They say that Charlie Balvak never forgets. I'll tell you, I won't forget this in a hurry.'

The West End Central area car came slowly into the square. Cheesy Fowles and Bob Paine got out and stayed by the car, like a couple of bodyguards as Big Toe Harvey, wrapped in his thick belted overcoat, wearing his grey trilby, got out. There was plenty of light coming from the blaze and Charlie Balvak walked straight across to Harvey.

'What you going to do about this then, Toe?' He reached up and for a moment put his hands on the lapels of the policeman's coat. 'It's a dead liberty, Toe. Someone's trying to take my livelihood away, me and Con's livelihoods. I want to know what you're going to do about it?'

'Take your hands off my coat, Charlie,' Harvey muttered not moving his lips, so that only Charlie could hear him. The body language, however, was clear as crystal, sending Fowles and Paine forward willing to take on anything that threatened their senior officer.

Big Toe went on speaking, and Charlie was still the only one who could hear him. 'Don't louse everything up, and take your hands off of my coat or I'll have to nick you, and we really don't want that, do we, old friend?'

For a full half-minute it could have gone either way, then Charlie smiled – a kind of smirk, not a proper grin – and did something he could have only seen in a B-picture, supporting feature, up the Odeon. He smoothed down the lapels of Big Toe's overcoat, then brushed them off, sort of gave a little tug to each lapel then flicked at them with the back of his fingers as though getting rid of some lint.

Connie watched his brother standing there with Toe Harvey towering over him and doing that business with both hands, then with fingers slightly opened in a Greek curse, he laid his hands on the lapels and pulled them back as if to say, 'Okay, no problem.'

Connie felt a wave of love sweep over him, a big surf-flecked breaker of pleasure sweeping towards his brother. He grinned because he recognized the bit of business Charlie had done with the overcoat's lapels. Saturday morning pictures when they were kids together in Camford. They'd come home after, to the Duke of Wellington pub where their dad was king; have what they could grab for lunch, what their mum had left in the kitchen; and their mum, Nellie Balvak – sour, mean and foul-mouthed – wasn't much of a cook, or a homemaker come to that. Then, in the afternoon they would be with their friends: Jack, Duggie, Gunner, Jack's cousin Sue, a boy called Carter and Porky Pine, only those days he was called Pudding Pine.

Together they would re-enact the B-pictures they had seen in the morning, or during the week because there was always a double feature and the show changed on Thursday night, which meant four films a week, not counting the cartoon, *Time Marches On* and the *Gaumont British News*, or *Pathé Pictorial*.

Oddly it was the B-pictures they liked best: *Custer's Last Stand*, *Secrets of G-Men*, *The Frog*, *The Boss*, *King of the City*, *Outlawed*, *Blue Steel*, *They Came From Chicago*. Oh, dozens they'd reinvent, shooting each other with cap pistols, screaming around on their little bikes, imitating the sirens of the motorcycle cops of the USA, and dying violent deaths, twitching and coughing on the ground in the yard behind the pub. Great days, happy days because they had both known the violence would come for real very quickly. And it did, by the time they were seventeen and smashing up shops who wouldn't pay up, and doing a bit more besides: thieving and the like.

'Get the girls, Con, we're going home,' Charlie called over his shoulder. Jacky and Cresswell fell into step and they went slowly through the smoke and thickening fog, past the burned bodies laid out under sheets courtesy of the ARP, slowly feeling their way towards South Audley Street.

'Home is the hunter,' Charlie said as they stepped inside their front door. Behind him the lift was coming up again with the girls in it, being looked after by Jacky and Cresswell. They had started to be a bit chirpy now, the girls, realizing they were lucky to be alive.

'Remember what we did to those two young girls when we were kids, Connie, out in the Duke's yard, out the back?'

'What, with the fizzy lemonade and the clothes line?'

'Oh yea. They didn't forget us did they?'

'We were horrible little buggers.'

'What d'you mean, *were*?'

'I find the bastards who did the club, Connie, I'm going to do something pretty basic to them an' all.'

'The poker, Charlie. You could use the poker.'

'Yes. First the pliers for the nails, then the poker – slow like they'll be praying for death before I'm finish.'

'What about the electric an' all, Charlie. That'd be good, give their balls some sparkle.'

The girls were being shepherded out of the lift cage, then coming in the front door with Ooh's and Aah's on account of the décor and the two big pictures on the wall, the old man and woman, done in oils, in Victorian gear Little Nell had picked up for them.

'Get 'em through, Connie, and show Cresswell were the booze is. Party, okay? I got to have a couple of minutes on the dog. Then a nice party, take the taste away.'

Charlie Balvak doesn't miss a thing.

'Matt?' he said into the phone, once he'd got past Mrs MacGregor who ran the Sunlight Private Hotel (Free cruet). 'Good. Now, are the builders on the way back to London? Tomorrow? You're sure? Yes, we got a problem . . . No, when I see you. You come here . . . Yeah, not too early though. And you're not to do anything else . . . No, no, forget about the wop. Plenty of time for Falconetti. Forget about him till later. We got a war on, Matt. Nasty, but someone's trying to play Hitler to my Churchill and I ain't going to stand for it. Blood,

183

sweat, toil and effing tears. Oh, there'll be tears alright. Mark my words. Don't you worry about that, and get those builders back. Tomorrow, Matt, okay? Make it around nine, give or take ten minutes.'

Porky Pine was flattened against the wall, back in the doorway of the office building directly opposite the Edwardian block on the other side of the street: the one that contained WDS Mountford's flat on the fifth floor, the one into which the upper-class copper, Tommy Livermore, had disappeared. Tommy Livermore, Porky mused, the head of Scotland Yard's so-called Reserve Squad.

The fog was thickening, if it kept up he wouldn't be able to see the other side of the street if or when Livermore came out. Come to that, Flash wouldn't get the GPO van up to a handy spot in the vicinity. Not in this fog.

Porky had stolen the GPO van during the Blitz. One night it was sitting behind the Post Office in Henrietta Street and he just drove it away. It was written off as destroyed. The Twins had been grateful because they'd been able to use it in numerous ways. Also they loaned it out for robberies – once for a smash and grab on a jeweller's shop in Kensington, and another time for that famous Post Office hold-up where the villains walked in and took the registered packages straight out of the sorting office in Maida Vale: Charlie, Conrad and Porky were all on that one. Nice little salary out of the envelopes. The GPO van was great to sneak around in and you could follow people and they wouldn't cop on because it was an official vehicle and they had a load of different number plates.

Finally, Flash brought it up from the lock-up the other side of Charing Cross where they kept it and it took over an hour, parking it round the corner from where they were watching the Woman Detective Sergeant's building.

'Stan, it's getting as thick as shit out there.' Porky was getting antsy, afraid they would miss something: lose the Honourable cop. 'I'll go across the road; get a better view in this murk.'

He set off across the road and halfway over, realized that he was guiding himself by intuition: couldn't even see the tiny blue glimmer light above the door of the block. He reached the pavement, went to the corner of the entrance with the blacked-out windowpanes studding the double doors; bumped his foot against the sandbags bolstering the recess. He walked quietly to his right, one hand out against the wall, guiding himself. Four paces along, he came to the alleyway that led through to the back of the building: a tiny slit separating the Edwardian apartment block from the neighbouring six-storey office edifice.

The alley was so narrow that Porky had to turn sideways to make any progress, shuffling down until he reached the far end, finding his way hampered by sandbags closing off the way out into the bushes and grass that made up the ragged open area directly behind the building. Cursing, Porky edged his way back up the alley and out on to the pavement. There was the muted sound of a car approaching, and to his left there were traces of its opaque headlights flaring in the fog. He stepped back into the alley just as the ghostly shape of the big Wolseley purred up to the kerbside.

It was between three and four o'clock in the morning he gauged, looking hard at the dim outline of the car, watching as the driver climbed out, left the door open and disappeared into the recessed entrance, using a hand torch to find the right bell, then striding back to the vehicle.

A couple of minutes later came the noise of the main doors opening and a voice calling, 'Brian?' Educated. Oxford accent, as they said.

'Here, Chief,' the driver shouted, low, from his open window.

Porky could only see the dim outline of the figure crossing the pavement to the car, knowing it had to be Tommy Livermore. Then he clearly heard the exchange as the detective chief superintendent opened the rear door.

'Newbury again, Chief?'

'Molly rang me. She's got a result from the girl. From Sybil. Wants us down there at the speed of light.'

'Well she'll have to make do with the crawl of light in this fog.'

There was another sound, the building door opening again

and a female calling – 'Tommy? The chocolate to take down to Mummy. I'm sorry I forgot, darling.'

Porky knew the voice, the one that had frightened the life out of him in the Dog & Duck, Bateman Street. 'Porky, we need to talk,' she had said, badly putting the wind up him. Told him that he'd been seen coming out of the Scout Hut the night Falconetti got his fingers caught in the door. The WDS saying that a beat constable had seen him coming out of the Scout Hut.

It was her all right, WDS Mountford consorting with Dandy Tom, saying, 'Be careful, sweetheart.' This would interest the Twins, specially that they were standing out in public, wrapped in fog, lickspittling. Quite a sight, see two coppers wrapped in an embrace. They'd soon find out where the female copper's mother lived; find out that and they'd have the girl bang to rights, Sybil.

Tommy had been distracted when he'd come in after midnight; didn't react as he should have done to her dressing gown falling open, revealing her naughty underwear and the long sheer black stockings she'd been saving up for a rainy day, or better still a foggy night. Should've worked; should've had him in the best of moods; usually did. But tonight it didn't.

'Pretty,' he said. 'You look nice, heart.' Gave a little smile, flashed on and off then passed his right hand across his brow.

'Tommy love, you okay?'

'Not really, heart. Concerned. Tired. Sybil's put the Twins slap-bang in the frame. She saw it, knows exactly what happened, but she won't sign a statement and won't appear in court. Tells you everything, then denies it.'

'Who was it?'

'Conrad. Stamped him to death. Had boots on with bloody great steel toecaps and steel on his heels. Danced on Buller Bellman's face.'

'Jesus.' The nuns would have a fit if they could hear her now. She blasphemed almost as much as Tommy.

'I suppose you can't blame Sybil, thinks the Twins're going to dance on *her* face. Heeds the warning – need a long spoon to sup with the Twins. See her point.'

'Come to bed, Tommy.' Pause while he scratched his head, walked towards the door, then came back again. Like a panther padding up and down, her lovely Dandy Tom.

'Yes, I will, heart, I'll come to bed but there'll be no making the beast with two backs tonight. I'm knackered.'

'Okay.' But she wondered if it *was* okay because it was a good ten days since they had, as Shakespeare once said in *Othello*, made the beast with two backs; and hell it used to be twice a night and three times on Saturdays not including the quick nice one over the kitchen table sometime during the afternoon and the one they had on Sunday morning while they were reading the papers. Is he getting tired of me or is he just getting tired? I'm still so inexperienced.

'Why don't you have some of that hot chocolate from the American food parcel, Tommy? I've got milk. I'll make it for you if you like. You know how that relaxes you.' The food parcel was from her old school chum Ruth who'd gone out and married a dull young American she'd met the year they left school: in banking. Ruth was always one to catch the scent of money. The young bride still kept in touch, but if you asked Suzie, Ruth was pretty dull as well.

He was standing by the door. 'Heart, that would be wonderful. Clever girl. Put a double Scotch in it, that'll really do the trick.'

And it did, sent him straight to sleep.

Suzie had felt guilty many times and she felt guilty now. Was it natural for a girl – a woman – to feel like this? To want the male shaft so much. She remembered her sister, Charlotte, saying that their mother had told her on the day before her wedding that she should never refuse her husband, *It gives men great pleasure*, she had said. *A woman just has to put up with it.* Was it really okay for someone like her to get enormous pleasure from it? The kind of pleasure so many women thought was the prerogative of men. To enjoy it was to be – what was it the Book of Common Prayer said? – like the brute beasts of the field. She had come to rely on the pleasure that Tommy gave her. Another guilt, they were not yet married. Tommy's breathing next to her was deep and steady. Not so often these days. After all he was a good ten

187

years her senior. Was that it? Was he going off her? Getting too old.

Her mother came back into her mind.

'I shouldn't have promised Mum the second tin of chocolate from the parcel.'

He grunted.

'I said the next time one of us went down to Larksbrook we'd take it.'

He grunted again, sound asleep until the telephone clattered them awake, three fifteen in the morning.

He grumbled. It was his phone, the special one he'd put in so he could stay with Suzie and people would think he was in his sordid hovel of a flat across town.

It was Molly.

'She's done it,' he said and did a sleepy little war dance. 'Sybil's made a statement and signed it. We can bring her back; I'm going down tonight. Tomorrow or the next day we can put the Twins in the bag and throw away the key. Coup for Tommy Livermore.' Peeped out, pulling the blackout curtain back. 'Can't see a hand's turn out there. Fog's thick as glue. Going to need a boy walking in front of us with a red lamp.'

He rang Brian.

Brian came in the car, so Tommy kissed her and left. Then she saw the tin of chocolate sitting on the table, so she grabbed her dressing gown and charged after him, out into the pea soup.

'. . . The chocolate to take down to Mummy . . . Tommy.'

'Right, heart. Get inside, you'll catch your death, you're not dressed. What a hussy, Brian. No shame, out on the pavement without a stitch on.'

'Take care of him, Brian.'

'I will, Sarge.'

Suzie turned and went slowly back to the big entrance with its recessed porch and the panes of glass blacked out. Didn't feel right though. It felt as though someone was watching her, could see her clearly through the wall of choking yellow fog.

The fog was a boon to the Ghoul: hid him, blanketed him as he felt his way, like a blind man through the streets he knew so well. He had wakened at two o'clock and was out now, searching for someone to look after, to spend a vigil with in his cellar.

But tonight nobody was about. Not a corpse in the eyeless street; only a policeman on the beat and he was aware enough not to tangle with a copper.

He wondered if he should go deep into the West End; or perhaps we could find someone in Soho. No, it was too far to go.

Dejected, the Ghoul returned to his place empty-handed and frustrated.

Fifteen

'I can't think who'd want to do this to us, burn down our best club, blow it up.' Charlie lay on the bed, nothing on but his silk dressing gown and that was open. He smoked a cigarette and Wanda, the Chink bit of crumpet, lay next to him with no clothes on.

'We're everybody's friends, my Connie and me, eh Wanda?' He took a deep drag on his cigarette and blew the smoke out in a long stream towards the ceiling. 'Nobody has a cause to do anything like that to us. Like I said, we're everybody's friends. Aren't we?'

'Could it be jearousy, Cha-ie?' He had told her to call him Charlie earlier, just when they were getting down to a bit of the horizontals, bit of nookie. The other girls had left and Connie was in his bedroom with the pretty young waiter. Roses in June, Connie had called him. 'He's a lovely bit of peach fuzz,' he whispered to Charlie. The guy was very young, the waiter.

Charlie didn't really approve of his brother being a poufter but what could you do? That wasn't quite true because Connie was only half a poufter. Like the Circle Line on the Tube, he went both ways. It worried Charlie because it was against the law, well the queer side of it was, and if he got nicked and sent down he'd have a rough old time. He worried because in stir Connie would probably see red, lose his temper and kill someone, quick as kiss yer arse: they'd do that an' all. But blood was thicker than water, he reflected. As long as Connie didn't do it in the streets and frighten the horses.

'Jealousy?' he queried now. 'Who could be jealous of us? We treat everyone right. Take what's our due, keep the riff-raff off the streets; give value for money – well almost. Who'd be jealous?'

'Wha' abou' Percy Hodges?'

'Percy Hodges? No. No, he operates other side of the river. Wouldn't move against us.'

Percy Hodges ran a firm in what used to be the badlands, deep in the East End. That was his patch. They'd had some dealings with Percy in the days when they only ran the territory around Camford, but things changed. Percy was a hard man, had a tough gang around him, but knew the rules.

'Don' be so sure,' Wanda turned on to her left side and looked down at his face. He thought he could detect stars in her eyes. 'Cha-ie, I work for Perce a few weeks rast year. He always say rife not fair. He say if he'd had his way he'd be the one sitting in a West End house, king of crubs, the gir's, and the plotection, not the effing Ba'vak twins.'

'Never?' Surprised.

'He whine on rike a se'aphim.'

'A what?'

'Se'aphim, rike in the Good Book: chelubim an' se'aphim continuary do cly. Percy moan and cly all fucking time.'

Charlie gave her a sly look. 'You a friend of Little Nell when he was alive? He was always spouting the Good Book and the prayer book an' all.'

'Nell Bellman? He was murder', weren't he?'

'Sunnink like that. Percy Hodges really was jealous of us?'

'Yea.'

'And you worked for him?'

'For while.'

'Why did you leave?'

'His girls were made to do plactices of wha' I didn't approve.'

'What kind of practices?'

'Like the gamalouche. I don' rike that. I think it dirty.'

'Oh, that's a shame. I was hoping . . .'

'No, Cha-ie. It okay with people you know, or people you feel sunnink for. But Percy expected his girls to do it any customer, off the streets, and that's not light.'

'No, it's not right. Anyfink else?'

'Well, I'm not turned on by the sadistic stuff.'

191

'What the whips and chains and that? Handcuffs?'

'You never know, do you? Could be in dead schtuck with the wong bloke. I mean a bit of right spanking I quite enjoy. That can be turn on. I rike a bit of spanking occasionally, that's natural, but the whips and handcuffs an' that. Not on your nerrie.'

Charlie smiled up at her. 'I think I ought ta get you out of the clubs, Wanda. Get you a little place on your todd. Somewhere near here. Where I could come and see you regular. Take you out. Only loan you out occasionally to your visiting firemen: people I know.'

'Oh, would you, Cha-ie? Would you reery?' She sounded truly enchanted.

'Why not? Morrie did well getting you to work at the club. You're a bit tasty, Wanda. Exotic. A touch of the Mystic East. You'll do a treat.'

'Touch of Mystic East?' she laughed. 'The furthest east I been is Wapping Old Stair.'

'The visiting firemen ain't to know that, Wanda. All they'll know is that the story ain't true.'

'Wha' story?'

'That Chink girls are made horizontal. After you, they'll know you're the same as anyone else: you got the vertical smile.'

'But I'll be mainly with you, Cha-ie, right?'

'Why not? And if you're nor a good girl . . .'

She giggled and crossed her hands over her breasts. 'Oooooh Cha-ie. Help.' She moved her hands and rubbed her little bum vigorously going 'Yow-yow-boo-hoo! Good hu?' Grinning and snuggling against him.

The telephone rang and Charlie's hand shot at it like a rock from a ballista. Picked it up. Didn't speak. Never liked to speak until the caller identified himself.

'It's Porky.'

'Yea, right, Pork. What's going on? I'm a bit busy at the moment. Bit tied up with some stir-fry.'

'You sitting down, Charlie?'

'Why?'

'Because we have more news.'

192

'Yea? Well tell me.'

Porky told him that as well as the cop they called Dandy Tom – head of the Reserve Squad, Scotland Yard – visiting the Female Dick, as he had taken to calling Sergeant Mountford, he now knew they were on very lovey-dovey terms. 'There's more. We know where the girl Sybil is: we figure she's down in Newbury staying with the Female Dick's mum. If you can find Mountford's mum's address, then you've got the girl on toast.' He went on telling Charlie that Sybil had made a statement and signed it. DCS Livermore was on his way up there to bring her back.

'At this very moment. Right?'

'You didn't follow him?'

'You joking, Charlie? The fog's as thick as arseholes out here. Livermore's gone down but it'll take him most of what's left of the night.'

It was just gone four o'clock in the morning.

Charlie said, 'Porky, go and have a wash and brush up then come over here for breakfast. 'Bout six, six thirty. Okay? Bring Flash.'

'As you say, chief. Breakfast, okay.'

'I make you bleckfast?' Wanda offered.

'If you can cook proper food, darlin'. I mean we don't want any of that Egg Foo Yong, or your Chicken Chow Mein. Not for breakfast.'

'That only for visiting fi'men,' Wanda grinned.

'So what can you cook?'

'Nice clispy bacon 'n' egg, bangers, mushloom, so tey potato, fly tomato, fly srice, toas' 'n' malamade good. Big eats. Also can do steak, egg 'n' chips. Fill your boots Jack, okay?'

'I'll let you cook bleckfast then,' Charlie capitulated.

He rang Big Toe Harvey at home. Big Toe was furious. 'Hell's effing bells it's the middle of the night.'

'Calm yourself, Tony.' Charlie sounded very hard. 'I got something for you'll warm the old cockles. Now listen. Do you know where that WDC Mountford's mum and dad live?'

'Mountford's mum and dad? Yes, I have it somewhere. Somewhere Newbury way, I think. It's her mum and *stepdad*. It's out in the sticks, where the deer and the antelope play.'

193

'No discouraging words or anything, eh? It's important, so bring Mountford's parents' address with you. Come and have breakfast with me, seven thirty sharp. I got a new breakfast chef. Come to that I may be falling in love. There's lots a good news.'

They went back to bed for a quickie and nodded off after; woke with a start and were sent rushing around like blue-arsed flies. Wanda bustled around the kitchen wearing a long apron and precious little else.

'Get some shoes on, my little water chestnut, you'll splatter all over your feet.'

'I make best bleckfast you ever have, Cha-ie.'

He patted her lovely little backside and she squealed and giggled.

Going to play house with you, Wanda, he thought, then told her there'd be three sittings for breakfast. First it'd be Porky and Flash Stan. Next would come the Law, and last – if he timed it proper – would be his Geordy mate Matt 'Newcastle' Brown.

Porky and Flash arrived and Wanda came in with everything beautifully presented: clispy bacon 'n' egg, bangers, mushloom, so tay potato, fly tomato, fly b'ead. Big Eats Jack. Get in, pig, it's your birthday.

Charlie had a banger and a fly tomato because he still had a couple of bleckfast to go, but Porky and Flash Stan filled their boots, ate the lot.

Big eats, Jack. Fill your boots. They did a double take as Wanda left the room, her buttocks going like a pair of windscreen wipers.

'We're in a war,' he told them. 'Not the one that's being fought against Hitler, Musso and the Japs. But a private one. A shadow war, 'cos we don't know who we're fighting, but I've had a tip off that maybe it's Percy Hodges.'

Porky and Flash Stan looked at one another, then nodded all grave and serious. If this was a Western film Percy Hodges would be wearing a black hat, black as a badger's whatsit. He'd be a bad hombre. They liked Western films.

'Seems to me last night was the opening shot, the attack on the On & Off. There's more to follow, so don't trust nobody.

The pair of you.' He paused to let it sink in, then – 'Now, what I want you to do is get someone you really trust and send them across the river.' Porky saw Flash Stan begin to open his mouth, so he kicked him under the table and let Charlie continue. 'Get 'em to keep their eyes and ears alert. Find out if it really was Percy who dumped the bomb on the club.'

After that he quizzed them on the question of Sybil and what they'd heard in Upper St Martin's Lane.

'Cushti,' Charlie concluded and sent them on their way to organize putting a spy in Percy Hodges' camp. 'Who you going to use?' he asked.

'I reckon Monkey. He's clever, they trust him over there and he stays shtum.'

Monkey's real name was Ollie O'Grady, and when they didn't call him Oily O'Grady they called him Monkey because he was trustworthy – heard nothing, saw nothing and said nothing – like the three wise baboons – after he'd sussed out what you wanted.

Connie came out of his bedroom when Porky and Flash Stan had left. Roses in June was mincing along following Connie. 'Cor, Charlie, there's a wonderful smell of bacon . . .'

'Yes, there is. I got three working breakfasts and we got a new chef and you'll keep your hands to yourself if you go in the kitchen, and Roses doesn't go in there at all.'

'I was going to tell you, Charlie, Misty's going to stay here for a few days.'

'Misty?'

'Yea, his name's Martin Dawne – wiv an E. The other lads call him Misty. Misty Dawne, see? Play on words.'

'I know what it's a play on, but he ain't staying here, Con.'

'Oh, Charlie, come on. He's a very nice boy. He could even be your galley slave.'

'I got a galley slave, Con. Do yourself a favour and get rid of Foggy . . .'

'Misty.'

'To me he's Foggy, right?'

Misty was pouting and sliding his right foot in an arc around the carpet. 'Come on, Foggy,' Charlie said, shoving his face near the young waiter's nose. 'There'll be plenty of other times. I'm not averse to you sleeping over, but not every night.'

The doorbell rang.

Charlie chased his brother and his friend back in the direction of Connie's bedroom.

It was Big Toe Harvey from West End Central. He came in and glanced around nervously. 'You got nobody else here, Charlie?'

Charlie had never seen Big Toe nervous. 'Only my brother and his friend,' raising his eyebrows and making a limp-wristed camp gesture. 'I've told them to stay out the way. And my new girlfriend's here as well, but she won't hurt. She's dead good at staying silent if that's what you're worried about.'

'I don't particularly want to be seen in your company, Charlie.'

'I can understand that. You got Mountford's mum's address?'

Tony Harvey gave a brief nod, curt, taking off his coat and hat, so Charlie called out, 'Wanda Lee Fook!' So loud that Big Toe winced. Charlie continued to shout, 'Bleckfas' chop-chop.'

'Bleckfas' coming up,' Wanda called back from the kitchen and Charlie shepherded DCI Big Toe Harvey through to the elaborate living room, where the usual table was laid for two.

Harvey looked towards the far end of the room and saw the long shards of glass which had not yet been swept up and safely stowed away.

Charlie said, 'This'll make your eyes water, Toe.' Referring to the rear view of Wanda after she'd put the full bleckfast on the table.

Wanda came in all smiles with the goodies on a huge platter. This time Charlie had the clispy bacon 'n' egg with mushlooms. When Newcastle Brown came, he would only have toas' 'n' malamade.

Big Toe's eyes followed Wanda, watching the dangerous curves, and it was only after she had served him that Charlie realized she had, to some extent, been taking the piss. She bowed low over Big Toe's plate saying, 'I think you likee bleckfast velly muchee. I thinkee you Rondon Poricemen are wonde'fu'.'

Harvey looked over at Charlie Balvak and raised an eyebrow. 'Your latest bit of squeeze?'

'Mountford's parents, Tony. The address.'

Harvey smiled, 'It's *that* important, uh?'

'I think you'll find it's more than important.'

'Tell me.'

Charlie gave him the look, then said, 'Is my memory at fault, Toe, or did you tell me that the WDS came to West End Central after an unfortunate blow up with Dandy Tom Livermore head of the Reserve Squad? A dangerous man.'

'Yes. A real Jews' friendly. Apparently a lot of people heard it happen. Screaming at one another, I hear, and that's about the worst thing you can do with Lord Snooty, Dandy Tom. Why?'

'Because I think you should know they either made it up or it never happened. Mountford and Livermore are still seeing each other. Livermore went into her flat at midnight plus twenty-one last night and left around four this morning. I heard it from someone who was close to them, hidden by the fog. He said they were very lovey-dovey. Didn't hide it. Even in front of Tommy's driver – a constable called Brian.'

Big Toe Harvey had speared a quarter of an inch of sausage smeared with mustard, then dipped it into his egg yolk. He had the fork almost to his lips when Charlie told him about Dandy Tom and Suzie Mountford. The fork remained poised with some yolk dripping back on to the plate. Big Toe's hand trembled slightly and his cheeks had a highly unnatural colour.

Tony Harvey who said, 'Shit!' Then he said, 'The bitch. That bastard Livermore. The tart's been put on my back.'

'Really?' Charlie said. 'I'm sure, knowing you Toe, it won't be terminal.'

Harvey popped the piece of sausage in his mouth and chewed. 'No, not terminal, Charlie. But I'm angry with myself. Should've seen this coming, spotted it a mile away. I'm a fool and didn't even suspect her. I use your phone?'

'Help yourself. I like to assist the police in their enquiries.'

As he was dialling, Big Toe said, 'They tell me that eventually we'll know who's dialling us before they make the connection. Death-knell for the married man.' Someone

197

picked up at the other end. Toe asked for CID. 'Don't react, Cheesy,' he said. 'You know who this is? Good. Tell me, is WDS Mountford in yet? When is she expected? Yes. Right. Midday. No. Do me a favour, Fowles. Have a word with Detective Chief Superintendent Battescombe, will you? Tell him I don't think I'll be in at all today. Not feeling too bright. I'll give him a bell later, okay?'

He cradled the receiver then came back to his place at the table; took another mouthful of food and looked hard at Charlie Balvak. 'Charlie mate, I want to teach that young woman a lesson. Something that won't kill her but'll scare her so witless that she'll forget about me: forget about West End Central nick and leg it back to Mum.' He was mopping up the egg yolk with a piece of toast. 'Her and Tommy Livermore?' He rolled his eyes. 'I can hardly believe that. He's soddin' aristocracy.'

'Tony, I expect she's inflamed with lust for him. It happens.'

'I need it taken care of: can't do that by myself.'

'What d'you think I want Mum's address for, Toe?'

'I mustn't be involved of course, no fingerprints; not a whisper that can lead back to me. Nothing. You do that for me, Charlie, for old times' sake, eh? You know if I go down you're not going to be left standing either. You can do it?'

'Course I can do it. How long you reckon we got, Toe?'

'Oh, couple of days. Three at the outside. No rush.'

'We'll get to it then, but at the moment, Tony, you got a more pressing problem.' He leaned forward and touched Harvey's left forearm, making the policeman lift his head, look at Balvak as though he had made some terrible social gaffe, withdrawing his arm and almost pressing himself back in his chair.

'What more pressing problem?'

'The reason I'm after Mountford's parents' address.'

'Which is?'

'The girl, Sybil, from the Nightlight. She's down there. She's got the truth about Connie an' all, which means she also knows the time when you were there. To tell the truth and hope to die, Tony. She's a menace to you. Screw you up and spit you out, my old mate.' He paused while Harvey took another forkful of food. 'So give me the address, old love.'

Harvey gave another nod. 'They live in a Georgian house

called Larksbrook about four miles out of Newbury on the Kingsclear road. It's on the left-hand side. The garden is walled and the stretch of road it's on could be described as tree-lined. Through the gates on the left side there's a converted stable block. The father's dead, but the mother's married again: she's now Mrs Ross Gordon-Lowe. Okay?' He slid a piece of folio-sized typing paper from inside his jacket pocket. 'The things I do for you, Charlie. Here, look, I've even drawn a map. Now see. The Kingsclear road . . .'

'I've got that, Tony.'

'Interesting, Kingsclear. The weather vane on the church tower, there's a metal replica of a bed bug. A king – I forget which – stayed the night in Kingsclear and slept with bedbugs, so he gave them a bedbug for all to see on the weather vane. Funny, I remember things like that. I've got an encyclopaedia of useless facts stuffed in my memory.' He gave a tired sigh, as though everything was too much.

'Thank you, Tony. I'll get it done today, I promise you. But there's still the question of the Mountford girl. If we're to get her off your back, scare the arse off her, there has to be a threat. Your name'll have to be mentioned. You understand that of course. There's really no other way.'

Big Toe gave him his hangman's smile and nodded gently. 'It's a service we'll both profit from, Charlie. You and me, both.'

And at that moment they heard the noise. First the reverberation, like one of the underground trains going right under the building: you got that in some of the theatres round Shaftesbury Avenue, the whole place shivering even while a performance was going on. There was a story about a drunken actor improvising, shouting, 'Mind the doors please,' middle of a love scene. Here and now the windows rattled, the glass rippling away. The rumble went through the ground then the noise, like a pair of bass drums being pounded, flat and with a double thump: ker-whump!

'Jesus,' Charlie said.

Big Toe walked to the telephone, dialled then spoke, 'DCI Harvey. I'm just west of South Audley Street. I heard the explosion. Do we know where and what yet? Yes, I'll hold on.' Charlie, half standing, counted twenty-three. Then, 'It is? Where? Yes. Yes, I'll take a walk in that direction.' He put the phone down then turned to Charlie. 'You seem to have a persistent enemy, Charlie. That was another club, the Nightlight, corner of Brewer and Warwick Streets. Greek Rose's club.'

'What—?' Charlie began.

'A bomb, they said. Blown the innards of the place to buggery. I'll go and take a look. You get organized dealing with that policewoman and the girl Sybil. Right?'

'Greek Rose,' Charlie said. 'Poor old Greek Rose.' He heard the flat door close and the whine of the lift mechanism as Harvey made his way out of the building.

Then he made one quick telephone call. Less than a minute on the line giving orders to Cresswell Smith, telling him to stand by with one of the cars. 'The Daimler'll be best. And get yourself a shooter.' A picture of Cresswell went through his mind and he recalled he'd first seen the well set-up lad in Southampton, where his father ran a ship's chandler's business for visiting yacht owners.

'Right, chief.' Cresswell was a bit of an arsehole creeper. 'By the way we took care of the ghost haunting your rubbish bins last night.'

Charlie gave him a terse 'Good,' and didn't continue with the conversation. There had been someone prowling the flats' rubbish bins at night. He had heard them again last night while they were whooping it up after the bombing of the On & Off. He'd told Jacky and Cresswell to deal with it and chase anyone off. He took a deep breath, then went through into the kitchen, where Wanda was cleaning up and preparing things for the third breakfast sitting.

'Cha-ie,' she shrilled. 'Cha-ie you plomise to get me flat. When, please?'

'Soon as I can find one.'

'I have difficu-ty,' she began. 'Need new prace now: this instan'. I share small flat in Bloadwick Street. I can't pay rent now crub is crosed.'

'Yes, Wanda. Crub is crosed. Stay here for a bit, eh?' he laughed at his unintentional joke.'

'Cha-ie, this okay?' Spoken on a rising sing-song. 'This wha' you wan'?'

'It's wha' I wan' now crub is closed,' he said slowly in imitation.

The doorbell rang, and Charlie went down, opened up, letting a sombre Newcastle Brown inside. The timing was immaculate.

Wanda served breakfast and Charlie poured the coffee.

'I want you to go down to Berkshire and do what you do best.'

'What's that, man? Drink strong beer and satisfy lusty women?'

Charlie looked serious and shook his head. 'No, I want you to effect an introduction.'

'An introduction? Why aye, who're the lucky people?' *luckee peeple.*

'A young woman who's causing me a lot of bother. You'll have to introduce her to your good friend the Angel of Death.'

Matt Brown went very still. 'Who's the woman?'

'You've never heard of her. Girl by the name of Sybil Harris. Can do us a lot of damage. She's being held down near Newbury. Held by the law.'

'Where can I find her?'

'Newbury. Well, just outside Newbury. I'll give you the details.'

Matt Brown had gone cold and still inside. This was the last thing he wanted. It would interfere with plans of his own.

'There's not much time, either,' Charlie continued.

'How much time.'

'Matter of hours.'

'If it's a matter of hours, how'm I going to get down there.'

'One of my lads'll drive you down. Anything else you want?'

'Such as?'

'I can get you a Tommy gun.'

Matt Brown gave him a look of splendid condescension. 'Anyone can get me a Tommy gun,' he said and that gave Charlie pause, as they say, made him feel uncomfortable.

Matt Brown said, 'I got something smaller'll do the job a treat, pet. Now give me the details so I can get on with it.' Smiling his lantern smile. To Charlie his friend Brown had never looked as hard as he did now. The smile stayed in place but the eyes had narrowed. Someone else had used the expression – eyes like piss holes in the snow. That's what Newcastle Brown's eyes looked like now as he headed off to meet up with Cresswell, who had been told to pick him up in Curzon Street: by the arch leading into Shepherd Market.

'Dead romantic,' Brown said, and for a moment his smile slipped from the pumpkin of his face altogether.

Sixteen

When Suzie came in to work that afternoon they told her that Big Toe was off duty, called in sick but had been seen looking perfectly fit up Brewer Street where the Nightlight had been bombed out this morning by person or persons unknown.

'That's two clubs removed in twenty-four hours. Sounds contagious,' DC Billy Hobbes said to her. Billy really hadn't yet got over the incident concerning Little Nell's head stuck on an assegai in his bathroom. He kept going round the CID office shaking his own head and muttering that he never liked the man but you wouldn't wish that on your worst enemy.

She had been in less than half an hour when Billy was called out to a beat constable who had found something disgusting on the bombsite off Dean Street, the bombsite where St Anne's Soho had been: the church. The something disgusting turned out to be the female down-and-out they called Tatty Macintosh. She had been bad enough in life and was even more filthy in death because someone had taken a blowlamp to parts of her body and stitched up her lips with twine and a sailmaker's needle. She smelled something awful and looked less than human now she was dead. Billy Hobbes was sick into the static water tank they'd erected on the site, almost where the font used to be. In the summer they'd even caught kids trying to swim in the static water tanks put up all over the place to help the AFS in the event of more incendiary raids.

Billy couldn't make out why anyone would do such a thing to a down-and-out. He wondered if he should talk to DCI Harvey, tell him maybe he wasn't cut out for this kind of work – well, the kind that meant you looking at mutilated bodies.

Darkie Knight said it was sad the way some folk ended

up. The one they called Tatty Macintosh had been a really high-stepping whore at the turn of the century, look at her now, burn marks all over her old wrinkled jugs, pubes singed off and her mouth sewn up with a sailmaker's needle and twine. Darkie knew everything, knew what Billy's mum used to call the far end of a fart.

'Apparently she was mistress to half a dozen titled men,' he told them when they were gathered in the canteen and the talk turned to characters of old Soho and what we know about them. 'Wouldn't surprise me if she'd been mistress to King Edward VII, God bless him.' Darkie had absolutely no evidence to back up this last remark but it was a cherry on the cake, and Darkie always told good stories.

Suzie heard about Tatty Macintosh and immediately felt guilty. Perhaps the Twins had seen her snooping around their rubbish bins and set the dogs on her. She also felt sad because she'd planned to talk the old girl into going to hospital: just for a few days, get cleaned up and checked over.

Take a look in their bins would you, Tatt? she'd said the last time she spoke to her. The Twins' rubbish bins she meant. And it was the last time; never spoke to her again.

'Before *ITMA* and Tatty Macintosh they used to call her Stinking Sarah. That was her real name, Sarah Emily Evans, married to a dwarf called Frank who was her pimp,' Darkie told them.

Big Toe was off somewhere today she was told, so what better chance did she have to catch up on unfinished business? She'd complete her current paperwork, then go down the Dilly to the Regent Palace and have another word with Brenda Marks. She had a few questions to ask Brenda, such as who tipped off the three boys who called themselves the Trinity Building Co. They were happy as Larry until she was going to have a chat with them and as soon as they knew it, they were away: up to Newcastle, Geordie land, fresh pastures and new building to do. She'd counted five people who knew she was breathing down the builders' necks, each of them a copper or a professional grass. Five people and Brenda Marks, or the Reception Night Supervisor, Susan Wood, smart, intelligent and, as Tommy would say, piss-elegant. Come to think of it,

Tommy was taking her for granted these days. Last night had been a case in point. The gaps were getting longer and he was turning a shade condescending.

No making the beast with two backs tonight. I'm knackered.

Then, when she gave him the hot chocolate with the double Scotch in it, *'You're a clever girl, heart. Set a fellow's pulse racing. Clever, clever little temptress.'* If that wasn't condescending I'll be a monkey's uncle. In her head she heard a high-pitched jabber – whu-hu-hu-hu, and there was an itch in her right armpit.

So, she'd walk down to the Regent Palace, deal with that, then visit Carlo Falconetti who was out of bounds, which was exactly why she wanted to talk to him.

She collided head on with a young Raff officer as she got through the hotel's main doors; stepped back, realized that she had seen the same young man when she'd last been in the hotel and was trying to place him, looking at his back. Now she saw his wings and the medal ribbon, DFC with a bar.

'I'm awfully sorry,' he said in a splendidly educated accent. She could imagine him saying 'Right chaps, bandits at angels one-five lets go and get 'em', and she gasped, off-balance.

He said, 'What a stunning girl. Gosh, but you're . . . thing. Police. Detective. Suzie, it is you isn't it? Suzie Mountford?'

'Yes. Fordham. I'm sorry,' because she had never called him by his name only; corrected herself. 'Squadron Leader O'Dell. I saw you in here the other day. Saw your back, sort of recognized you.'

'Then why didn't you come over? Wake me up? Kiss the sleeping Prince. Oh, gosh it's good to see you. Middle Wallop, you shot me down in flames, Suzie. I'm on leave. Nowhere as lonely as a city without friends when you're on leave.' And she didn't believe that for a start: Fordham O'Dell without friends was omelettes without eggs, bread without cheese.

She realized he was holding her shoulders, looking at her with those big brown eyes that had seen so much excitement and weeks of pain, the soft sandy hair now neatly cut, which it hadn't been when she last saw him. She smelled leather and aircraft dope, oil, smoke and the scent of the 'A' Flight

205

Hut. She could hear a Spitfire like an angry huge insect with a whine added to its singular sound. Her mind recaptured the scents of when she went to interview him after the murder of his dear school friend Jo Benton, her first serious case, in out of her depth, over her head. The aerodrome at Middle Wallop. 'A' Flight, 609 Squadron, a clear, sharp December day, just before Christmas last year: just before the horror.

He had sat in his Flight Commander's office and sobbed like a child and she felt useless, impotent, unable to help him.

'Come to lunch,' he said with an enormous grin. 'I know a little place'll do us proud. Please.' The eyes glistened, still weary but mobile, used to searching the skies for the black dots that grew so quickly into Messerschmitts, huge in his gunsight.

'I'm,' she said fumbling for the right words. 'I'm here on police business. I'm sorry Squadron Leader . . .'

He said, 'Fordy, or if you want to be formal, Fordham. Lunch, then whatever your business is, how about that?'

They had moved back into the entrance, inside the hotel, people buzzing around them on a chatter of talk.

She looked at him again, and changed her mind in a second. She said, 'No. You wait here. It won't take long. I'll be as quick as I can.'

So, I'm inexperienced. Catch up now.

'You'll have lunch with me?' He did not look as ridiculously young as she remembered. All of twelve she had thought at the time, the eyes older in the young face, the slight tremor of his hands.

'Yes, of course I'll have lunch with you.' It was as if she was grinning with her whole body. What a lovely surprise, she thought. How wonderful. He actually remembered me.

And Suzie went off to work, to see Brenda Marks among the leather chairs and the couples clamouring to be alone together. She thought:

In Room Five Hundred and Four. A female vocalist she couldn't name. Dorothy somebody.

She asked for Brenda Marks at Reception, and the girl said, 'I'm sorry, Miss Marks isn't with us anymore.' Not she's off duty, but she's not with us anymore; she's gone, vanished, vamoosed, been fired.

She showed her warrant card and asked to speak to whoever was in charge, taking the initiative, wondering why she had a new confidence; and the piss-elegant Susan Wood came out of the office behind the long reception desk.

'How can I . . . ?' she began to say. 'How can I help . . . Oh, we've met? Miss Mountford, isn't it? You've been on my mind this morning. I've been on the verge of telephoning West End Central. That is right, isn't it? You're from West End Central?'

'Yes. What'd you want to talk about?'

'Come into my office,' and to the little dark Jewish receptionist, with the jet black hair, ringlets down to just above her shoulders, 'Let Miss Mountford in, Jessica.'

The girl went to the door at the side of the closed-in Reception area and opened up for Suzie, muttering, 'Yes, Mrs Wood,' in a voice full of displeasure. Maybe Jessica's mother had been frightened by a police horse.

When they were settled in the office, coffee ordered and cigarettes offered from a silver box, Suzie asked if there was a problem.

'No, and it's really nothing to do with the hotel.'

'Well?'

'The three lads you wanted to interview. The Bishop brothers and Derek Green?'

'What about them?'

'They're not at the hotel but they're back in London. I saw them this morning.'

They were stopped just the other side of Reading, in the smart Cambridge-blue Daimler, Cresswell and Matt Brown making good time through the patchy mist on their way to Newbury on a deserted stretch of secondary road.

The police regularly stopped cars on the road: asked them for identity cards, why they were driving, what authority they had to be out on the road at all, wanted to see all the papers: insurance, petrol coupons, the lot.

'Go, canny bonny lad,' Matt Brown said to Cresswell. 'We got a speed cop coming up right behind us.'

The speed cop overtook and flagged them down, asked

them to step out of the car and began his routine, a laugh a minute. He started with Cresswell: wasn't he old enough for military service? Why wasn't he with HM Forces? Let's see the driving licence. Where were they going? Wallingford, they said producing documents. Going to suss out a job. They worked for a building firm, Erection and Demolition Ltd. 5 Standbury Gardens, Croydon – a firm set up by Charlie Balvak, a dummy but with all the paperwork. There was nothing the speed cop could do; everything seemed all Sir Garnet.

Matt Brown had to squeeze past him to get back into the car. Matt bumped against the speed cop, who felt something hard and heavy inside Matt's breast pocket.

'What you got there, then? Tool of the trade?'

'Yes,' Matt said. 'Want to see it?' Bobbies always liked to see tools and knew what to look for, what could be used for housebreaking.

'Whatever it is, get it out,' the speed cop said, not knowing what he was doing.

So Matt Brown pulled out the German Luger automatic pistol and shot him right between the eyes.

It took time to drag the cop behind a hedgerow and cover the BSA bike with branches and tuck it away where they could find it again.

'Can't take it now, Newcastle.'

'Pity, that's a canny little bike.'

In his head, Matt Brown thanked a friend who had brought the Luger back from Dunkirk, took it off a dead German officer and thought it would be a nice present for his old friend, Matt Brown.

Took them almost twenty minutes from being stopped to getting on their way. 'Try and pick up the bike on the way back,' Matt said. 'Good job he was on his own. Would've been difficult if it was a combo setup. They use them up round Newcastle. Bike and sidecar, twa bobbies for the price of one.'

Cresswell concentrated on driving. The way old Newcastle Brown had shot the speed cop, not a moment's hesitation and not a hint of emotion. Cresswell was shaken rigid. This was a cold-blooded killer, Matt Brown.

208

The only traffic they saw was military and the occasional bus, rarely a private vehicle. Cresswell told Matt that they'd come to Kingsclear first, so he'd have to reverse the route: when they got on to the Newbury road from Kingsclear the house, Larksbrook, would be on the right-hand side, not the left.

They were in a country lane and the fog had nearly all gone, just a touch of mist but cold with it, and hanging in the trees, damp.

'Pull in here,' Matt told him.

'Why?'

'To take a slash, bonny lad. Last chance, the bushes here on the left. Better have one yourself while we're at it.'

So Cresswell went with him, not saying much and they stood side by side as though they were in a public urinal. Matt got to shaking the dew off the lily and stepped back before he had even buttoned up, Cresswell glancing at him but seeing he still had his dong out, shaking it. Behind him now, Matt Brown slipped his free right hand inside his jacket, drew out the Luger and shot Cresswell in the back of the head, the little hollow in the base of the skull.

Cresswell went down like a poleaxed cow; didn't know what happened, went from life to death in a second. Taking a pee, then dead. Matt buttoned up, kicked Cresswell's body, rolled him over caught against the tuft of bushes between the taller trees. Matt Brown liked to think he was humane, stripped him of all the documents, give the Law a bit of work to do for a change.

He got back into the car, started the engine turned it round and drove back to Reading, where he caught a train to London. Left the car in a small free car park about a mile from the station. In London he walked out of Paddington Station, went to the nearest pub off the station concourse, over Praed Street down near Sussex Gardens. Matt needed a drink. The timing wasn't bad, he thought. Never intended to take the girl, Sybil. Far too close to home. He had other things to do, so he would let Charlie and Connie hear about the speed cop and Cresswell when they listened to the news. He sat there sipping a small whisky; looking at his watch. It was half-past one on the nose.

Quietly, Matt Brown said, 'Boom!'

* * *

209

At the Melody Club in Frith Street, Bankie Blankovitz, manager and titular owner, had just appeared, bringing with him the daily float; in his office putting the locked cash box into the safe then shouting to Barbara that he'd like a cheese and onion sandwich. The barman, Edgar, had also just come in and two of the girls were sitting in the bare, spartan dressing room. They liked to have a few staff around in case any military geniuses came into the street looking for a drink, a strip show or even a bit of nookie during the afternoon hours. Charlie and Connie both maintained that it was better to be ready than be left with a lost chance.

Bankie looked at his watch. It was half-past one on the nose. Boom.

The biscuit tin was smaller than the one that had virtually destroyed the On & Off. The tin inside it was rigged up in the same way but the basic propellant was black powder not guncotton. There was also a little more magnesium in the mixture, which meant there was more fire in the initial explosion.

The tin had been slipped under the bar and next to eight bottles of spirits: cheap and basic spirits admittedly but spirits all the same. When the device exploded so did the bottles of spirits. This killed Edgar who got a shard of glass straight into his carotid artery – the right-hand side – and was set alight by the tongue of flame that started a merry cracking fire quickly doing a great deal of damage. Everyone else got out and Bankie, a man with little patience, was the one who got to tell Charlie Balvak of the disaster that had befallen the Twins. Two clubs gone in one day.

It was soon to be three.

The girls liked working at the Bandbox in Kingly Street. For one thing the manger, Cab Carter – titular owner of course – was a kind, relatively honest and marginally good guy; a family man with the set: wife, girl, boy, dog and mortgage. He was also well-built, with distinguished looks, hair greying at the temples and matching eyes. The dressing room for the girls was nice as well: cool in summer and warm in winter it sported three big stuffed easy chairs. Two girls sprawled in two of the easy chairs. The biscuit tin had been slid under one of the chairs. The two girls, Stella Bartlett and Monica Masterman, one blonde, the other mouse but tarted up with henna, sat in the dressing room talking boyfriends, the war, and where were they going to get the next pair of stockings? Unfortunately Monica's chair had the slim long biscuit tin slid underneath it, an old chair with horsehair stuffing. When the bomb exploded at two o'clock on the nail poor Monica was engulfed in flame, hardly had time to cry out. Her friend Stella was not over blessed with common sense and just stood there screaming. Then ran for her life.

All of the Twins' major clubs were now gone with the wind.

In the pub near Sussex Gardens Matt Brown could hear the music from the film *Gone with the Wind* playing away like mad, swelling and sweeping him along, music by Max Steiner, which Matt loved. He thought that music was the best classical music of all time, helped him get over many sticky patches. As he sat there now among the grey dreary-looking business men drinking his whisky the strains of the *Gone with the Wind* theme mixed with his feeling of a job well done and he seemed to be riding on the clouds listening to the music in his head.

Suzie Mountford told herself to snap out of it. Fordham O'Dell was taking her to lunch and she really must divorce herself from the news Susan Wood had given her. Mrs Susan Wood, married to an architect who made a mint of money though she preferred to work. 'I've no ties and I'm good at this job,' she had confided. 'And it keeps me from going into the ATS, the WAAF or the WRNS. Don't fancy all that business of living cheek by jowl with thirty other females in a Nissen hut. My dear, you never know where they've been,' lighting her cigarette and then Suzie's, using a heavy silver lighter with initials engraved on one side. 'Isn't it hell trying to get petrol to fill these?'

Then down to the nitty gritty:

'Sheer coincidence,' she told Suzie. 'Director's meeting here this morning, crack of dawn. One of them coming in from Glasgow, the Night Sleeper, Sir Andrew MacCormick.

Duty Manager was supposed to go down in the company car, meet him. Not well. Tummy bug, lot of it around. I drew the short straw. Terrible old bore, Sir Andrew. I collected him and tucked him up in the back of the Bentley. Got in the front and who should be walking off the platform, bold as brass, but the Bishop brothers and Mr Derek Green. Plain as a pikestaff and with a porter, luggage on a cart. More luggage than they left here with. I thought, Hello, I know you lads, then remembered. Thought I'd better give the sergeant at West End Central a buzz, what's her name? Hadn't got around to it yet, then you come waltzing in.'

That was the gist of it, but Mrs Wood went on talking, and that's always good 'cos you never know what could come out – that's what they taught and Dandy Tom had told her, never stop somebody with an urge to tell you things. Pity it was all mundane except when they got to Brenda Marx. 'What happened to her?' Suzie asked.

'Yes, Brenda left. Under a little cloud, I'm afraid. Special favours to certain guests. Leave it to your imagination, Sergeant, eh?'

Now Suzie was sitting in a restaurant called Moulin Blanc surrounded by French military men with mostly English girls, but the cream of the crop, and across from Fordham O'Dell, looking impossibly young in his Royal Air Force blue, the wings over his left breast and above the cleaner medal ribbon.

The restaurant was on the outer fringes of Soho, in Coventry Street, only a small place, around fifteen tables, but French waiters with London accents and all the gear, the black trousers, white shirt, waistcoat and the long white apron, four of them serving, taking orders doing the *Oui, monsieur. Non, monsieur. L'Addition, monsieur? Certainement, et tout ce jazz.*

The food was well above average, the bread tasted like real French bread she remembered from holidays with her mum, dad and sister: pause for a moment while she thought sadly about her sister and her dad, still missing both of them, often shed a tear, sometimes dreamed of her dad.

The onion soup tasted as good as when she made it, possibly better and the salade Niçoise, well, they were probably using tinned tuna but the salad seemed to be fresh. Where the hell do you get fresh lettuce, tomatoes and beans now in 1941?

'You okay, Suzie? Everything alright?'

She dragged herself into the present, Fordy sitting across from her with a slightly lopsided smile, eyes twinkling.

'I'm sorry,' she said. 'Oh, Fordy I'm so sorry. I'm wool-gathering. Bit of a surprise from the lady I interviewed in the hotel.'

'Something good and juicy? Come on, tell me.'

'No, I can't, it's a case I've been working on. I'm being very rude, sorry.' A ripple ran through her body – *come on Suzie, pull yourself together.*

'How's your Spitfire?' She smiled back at him, then saw the rings on his sleeve. 'Oh, Lord you've been promoted.'

'Yes, demon Wing Commander, but don't worry about that. Are you really okay? I read the reports of the trial. You had a terrible time with that fellow, the creepy bloke.'

'He was creepy alright. Locked away safely now at His Majesty's pleasure. In a place for the criminally insane.'

'Pity they couldn't hang the blighter. I suppose the tax payers're going to keep him for the rest of his natural.'

'That's how it is. How's your Spitfire?' Repeating the question, turning the conversation away from the events of last year and the Old Bailey trial in the spring.

'Pranged it, I'm afraid.'

'Fordy, when?'

'Early September. We split-arsed over to the *pas de Calais.* Shot up some Jerry aerodromes and suddenly clang, bump, the old Merlin's not as smooth as it should be. I caught a bit of flack in it. Tried to get back over the ditch, then the glycol came streaming out, couldn't get any height, so I belly flopped, got out – a floater wearing the old Mae West, bobbing around singing "Oh, I do Like to be Beside the Seaside". Rescue launch putters in and they pick me up. Hot soup and a glass of rum, then along comes a truck, drives me back to Middle Wallop. The Groupie tells me not to be so stupid next time. That's enough of my line shoot.' He looked away, bashful, then back, squinting. 'Last time I flew my old Spit.'

213

'You're not flying . . . ?'

'I'm not flying my old Mark II. Got a brand-new one now. New type of Spit. Hush-hush. Got a bit more firepower.' He laid his forefinger alongside his nose.

After a while Suzie said she'd heard about Jamie Simnel, the young man she had met on her trip to Middle Wallop, killed soon after.

'Tough,' O'Dell nodded, not looking at her square in the eyes. 'Last one. Last of the fellows I came into the service with. All gone now.' His eyes clouded over. 'Gone.'

They talked as so many people talked these days, about how Hitler's invasion of Russia seemed foolhardy. 'Fighting on two fronts,' O'Dell said, 'Bloody silly way to run a war. Jerry's been unstoppable so far. Thinks he's leading a charmed life, but now the Yanks are in . . . Well . . .'

She said it was an odd feeling, last December when she had come down to interview him. 'Cold but a lovely day, blue sky, trees looking sharp against the sky. I thought how detached it all was – detached from the war. I looked at you all and the boating song went through my head. Eton boating song. You all looked like senior boys still at school. But you'd really been up there, fighting what we now have to call the Battle of Britain.'

'Like a dream,' he told her. 'Like living through something and thinking now that it was all dream time, the friends you knew who disappeared: they were dreams as well. "Merrily, merrily, merrily merrily, life is but a dream." D'you know what I mean?' Then, 'Tell me about your people.'

Looking at him, listening to his voice, Suzie understood why he'd been so attractive to women, the effortless charm. Tommy had charm in spades but she suddenly realized that his age showed against the young pilot. Tommy Livermore was ten years her senior.

She told Fordy about her beloved father who'd died in that stupid accident and how her mother had gone and married someone she thought quite unsuitable because Daddy hadn't left much in the way of cash and Mummy was determined to see her brother James through school.

'One doesn't like to think of one's parents being like

214

other men and women. *Vive la différence* and all that.' He chuckled.

Suzie told him about a maiden aunt who'd said to her at her mother's wedding that she for one couldn't put up with all 'that bedroom unpleasantness'. 'Funny how that generation thought sex was somehow nasty, unclean.'

Fordham grunted, tucking into the baked apples. 'Frogs're clever little buggers aren't they? What they do with food . . .' he picked up his glass of Chablis, sipped, '. . . and drink.'

They both laughed and Suzie scooped up the last of her baked apple, done with brown sugar, sultanas and some kind of liqueur, *Pommes Rive Gauche* the menu called them.

'Where the hell do they get brown sugar from, Fordy? Sugar's difficult.'

'I think they have some special arrangement, and I suspect there's a good black market.'

She looked down at her plate, thinking maybe she shouldn't be eating this.

When she looked up again she had this strange sense that everything suddenly seemed sharper, the things on the table, Fordy's greatcoat hanging on the coat rack near the door. Everything seemed cleaner and she had the unusual feeling that she'd been with him before, sat in this restaurant, and she looked at him for too long, dangerously long. He reached across and took hold of her hand. 'Dinner tonight?' he asked and she nodded, 'Can't get away until around half-eight, nine.'

'Good show,' he grinned. 'I'll be in the Ritz. The American Bar. Can't afford to stay there but at least we can have dinner, show off, eh?'

The first time she dined with Tommy Livermore had been the Ritz.

Walking back to West End Central she went down into Piccadilly Underground and put in a trunk call to the stables at Larksbrook. Molly answered.

'The Chief there?' Suzie asked and Molly was a shade on the monosyllabic side.

'Just caught us,' Tommy said. 'Bringing her back to the smoke, putting her somewhere safe. Hear you've got a territorial battle going on.'

'So it would seem.' The headlines of the *Evening News* scrawled on a poster read 'Crime War Bombs Destroy Soho Clubs'. 'Blowing up sleazy clubs has pushed the real war off the front pages.'

'No, I mean what's going on down in these parts. I think they were coming for us.'

'What?' Bewildered.

'Policeman shot through the head and the body of one of the Twins' heavies found behind a ditch. Looks like the same geezer did both of them. I'll see you later.'

Her own answer surprised her, just came out automatically. 'I could be late, Tommy. Maybe not back at all tonight.'

'See you when I see you then.' He didn't sound concerned.

Had she really said that? Well, maybe. From the back of her mind came the idea: I've only had one man in all my twenty-four years, so why not?

As she walked briskly back to the nick, she thought that she had yet to tell Tommy about Molly Abelard and Brian. If she was going to tell him. She thought of Fordham O'Dell and his cool, calm manner. Shit, she wondered, why did I tell Tommy I might not be back tonight?

She knew why and felt ashamed. But not for long.

Seventeen

W hen Suzie returned to West End Central, Sergeant Will
Bowden was on the front desk, dealing with a Raff erk
who was giving his name and address, which made her think
of one of her favourite children's programmes on the BBC
Wireless when she was little: *Toy Town*. Ernest the policeman
was always threatening to take Larry the Lamb's name and
address. Time was when the worst thing that could happen to
you was having your name and address taken by Ernest the
policeman. He would say, 'Take care, my Lamb, or I'll have
to take your name and address.'

The erk was saying, 'I've got a new billet in St John's Wood.
I become an officer cadet in a day or two.'

'That'll be nice for you,' Will Bowden said straight-faced.
'Name, please, and the new address.'

'Cummings. Gordon Frederick Cummings.' Then he gave
the address and Sergeant Bowen said they'd let him know if
the watch turned up, but in his experience ladies like that rarely
returned property left in their rooms. He raised his eyebrows
as Suzie went past.

There was nobody in the CID room when she got down
there, but her nemesis, DCI Harvey, sat in his office with the
door open.

'Susannah, where the hell've you been?'

'Following up on something, Guv. Thought you weren't in
today. Off sick.'

'Well you thought wrong, Susannah. Bloody criminals
almost fighting each other in the streets and you're swanning
off on some personal little jolly while I have to get up from
my bed of pain and sickness and come in.'

'Not a personal jolly, Guv,' she answered, a tiny worry in

217

the back of her mind: had she been seen with Fordy? Fordy had certainly become her personal mental jolly. She couldn't get her mind off him: what it would be like with him, of course that was daydreaming, nothing was going to happen between them – how could it?

'What've you been up to then?' Coming out of his office now, eyes everywhere, sneaky, suspicious. Behind her as she sat at her desk.

'Sorry you're not well, Mr Harvey, but I've really been following a lead.'

'Well, tell me about it, woman.' Gruff. Snappy.

That made her turn round; swivelling her chair; clumping it round on its four legs.

There was something up: she could see it in the way he stood, placed his feet, squared his shoulders, aggressive as hell. She didn't like discussing matters marginal to the Twins, but she had no option.

'I don't know if you remember it, Guv, but some time ago we took a look at three young men working in the West End – well, Soho to be precise. Called themselves the Trinity Building Co. Recall that, sir?'

'Vaguely,' not committing himself and it was only a few days ago. Tony Harvey regularly steered clear of things or people that had some kind of a link with the Balvak twins, of whom he constantly said, 'I wish I could get my hands on 'em, the Twins. I had the buggers once, in Camford and couldn't pin anything on them. I seem to be the only bobby who's actually felt their collars and much good it did me.'

Suzie thought: Yes, I was around while you were setting up that arrest in Camford, Guv.' You made damn sure you wouldn't be able to even get them into court: set up a pattern for the future.

'We thought they were possibly squaddies gone AWOL. Did a lot of work for the Balvaks, sir. The paperwork went to you, Guv, you may not've got round to it.'

'Oh, I do recall. Were they the ones did all that work on Falconetti's new place?' Pecking at it, really vague because he had never heard about that from her. Got it from the Balvak twins.

'Yes, sir. *I* discovered they did the work for Carlo Falconetti.'

'Yeah, well, what about them?'

'They're back in town, Guv. They got back this morning.'

He didn't even know they had left. Or if he did it was from the Twins.

'Keep your eyes open then.'

'I'm doing that, Guv. What was it you were saying about criminals fighting each other in the streets? You talking about the club bombings?'

'Partly. Everyone else is out there following the clubs getting done. Sniffing around. I'm off shortly to take statements from the Twins, see if they know who's breathing down their necks.' He gave a grim smile and looked at her, eyes trying to gimlet their way through her. 'You'll be pleased to hear that we've got some of your old colleagues on the manor helping us. Called in the Yard as they say. You know a WDC Cotter and a DC Worral, Ronald, I think his name is?'

'Laura Cotter and Ron Worral? Yes, Guv.'

'They're said to be wizards of the forensics field and know a lot about explosives.'

'Yes, Guv, Laura and Ron're bang on when it comes to explosives.'

'So your former boss told me.' He gave her his executioner's look. 'He didn't ask after you if you were wondering.'

'No, sir, I don't suppose he did.'

'Really?' He let the word hang in the air and Suzie thought to herself, He's scented me. If he doesn't actually know, he certainly suspects.

'So, it's only partly the clubs is it, Guv?'

'You haven't heard the developments? No, well I'll tell you. A motorcycle patrol officer's been found shot dead out your way, Hampshire. That is your way, isn't it?'

'Used to be. Yes, sir, near Newbury.'

'Yes, sir, near Newbury. That's where the officer was found: and there's more. A bloke called Cresswell Smith – ring a bell? – has been found nearer to Newbury. One bullet through his head. In a ditch. Could be the same chap wielding the gun. Cresswell Smith? Heard of him?'

'He's one of the Twins' bruisers, isn't he, sir?'

'They have a saying in the theatre, Susannah. An actress – or an actor – can be a quick study. Means he learns his lines fast.'

'I'd heard that, sir, yes.'

He nodded, gave her the grim smile again and walked slowly to the door. 'You watch how you go, young Susannah Mountford. You may be a quick study, but so am I.' Harvey turned and locked eyes with Suzie. He whispered, 'If you know what's good for you, you'll – no, why should I give you advice?' He left the room, closing the door quietly behind him.

She had no doubt he was warning her. For the first time since she had been at West End Central she smelled fear and felt it in her bones, running through her body like a disease. The Twins had Tony Harvey in their pockets, and the Twins controlled a large portion of the West End. They had resources, a small army of toughs and sleazy small-time crooks, they had a steady income from the bars, dives and strip joints and they took a high percentage of other incomes – the whores, tarts, strippers and the more skilful criminals who worked the scams, robberies and confidence tricks across the centre of London. Give them a reason and they could reach out and have her snuffed out like a candle.

She got her trench coat and the blue beret she was wearing, preparing to go and take a look at Carlo Falconetti as she had originally planned. Hanging on to the hope of getting the Italian to admit that his fingers had been broken by Porky Pine, hard man to the Twins. And if Tommy was really bringing Sybil back into London with a statement naming the Twins as the killers at the Nightlight club, then their days may well be numbered. But she couldn't be certain yet. One of the bywords in policing well-organized crime in the heart of the capital was never count your banged-up villains until the appeal's been turned down and they were locked away for a long stretch on the Moor.

Her hand was on the doorknob when her telephone began to ring. She waited, indecisive, uncertain about answering. Then she picked up.

'Suzie,' Fordham O'Dell said, 'glad I've caught you. Slight change of venue. Can you make it the Savoy not the Ritz?'

She really couldn't understand why her step felt so light, nor why she gave a little dance step as she reached the front counter.

Percy Hodges controlled a manor that ran from the Elephant and Castle to Lambeth and Vauxhall Bridge then through Kennington to South Lambeth and as far as Deptford: a large slice of London south of the river and a reasonable living, kept the wolf from the door, but not as lucrative as those Balvak twins in the West End. Percy often alluded to them in terms of envy.

Percy's favourite hangout was in the upstairs private rooms of the Black Prince, off Vauxhall Walk, down near the river. Everybody knew that Percy controlled his little empire from upstairs in the Black Prince, where he regarded the rooms as his private club. So it was to the Black Prince on that misty afternoon that Ollie O'Grady, also known as Monkey, made his way.

Porky Pine had caught up with him in Lyons Corner House close to Leicester Square, where he often had his baked beans on toast and, when they had them, a poached egg, round about one o'clock in the afternoon. 'Fifteen 'undred ours' as Monkey called it.

'Twins've got a job for you, Monkey,' Porky told him and Monkey winced because he didn't really like doing jobs for the Twins. There was always the possibility that he'd get his legs broken if he didn't do the job to their highly exacting standards.

The nippy came by, so Porky said he'd have what Ollie was having, double baked beans on toast and a poached egg.

'Eggs're off,' said the nippy. 'You've just missed them, love. We've got some pilchards though.'

No, Porky wasn't partial to pilchards. 'Just the baked beans then, love.'

'Right, I'll give you some extra 'cos you're a growing boy,' and she gave him a knowing nudge with her elbow. Play his cards right and he'd be in there, Monkey told him and Porky Pine shook his head slowly. 'I'm hard up, but not that hard

221

up,' he responded wittily. That was wit as far as Porky was concerned and Monkey told him that if wit was . . . never mind: you had to be there.

Monkey asked, 'Have I *got* to do whatever it is, Pork? You could say you weren't able to find me.'

'That would be an untruth, and I am not one who enjoys untruths.'

'Means I've got to do it, dunnit?'

'I'm afraid so, Monk. We're in a bit of bother.'

Bit of bovver.

'I heard. Places burned down; places razed to the ground; staff not paid – strippers without a nicker to their names.'

'Yes, and we've just lost one of our best men, rising star, Cresswell Smith, maybe you heard.'

'No.' Monkey looked blank. 'Cresswell Smith, was he the Southampton lad, father was in the seafaring business?'

'I believe so. Shot through the back of the head in Berkshire.'

'Berkshire. No, I try not to move out of London myself.' Monkey had a long lugubrious face that seemed to get longer. 'So, I haven't got an option, Porky?'

''Fraid not.'

'What do they want?'

Porky told him, and he nodded with some gravity. 'I'll find out,' Monkey said. 'Who do I report to?'

'Me. If I'm not at my place, I'll be with the Twins: they'll no doubt be having a council of war.'

Monkey had this good reputation: loved children, kind to animals, mixed with criminals of all creeds and classes, but stayed clear of a criminal record of his own. Had plenty of gramophone records, mainly Gershwin, *American in Paris*, *Rhapsody in Blue*, liked the big orchestra doing those jazzy bits, 78 r.p.m. No criminal records though. There had grown up around him this reputation – you could trust Monkey; he would always keep shtum, he could do business and act as a go-between on any level of the criminal hierarchy. The trick was his basic honesty. If something had to be found out he would first go to the party concerned and ask him for the truth, straight up. He was great as an intermediary: just the thing they needed in the present circumstances.

222

So on that afternoon he arrived at the Black Prince in a calm and contented frame of mind.

There were faded photographs up the stairs to the private rooms, pictures of darts teams on day trips, and snooker champions competing for the Black Prince Trophy in days gone by. The photographs mostly had an Edwardian aura about them: sepia, dated clothes, the women in long skirts and outrageous hats.

There was a queue stretching down to the first turning in the stairs: three or four people, male, female with or without a couple of snotty-nosed kids all waiting for a judgement from Percy. The people on Percy's manor came to him, after the manner of people who went to the wise elder of the village or, as Percy thought, restless for the Wisdom of Solomon. Know what I mean?

They came for advice when the landlord was getting antsy for his rent, when they were having problems with neighbours, when a husband in work with Percy was sent away, banged up for a five or ten stretch on the Moor or down the Scrubs – the wife would drop round to see what the deal was about money, stuff like that.

Monkey could bypass the queue, and knew it. Monkey, with his lugubrious face, heavy black-rimmed specs, long black coat, white scarf – to show he came in peace – and a slightly battered Anthony Eden hat, would say, 'Excuse me,' tip his hat to the ladies and walk calmly into the room, closing the door behind him.

Percy Hodges sat at a long table facing the door. On his left was Fat Florrie who handled all the cash for Percy; on his right 'Crazy' Colin Combes, henchman in charge of muscle; behind him stood Harry Henshaw and Albert Mint, clubs and protection respectively. All three of them at the moment too old for call-up in His Majesty King George VI's Armed Forces.

When Monkey came in they were just finishing off a case concerning 'Hard' Sam Jacobs who'd been sent away for twelve months for Street Trading without a Peripatetic Licence. 'I agree with you, Mrs Jacobs. Sadie,' Percy said. 'I agree wholeheartedly. The magistrates took a diabolical liberty in sending Sam down, but I think we have to be realistic about

223

this. They done it, and he can do his bird and that's all there is to it. Sam's a good boy and I'll see that you get a fiver extra now and again, regular. No need to bother yourself about it. I mean I did speak to one of the magistrates but he told me there was nothing to be done, seeing as how his colleagues wanted a longer sentence. I mean there was the question of the Find the Lady routine and other games of chance.'

Sadie Jacobs didn't look happy, but she could see the problem. Percy had done his best.

'So, Monkey, what can we do for you? Come over. Sit down.' Percy had, in his time, been a middleweight wrestler of some skill. He was on the short side but powerful in the arms, shoulders and legs; had a barrel chest, bullet head, a small crooked nose and what was often called a firm jaw. In fact the jaw jutted a shade and was, as many said, a glass jaw, reason for giving up the wrestling; always getting broken. In spite of his appearance, Percy adopted a 'hail fellow well met' personality that worked with most people. He also had an exceptionally nasty side, but not showing at this moment.

Monkey had recently seen *Fire Over England*, starring Flora Robson and Leslie Howard – about how Queen Elizabeth and her court defeated the Spanish Armada, Laurence Olivier was also in it. Monkey had been greatly moved by the film, seeing himself as a courtly English noble working for Good Queen Bess, all of the swaggering about and using flowery language.

Now he said, 'I come as an emissary,' a statement that took Percy by surprise.

'An emissary?' Percy asked.

'Emissary for the Twins,' Monkey explained.

'Ah. I hear they been having a spot of bother.'

'Indeed,' he wanted to add, 'sire,' but felt that'd be going over the top. 'They've lost four clubs and had one of their top men killed. All in a couple of days.'

Percy nodded. 'What's this got to do with me, Monkey?'

'I don't think it's got nothing to do with you, Perce. But Charlie Balvak heard a whisper.'

'Little Sir Echo, was it?' Little Sir Echo had been a popular dance number a couple of years ago – summer of '39.

'It was rather nasty, Percy. Someone whispered that it was you causing trouble on the other side of the river.'

'Me? Me personally? Or my . . . ?'

'Emissaries, yes.'

'What could've given him that idea? I would bother to trail people over the bridge and let them tramp about the Balvak's manor? I should co-co. Charlie gone marbles and conkers, has he?'

'I think he's under a lot of strain, Percy: there was the Battle of Britain, then the Blitz. He worries.'

'Well, Monk, you've got ta go back and tell him he's no need to worry, not on my account. If I wanted his manor I'd come across the bridge and tell him to his face. Get back to him, Monkey, and don't bother me no more. If he's got people killed he should have went to the coppers. Should know that.'

'Right, Percy. Thank you, Percy. I knew it couldn't be you.' Monkey gave him a grin and backed away, tipped his Anthony Eden hat, then closed the door behind him.

They could hear his feet retreating down the stairs.

Percy said, 'Colin?'

'Yes, Perce.' Crazy Colin Combes was a big fellow, big, dark and ugly. You take one look at Colin and know he's trouble.

'Colin, this is interesting.' Percy settled back in his chair.

'Very interesting, Percy.'

'Things are bad in the West End, round Soho. We know that, but they must be very dodgy if Charlie and Connie have to send Monkey over here to ask if we're causing him any bother. Means they must be in a right two and eight. Nip over there, Colin. Nip over with some of your lads. Could be that the Balvaks've bit off more than they can chew. Always fancied being up West, managing it all.'

'How many of the lads should I take, Perce?'

'Just enough to suss 'em out, Colin. Three. Four. I mean the Balvaks're mob-handed over there but see how the land lays then come back for more. Quite fancy myself over there. Be a nice step up at my time of life.'

*　　*　　*

Big Toe Harvey walked in on the council of war the Twins were holding in their large flat west of South Audley Street. Before he arrived a lot was going on. Charlie sat on one of the oxblood-leather buttoned chairs like a potentate – one foot drawn back, the other extended – with Wanda Lee Fook on the floor, literally at his feet, her arms wrapped round his legs as if declaring ownership. Connie sat close to his brother in the other oxblood. There was no sign of Roses in June, but the room was full of henchmen: Porky Pine and Flash Stan, Jacky Russell, sleek Sid Silverman, who looked after the girls on the game, took the Twins' percentage each day and had two burly lads working under him (Fast Eddie Ellis and Martin Beck). Also present were four of Porky's muscle men, Slammer Hammond, Jock Barty, Collie King and Frenzied Freddie Nolan, who was also known as the Dynamo on account of his incredible energy. Missing from the party were Cresswell Smith and Little Nell. Charlie had never liked Little Nell but would be the first to admit the small man was very good in the event of panic.

Charlie was close-questioning Maurice Benoit also known as Morrie Baldwin from Harrow, major domo of the On & Off.

'So, we've established you saw nobody suspicious in the club before we arrived that evening, Morrie?' he asked.

'On my life, Charlie, nobody. I mean, yes, Freddie looked in for a few minutes around six thirty, and that big fellow you've got down from Newcastle, he dropped in with a big tin of biscuits, what's his name . . . ?'

'Newcastle. Newcastle Brown? He was carrying a tin of biscuits?' Charlie exchanged a sharp look with his brother, as though there was an electric charge between them, flash of lightning, a crackle in the air inside their overdecorated living room.

'Bastard!' Connie said. 'Bastard. I'll stamp him out of existence. I'll trample his face under my feet, squash him flat.'

'You see what he did with this biscuit tin?' Charlie asked Maurice barely controlling the shake in his voice. 'You make no comment to him?'

'He brought it for one of the girls, that's what he said. Had it when he went into the office, gone when he left. I saw him both times. Very popular Matt was. Very popular with the girls.'

'I'll pulverize the little bugger,' Connie continued. 'I'll take my bayonet to him, skewer his gizzard. Shit 'n' abortion, I'll fill him in.'

'I rike Newcastle Blown,' Wanda said, rolling her eyes and posing in a kind of Betty Boop fashion. 'He is ve'y funny man. All a time calls me hinny.'

'He called every woman hinny, or pet, or petal. Geordie words. Anyway, nobody asked you, Wanda. You speak when you're spoken to, girl.'

'I just say I rike him, Cha'ie. Surey I'm ar'owed say that.'

'How well did you know him?' Charlie was irritated a shade.

'Oh, just a rittle. Massage middle piecee two time.'

Charlie's reaction was masked by the doorbell ringing. 'See who that is, Jacky.'

It was Big Toe Harvey large as life and wanting to talk privately with Charlie, looking at the others as though he was memorizing exactly who was there and making notes. Suspicious that he'd walked in on a meeting planning some huge criminal endeavour. Maybe they were going to pull the crime of the century, steal the Crown Jewels, blag a few million from the Bank of England, hold up a mail train.

'So what's up, Tony?' Charlie asked him when the others had gone from the room. He suspected they were all crowded in the hall, some of them with their ears pressed to the door. Or even with a water tumbler, trying to follow what was being said.

'I didn't notice your friends the Trinity Building Company.'

'Where? Here?'

'Yes, didn't notice them.'

'They're up North. They're in Newcastle.'

'Oh no they're not.'

'Then where are they?'

'I heard they were back here, up the smoke that's what I was told. Back this morning. On the night sleeper, seen getting off the train at King's Cross. Come down from Glasgow.'

'I'd have heard.' Charlie looked pale and worried. Stricken was the word Big Toe thought of.

'You obviously haven't then.'

'They were supposed to be back today, I know, but there's something funny going on.'

'I'll say there is. Something fucking hilarious is going on.' Harvey didn't even smile. 'You know about a Daimler car? Registration EOC 702?'

'What colour is it?'

'Come on, Charlie I've given you the reg. It's Cambridge blue. Four-door saloon.'

'Oh, that one, yes. It's registered to me but I let people use it all the time. Why?'

'You got to be careful, Charlie. I don't know how long I can keep things under my hat.'

'What's it matter?'

'It's been traced to a car park in Reading, that car. Someone responded to our message about seeing anything suspicious on the Reading–Newbury road.'

He told Charlie that someone had called in and reported a Cambridge-blue Daimler stopped by the side of the road and two men, driver and passenger, talking to a speed cop. 'Everyone calls them speed cops, don't they? Really they're motorcycle police patrolmen. Your car? Right Charlie? Who was driving?'

'Cresswell Smith.'

'And who was the passenger?'

'I wouldn't know.'

'If he's got form they'll have his name in a matter of hours, if not sooner, and there's no way I can stop that coming out. He left his dabs all over the car. Steering wheel, glove box. Everything, everywhere.'

'Shit!' muttered Charlie.

'So who's burning and bombing up your clubs?'

'How should I know? It's all come outa the blue. Someone said maybe Percy Hodges.'

'Could Conrad have got jealous and started doing things behind your back?'

'Don't be silly, Tony. Connie handles the violence, he

doesn't work things out; he's not a candidate for the Brains Trust, he's more your Stainless Stephen, en't 'e?'

'I'm just trying to think of everything. You sure you don't know who was with Cresswell?'

'Matt Brown?'

'You mean Matthew James Brown? Newcastle Brown who's done everything from buggery to burglary and back? Matt Brown of great renown who has never had to stand in the dock only once and that time he beat it? Jeeerusalem, Charlie, you don't half pick 'em. The man's a walking horror, a fucking nightmare.'

'I know,' Charlie said, 'but I thought he was on my side.'

'The only side Matt Brown is on is Matt Brown's.' He laughed, then frowned. 'And you wonder who's burning and blowing up your clubs? Ye gods!'

'I always live in hopes. A wise man wrote it is better to travel in hope than to get to Fenchurch Street, or something like that.'

'Charlie, does this mean that *my* current problem isn't going to be dealt with?'

'Your feminine sergeant problem?'

'The permanent thorn in my thumb. Yes.'

'It'll be taken care of as long as you go on protecting Connie and me.'

'She's got to be frightened off for your sake as much as mine. I'll look after you as long as I can. But it can't go on for ever.'

'You're satisfied with what you're getting?'

'Envelope arrives every first of the month, Charlie. Thank you, have I ever sent it back?'

The telephone started to ring and Charlie moved towards it slowly, muttering who the hell was this now? More bad news?

'Hello,' he said. 'Yes, he's here, who wants him? Monkey, this is Charlie, you can talk straight to me.' (Pause while he listened to a voice yacking on.) 'You're sure, Monk? Positive? That's good enough for me. See Porky about the doings, will you? Whatever you agreed. Thanks, Monkey. Right.'

He put the phone down and turned to Harvey.

'It's not Percy Hodges,' he said.
Big Toe said, 'There you are then.'
Charlie Balvak never misses a thing.
Maybe this time.

Eighteen

Suzie Mountford stood for a moment at the top of the steps of West End Central Police Station, allowing time for her eyes to adjust to the cold and damp of the gloomy, darkening early evening. She walked down into Regent Street, decided to get a bus at Oxford Circus and crossing the road turned left and began to walk in that direction.

Now that the light was fading she couldn't quite see the pallor of her fellow Londoners' faces, nor the strain in their eyes and the greyness and washed-out colour of their clothes and surroundings as they trudged and queued at the end of a day's work.

Yet life wasn't nearly as bad as it had been this time last year. Nowadays the bombs only came occasionally, though people still went down every night on to the Underground platforms to sleep, not wanting to be caught out if the *Luftwaffe* decided to plaster London again. But this year there were differences: the increased problems of rationing, the shortages that slid into daily life, the chilling routine and the mounting number of restrictions that had to be faced by the ordinary man or woman in the street. Then there was the added worry of having a son off in the Army, Navy or the Raff. The Navy and Raff boys were dying every day and night, the army was engaged in the western desert and the telegrams never stopped arriving and in so many cases the dead could not be buried.

WDS Sheila Cox, who had been a real mate at Camford nick, had a cousin, very close but was killed on a training flight. The family went down to the funeral, Christ Church, near Bournemouth on the south coast. When the coffin was brought into the chapel her cousin's mother broke down and started raving on, that couldn't be Harry because the coffin

231

wasn't big enough. Sheila said nobody could explain to her that Harry really didn't exist anymore, only bits of him.

She went past the dark windows of Liberty's to the corner, waited, crossed the road, stood in the queue for a bus – preferably a 73 or a 25. Shuffling along, waiting her turn, climbing on to the platform of the big double-decker, the clippie telling everyone to watch their step, 'Don't wanner do a header orf there darlin', do you? Pass along inside, blimey you'd make lovely sardines. Plenty of room on top.' *Click-click* on her ticket clipper. 'Wouldn't mind being a sardine with you, darlin',' says a sprauncy young fellow smoking a cigarette on the platform.

'Smoking on top only,' the clippie sings out.

'Give me half a chance.'

'Get up them stairs. Plenty of room on top. Any more fares, please?'

Ting-ting went the bell, signalling the driver.

And so off they went, swaying and rumbling up to the corner of Tottenham Court Road. It was amazing really how disciplined people were in the queues for buses, food, anything. Folk just stood patiently waiting their turn, docile as donkeys.

It was completely dark by the time she descended from the bus and started to walk along Tottenham Court Road, the glimmer lights were on and there was the almost ghostly glow from the slits on the headlights of vehicles as they moved to and fro along the road. Dark and chilly, the breeze whipping at her, icy. In her head she remembered a poem from her schooldays.

> *No sun – no moon!*
> *No morn – no noon*
> *No dawn – no dusk – no proper time of day.*
> *November!*

Something like that, eighteenth century, Thomas Hood, she thought. Only it was December now and the play on words didn't quite work if you substituted December.

People appeared to float along the pavements and occasionally she glimpsed a square of white material sewn to the back of a coat to make the wearer more visible in the blackout. There were white painted dashes along the edge of the pavement on the kerbstones, and white rings low around trees. Two taxis went by, visible, painted grey, commandeered for ARP duties. Ahead she saw the two streetlights at the junction, their pinhole starlights sending beams straight down, pricking the pavement. Somewhere ahead a door opened spilling a sliver of light on to the pavement and she caught a shadow moving out towards the street: there for a minute and gone like a wraith.

She turned into Goodge Street, the darkness even deeper and Suzie was aware of another door opening, a shaft of light painting the paving stones again and a shadow there and then almost gone, the outline lingering ahead of her. Was it? No, Big Toe Harvey couldn't be here, she knew where he'd end up tonight, with his cronies, with the Twins. But she was concerned, the tall figure still walking ahead as the shrouded lights of a car picked him out. She knew the walk, heard the footsteps. Then, suddenly, the man was gone.

Turn right again, into Charlotte Street, crossing Tottenham Street, everything muffled by the darkness.

She walked by a figure standing silent in a doorway and didn't realize until she was almost past: felt the curl of fear in her stomach and, for a second, heard that terrible grinding of metal she had heard on the afternoon her father had been killed. Dear heaven she was edgy. Another two buildings and she'd be at the Falconettis' restaurant: Tosca.

Beryl Falconetti ran up the stairs and pushed open the door to their living room above the restaurant. 'Carlo,' almost whispering. 'Carlo, quickly that policewoman detective, she's just coming in the restaurant. You don't want her up here, *do* you?'

Carlo, sitting with two other men turned, his lips framing an O.

'You certainly don't want any policewoman up here, bonny lad,' said one of the men. The other shook his head and they all looked as though a funeral cortège had just gone past, body of a beloved family member on its way to the cemetery.

Downstairs, Suzie pretended she had not seen Beryl slide

from her desk and almost run up the stairs. What had Preece called it? Sitting at the receipt of custom. Biblical.

Now Carlo was coming down the stairs, smiling when he saw Suzie. She had the impression that he was putting on an act, playing a part specially for her.

'Detective Sergeant Mumford,' he said, short bow from the waist. 'How nice to see you.' Accomplished, sounding genuinely delighted. *Little wop liar*, she thought.

'Detective Sergeant *Mountford*,' she corrected.

'You come for a dinner, or . . . ?'

'Just passing. Thought I'd look in. See how the fingers're getting on. Not official.'

'Sit down. Have some coffee. I still have the good stuff.'

Only two of the tables were occupied. Navy at one, two young officers, one with a dark growth of beard, the other with tired eyes, and an Army major with a young ATS officer, whatever they called a subaltern in the ATS. She looked shy, little turned-up nose and wide mouth, early twenties if that, glancing up with a slight hostility, looking at Suzie's trench coat and beret: a civilian, a smudge of contempt in the ATS officer's eyes.

They sat at the table right at the back of the room. Suzie asked about his hand.

'Too early to expect much change yet. Thank heaven for the pain killers. Sleeping's difficult.'

She looked up at him. A quizzical, amusing look they'd call it, with a smile just showing at the corners of her mouth. 'And when're you going to tell me who did the fingers? When're you going to tell me it was the Twins' man, Porky Pine?'

'If you know it already you don't need me to tell you.' Playing with her. 'I hear they've got problems, the Twins. Things that go bump in the night – and in the morning also.'

'I've heard that,' she said. Then, 'How long've you lived here, Carlo.'

'In England? 1922. Autumn. End of October, early November. Left Italy night of 28th October, after my father was killed. Murdered.' He took a deep breath and then gave her the story in a series of quickfire sentences. 'Time of big trouble. Political trouble. My father kept a small hotel in Milan, Albergo Ricci –

my mother's maiden name. The hotel was close to the square in front of the cathedral, a stone's throw away.'

He told her that his father had been vociferous in the condemnation of Mussolini, head of the Fascisti, the Fascist Party. He spoke at meetings and rallies in Milan and the Fascists hated him. 'Now, on that day in 1922, the Fascists had their chance of power. Before they headed for Rome they settled old scores.

'I still remember it,' his eyes hinting the sadness. 'My father being dragged out of the hotel, beaten to death by the Fascists in the little garden in front. The garden where I'd play.' He shook his head. 'My mother screaming, and all the time an opera on the radio – *Tosca*. Beginning of the last act. The sound of the shepherd, playing his pipe and singing as dawn breaks over Rome, and the bells of Rome ring out, the dawn of the day that will bring Tosca to tragedy and death.' A sad smile and another shake of the head. 'Is why I call my little restaurant here Tosca.' He told it with just the bare facts, pausing as a waiter brought their coffee and poured it. And again when a new pair of customers arrived, and he got up and greeted them –

'Ah dottore, and madam. How are you? No, I cannot shake hands. I have damaged fingers. Luigi, the dottore and madam. You look after them well, yes. Good.' He came back to the table with a sparkle in his eyes, just walking off stage.

She said, 'Carlo, let's stop playing about. We need you to sign a statement about Porky Pine. Peter Porteus Pine. Snobby little name. Please, Carlo.'

He spread his hands apart in a gesture of hopelessness. 'How can I?' Dropping his voice. 'You expect me to risk my life by naming these . . . these . . . bastardo. Sure, they could have problems now, but they'll pass. They always do for people like the Balvaks.'

'I think we've got someone willing to speak up. A confession's been signed. Witnessed and signed.'

'Yes. The pigs might fly also.'

So it went on, round and round until he said he had work to do. 'I'm sorry, Sergeant, but I can't do it. You put those two in prison they'll still be able to reach out and take revenge.

Same as the devil. What they say? Eat with him you have a long spoon, yes.'

She knew how he felt, knew that they'd promise the earth, tell him there was no way the twins could hurt him once they were on the Moor or wherever. Then he would be found carved up, or shot, or shived up a back alley on a dark night.

'I'm sorry, Carlo.' She finished her coffee.

'I am also sorry, but it's how things are.'

'I know,' and she left, headed back up to Upper St Martin's Lane. Time for a bath, change of clothes, ready to meet Fordy. The strange leap of her heart, like a salmon leaping inside her chest. Why?

Outside it had started to drizzle, beginning to turn bitterly cold, the breeze slashing spray at her, and the shadow was still in the doorway, so that she moved out, towards the edge of the pavement with its white painted stripes and hurried on until she was past.

Was the Ghoul out in the night, prowling the streets and the bomb sites for bodies? Suzie hadn't even heard of the Ghoul: didn't know of his existence.

Not yet.

'See, there's only one way to deal with this scurrilous business.' Charlie Balvak had started using long words and the usual suspects sat around his living room listening, and not forgetting that the Law had been in earlier, Tony Harvey, detective chief inspector of this parish. *Never trust a copper.* 'Only one way with the clubs,' Charlie continued, 'lose a few, so grab a few more.'

They nodded as Connie repeated, 'Grab a few more.'

'Some time ago we made a list,' he waved a piece of paper in the air, high above his head.

'. . . a list,' parroted Connie. Nobody mentioned that it was Little Nell who had prepared the list for them. The object? A takeover of certain clubs and premises in Soho because 'when the Yanks come – as they must come one day – there'll be a killing here.' Little Nell had said it long before December 7th, date that will live in infamy. 'They'll come like tourists,' Little Nell'd said. 'They'll want exactly what all tourists would like in a strange land without their wives to keep them on the straight and narrow. They'll want drink available twenty-four hours a day, and they'll want women to look at, to drink with and finally to go home with, get into bed with, have their wicked way with. A standing prick has no conscience.' That's what Little Nell had said before someone took off his head and stuck it on an assegai in his bathroom, and Charlie Balvak was saying something similar now to his assembled troops, stating his battle plan.

'The Silver Fork in Frith Street; Drum's Coventry Street; Swallow's Nest Beak Street; Pay-21 and the Golden Fleece in Lexington Street; Hexie's Place in Warwick Street, and Mona's Garden in Sherwood Street.'

Fast Eddie Ellis cackled. 'Couple of bloody window boxes on the inside and they call it a garden. Mona's not much of a flower, either.'

'These,' Charlie raised his voice, '– These are our obvious targets. Seven small places, run on a shoestring and owned by six independent people, people who run the rooms themselves: no real experience, no muscle, just please themselves, use transitory crumpet, mysteries you can't control, and migrant talent. Tomorrow we'll start changing that. We'll go in and take some of them under our protection. Tomorrow evening we'll begin: show 'em they can't push us around. Tomorrow.'

'Tomorrow,' Connie repeated.

'And we'll be using our influential friends an' all: some of them highly placed.' Charlie looked around. 'I reckon we begin with the two clubs in Lexington Street – Pay-21 and Golden Fleece – and we'll also take in Mona's Garden. Right? Porky, your job is to wander into Pay-21 round about nine o'clock. You and three or four of your boys. You have a drink and Connie and I'll come in round ten. Make your presence felt, nothing heavy, just let people know they're not really welcome, all right?

Porky said, 'That won't work.'

'Why not?'

'Tomorrow night's Saturday. Those smaller joints'll be full seeing as how we won't have anything open.'

'Okay, just control them then. You can surely control a

crowd drinking in a small place like Pay-21 or Golden Fleece. Just keep them quiet while Connie and me talk to the fellow who owns the place, bloke called Joe Chalk, convince him that it's in his interest to let us take over – the usual insurance chat to start with, protection and that. Then we'll move on.'

'Move on,' from Connie.

Flash Stan Page was to take some of the lads into the Golden Fleece at nine thirty and run the same routine; Joe Chalk owned both places. Charlie and Connie would come in at about ten thirty while Porky would leapfrog up to Mona's Garden for the same business.

'Catch Mona with her knickers down,' Connie declaimed with a schoolboy snigger.

Charlie looked around the room, saw Sly Sid Silverman and told him he wanted a private word. 'Something needs great tact.' Inclined his head towards the door and led the way to the small boxroom at the back of the flat, the one with the desk and a private-line telephone, the one few people ever got inside.

Sid Silverman was like his name: silver haired and silver tongued. He was only in his late forties, so he helped the hair along and was always well dressed – after his own fashion: sharp suits, grey or charcoal with the hint of a stripe, shoes hand-made by a man he knew in Chelsea, silk ties and shirts. Immaculate, that's what you could call Sid, who liked to be around ladies, his job really.

'Sid, you know that Carlo Falconetti?'

'Charlotte Street. Restaurant called something, Tosca? That it?'

'That's the one. Doesn't like us at the moment, caught his fingers in a door, only Porky helped him do it.'

Sly Sid Silverman winced, then nodded as though he understood. He said, 'It could happen to anyone.'

'I want you to take one of your ladies there, to his restaurant, tomorrow night, dinner, say seven, half past and linger until around nine thirty, ten. One of your girls must deserve a little something.'

'Sure, Charlie.'

'But first you must ring the restaurant. You must make

certain that Carlo Falconetti is going to be there. You tell them you heard Mr Falconetti's a wonderful host and you want to talk with him about a special party you going to hold Christmas week. Then tell him what you like. Got it? Run him around, keep him there.'

'You're a sly dog, Charlie. Yes, I'll keep him busy, don't worry.'

'Then of course I'll need you at some point because we want to put girls in those three clubs quick as kiss your arse when we've taken over, done everything but pay for them.'

'You'll have the cream of my cream, Charlie. Could I perhaps borrow Wanda to help out?'

Charlie gave him a charmless smile. 'There's something you have to learn, Sid. Wanda's mine; my own special dancing partner for the immediate future. Understand, Sid?'

Sid indicated that he understood very well.

Charlie dismissed him, saying, 'Oh, and Sid, could you ask Porky to step this way.

Porky arrived a couple of minutes later. He had only been in this room once before. Special honour, he thought. Aloud he asked, 'You wanted me, Charlie?'

'Yeah. That place of Carlo Falconetti's. The old scout hut?'

'Going to call it Ursula's Place, yes, Charlie.'

'Could you still get in through that back door? Could you still open the door and get in, Porky?'

'You know, Charlie. I can get in most places.'

'That mean yes?'

'Affirmative – sure, Charlie.'

'Good. I want you to select three strapping young blokes – your lads, three'll be quite enough, well set up and ready to take on any woman they bump into. I want you to chose them and be ready tomorrow night, do a special job for me, you leading them.'

'Of course, Charlie. Before we start in on the new premises in Lexington Street?'

'No, after we've laid claim to those three little clubs, want to get them squared away first. Nice job for you though. Cause a stir, okay?'

'Right, Charlie.'

'Listen then, what you're to do . . .' And Charlie Balvak told him in detail what the job was, what he expected, and where and how they were to do it.

Porky grinned his porcine grin and said it would be a pleasure.

When he was left alone, Charlie Balvak picked up the telephone and dialled a number from memory.

'Toe,' he said in an oily voice, pleased with himself. 'This is what you do . . .'

Late that afternoon on the fifth floor of New Scotland Yard, where the Reserve Squad lived, moved and had its being, DCS Tommy Livermore took a telephone call that lasted a little more than three minutes.

After twenty minutes thought, he called Billy Mulligan, his executive sergeant, into his office: the room which he had made comfortable for himself by bringing in some deep leather chairs from Kingscote Grange, the family retreat, and hanging three rare 'Wanted' posters on one wall and two front pages of the *Police Gazette* from the late nineteenth century on another.

'Billy,' he said when they were seated, 'I've just had a tip and I don't know if it's genuine or not.'

'Who's the grass?'

'I have no idea. Phone call out of the blue, says Saturday night's going to be a milestone; also says that on Saturday night someone, or some people, is going to take a crack at the Twins. My instinct tells me that it's real and we should plan accordingly.'

'Your instinct's always good enough for me, Chief.' Billy was hunched forward. 'I'd act on it if I were you.'

'Yes,' said Tommy, and again, 'Yes.'

Suzie lay back in her bath and warbled, 'Hi-ho, hi-ho, it's off to work we go,' seeing in her head the Seven Dwarfs trotting along, coming home from the mine where a million diamonds shine. While she sang, Suzie thoroughly soaped herself, then got the loofah out and washed the soap off with the steaming hot bath water, nothing better after a day in the salt mines.

She wished she had a yellow celluloid duck to play with, like she had when she was a kid.

Her brother, James, had a submarine for the bath at Larksbrook even at his age. A submarine in the bath; she wished she had a submarine to play with in the bath, suddenly thinking a wicked thought and giggling.

She got out of the bath, rubbed herself down with the big rough towel, dusted herself off with talcum powder, went through to the bedroom and began to dress, taking a look at herself in the blue, lace-trimmed underwear that Tommy liked so much. Would Fordy like it? What a terrible thing to think. She really shocked herself, peeped at herself again as she buttoned her stockings to the matching suspender belt, running her hands down her legs, adjusting, straightening the seams, thought, You hussy, Suzie! She had chosen the deep-red dress with the wide skirt, pinched waist and buttoned top with frogging. Couldn't get wide skirts any longer. The red dress was her best buy in the autumn of '39 when the war started. Now you had to conserve every bit of material. Austerity they called it, drab and dull.

She needed something to cover her head, the wide red and sparkly shawl thing with sequins. Not quite the right shade of red for the dress, more a claret, but that would be fine, never worn it before, given to her as an extra present after the horror of last Christmas, given to her by the Galloping Major. He'd been all embarrassed about giving it to her. 'Got it on me travels,' he had said, handing her the tissue-covered packet, thick and heavy for a shawl. When she had opened it and said, ooh and aah, he told her they used to call them fascinators. It was a fascinator, and she never believed it. Fascinators were for old ladies. She wound it round her head, throwing the right-hand length across and over her left shoulder: looked dead mysterious, went to the mirror and fiddled with it, feeling good. There was a truce between her and the Galloping Major at the moment because he had shown he cared for her mother, still didn't mean she liked him, pompous fart that he was.

She wondered where Tommy had got to. Was he settling Sybil into somewhere safe, tucking her away with Molly Abelard, tooled up, ready to shoot the lights out of any intruder? Again she asked herself if she should talk to Tommy about what she had seen, Brian and Molly wrapped together outside Molly's house. Hadn't even told him about there being no Mrs Abelard admitted to Dulwich Hospital. Don't really get to talk to Tommy these days . . .

The claret-coloured fascinator gave her a dramatic look, a shade dark for the red dress but it couldn't be helped, and she'd be wearing her big overcoat, the long one with the fur collar that she'd bought at Fenwicks. Madly expensive, paid for with the cash she'd hoarded from birthdays and Christmas presents over two, three, years. Almost a hundred quid, king's ransom. She always thought that when she looked at the coat with its high fur collar and its rather military cut. It had been costly but well worth it. Tommy had taken her to some special meal and a woman had leaned out of her chair from another table just to touch the fabric.

In the coat over the red dress and wearing the silky underwear next to her skin, Suzie felt luxurious: very expensive. She felt dangerous as well, first time out with anybody else but Tommy: her Dandy Tom with whom she'd fallen in love quite hopelessly and he had taken her up on it: a year now and they'd been together ever since, the only man, the one who had made her a woman and to whom she'd vowed to be true for the rest of her life, but not in front of a priest because he had promised it but not followed through.

She remembered the last pantomime she had seen around 1938 – 'Cinderella you *shall* go to the ball,' and the wonderful transformation scene. It was happening again now in dusty half-ruined London.

Fordham O'Dell was waiting for her in the foyer of the Savoy: pleased to see her, like a dog with two tails. She left her coat with the woman in the Cloakroom, kept the fascinator over her shoulders.

Fordy looked really dashing, his best uniform, the wings and his medal ribbon bright as if just given to him. He's so nice, she thought as she took his arm and they walked down to the restaurant, stopping just short of the entrance as she spotted a figure seated halfway up the room, his back towards her, a very young blonde, latest hair style like Francis Day, leaning across the table, eyes only for him and laughing at some witty remark. Laughing and reaching across to place her hand over his on the table: a gesture of some intimacy. Her eyes only for him, gazing at him as though her entire world depended on him. You could tell even from this angle that the pair were having a splendid time in and out of bed.

'Fordy,' she pulled him back with her hand on his arm. 'I'm terribly sorry, I can't have dinner here.'

'Oh,' face crumpling the tinniest bit. 'Oh, why on earth not?'

She shook her head, biting her lip, turning away from the picture of Tommy Livermore and the young blonde girl seated in unrelenting intimacy while the orchestra in the Savoy restaurant played 'This Can't be Love'.

Nineteen

Fordham didn't make a fuss, acted as though this was a regular occurrence – which it might have been for all Suzie knew. Taxis were, as ever, thin on the ground, but the commissionaire got one for them and Fordy almost elbowed him out of the way to hold the door open for her, whisking her off to the Connaught, where she cleaned up her face, tidied her hair and set out to have a damned good time. Sod Tommy, she thought, and worse. Damn him. Who the hell did he think he was? Playing silly buggers.

Suzie darling, I do hope you're not compromising yourself, her mother had said.

Well, Mummy, yes. Yes, I've been compromising myself totally and now I'm shafted. You were right, Mum. What do I do about it now?

She tried to make some sense of it. Was there a reasonable explanation? Was the girl connected with a case? No, the fact remained untrammelled in her mind: the girl, blonde, a lot of hair sweeping in two waves from the top of her head, beautifully kept, like her teeth, just visible in the loving smile, the lips perfectly painted and her cheeks smooth with foundation powder and a tiny touch of rouge. Her eyes? They were turned towards Tommy, deeply adoring. If the girl had been an actress feigning love she couldn't have done better. Above the eyes the eyebrows were neatly tweasered out, plucked and curved and highlit with a special pencil for eyebrows only.

Suzie ordered automatically: she'd have the *Melon Charentais*, she took in that it was seven bob a pop, so what? she thought. Wing Commander O'Dell wanted to take her out, he could afford it. 'And for the entrée, madame?' She wanted to say *les arseholes en croute* but rose above the vulgarity that came straight from Tommy's influence. She'd have *Le Chicken pie en Gelée, Pommes Purée* and *Haricots verts*. What a patronizing bloody menu, she thought. Mashed potatoes and green beans tarted up as *Pommes Purée* and les beans green!

'You're very quiet,' Fordy said. 'What's wrong, Suzie? This is not like you.'

'How do you know?' she asked, having a bit of a smoulder.

'We've only met twice. The first time I asked a lot of questions, then we had lunch today. This is the third time, so how'd you know what I'm like?'

The truth was that she had tucked herself away in her own brain thinking about Tommy Livermore and the lovely young girl with whom he was having a splendid dinner at the Savoy Hotel.

'Marry you tomorrow, heart, if that's what you really want. You know that.' That's what Dandy Tom had said.

You bugger, Tommy. You absolute horror. Tommy you're so low you'd need a stepladder to get under a snake. She was becoming more and more angry, alone there in her head.

'Announce it tomorrow, heart, and by Tuesday morning they'll have you out of here. Lands End or John a thing . . . Groats. Just won't let us go on working together. Move us to different ends of the planet.' That was Tommy Livermore's excuse. How many girls was he running on the same string? Tommy how could you do it?

And in a rush she suddenly came partially to her senses and looked across the table at Fordy. Deep breath. 'I'm terribly, terribly sorry, Fordy. Unforgivable of me.'

She saw the girl again, in her head, the blonde. She had a large aquamarine set in a triangular gold piece, the point attached to a slim gold chain, hanging round her neck the stone picking up the burnished corn colour of her hair. Wondered if that was a family heirloom Tommy had given her, a keepsake. If it was he'd never given *her* a keepsake. Food from the Home Farm, yes, but *she* usually had to cook it. Tommy didn't do a hand's turn in the flat.

'You've got a problem, haven't you, sweetheart?'

She reflected sweetheart was better than heart. Tommy was

beginning to get her down with his 'heart' recurring every other sentence. Fordy could call her sweetheart whenever he liked. But never bloody heart because that got on her tits, as Tommy would say. Inside she was a seething volcano. No. Stop it.

'A shock, yes,' she said. 'A problem, no. I just carve somebody out of my life, that's all.'

'Want to talk about it? Helps sometimes.'

She thought how tantalizing his mouth was, set in that ghost smile, a fund of humour just behind the eyes and the slight quiver of the lips. Lord it was an attractive mouth and if he tried to kiss her she'd let him, even give him a bit of tongue back, just a bit, try some fencing with him, lick him to pieces. She felt the old devil wink in her loins.

'Been having an affair,' she told Fordy. 'More than an affair really. Been living with a fellow. Another police officer.' Didn't mention his name, why take it any further? 'And now . . . Well . . .'

'You walk into the Savoy, and there he is wining and dining another popsie,' as though he could read her mind.

'How did you . . . ?'

'Work it out? Didn't take an R. J. Mitchell to work that out.'

'Who's R. J. Mitchell?'

'Boffin. Designed the Spit. Every schoolboy knows that.'

'I'm not a schoolboy,' almost laughing.

'No need to remind me, sweetheart. I have the evidence of my own eyes, sitting here looking at you.'

The waiter brought the melon for her, seven shillings a go, and a bowl of green-hued soup for him: five shillings. Twelve bob for their starters here in the luxury of the Connaught. Expensive.

'There we go,' Fordy said. 'Big eats.'

'Big eats?'

'That's what they say in Malta. Friend of mine in the Navy told me, went though Malta a year ago. They've got this street there, King George V Street, runs downhill, lot of steps, lined with all sorts of strange places, cafés, show places, naughty ladies showing you their wares, lady does it with a donkey . . .'

246

'Really?'

'So I'm reliably informed. They call this street "the Gut". Top of the street blokes stand outside their cafés trying to lure you in, "Hey Jack, come in. Big eats. Steak, eggs and chips, Jack. Big eats. Fill your boots." I reckon that was when they had plenty of food.'

He pulled such amusing faces that, against her depression and the fury of having been cheated on by Tommy, Suzie smiled. Then she laughed, tucking in to her melon feeling a smidgen better. Fordy asked if there was any chance the gorgeous young girl she'd seen with her chap was some relative, or an essential witness to a case he was pursuing.

'Not a hope,' she told him. 'The bitch was looking up at him as though she'd found the Holy Grail and the antidote for the Curse all in one go.' She could still surprise herself with the language she seemed to be using effortlessly, and without shame – Tommy's influence again.

He asked, 'Talking about the Curse. Is it true that girls with a bandage round their ankle have the Curse? Sort of signal?'

She laughed. She'd heard it before. 'Old wife's tale,' she said, 'along with the great fact that you can't get pregnant the first time you do it.'

'I knew about that one.' Getting into cheeky territory. 'It's not true about girls wearing red hats either, is it?'

'Never heard that one.'

'Girl wearing red hat isn't wearing any drawers.'

'Certainly not!' slightly shocked. Then, 'Is that what they say?'

'All the time.'

'My goodness.'

'Stick with me and you'll learn more useless gen than you've got house room for.'

'What do I do about the bastard, Fordy?'

'Your lover boy?'

'Yes.'

'Nothing you can do. It happens. Years ago I learned that if the girl you love, have feelings for, whatever you call it, wants to go, well . . . You learn she wants to leave you, there's nothing you can do about it. You can rant and rave, bay at the

247

moon, all that kind of stuff till you're blue in the face. Won't do any good. When someone's mind's made up, you may as well sit back and let 'em go. Must be the same for girls whose bloke walks out.'

She nodded, feeling very old and experienced.

'Mind you,' Fordy gave her a splendid smile. 'Mind you, it ain't easy. I mean I've been told this by my elders. Doesn't mean I could do it, sit back and smile. With men it's a personal affront when a woman walks away. Means to a man that the other fellow's better with his whatsit: his technique of loving, all that. It's an insult to his manhood for the girl to walk out.'

Fordham O'Dell was very wise, she thought. Tommy was wise about some things, police things, how you coped with an investigation, the psychology of criminals, stuff like that. Fordy would probably be very good in his Spitfire saying things like, 'Bandits at one-zero. Right-ho chaps, let's get 'em,' drawling it out then swooping down on the enemy.

'Do you ever get afraid when you're fighting the Hun?' She said Hun because she had heard somewhere that they called the *Luftwaffe* the Hun. Beware the Hun in the sun, she had read somewhere. 'I mean really afraid?'

He nodded, grinning. 'Too right. Yes. Shit scared, if you'll pardon the expression. But you try not to show it. Bad show if you do. You carry on and, when you start the fighting, when you're up there blasting away at some poor bugger in an ME 109 . . . well, you forget about it, you get carried away until you come down. After you've landed, that's a different story.'

'What d'you mean?'

'First time I was in a scrap, I got back to the base, felt fine, excited. Landed, unbuckled and climbed out, then my knees sort of gave way. Couldn't walk. Like a drunk, you know, weaving around all over the place. Couldn't stand up for a few minutes. Some poor devils get so scared that they can't carry on though. Damn difficult.'

'What do you mean they can't carry on?'

'All sorts of things happen. They go sick, they collapse. We had a couple who baled out as soon as we spotted the Hun.

248

They had to go of course. Didn't see them again: Adj just sent them on their way. Then we had one poor fellow went blind. Well, we never knew the truth of that. Said he went blind. Quack came along took him into hospital. Didn't see him again either.'

'You said you were frightened, Fordy.'

'Sure. Yes. Course I was frightened, but the only way to behave is to carry on, do your job. No point chucking in the towel. There're guys who're taxiing out for take-off and they upchuck, straight out of the cockpit, over the side. Throw up their heels and toes and they're okay after that. But you've got to treat it as a job, go and do it. Even make light of it. Flying the aeroplane takes enough concentration, let alone people trying to kill you.' Pause for a couple of seconds, then went on.

'You'd get a fellow shooting a line about what happened to him, how brave he was: "Baled out at four thousand, nothing to it." Someone says that and all the chaps near him will go into a line-shoot chant, they'll say, "There I was, upside down in a cloud, on fire, nothing on the clock but the maker's name and that was blurred . . ." Make a joke of it. That's why you hear all this balls about fighter pilots being super-composed, dead relaxed. That's just a joke, way to behave. Pretending it's not happening, I suppose. Empty chairs in the mess means they've gone on leave, don't come back, you know someone says, "Where's Jamie?" And you say, "Gone for a Burton."'

'*You* ever get frightened when you're doing *your* job, Suzie?'

Porky Pine decided that he'd do a recce, as he'd heard people call it, having a look round, going on a bit of an exploration. So he dressed up, put on his check sports coat over a blue Airtex shirt, grey flannel trousers with his lace-up boots, combed his hair, short back and sides, and went down to Pay-21 in Lexington Street, right the other end from where Little Nell'd had his house.

Friday night and there were quite a few people about, squaddies not saluting the young officers sniffing around for a bit of nookie because it was too dark to see anything, people were bumping into each other, knocking people over in the

249

blackout. Some had torches with two sheets of tissue paper over the glass. The whole of Soho seemed alive in the dark, crawling with people wanting the time of their lives. Popping into the places, restaurants and the like, that were now allowed to advertise in lights – not too bright.

Pay-21 was down some area steps, like the Nightlight had been, a couple of girls standing by the steps enticing people down. They didn't say 'Big eats, Jack,' like the Maltese down 'the Gut'. They said things like, 'Nice drinks, nice girls, come and take a look, darling, come on. Best girls in town. Take me down for a drink, darling, you won't regret it.'

Sly Sid Silverman spent half his life chasing girls off his territory, where he ran the Twins' girls, Porky thought. Sid's girls were after one thing, selling their bodies, as opposed to the girls who were only after suckers to take them down the club they worked for. Sometimes there were as many as four or five girls standing around near a club like Pay-21, luring men in, promising the earth. Once inside they'd ask the bloke to buy them champagne and have a drink themselves. The bloke would say he thought they were going to a room with a bed, just the two of them.

'All in good time, darling,' the girl would say. 'No need to rush. Have a drink first,' and before the bloke knew it he was looking at a bill for ten, fifteen pounds for drinks that tasted like coloured water, and the girl wasn't there anymore. Hadn't even had a dance to the nice music they were playing on records behind the bar or rendered by some clapped-out old boy banging away on an antique piano in the corner, off key.

Porky blundered along until he found the area steps to Pay-21, where a girl, looked about sixteen in the dark, said, 'Oooh, you're a big boy, darling, want to come down the club with me, have a drink and afterwards, won't regret it.'

'Do me a favour,' Porky said. 'I'm in the business and I don't want to wake up in a queue at the pox doctor's surgery.'

'That's not very nice,' the girl says, but she gets out of his way. After all, as she had observed, he is a big boy.

Just inside the door there's another woman talking about club membership. Porky grimaces and says, 'Do me a favour, eh? Just let me in. I got a life membership.'

'Can't let you in without seeing the card, darling,' the girl says.

'Right,' says Porky and pulls an ace of clubs out of his pocket, says, 'Aces high, right?' Then he goes in anyway without a membership or the girl's by-you're-leave. Which is not surprising because Porky is incredibly confrontational. He's not drunk and he's on his own, so the girl lets him go. There's also a possibility that she knows exactly who he is.

Porky walks into a room that, at a push, would take one billiard table, a bar billiards game and one each of Shove-Halfpenny and a Crown and Anchor board. Not large, accommodates only around five tables, maybe just six tables and the battered old crone playing a battered old piano in one corner, playing 'Somewhere over the Rainbow', and girls in short wispy clothes dispensing drinks from a small bar in the other corner. Just enough room to swing maybe two proverbial cats. Just about. So here we are in London, December 1941, in the blackout and all this suppressed villainy going on.

There, sitting quite close to the bar is Crazy Colin Combes from across the river, one of Percy Hodges' heavies.

'Colin!' says Porky, sounding surprised to see him here.

'Porky!' says Colin, not surprised to see him.

'You on a day trip to sunnier climes?' Porky helped himself to a chair and sat across from Crazy Colin.

'Just thought I'd take a look at what's going on. I hear people got hurt in a fire and a couple of small bombs.'

Porky smiles and takes a look at what's going on and a girl stops at the table and says, 'A drink, sir, and would you like one of our lovely young girls to keep you company? Won't regret it, sir.'

'Don't want anyone to keep me company, not even if it helps with the war effort, darling. A drink, yes, and make it a real one: a whisky out of a proper dimple Haig bottle, not tampered with, not a forgery and tasting proper. I'm in the trade, darling, so be careful and don't bugger me about, otherwise . . .' and he lifted the forefinger of his right hand and waggled it about – the gypsy's warning.

251

'So, mush, what're you doing in this neck of the woods?' Porky asks, having heard the expression in a Hollywood B-picture.

'I told yer,' Colin says. 'Coming over for a look-see, heard bad things, danger afoot.'

'Hope you're not doing anything iffy over here, young Colin.'

'Don't be silly, Porky. What kind of iffy would I do?'

'There's iffy and iffy, Colin. What would I know? I shall have to tell Charlie and Connie.'

'Tell who you like.'

Porky felt uncomfortable so he drank up and left the club, going to the Golden Fleece, two doors up. 'I don't want the goods,' he told the girl outside, and to the girl on the door he said, 'Just looking for a friend.' Peeping inside, he saw one person he recognized: bruising tall bloke known as Harry Henshaw, Hard Harry Henshaw who did protection for Percy Hodges across the river working out of the Black Prince just off Vauxhall Walk. Hard Harry was with a geezer Porky sort of recognized as a known villain from Lambeth but couldn't put a name to him.

It was enough. He didn't like the smell of this, Percy Hodges' blokes over this side of the river, sniffing round unadopted clubs.

He rang Charlie, who told him not to worry. He'd pass a little warning over to Percy, see if he cared.

They didn't stop talking from the start of dinner to the end: as Laurel and Hardy would have said 'from the soup to the nuts'. Suzie told him about her happy life until her late teens when her beloved father died and her mother remarried, big bone of contention.

Suzie swapped her story for Fordy's tale of misery at his first boarding school, where he was bullied to within an inch of his life and only happy when he was finally shipped off to Farnham Place, a modern and radical school where the pupils ran the organization on behalf of the pupils. 'Thrived there,' he said. 'Probably did all the wrong things but I was deliriously happy. Don't know if I learned much, but what I did manage to

252

pick up appears to have prepared me well for the vicissitudes of the grown-up world.'

She'd heard most of that when she interviewed him at his base, Middle Wallop, in December '40: a year ago. But now he got on to his present job: low-level attacks on northern France – 'Shooting up airfields. Other targets. Wizard fun. You come back exhilarated.'

They both appeared to be entranced with each other's stories. Time flew and before they realized it they had drunk coffee, the bill was presented and they were on their way, waiting outside for a taxi.

'I suppose it would be silly to ask, "Your place or mine?"' As he said it, the back of her hand just scraped the back of his. Suzie grabbed, felt her fingers lace with his and their palms kiss. *Hand to hand in Palmer's kiss*, she heard in her head, her most choice moment in Romeo & Juliet, her absolutely favourite Shakespeare play, if truth be told the only Shakespeare play she knew anything about because she'd done it for Eng. Lit in School Certificate.

'It can't be my place,' she looked at him, Lord, I'll drown in his eyes.

The taxi arrived and he said, boldly, 'Regent Palace Hotel.' And Suzie knew this was her undoing. Fordham De Vitre O'Dell would be her second lover ever in the whole world, and she was going shamelessly to the slaughter, a willing lamb.

She thought of the song again, 'Room Five Hundred and Four'.

That seventh heaven on the old fifth floor.

It was nice. Later, when Suzie had a chance to think about it, she wondered if she had dreamed it all. Later still, she realized that it had been in some way like dying and being reborn: she was swept off her feet, taken a long way out to sea and then borne back again to something that was perfect peace; contentment; that mythical island where we'd all like to go and just be. There were no fireworks going off in her head, but it was comforting.

It had nothing to do with the way Fordy made love to her, or that Tommy had not been as good a lover as him. It had everything to do with how they made love to one another: light, easy, their bodies coming together as though they were meant only for one another. She thought to herself, That's sentimental cow dung. Then she thought, No, it's not, its how I feel: how it should be.

The point was that in an instant Fordy possessed her, and as she followed in the dance that some uninspired poet called the world shrunken to a heap of hot flesh straining on a bed, she felt the lightness of being herself joined to a man, flying from the humdrum of daily life, transported by his body within her and her body enveloping his.

So they went to this place they discovered and they stayed there most of that night. Fordy said, 'I've never ever . . .' and she laid a hand across his lips, shook her head and said, 'Don't spoil it.'

In the early hours he asked what they should do next and she said she didn't know. 'Nothing to begin with,' she told him.

She was working the next night, so knew she could not see him until Sunday at the earliest, and even then didn't know if she wanted to.

'I go back first thing on Monday,' he told her and it was as though there was a time limit on everything.

'I'll see you,' she said as she left. No plans, no restraints, no promises. 'I'll see you.'

She fiddled with her key, she so wanted a cigarette but couldn't smoke in the street, something a girl could not do: girls and women never smoked in the street, just wasn't done.

It was eight thirty when she walked in. The flat was empty, so she stripped and began to run a bath. Then, wandering around, she saw the note on the kitchen table. Across the top, Tommy had scrawled – 'Well you didn't make it. Pity, we had a great time and you can meet at some point soon. Alison's so looking forward to meeting the woman who's brought her big brother to heel. Phone me. T.'

Then the body of the letter was timed at 7 p.m. last night. She hadn't even come into the kitchen she was so occupied in bathing and dressing up to go and meet Fordy.

Darling Heart,
Hope you get back in time to take me up on this. My

254

baby sister's turned up in London – Alison, don't ask
for details, big falling out with the parents four years
ago. Name never mentioned that sort of thing. She's
been through hell and back with an idiot man in France.
Survived the occupation and has had one devil of a
journey, managing to cross from Perpignan to Paris and
from there, after adventures with resistance fighters, has
made it to London. Actually she's been in England a
couple of weeks but the funnies have been interrogating
her at some ultra secret place, very hush-hush. She says
she's going back to France soon!

She looks as though she's come straight off the catwalk
at Schiaparelli or Chanel. Perfect and beautiful. She's
dying to meet you so hope you get off in time to dash
down to meet us at the Savoy. I've booked a table
for three.

Ever with my deepest devotion and love to the ends
of the earth.

Tommy.

The world turned and the great breakers of guilt crashed in
on her, knocking everything out of her, winding her standing
there naked in the kitchen.

The telephone began to ring, brash through the flat, making
her jump and releasing a thousand butterflies into her stomach.

Twenty

I t was Tommy on the phone.
  She felt her stomach turn over then fall right through the
floor. 'Tommy,' she said, knowing her voice had gone tiny and
husky. She could hardly get the words out, her throat suddenly
parched; reminded her of school, when she had to read aloud
for Sister Mary Joseph, or own up to something. 'Tommy,'
she said again, not getting anywhere. Feeling suddenly terribly
young and remembering Tommy saying she was too young to
be involved in a murder inquiry, over a year ago. She'd got
very snotty with him: thought she was grown up and knew
everything; in your early twenties you're never going to die,
it's not going to happen – ever.

'Heart, I'm sorry to bother you. Hope I didn't wake you.'

'No. I haven't been in long. I'm sorry I missed last night.
You never told me you had a sister.' Blurt, she thought, slow
down, Suzie, you silly cow.

'There'll be other times, she's here for a month. Unexpected
and, for me, wonderful to see her again,' he said quietly and
with the same old confidence. In her head she said, Tommy, do
it or shut up, it's been a year since you popped me, promised
me the earth and the wedding, the whole business. Now its
time, Tom. But she didn't say it out loud. She was confused.
To quote Tommy, she didn't know her arse from Easter Day,
didn't know which was north, didn't know who was Prime
Minister, thought Beaverbrook was the name of a beauty spot,
didn't know any bloody thing.

'Tommy, we've got to talk.' Oh shit, she thought, the 'talk'
came out more like 'squawk'.

'Yes, later, heart. Time's running out, important things've
got to be done.'

'Things?'

'We're aiming to arrest Harvey tonight.'

'Tonight?' Coming to the crunch so soon?

'We've got all sorts of things going on. Bit concerned about your safety, heart, to be honest.' Tommy said that to start with, Laura Cotter and Ron Worral were still nosing around. 'They're supposed to be working on the bomb at the On & Off up Golden Square, truth is they've more or less finished there. They're having a good sniff around. Seen some strange people running about as well. People from across the river; people usually work for Percy Hodges – names like Colin Combes, Harry Henshaw. Heard of them?'

'I've heard of Colin Combes – *Crazy* Colin Combes?'

'That's the one. Some of their sidekicks as well: Porous Pat Jansen, Nutty Fryer, Willie Watts – great big fella – and Cliff Sweeney.' Suzie knew that porous was Raff slang. If they said someone was porous they meant 'porous piss'. Dandy Tom was still speaking. 'Word is the Twins're organizing a take-over of clubs: what you might call privately owned clubs. Whole thing's starting to blow up in our faces.'

'So you're going to feel Harvey's collar tonight?'

'Probably. Someone'll go in, nick him and bring him to Marylebone, somewhere like that. Maybe even as far afield as Harrow Road. Somewhere he's never worked. Arresting officers'll be people he doesn't know. Rubber heels.'

'And you'll be waiting to talk to him?'

'Interrogate him, yes. Lay the facts before him and ask if he would like to tell us things.' She could picture Tommy giving his ratty smile, a bit of a gloat. 'Big Toe's career's over. What a pity, could've been a fine officer.' She could feel his smile as he said it.

'You just rang to warn me, Tom?'

'No, need to ask you about your statements as well, heart.'

She had made a long statement about the three hours Harvey had conveniently lost from the Buller Belcher murder at the Nightlight. There was another regarding the information about Little Nell betraying the Twins. Tommy had said, 'I know they've got a watertight alibi, but I'd bet you a pony that they did Little Nell. Particularly after you told Toe Harvey what Sybil Harris had said.'

Pass him on to Harvey, and Harvey will pass him on to the Twins and we can all watch the fur fly. Give it to him as though it's an afterthought.

So she'd told Harvey that the girl Sybil had let it drop that Little Nell Bellman was plotting to betray the Twins, had an organized swindle going, creaming money from the clubs, inferring that Nell was on the fiddle throughout the organization, threatened to bring them down. Tommy believed if the Twins got strong information from Harvey they would, in his words, '. . . do Little Nell to death.' Sure enough, Little Nell *was* done to death, head sliced off and stuck on an assegai. Claret all over the place.

'That woman,' Tommy said, changing the subject by a couple of degrees, 'the woman they called Tatty Macintosh, used to call her Stinking Sarah way back. Did you have an understanding with her?'

Normally you never gave away an informer, a grass, even to a fellow officer, but Tatty was dead, so what could she do? 'She was a grass of mine, yes,' Suzie acknowledged. 'I'd asked her to pick through the Twins' rubbish bins out the back of the flats where they lived.'

'So they had a reason to top her?'

'They had a good reason. I feel . . . I couldn't tell you how I feel about it. Empty . . . I'm responsible . . .'

'We're all responsible, heart. The bloody war's responsible. It's a bugger, heart.' Pause, 'Any idea who did her?' Turn on a sixpence Tommy could.

'Obviously one of the Twins' people. Top of the list would be Cresswell Smith.'

'Why?'

'Cresswell used to be a sailmaker. His father ran a ship's chandler's business and taught him the trade. Old Tatty had her lips sewn up with a sailmaker's needle. Twins getting eloquent all of a sudden.'

'And Cresswell's now gone to the great sailmaker in the sky. Did *he* know Harvey?'

'Must have done. But Harvey's supposed to have the dope

258

on Little Nell from someone. He told us that there were Tommy guns hidden in the Lexington Street house where we went, found him dead.'

'Harvey the omniscient,' Dandy Tom said pointedly.

'He threatened me since I last saw you,' she told him. 'I couldn't prove it but I'm sure he knows about me. Someone's talked.' She suddenly wondered about Brian and Molly Abelard, so she took the plunge, it was difficult enough talking to Tommy on the telephone anyway. 'Did you know that Molly and Brian are having a gallop round the park?'

'They are? Really?' A drop of jealousy? Molly was Tommy's biggest fan.

'Definitely, and no Mrs Abelard was admitted to Dulwich Hospital.'

'Really? Oh, naughty Molly.' Distant. 'Ah well.' Pause, then, 'Your statements, heart? Stand by them, do you? Get up in court and swear to them? On oath?'

'Of course.' Naturally. Didn't he trust her anymore? Not for the first time she thought, Lawks, if he knew he'd have no reason to trust me.

'Big part of our case against Toe, your evidence.'

'It's about all you've got against Toe.'

'No. No, not quite all. Young Sybil has things to say.' He told her that Sybil Harris had owned to seeing Harvey with the Twins on many occasions. Saying they were close. 'Described them as being thick as thieves. Bit of a cliché but good stuff all the same.' Then, 'You're absolutely certain about Molly and Brian?' Harping on it. Molly on his mind, she thought and a scrap from a tune went through her head, 'Molly on the Shore' – she thought it was by Percy Grainger who collected folk tunes.

'Hundred and fifty percent, Chief.' She was very firm, only called him Chief when they were alone if she wanted to get his attention. In the Squad they all called him Chief, mark of respect. She could see him at the other end, in his office on the fourth floor at New Scotland Yard with the framed old 'Wanted' posters and front pages from the *Police Gazette* on the walls.

'Ah well,' he said again. 'All things betray thee, who betrayest Me.'

'What Tommy?'

'"Hound of Heaven", heart. Francis Thompson. Christian poem, "Hound of Heaven". Jesuits used to beat it into us.'

'When will you know?' she asked. 'When'll you know definitely?'

'Know what?'

'Know when you're going to feel Harvey's collar.'

'Tonight. Count on it, heart. And stay clear of him. If by chance he *has* got wind of you being the channel to me . . . Well. Death too good for you, his view.' He left it trailing in the air, floating off, and she thought, Yes, and it would be your view if you knew what I'd been up to. Stupid, stupid girl, Suzie.

'I'll try, Tommy.' Her little voice.

'Watch your back, heart. My love.'

'I love you, Tommy.' Oh my God, what have I done? *Tommy we have to talk.* Do we? she wondered. What is it? Confusion swamping her. Was it because she was so damn young and inexperienced? A couple of days in the orbit of Fordham O'Dell; Fordy O'Dell; Hawk Eye O'Dell; O'Dell o' the Dell; she could hear the young pilots' voices chanting his nicknames last year in a pub. A few hours with him, Suzie, and there you are, listening, and looking at Fordy with eyes all out of kilter wearing rose-coloured spectacles. And now, dear heaven, what was she thinking of?

Suzie, bewildered, went to the bathroom and lay for an hour or so in her bath, warm and safe, surrounded with sweet-smelling water. She'd always done this when she wanted to think, make up her mind: spent afternoons during her disoriented teen years lying in a bath, topping it up with warm water, letting cold out putting hot in; had been known to consume toast, even sandwiches, while lying there working out what was true about life, and what was not, and she was doing it again now. It used to be her equivalent of doing 'he loves me, he loves me not' with the petals of a giant daisy. She got out, shook herself like a dog and dried herself with a big rough towel, one of the towels that her mum used to take on holiday.

Finally she put on a long crêpe de Chine nightgown,

luxurious, and curled up in bed; couldn't settle, so went out into the kitchen, put on the kettle and filled a hot-water bottle, had a cheese sandwich. The days were getting as cold as the nights now as Christmas loomed. Tommy at Christmas, he was taking her to the family seat, Kingscote Grange. Christmas in Gloucestershire. Going to be with the lord of the manor – the young master anyway – doing all those lovely Christmas things, being Santa for the estate children, being at the carol service, welcoming the Waits, putting up the tree in the great hall, bringing in the Yule log: Suzie had a great imagination fuelled by fiction. She pulled Tommy's leg about his duties at the country seat: flogging the peasants she called it.

She curled up warm with the hot-water bottle and sank into a drowse, not a real sleep because the question kept revolving in her mind: Why the idiocy with Fordy? She was an immature baggage who had set herself up with Fordy because she wanted a change, needed an adventure and had got in over her head, drowning in the shallows of emotion she thought with great drama. She thought in purple passages when she wanted drama and it was as necessary to her as air.

She wished hard that she was married to Tommy, it would make so much difference, she thought. In love with the idea of love she imagined. The old 'Room Five Hundred and Four' syndrome. Dorothy Careless, she remembered, she was the singer who'd recorded it.

That seventh heaven on the old fifth floor.

Slowly she sank into a deep, dreamless sleep. Like Jesus at Christmas.

Porky Pine was over near South Audley Street in the flat going through the last bits and pieces with Charlie and Connie Balvak.

'Can't be just a coincidence, Percy having so many people over here, place is teeming with them. I seen several last night and I seen three more this morning, lad called Parker, Phil Brewer, punchy looking geezer, walks with his head cocked on one side, and Martin Fee, Scotch, I think, little tough fellow use to help Florrie Findlator count the money. Got a cauliflower ear.'

261

'Well,' Connie said, deadpan. 'If they're thick on the ground you'd better offer them a job. Many hands make light work.'

'I might even do that,' Porky said with a grin.

'You seen anything of them three builders?' Charlie asked.

'Neither hide nor hair of them.' Shake of the head. His mum used to say that, he remembered: haven't seen your father in three years, neither hide nor hair of him.

'Well, keep looking. And you're clear about tonight? I want her so bloody frightened that she'll pick up her skirts and run from the West End, but I don't want her badly harmed. Know what I mean?'

'She'll pick up her skirts alright. It'll be her worst bad dream ever.'

'And you've chosen wisely, the blokes, I mean.'

'Got three of the heaviest, horniest men on the manor,' Porky grinned, thinking, 'and we've got a special an' all.'

Out on the darkening streets again, Porky turned over the Twins' plan in his mind, made sure he had every eventuality covered. Slammer Hammond, with Jock Barty and Freddie were going to be at Pay-21 by six o'clock, inside, having a drink, so that he could walk in just before the Twins arrived to confront Joe Chalk and set him up with a deal. Not enough room in the place to swing a cat, but if necessary they'd swing Joe Chalk. Then on to the Golden Fleece by prior arrangement. Last, up to Sherwood Street to Mona's Garden owned by a little Ikey called Abe Green who would be easy meat, they reckoned. Flash Stan said, 'Hold a leg of pork in front of him he would even sign the pledge.'

It was miserable out, cold and drizzling, already starting to get dark: when Double British Summertime ended, last weekend in October, it started to get dusky in the evening, not as bad as it used to do when it went from Summertime to winter, back an hour, but now they had Summertime the year round and *double* Summertime from end of March. Porky missed Double British Summertime. He walked slowly, keeping his eyes open along the streets, saw the kerbstones with their white dashes; soon it would be blackout and he'd need his torch, two pieces of tissue screwed under the glass.

Porky went into the Blue Posts pub, top of Berwick Street,

already crowded in the public bar. The pubs did a roaring trade in the early part of the evening. On a Saturday people went in around half five and stayed an hour, maybe hour and a half, people from the market, by seven most of them would be gone and then it was just the casual trade. But by then most of the beer was gone as well. Some days there was beer, some days there wasn't.

He looked around, moving his head, peering sideways and over people's heads. Crammed close to the bar were Colin Combes and Phil Brewer, 'Crazy' Colin and 'Hoppy' Brewer. Talking animatedly, laughing, tipping back their pint glasses, enjoying themselves even though they were a long way from home.

Porky smiled and went off in their direction, sashaying his shoulders, cutting a swathe through the drinking, chattering crowd, all seeking a little distance from reality with the aid of alcohol, Porky creeping up on them until he was directly behind the pair.

'Just the people I'm looking for,' he put one large hand on Colin's left shoulder and the other on Hoppy's right, pulling them closer together and encircling them.

'How are you?' he asked. 'You don't look pleased to see me, and I came to offer you jobs over this side of the river: double what you're getting from Percy.'

Colin Combes, swivelled his head and gave Porky a sinister grin, sly and unpleasant, his lip curled back and his eyes freezing cold. 'We already got new jobs over here, Porky,' he half whispered. 'And you'll soon be out of business I'm told. On your bike.'

'Yeah, on your bike,' added 'Hoppy' Brewer, baring his teeth, for a second like an animal, so that Porky thought he was going to get bitten.

Then Colin Combes lifted his right hand, fingers bent like a claw, grabbed Porky round the wrist, tight and painful, a vice on his arm, the man's breath evil-smelling and his face pushed close to Porky, eyes like chips of ice. 'Get your fucking hand off me, Pine,' he hissed. 'Then when you've done that, get the hell away from me and sling your hook. Do something with yourself. Disappear.'

Porky stood there nodding, as though agreeing to everything. 'Be well, Colin,' he said and shrugged his way out, no good arguing with a bloke like that. In his head he was planning to kill Colin Combes. He was also wondering what the man had meant, 'We already got new jobs over here, and you'll soon be out of business.'

On his way from the Blue Posts to Dean Street, to meet the lads in the French House, Porky stopped off at a telephone kiosk to phone Charlie Balvak, he had been so affected by Combes.

'Take no notice of him, Pork,' Charlie said after Porky had told him about the aggression and the words used. 'You know what he's like: the great I am. That's why we call him 'Crazy' Colin. Always wants to be part of some mystery play. Forget about it, ain't worth bothering about.' *Bovvering abaht.*

Yes, well, Porky thought, it was easy for Charlie to say – or Connie, for that matter, whom he heard parroting away in the background as Charlie spoke on the dog.

Something still wasn't right, he could feel it in the air, all round him. Were the bombers going to come again tonight? The feeling was like in the worst of the Blitz, that sense of not knowing if you'd see the dawn again. Worrying. It was an itch that needed scratching. He was concerned. Seriously worried.

So he thought as he headed to the French House, in Dean Street, with all its pictures of boxers on the walls, great bare barn of a place where the lads were sitting at a table nursing half pints of mild ale.

'I told you no drinking beforehand,' Porky said, well annoyed that they hadn't obeyed his orders.

Billy Joy-Joy, part Chink, said, 'S'awright Porky, just the half.'

'Well, you mind it is, lad. All of you, only the half.'

They were well set-up lads, Billy Joy-Joy, Gerald Moke, with the scar over his left eye he got in the boxing ring, and Harry Seymour with his shock of red hair. All of them had wide shoulders and plenty of muscle where they wanted it an' all. Moke and Seymour would be in HM Forces come February unless he got the Twins to do something about it. Be a prize for them.

264

Porky went over and had a talk with the barman, ordered himself a pint of bitter, it was okay for him to have a drink but not for the three lads who had heavy work to do before the night was over.

Never could be too certain, so he went back to the table and went through everything one more time. 'You speak, then you have to speak gruff,' he told them. 'Gruff enough to put the fear of God in her. After it's over, if you want to put anything else in her that's up to you.'

Billy Joy-Joy sniggered and Porky went off to meet the others at Pay-21.

It was still light when the Ghoul woke up and thought to himself that this was odd, couldn't remember that side of himself catching him unawares in daylight. He was a Ghoul in daylight now and he was usually only a Ghoul after dark, like vampires, only vampires didn't exist. Vampires were figments. Not so Ghouls. Then he remembered what he was doing that night and knew why the two sides of him were coming together, surrounding him making him twice as dangerous.

There would be dead bodies tonight, at least one, possibly two, maybe more. Depended how things worked out.

Twenty-One

J oe Chalk was a big fellow, an abundance of fat straining his suit jacket, his shirt collar almost choking him. He had big hands resting on the bar, and a wide open face. The face was a bit of a swindle because Joe Chalk was far from being open in his dealings. On the other hand he was as wide as they came. You went up to Joe, he'd always greet you with this wide grin, his hands about two feet apart, welcoming you into his world. This was not to be trusted. Joe Chalk was indeed a wide boy who had reached his pinnacle: owning and running two small, seedy clubs, both of which were dying on their feet for lack of funds.

Joe had come into Pay-21 early because he was training a new barman, bloke called Eastlee not blessed with much common sense. That didn't matter to Joe Chalk because Eastlee came cheap and there was really very little for him to learn.

Porky met up with Flash Stan directly outside the door of Pay-21, huddled up to a pair of downmarket girls damp with the drizzle. Porky was more than usually concerned because he thought he'd caught a glimpse of the three builders, Dave, Dick and Derek, Trinity Building Co. as he'd crossed over Berkeley Square, where that nightingale squawked all the bloody time. Saw the Trinity Building Co. Dave, Dick and Derek cross in front of him in the murk, heading towards Regent Street. Gave him a nasty turn because he tried to catch up with them, but when he got up there, in Regent Street, they had gone. He thought of the *Marie Celeste* and the ghosts in the Tower of London, their heads tucked underneath their arms, and wondered if this was a case of a further apparition he could talk about. Ghosts and spectres of old London being one of his best subjects. Perhaps they, the Trinity Builders, had really died in some accident and were now doomed to walk the earth dragging along the chains they'd forged in life. Only he hadn't seen any chains, let alone heard them.

'Everyone here, Stan?' Porky's eyes were on the swivel, looking out for the Twins.

Flash Stan's response was to nod at the door, signifying that everything was hunky-dory. 'Listen,' Stan said. 'I'm bloody glad Chalk is in there already. I was dreading having to go over to Waterloo and fetch him.' The plan had taken into account that Joe Chalk would possibly not be in the club at this time of the evening. In that case Stan and a couple of the boys were briefed to go over to the flat he shared with his wife and daughter on the other side of the river within minutes of Waterloo station.

'Get round the back then, mate. Just in case he takes fright when I lay the news on him.'

Flash gave a knowing nod, which Porky couldn't see because of the dusk coming down quickly now. Flash touched Porky on the shoulder and disappeared off into the gloom. Porky went inside and saw Joe Chalk, wide smile and all, while he explained matters to Eastlee – the girls always got champagne and punters could have anything they liked as long as it was whisky and soda. The whisky came by the thimble-full and the soda came from a large siphon, 'a big splash,' Joe told him. 'Drown it. The whisky's for show only, so the punter gets a taste.' The champagne was carbonated white wine that Joe Chalk bought from 'a little man in Walthamstow'. The little man had others who helped make the big – gallon-sized – carboys that were brought down full of carbonated wine at half-a-crown a time and sixpence back on the carboy. The wine was made in a disused factory by four men who had taught chemistry years ago and were now known as the Winos of Walthamstow. You could get forty or fifty glasses of champagne out of a carboy, so it was a reasonable profit: ten pounds for the first drink, 'after that it gets less expensive, darling,' June-Mary Humbolt, Joe Chalk's waitress at Pay-21, told the punters. She didn't tell them the second drink was eight pounds. It was *very* expensive but if a punter complained they would tell him that this was the West End so you had to expect

West End prices. They didn't tell him that drinks were cheaper at the Savoy, or even the Ritz.

Tonight, at around six fifteen, Joe Chalk was pleased: already he had three people in, each sitting with one of the girls and each paying his ten pounds initial drinks charge and the girls were saying, 'Come on, darling, drink up it's a party. Let's have a good time. There's going to be a cabaret shortly.' The cabaret being aged Andy Evans playing songs like 'Red Sails in the Sunset' and 'T'was on the Isle of Capri that I Found her'. Andy was heavy-handed with the keyboard and quavering with the songs, which didn't make for a sophisticated performance. To tell the truth, you could get better in a knees-up of a Saturday night in practically any other London boozer having a singsong. Most London boozers had much higher standards and boasted that their booze-ups showed the spirit of London that defeated the Nazis in the Blitz. 'We can take it,' they all said.

That the three punters looked familiar didn't worry Joe Chalk. He was really only interested in the cash turnover.

Slammer Hammond, Jock Barty and Frenzied Freddie Nolan each sat with what was euphemistically called a hostess, these hostesses picking up money for every punter they brought into the club.

'Come on, darling,' Cynthia – Cyn for short – was saying to Slammer Hammond. 'What you waiting for? Get another drink in, I'm parched.'

Slammer said, 'Right. I'm all for a party,' doing his punchy move, nodding the head, punching air.

'Well, get the bloody drinks in,' Cyn pressed. 'Whatcher bring me 'ere for in the first place if you're not going to drink.'

'Because the night is young and you're so beautiful,' the Slammer chanted, deadpan and on a single note. Dead romantic.

Jock Barty and Freddie Nolan had hostesses called Annie and Hilda respectively. Annie wore her hair in one large Victory Roll in front while Hilda wore hers short and would rather have been a Waaf. Neither could be called stunningly attractive, but in the blackout you had to take what was around.

At this point in the war there wasn't that much choice because the best talent was either higher priced or in HM Forces doing their bit, which was exactly where Hilda wanted to be.

As Porky walked through the door, Annie was saying to Jock Barty, 'Just buy me one more drink, darling, then we can go back to my place later.'

And Jock was replying, 'You couldn't anaesthetize a flea with this pissy drink.' Charming.

'Oh, it's you, is it, Porky?' Joe Chalk said as Porky walked up to the bar, saying it nicely, with the wide welcoming smile and the hands in the 'hail fellow well met' position, looking like one of those saints in a stained-glass church window getting ready to receive the bird on fire coming down with the heavenly host poised over their heads.

'So what can I do for you, old chum?' says Joe Chalk while Porky turns from the bar and grins at Jock Barty, 'Jock, nip orf outside and keep the punters at bay.'

Jock picks Annie up from his knees where she'd been sitting and puts her down in a chair, where she makes a wailing noise. 'Stop that caterwauling or I'll thump yer,' says Jock heading resolutely to the door, obeying orders.

'What's going on?' asks Joe Chalk, looking bewildered, as well he might.

'You've got important visitors any minute,' Porky informed him, and Joe Chalk looked furtive, his eyes sliding about all over the place.

Porky said, 'And if you try to get out the back, I've got someone out there and I'll nail your hands to the bar if I have to.'

Joe Chalk looked at him and knew he meant it. 'Who's coming to see me then?'

'Wait and see.'

'I might not want to see whoever it is.'

'Whoever *they are*,' Porky corrected and the Salvation Army started up outside with their band, the tambourines, everything, the rank and file singing Christmas Carols – 'Once in Royal David's City', the girls in their bonnets doing a descant.

Porky turned to Frenzied Freddy and told him to chuck a fiver at the Salvation Army, ask 'em to move on. But it still took the last three verses of 'Once in Royal David's' and a big finish with a flourish on the tambourines before they left.

After that the Twins came in, dressed in their camel-hair coats and trilby hats, Jacky Russell and Fast Eddie Ellis bodyguarding and Collie King in the rear acting on behalf of Sly Sid Silverman, who was getting set up to have dinner at Tosca and talk to Carlo Falconetti, just as Charlie had told him, taking Blondie Beauchamp with him because he thought she looked as though she needed more flesh on her bones, though she was also a fabulous lay and much requested by the sophisticated end of Syd's private clientele.

As soon as Joe Chalk saw the Twins he began to look more furtive than ever, realizing he was surrounded by a horde of gangsters and heavy men: people he tried to stay away from because all he was interested in was money and he never had any.

'Over here, I think, Joe,' Charlie pointed to a table at the far end of the little room. 'Have a nice little talk, eh?'

'Nice little talk,' said Connie, reaching out as if to usher Joe to the table.

Joe Chalk had the nous to offer them a drink which they both refused, 'Seldom touch it except special occasions,' Charlie told him.

'Better off without it,' Connie said. *Better orf wivvout i'*.

They handed cigarettes round and Jacky Russell lit them in turn like a flunkey.

'See Joe,' Charlie began, 'you've got a nice little site here. Not big, I grant you, but pleasant and has what they call potential. I mean it's a nice area.'

'Nice area,' repeated Connie. 'Nice area and you've got some nice restaurants and cafés around, like that lovely place up by the Lex Garage.'

'They all close up when it gets dark,' Joe had a whine in his voice. 'In the old days, I lived with my mum in Kingley Street and there were really good places, international, lights on, stayed open till late, sold any food you asked for, all sorts. At night lots of flares and things, naked flames, naphtha torches I remember before the war, at Christmas time, it was lovely. Shops lit-up, decorated.'

'Yeah, well, Joe, we thought as how we could do you a favour.'

'Oh yes?' Joe going all sneaky again, recalling how the Twins had been bombed out of their three prime places and not by Hitler either.

'Yes, Joe. We can give this place some class. Give it a lick of paint, get some high-class girls in, allow the punters to have a couple of real drinks now and again . . .'

'. . . altogether change the ambience,' Connie said and got a strange look from his brother.

Charlie said, 'See, Joe, there's sunink else you got to keep in mind. Real important. The Yanks are in it now, and we've got some privileged information.'

'Yeah,' Connie said. 'Pukka gen.' Charlie thought he'd have to stop Connie using all this Raff slang, pukka gen, wizard prang, all that kind of stuff.

'Next month, early in '42, the Yanks're coming.'

'Over there, over there,' Connie began to sing and Charlie told him to dowse the chanting.

'Listen,' Charlie was bright and full of energy, confident. 'You know what it means, Joe?'

'More trade?'

'Just a lot. There'll be rivers of silver flowing down these streets and the girls won't believe they're sitting on assets of thousands of pounds. See, Joe, they'll want entertaining when they arrive in London: strange city, far away from home, no Ma and Pa, or wife to keep them in line. What're they going to want?'

'Booze and pussy,' Joe Chalk gave his wide smile.

'Give the man a prize,' Connie chortled.

'They're going to want it like men lost in the desert'll want an oasis. Hey, good name for this place, the Oasis, how about that? And there's an added bonus I only just thought of.'

'Yes?' Joe was really interested now.

'Added bonus. The Yanks won't understand our currency, eh? They'll be sorting out the shillings, tanners, half-crowns, threepenny bits. They won't understand tanners, bobs, half-a-crack, two and six, five eleven three.' This last meant five shillings eleven pence and three farthings, which in turn meant

271

a halfpenny – pronounced ha'pny – and a farthing. Money could get very confusing because some older people still referred to a crown, which was five bob or two half-crowns, and the guinea was still much used – one pound one shilling.

'Farthings,' Connie went to the wrong end of the scale.

Charlie said, 'Pound notes, ten bob notes, when they get to the five quid notes they'll go barmy, won't know what's hit 'em. They'll be so confused they'll be giving out a fiver for a pint and not expect change.'

Charlie's grin split his face in two. 'We can start straight off, Joe. Take all the worries off you're head, put in our own people and give you back a whole third of the takings. In oncers, no cheques, cash on the nail. You think about it. You'll be getting just as much as this place is earning now, the take'll rise very quickly.'

'And we guarantee no nastiness,' Connie said with a beatific smile. 'I mean you imagine what dangers are around at this end of the market.'

'I haven't had any bother up to now . . .' Joe Chalk said, the sentence trailing off as he saw the possibilities ahead. You could bet that if he turned down the Twins' munificent offer there'd be all kinds of shit flying in his direction. A person could get his legs broken not going along with an offer from the Twins.

'You never know, Joe, you never know.' Charlie shook his head gravely. 'I've heard of terrible things happening to clubs . . .'

'Like getting burned down?' Joe asked cheekily and got the look from both Charlie and Connie.

'Yeah,' Connie said. 'Some places get really done over, people getting their arms and legs smashed.'

Good lad, Charlie thought. His brother was starting to learn the business besides thumping and kicking people to death. 'You gotta see, Joe, that this is all in your interest. You'll get a tidy sum once a week, like I said maybe more'n that you're making now, and we'll have the risk and responsibility. I can't see how you could turn it down. No bother. Think about it, Joe old son. There's no hurry. Ten minutes should do it. Just tell one of us as soon as you've made up your mind.' And he went off to fire Eastlee, the bartender, and tell June-Mary Humbolt she would have to smarten up her ways if she wanted to stay on under the new management.

'It ain't fair,' Eastlee said. 'Joe Chalk promised me the job; said he'd even get it fixed as a reserved occupation.'

'Shut it or I'll shut it for you, and reserve your occupation down the crematorium,' snapped Porky Pine.

They left Joe Chalk at the table and he tried to get June-Mary Humbolt's attention – nothing he'd like better than a glass of lemonade. He felt hot and sticky, nearly bursting out of his tight shirt collar. After a few minutes, Charlie came back to the table.

Joe Chalk said, 'I've got no option, have I?'

'I knew you'd see it as a golden opportunity, Joe. Hey, Connie, we're going to be partners,' and he drew a thick wad of paper, folded lengthways, out of the inside pocket of his suit. 'You have to sign in three places.' Charlie smiled happily. 'There, there and there,' pointing.

Joe Chalk felt the strain on his neck and ran a finger round his collar before he leaned forward to start signing.

'Porky, come on, make yourself useful, witness Joe's signature.'

'What's Brotherhood Associates?' Joe asked.

'Just a little company me and Connie have. All nice and legal. You're signing a contract to say we're partners. You now own one-third of Pay-21 or whatever if we change the name. Congratulations, Joe. Many congratulations.'

Joe Chalk felt he really might have done himself a favour until Charlie said, 'Now, Joe, I think we ought to go to your other place. What is it, the Golden Fleece? Let's go and sort that one out.'

Connie said, 'I wonder what Hitler's doing today? I feel full of power, just like that man, Adolf,' and he began singing loudly:

> 'Hitler has only got one ball,
> Goering has two but very small,
> Himmler is very simmler
> But poor old Goebbels has no balls at all.'

273

All to the tune of *Colonel Bogey*, to which he usually sang, 'Bollocks, and the same to you.'

Suzie got in to West End Central just after six thirty, and looked over the papers on her desk. Nothing important, so she began to map out her evening. Then Cheesy Fowles came in.

'Big Toe went off at five,' he told her. 'Got to take his wife to some party in Wimbledon or something. Left a message for you, Sarg. Now what was it? Wrote it down. There you go.' He changed his voice to the one he used for reading out loud. 'Would Sergeant Mountford please see Mr Battescombe as soon as she gets in. That's it, Sarge. Got it?'

'Certainly have, Cheese,' and she was off to DCS Battescombe's office down the hall: Sammy Batter 'em, as the lads called him, only he wasn't there. Ruby Newman, the WPC on Night Clerk duties was: sitting there, queen of all she surveyed.

'Sarn't Mountford, I got a message for you.' She looked up perky and full of beans. 'Mr Battescombe says you've got to nip up Old Compton Street after twenty-two hundred hours. Not before, he was most specific about that. They've had reports that kids have been breaking into the old St Ursula's Scout Hut: going to be some kind of club, been done up.'

'And he wants me to sort the kids out?'

'Thinks you're the very person to do it.' She didn't say that she'd got all this second-hand from Detective Chief Inspector Harvey – Big Toe Harvey – told her to say it came direct from Mr Battescombe. 'Don't forget, Ruby, I didn't say a word. If she thinks she's being instructed by me she won't go.'

'Right, later on then, okay.' Suzie Mountford thought of the long low hut, squeezed between buildings at the far end of Old Compton Street, owned by Carlo Falconetti. Carlo probably went to the top, to Sammy, didn't want any damage done in his precious new venture. She'd help Carlo out later on. Get her out of the CID Room after ten tonight. She'd have to wrap up warm.

Sly Sid Silverman came into Tosca with Blondie Beauchamp on his arm, Sid wearing his double-breasted overcoat and a suit in heavy grey material, beautifully tailored, a light-blue shirt from a place that did Turnbull & Asser lookalikes at a quarter the cost, grey silk tie looked Sulka until you peered closely: Sharp Sid Silverman. Took off his grey homburg displaying his iron-grey hair, smooth, as though someone had ironed it straight back from his forehead. Blondie Beauchamp looking as if she'd spent the afternoon in a beauty shop being washed, pressed and ironed, wearing a little black number with her waist nipped in and her tits on show under the thin gauzy material, would give people the impression that she was a model, not the expensive whore she truly was.

The waiters gathered round and Carlo Falconetti came over, glad to make his acquaintance and how good of him, *Dottore*, to do his restaurant the honour and when would he like to discuss this special dinner party he was planning? Sid told him later, and they sat down to study the menu, each with a copy in big leather folders, the menu about twelve pages thick.

'I bet most of this is off,' Sid muttered, and Carlo, standing near said haughtily that everything was on.

'How d'you do it, Carlo? I bet the Twins supply you with meat.'

Carlo Falconetti shook his head. 'No, but we have equally good suppliers, Mr Silverman. It's the secret, knowing you're going to get the meat and vegetables you need every week: meat and veg that people find difficult to put their hands on, what with the Ration Book ruling almost everything.' Sid gave him what was known as an 'old fashioned look', then asked what minestrone was, said he'd have that followed by spaghetti in a tomato sauce – 'Just a small taste of the Italy we used to know before it became tainted by Mussolini,' Carlo said – then the game pie and a salad. 'Right time of the year for game pie,' Sid remarked refusing to have the menu removed. 'Want to study this. See if it's a work of fiction,' he grinned.

Blondie Beauchamp said she'd have what Mr Silverman was having, 'and an ice cream to round it off.'

'You don't order the sweet till you've finished the main nosh,' Sid told her, loftily ordering a bottle of the house red – 'That is real wine, innit, Carlo?' – before going back to his menu studies.

He asked Blondie, 'You think these dishes they got are real? I mean what's this, *Osso buco*, that a real dish? *Spinach gnocchi*, what's that when it's at home? Or *Fungi Gougere*, could be just made up to look good on the menu.'

Sly Sid was sophisticated, but that didn't go very deep where food was concerned. These war years were just laying bare facts about other countries, what food they liked. For people like Sly Sid the epitome was fish and chips, boiled beef and carrots, brown Windsor soup, Sunday roast beef and Yorkshire pudding. He used to boast that of a Sunday he and his missus would have roast beef – which he got hold of through having connections – and he'd put on the gramophone, play the 78 r.p.m. records of Beethoven's Fifth Symphony. 'It's good, that's the English way: Beethoven and roast beef.' Sid Silverman didn't spot the incongruity.

'What's gnocchi?' he asked. 'What the hell is gnocchi? You're a girl, Blondie, you tell me about this.'

Blondie leaned back in her chair pulled up close to the table. 'Sid. I've made it a rule in life, from being a child, never to know much about food. If you know about food, sooner or later someone'll want you to cook, and before you know it you'll be cooking for every Tom, Dick and Harry.'

They liked the soup. 'They call this Minestrone, it's just like the veg soup my old Mum use to make,' Sid nodded. 'Just like it, with a bit of spaghetti chopped up in it. Really good. My condiments to the chef, Carlo.'

Carlo had just come back to their table. He bowed his thanks and said there was someone to see Sid. 'To see me? Who? Not Charlie?'

'Coming down the stairs now, Mr Silverman.'

Sly Sid looked up and his jaw dropped because walking towards him was someone he knew the Twins had been searching for. He half rose, as if about to engage the man in some physical violence, then subsided into his chair again as Newcastle Brown came lolloping towards him with his broad lantern smile.

'Why Sidney, bonny lad. It's nice to see you, man.'

'They're searching for you, the Twins. And the Law an' all.'

'Why aye man. I'm hiding out, back for one night only by special request. Come to give you some advice.'

'Oh?'

'Aye, sound advice an' all. If I were you, I'd keep away from the Twins tonight. Keep out o' the way of the Twins and anyone connected with them, you want to look out, man. Think of yourself.'

'Why should I look out?' Sidney now getting disturbed. 'I've always been a true supporter of the Twins. They've been good to me, I've been loyal to them.'

'Just marking your card, Sidney. This might be the time when you turn your back on matters connected with the Twins.'

'You're a bloody murderer,' Sid bridled. 'Cresswell Smith's down to you, and that copper.'

'That's as may be, bonny lad. But tonight sees everything change. Ah'm trying to help you, man. Don't go near a telephone either.' *Doan't go neah.* He was smiling his broad lantern smile and, to tell the truth, Matt Brown had always liked Sly Sid, liked his style. Now he was lost for words.

The big Geordie nodded and said, 'In a minute or two, Sid, there's people coming down those stairs at the back, some of them you'd never expect to see. You have a canny evening now, Sid, and don't be an idiot.' He stood up, said, 'Have a nice time, hinny,' to Blondie Beauchamp and turned to leave with the men now coming down the stairs and passing through the restaurant on their way out.

'Fuck me,' Sid said as he saw the three men, Dave, Dick and Derek – the builders. Then, 'Bloody hell,' as he clocked the next one down and saw Carlo Falconetti join the group and walk with them out through the front door, looking businesslike.

'You'd like your spaghetti now?' asked Beryl Falconetti. 'Safer you just stay here and eat your dinner, eh Mr Silverman?'

Sly Sid nodded, almost imperceptibly. He may be a bit of a prick at times, but he was no fool. Knew when someone was marking his card.

'When we've finished our meal, Blondie, how about a trip back to my place?' Telling, not really asking.

'Why not indeed. Was that who I think it was, went out just now?'

'I doubt it. Didn't see anyone go out. Neither did you, hinny,' copying Newcastle Brown.

They both laughed.

Twenty-Two

Fifteen, twenty minutes earlier they were preparing to leave the Golden Fleece, some haggling eventually led to a three-quarters/quarter split between the Twins and Joe Chalk. The split in favour of the Twins. That had taken some negotiating with Chalk going on and on about how the Golden Fleece, which was even smaller than Pay-21, had been his insurance, keep him in his old age. 'I planned to put someone good in to manage the place, he'd bring me the lion's share every Friday night, six o'clock on the nail.'

'Well, we're going to do that, Joe. You'll get a quarter of everything,' Charlie told him just like he told him before, about Pay-21. 'Quarter of the whole thing, including the dropsy. That could be way more'n you're getting now, at this moment.'

'Terrible things could happen here,' Connie was examining the locks on the door. 'These locks'd start waving flags of truce the minute you got within a yard of them with a set of pick-locks. Just breathe on them and they unlock. No contest.'

'Oh, I don't know. I really don't know,' Chalk wailed and that would start the arguments again. Charlie saying how fair the deal was and Connie going on about the place being a fire trap. 'One match,' he'd say. 'One match would do it and it would be goodbye Golden Fleece,' except Connie pronounced it Golden Fleas which annoyed Joe Chalk. 'Like a cinder box,' Connie said, 'it would go up like a cinder box,' and Charlie would hiss, 'Tinder, Con. It's *tinder* box.'

Connie would say, 'Whatever.'

Porky Pine was clock-watching because he was conscious about his next appointment with the three lads who were going to put the frighteners on WDS Mountford, everything

279

organized to a timetable better than GWR or LNER. So he was pleased to note that, as arranged, Flash Stan Page had followed up from the back of Pay-21 and wandered around keeping his eyes open. Slammer Hammond, Jock Barty and Freddie Nolan had drifted off, presumably to Mona's Garden, get their feet under the table so that Flash Stan could escort the Twins up there with Fast Eddie Ellis and Jacky Russell.

What Porky didn't know was the fact that Flash Stan had been nobbled. The day before, he had been on his way from Camford, where he still lived with this nice girl he'd saved from a life of prostitution, he thought, when he came up from the Tube in the Dilly, walking up on to the corner next to Swan & Edgar's, when he ran slap-bang into a posse, consisted of four people worked for Percy Hodges across the river. Porous Pat Janson, Nutty Fryer, Willie Watts and Cliff Sweeney, big fellows, well set-up and sprauncy with it, wouldn't take no for an answer and smash your face in soon as look at you.

They crowded around Flash Stan, patting him on the back, glad-handing him, telling him how great it was to see him again and how unexpected. These sentiments were quite obviously insincere, and would have made a nun blush with shame, but it gave the lads enough time to look as though they were meandering towards a couple of taxis that Nutty Fryer had hailed just as if he didn't know they were being steered around by Pete and Angelo Gurney, a pair of the best wheel men in the business.

Before he could say, 'Jack-the-lad,' Flash Stan was being driven to a prime location in the Tottenham Court Road, back room in an empty house, bare but for a couple of rickety chairs and a few drops of blood on the wall next to the rear window. In this room several people quietly explained to him what was going on: that the Twins were the object of a take-over bid. 'The people taking over would kill for their territory in Soho,' Porous Pat told him. 'Quite literally and you know what? The Twins are soft. No shooters, nothing. We think they're going down and the take-over people've got most of Percy Hodges' boys with them on loan, sale or return, if you know what I mean. We should know because we *were* Percy's boys, on his payroll. Now we're on a new payroll, double money and running back and forth across the river. Every day going to and fro and getting good gelt.'

This talk convinced Flash Stan on two counts. First he should do as he was told, don't listen to anyone else, just do exactly what they told him; second he would be dead if he didn't, if for no other reason than two of them – Cliff Sweeney and Willie Watts – had bloody great shooters, very clean, well-oiled and dangerous looking.

So as soon as Porky began nudging the Twins and saying he had to leave and the Twins had another appointment, Stan sidled quietly into the storeroom behind the bar where there was a telephone. He dialled a local number that happened to belong to Carlo Falconetti. 'It's Stan,' he said into the mouthpiece of the old sit-up-and-beg instrument, whispering, 'You were expecting me to ring. They're leaving in a few minutes, 'bout ten. Yes.' The job was done.

All that was left was for him to wait and see how strong the threat was to the Twins, knew he was doing the right thing but couldn't quite believe he was going to see the end of an era.

Charlie and Connie headed quietly out with their body-guards, Jacky Russell and Fast Eddie Ellis, Russell smoking this fat cigar just like Winston the PM – the blood, sweat and tears merchant they so admired – and Fast Eddie Ellis with his head almost permanently cocked to one side on account of the hearing problem, his right ear having been damaged in a fight, hit by a wine bottle. Good vintage though, a Côte d'Or '36.

The other lads, Slammer, Frenzied Freddie and Jock, had gone ahead, getting set up with girls at Mona's Garden.

Charlie and Connie were talking excitedly as Flash followed them along Lexington Street, up Brewer Street into Sherwood, where Charlie made some loud remark about Robin Hood – an old joke, 'They used to call me Robin Hood,' he crowed. They all joined in, 'Now they call me Robin bastard!' and everyone laughed, not because it was funny but because it was Charlie saying it.

The girls out trading in the dark streets shrank back into doorways as the cluster around the Twins plodded on its way to Mona's Garden, a small frontage straight off the street on the right.

Mona's Garden was a deceptive property, didn't look wide enough from the front, just like a narrow little two-up-two-down dwelling house. Inside it was a different matter: big main room, the club, originally three rooms, two rooms off it and another to the rear through big double doors; then there was the upstairs that Abe Green was just starting to convert into nookie rooms for the girls, rented out at five bob a bed; thought it would bring him a fortune – five bob for a half-hour.

They had told Abe to be there all evening, not to take any time off and Mona – Abe's daughter – was ordered to stay well clear, on no account to come near. 'We're expecting ructions,' her father had told her.

Slammer, Jock and Freddie were already settled with three girls, Laughing Nancy, Fancy Fiona and Lisa Leicester, sitting there at tables with drinks paid for but nobody tinkling the ivories or singing old 1939 songs. They were all set and ready, like a tableau, the kind they had down the Windmill in Great Windmill Street, except everyone had all their clothes on and there was a hint of tension and concern in the air. Truth was a few people already knew what could happen.

Almost as soon as the Twins and their entourage arrived, and Charlie greeted Abe – 'Abie, my friend, good to see you. You got a nice place here,' – the Salvation Army Band started up as if on cue. This time nobody told Freddie to drop them a fiver so they went on playing, 'While Shepherds Watched their Flocks by Night', playing it loudly and singing it like nobody's business. Fact was they'd been asked, with remuneration, to play out there very loud, drown any iffy noise, only the Sally Ann didn't know the reason.

'I hear you've taken over Joe Chalkie's places,' Abe Green, shook his head. 'Now I suppose you're expecting to take over mine.'

'At least hear us out, Abe,' Charlie told him. 'Would I do you down?'

'We plan a good, fair deal,' Connie said, and at that moment the big double doors at the back of the room flew open, just as the Salvation Army got to their well-rehearsed '*Glo-or-or-or-or-or-or-or-or-or-ria, in excelsis De-eh-eh-oh!*'

There was this little raised section, like a small stage when

282

you opened the double doors and Charlie actually gasped aloud when he saw Matt 'Newcastle' Brown flanked by the Trinity Building Co. – Dave, Dick and Derek – plus Collie King, who'd always been a Twins man, huge cauliflower ear and a broken nose he'd got in street fights years before.

'Evening, bonny lads,' said Newcastle with his wide lantern grizzly grin.

'You effing turncoat,' Charlie said and was mirrored by Connie saying something similar. 'I suppose you think you're going to push us out of Soho,' Connie said.

'Not me, bonny lad. Ah'm ganing back up Newcastle. There're others waiting for us to get out the way.' *Out the wey.* 'People better equipped to lead.' And for the first time they saw Carlo Falconetti step into the light as though he was in charge.

This was the point that Jacky Russell made his mistake, and there was no reason for him to do it: everyone could see the Tommy guns carried by Dave and Derek, plus the large automatic pistols in the hands of the others, including Matt Brown.

Perhaps Jacky really thought the weaponry was for decoration – after all he only had his little cosh, length of bicycle inner tube filled with sand and coins, that he had pulled out of his back pocket as he stepped forward, 'You treacherous buggers,' Jacky snarled at the group of men moving towards them and brandishing the cosh.

Matt Brown shot him in the face and some of his blood sprayed back over Connie, who made a little shrieking sound as Jacky went down flat on to his back, the body sliding a little with the force of the impact, like an animal slaughtered in an abattoir.

'Any more want to gan a couple of rounds with a forty-five bullet?' Matt Brown, still smiling, swept the room with the muzzle of his Colt. 'Fair take your breath away.'

Everyone went very quiet, the Twins and their people moving a few steps away, the girls slipping towards the back of the room, so that Matt had to warn them that there was a man outside ready to beat seven kinds of shit out of them if they tried to run. 'You're to stay here for the business meeting.'

So now everybody knew what it was about: a business meeting, nothing to get worried over.

Charlie and Connie both found themselves sitting down on the chairs vacated by Slammer Hammond and Freddie Nolan, who, together with Jock Barty, had done a sort of slinking movement to positions near the wall, and you'd have to be half daft and blind not to see that they, like almost everyone else, was waiting to line up on the side of whoever came out best. At the moment this looked like Carlo Falconetti, who stood looking happy, a little smile playing round his lips.

'I think we should take him into one of the side rooms,' Carlo nodded towards Jacky lying still and bloody in the middle of the room. 'It's a pity this had to happen, it was planned to be done with no violence.'

Fast Eddie, who had also been trying to look as though he was invisible, plodded forward, took hold of Jacky's wrists, flicking away the cigar clamped in Jacky's mouth, still smouldering though shredded into his face. Fast Eddie nodded, then tugged and pulled Jacky Russell through the door to his right, muttering something about getting a dodgy undertaker round, one they'd used before, Stiffy Sitwell, who ran a business over in Paddington. For a moment Charlie seemed to have lost his comprehension regarding the situation, and said aloud that he'd get Stiffy on the blower and set it up, while Abe Green was moaning on about cleaning the blood off the carpet. 'That's a good piece of carpet. Almost new.'

Under his breath Connie started to sing:

> '*Blood on the sideboard,*
> *Blood on the wall,*
> *And a great big puddle of blood on the floor.*'

'Stop the lamenting, Abe. I'm sure you'll get the carpet cleaned,' Matt Brown told him. Then, 'Let's get on, I haven't got all night you know.'

Carlo said no he hadn't because he was catching the night express back to Newcastle.

'You'll be looking behind you for the rest of your natural life,' Charlie said, eyes like broken glass in his head.

Connie said something about Newcastle rueing the day he ever took a step against the Balvaks, but Matt didn't seem at all worried.

'So, we've got an Eyetie running the manor now, have we?' Charlie really bitter and showing it.

'An Italian running the manor, no.' Carlo looked steadily at the Twins. 'No, not me. I only help a little. Chipped in, gave some advice. People been getting fed up with your greed. You've been taking too much from ordinary men and women who've nothing to do with the games you play. Good folk who live round here just want a bit of peace and quiet.'

'So who's going to step into the breach? I mean we can reorganize if you like, have a sit-down talk and take a democratic vote on how we should run things.'

'No. I'm afraid not,' the voice came from somewhere behind Carlo, whispering in through the dark, so that both Charlie and Connie felt ice running up the back of their necks.

'Who's buggering about?' Connie asked.

'You're fucking dead,' Charlie had recognized the voice, and Little Nell Bellman stepped from the shadows.

'You're fucking dead,' Charlie repeated.

'Not me,' the little man smiled, his lip curling in a sneer. 'Not me, Charlie. This is your problem, you don't look past the obvious. Nobody did, though I told you enough times.'

And Charlie got it.

My brother's a good eighteen months older than me yet we could be well mistaken for each other. Same lack of height, same quirky nonsense.

'Yes, Charlie. My brother, the eighth dwarf. Nasty. He was the one who was taken suddenly dead having his head removed from his body. Oh my God, didn't that make a mess, curtains, carpet, everything got blood all over, soaked.'

'He knows your business backwards, Charlie.' Carlo appeared to find this amusing. 'You were leaning on too many small people. People like me, trying to make an honest penny. Men and women doing an honest job, nothing to do with becoming involved in crime.'

'We never leaned on you, Carlo.'

'You were going to. Saw my club, Ursula's Place, as a potential gold mine, didn't you?'

'Yea, but we didn't do nothing about it,' Connie beginning to whine a little, getting concerned now about what they were going to do with him. Like many bullies, Connie didn't relish the thought of brutality and pain, let alone death.

'You didn't? What about Porky slamming my fingers in the door.'

'Just a warning, I expect.'

Charlie, livid, cleared his throat, hawked up and spat a great gobbet of phlegm on to Abe Green's precious carpet. 'You clever little bastard,' he said, the rage showing in his cracked glass eyes looking at Little Nell, and in the high colour of his cheeks and the twist of his mouth. 'You cunning little bugger. You went to all this trouble to get your hands on Balvak territory. What you do, Nell, lure your brother down here so you could cleave off his head in your sitting room, then go to ground making your plans?' He took a great laboured breath and as he did so, Little Nell laughed which made Charlie even angrier. 'And what you going to do about us, Nell? Eh, what you going to do with us because alive we'll never rest till we come back into this manor and screw you down in your coffin. You'll have to kill us first.'

Nell laughed again. 'All in good time, Charlie. I hadn't planned to do anything to you. Not just yet. Thought I'd let you leave peacefully, then, maybe next year, or the year after, I'd get it finished.' His little face crinkled with pleasure. Then a big grin, because it was all a big game to him and this showed, shining through his nasty face and the way he moved. 'Hey, Charlie, Connie, isn't this a bit dramatic? It's only business after all. We can do this in a civilized way surely.'

Charlie Balvak smiled, bitter aloes, wormwood and gall. 'Sure Nell, it's only business. Why not?' He looked around, suddenly realizing that Matt Brown had quietly slipped away, no doubt heading for the night express to Newcastle. Hope it's bloody late, he thought, and realized that Carlo Falconetti didn't seem to be around either.

286

'What you want us to do, Nell?' Connie seemed to be pleading.

'Just sign a few documents, put the real estate, the buildings into the hands of my company. Transfer them from Brothers Associates to the Death Nell Trust.' He gave an excited little yelp of delight. 'And you're wrong, I didn't scheme and plot and plan, Charlie. It just happened. I went home one morning and there he was, my brother Bartholomew, Little Bo Peep, sitting on my doorstep. Hadn't spoken to him in nine years and there he was, down and out, hitched all the way from Glasgow to see his brother, see if I could help him out with the pot of gold. End of the rainbow for Bartholomew Bellman. And it was. Worst place for him. Should never have come to me. Hours later, with money in his pocket, dressed in one of my jackets I took his head off, clickety-click, one stroke blood all over the auction and me. I was naked, could've taken my dick off with that axe. Terrible. He thought I was getting him a nice cup of cocoa, then he turned round and saw me:

> 'One, two! One, two! And through and through
> The vorpal blade went snicker-snack!
> He left it dead, and with its head
> He went galumphing back.'

'Thought that would be one of your favourites, the Jabberwock. No?'

'What's he on about, Charlie?'

'Fucked if I know, Con. Crazy.'

The little man's perky face lit up. 'Let's get the papers signed then. Get them out of the way, make out all the bricks and mortar to me.' He grabbed at the bulging music case, his badge of office and leaped nimbly from the stage on to the floor near the Balvak's table.

Carefully, Little Nell laid out documents in front of Charlie and Connie. 'You sign each of these in three places.' The grin again. Then pointing, 'There, there and there.' Capering around the table, looking like a dancing puppet.

Reluctantly Charlie took out his pen.

'It won't hurt,' Little Nell looked as though he was going to explode with excitement, like a child on Christmas Eve, waiting for Santa. 'Come on, come on, come on.'

And as if prearranged, the roof fell in. The door shattered open, there were shouts of 'Police. On the floor, everybody down.' And the club became alive, first one in Molly Abelard, brandishing a big Webley pistol and looking most determined.

It was almost a quarter past ten, about time for Suzie to take the walk along Old Compton Street, up past the old scout hut, see if kids were playing the fool up there. She told Cheesy Fowles where she was going and he asked if she wanted him to go along with her, keep her company, didn't take him up on it. She put on her white trench coat and the light blue beret, then went up to the front office, pulling on her new soft leather gloves, fully lined, bought at Derry & Toms, size 6, colour 'nigger brown', five-nineteen-three, a farthing short of six quid. Expensive.

She reached the front desk and there was Sergeant Knight – on night duty again, hilarious – talking to three smart and hard-looking men dressed in heavy clothes, two with mackintoshes and one, the tall one, in a greatcoat. They all wore trilby hats with snap brims, and still talking they looked up in unison as she approached.

'Sergeant Mountford?' The tall one touched his hat and Darkie Knight said, 'It appears you're the ranking officer in the station, Suzie. Mr Henderson's slipped out for a moment.' Inspector Ian Henderson was duty officer. In uniform.

'The famous Sergeant Mountford?' The tall one looked very steady and unsmiling, the kind of bloke you expected to bring bad news. Last year Suzie's name had been in the papers a lot and some of the old school hadn't take kindly to that. In fact they didn't like the idea of women investigating crime at all: didn't approve. This one was undoubtedly of the old school.

'More infamous than famous I'd have thought.' Suzie laughed, it was her way of turning things around.

'If you say so, Sergeant, who'm I to argue?' Straight and serious, not a line altering in his face, eyes grey and unforgiving as the North Sea. He didn't offer his hand as he introduced himself, 'DCS Topping, Internal Investigations Department.'

Well-well, she thought. The rubber heels.

'This is Inspector Rufus, and Sergeant Argyle.'

The inspector was older, moustache, and the air of one who had been passed over. The sergeant was the only one who smiled, and then only briefly, flicked on and off as though he was using some internal switch.

Suzie asked what she could do for them.

'We're looking for DCI Harvey.' No explanation, just the dour look that said they were on serious business.

'He's off duty, sir.'

'Well, he's not at home. We've just left his wife there. She told us he was here.'

'Oh.'

'Oh indeed, Sergeant.'

'I came on at half six, sir. DCI Harvey left at five. I was told he had to take his wife to a party in Wimbledon. That's what I was informed, sir.'

'By whom?'

'DC Fowles, sir.'

'Still on duty?'

'Yes.'

'Where?'

'Down in the CID office, sir.'

Topping said, 'Right we'll drop in on him.'

'It's down . . .'

'I know where it is. Thank you, Sergeant.' Almost all one word, deep and crisp and even. Freeze your arse off if you touched him.

The three officers strode off as though they were about to meet General Guderian's Nineteenth Panzer Corps and didn't think much of the Panzer Corps' chances.

'Little charmers,' Suzie spoke low to Knight.

'They're always the same, rubber heels,' Darkie said, looking concerned.

'Really, Big Toe been a naughty boy, has he?'

'What d'you think, Suzie. Never was one for sticking

289

to the rules. I'd better give Sammy Battescombe a ring at home.'

'That serious?'

'Nobody likes the rubber heels coming on to your manor. Reflects on everyone, don't it?'

Suzie nodded and headed towards the doors leading to the steps and the street, and had hardly got the door back when a grey Wolseley pulled up right in front of the station. Doors opened and Tommy Livermore climbed out with his large battered-looking Sergeant Billy Mulligan, who smiled up at Suzie. Brian was driving.

'Back inside, wherever you're supposed to be going, Sergeant,' Tommy said, obviously being careful because the job wasn't done yet. 'Come on, girl, back inside, fast, don't hang about.'

'The rubber heels're here, Chief,' she said quietly and saw him nod as he came back into the front counter area.

'Mr Livermore, sir,' Darkie Knight greeted Tommy. 'What a pleasant surprise to see you here, sir.'

'Not really.' Tommy was like a man batting at the crease putting the shutters up and playing everything safe, not taking any risks. 'Don't suppose your Mr Battescombe's in, or Mr Farquar, your station commander?'

'Mr Battescombe may be on his way, sir, We've got visitors from the IID.'

'Doesn't surprise me, sniffing out your rotten apple no doubt.'

'Sir,' said Darkie. What else could he say?

'Then who's your senior officer in the station.'

'You're looking at her, sir.' Suzie had the nerve to grin.

'Really? What is the Met coming to?' deep with their cover. 'Right, Sergeant Mountford. I did clear this with Mr Battescombe earlier but I'm calling in here to let you know that my people from the Yard are operating on your patch.'

'I knew Worrall and Cotter were here, sir . . .'

'Tip of the iceberg, Sergeant. My people, some of them armed, have been here for most of the evening. They've already arrested a club owner name of Joe Chalk and, at the moment they're raiding another club, Mona's Garden in Sherwood Street. Know it?'

'Heard of it, sir.'

'Right, well their job is to arrest Charles and Conrad Balvak and any of their associates. When they've pulled these unnecessary pieces of humanity, they'll take them along to Vine Street, where, eventually, I'll put them to the question.' Sounded better than 'interrogate them'. 'We are also looking for Neville Bellman,' he continued. 'Also known as Little Nell. One of the more unpleasant people living on your manor—'

'Sir, Neville Bellman's dead, sir. He was murdered, we found the body, decapitated, on—'

'No, sir, Little Nell is not dead, sir.' Tommy looked at her very seriously. 'Neville Bellman is alive and well and doing his dwarfish horrible deeds where he's always done them. They've had the body of the one you found out at Hendon. Examined the corpse there. Did numerous forensic tests. The prints don't match, the features are similar, as is the body, but what you have is Bartholomew Bellman, known in the north of this country as Little Bo Peep, an unsuccessful cat burglar, and he's as dead as a wooden Indian, a true deadhead. Little Nell is abroad and, I must presume, highly dangerous. Anyone who can cut off his brother's head, affix it on the blunt end of an assegai then take a bath with the head looking on has got to be suffering from that well-known psychological condition of dippy. Now, I must see how my boys and girls are getting on up Mona's Garden, so I'll bid you goodnight.' With that, Tommy Livermore, accompanied by a smirking Billy Mulligan, turned on his heel and headed towards the big doors with their glass inlays.

Plain-clothes police officers crowded into Mona's Garden, front and back, lead by Molly Abelard flanked by two particularly large uniformed officers, while the rear doors had been smashed in by DS Mike Stroud, a recent arrival in the Reserve Squad, now charged with bringing in Little Nell Bellman.

Ron Worrall and Laura Cotter had been on the Balvaks' backs all day, watching their flat near South Audley Street, then as time wore on, following them when they went down to Lexington Street and Joe Chalk's two clubs, and it was then that they called in the remainder of Tommy's lads, who came quietly into the area in ones and twos, in cars and bicycles but mostly on foot. Once there they followed the Balvaks because Tommy had told them to saturate the area. What Tommy didn't tell anybody was that his tip had come from the telephone call he'd mentioned to Billy Mulligan, and he didn't even tell him that the voice on the telephone had a very slight Italian accent, hardly detectable, background music really.

The Balvaks had made no secret of their presence: after all, who was going to follow them up to Mona's Garden? Both Charlie and Conrad considered their lives blessed by some magical ingredient making them above the law, untouchable, with charmed lives. They had been protected for so long, almost their whole lives, that they believed wholly in their invulnerability.

Now their nemesis had finally caught up with them. Four plain-clothes men surrounded the Balvaks, both of whom resisted. 'Get your hands off of me,' Charlie shouted as they held him and forced him on to the grubby carpet.

'What I done? Leave me alone!' Connie pushed, ineffectually at the people restraining him and snapping the handcuffs in place. 'What I done?'

'What you done?' Molly Abelard bellowed at him. 'What haven't you done? You've done the lot, Connie, and you'll be going up the dancers one bright morning to do the Tyburn jig with Mr Pierpoint.' And Connie started to wail like a child, crying to his brother to help him. 'I didn't do nothing, Charlie. Tell them. Tell them to stop. Helllllp me.'

When they found Jacky Russell's body, tucked away in the side room, Charlie began denying all knowledge. 'That wasn't anything to do with us. That was the Geordie bastard, Matt Brown. Just shot him dead. No reason. Mad-dog killer, that's what Matt Brown is. I'll give evidence when you get him: killed Cresswell Smith and that copper out near Newbury an' all. Gone off to catch the Newcastle train.'

Most of the other men and women, like the builders, Fast Eddie Ellis and the rest caught in Mona's Garden just quietly gave up. They'd had a lot of experience and knew what the law meant when a copper shouted, 'You're nicked!'

Of Little Nell there was no sign. As soon as the doors were broken in, Neville Bellman did a pitchpole somersaulting under the table at which he had been standing, supervising the Twins' signatures. Like many little people, Nell was an expert tumbler and from under that one table he squirmed his way under others, remaining in the end close to the wall, creeping out as the police were taking the Balvaks, their cohorts and those involved in the palace revolution out to the Black Marias waiting to take the prisoners off to Vine Street nick, where Tommy Livermore would be waiting to, as he would say, 'Put them to the question,' and in some cases charge them. In particular he was determined to see both Charlie and Connie Balvak charged with murder that night.

In fact Tommy was not sure which would please him more, the Balvaks on a murder charge or Anthony Harvey for aiding and abetting.

Suzie made her way slowly past the cordoned-off ruins that had once been the Admiral Duncan public house near the junction of Old Compton Street with Dean Street. It was now after eleven and nobody seemed to be about. Any kids would probably have gone home, but as she reached the old scout hut, Suzie was surprised to see that light was filtering out from half of the main double doors left partly ajar. She also thought she could detect movement from inside and hear coughs and the murmur of voices.

She put her hand on the door and stepped into the space between the street entrance in front of the solid big door that led into what was going to be the club and restaurant proper: the door in which Carlo Falconetti had trapped his fingers with the help of Porky Pine.

As she touched the metal handle she recalled something that Fordy O'Dell had asked, and thought she could even hear him inside her head.

You ever get frightened when you're doing your job, Suzie?
She swallowed, put her hand firmly on the door handle,
turned it and stepped inside.

The lights went out.

Twenty-Three

The lights went out and Suzie could smell the men, couldn't see them, but could hear them and feel them move closer, hear their breathing, smell their sweat and the tobacco smoke impregnating their clothes. Someone had thrown a cloth or bag over her head as she braced herself, getting into a defensive position, left foot forward, hands up, flat, left arm out, thumbs back to tighten the chopping edge of the hands, make them hard. It was cloth over her face, smelled like sacking.

She lashed out and felt her right hand brush harmlessly against clothing. Then they were on her. Five she thought, then reassessed to three, maybe four, already confused.

They overwhelmed her, hands taking hold, firmly smashing her back against the wall, someone's forearm across her throat. Grunting sounds, nobody speaking until – 'If yer don't struggle yer won't get hurt.' She didn't recognize the voice, wasn't quite sure of the direction it came from even, and as the men took hold of her and lowered her to the floor she knew what they were about to do.

She had been terrified of this happening, fearful since in the sixth form at school, when another girl, Beryl Trotter, had been accosted by a farm hand while walking alone in the woods near St Helen's School on a summer afternoon. The nuns warned their charges to be on the lookout, beware of a lone man. They started to go out only in pairs and the nuns failed to delineate the danger. 'You have to be very careful,' Sister Martha Mary told Suzie. 'Men have nasty habits and they can ruin a girl for life if they've a mind.' Suzie thought it strange, nuns talking about habits. One of their jokes was of a nun coming in out of bad weather and saying, 'I must get out of this dirty old habit.'

Beryl Trotter never told them what had actually happened, or how a man could ruin a girl for life. At school nobody talked about S-E-X and naturally there were inaccurate rumours. A bizarre mythology grew up until the true facts were revealed, often relatively late in life.

They began undressing her and she thought right, the worst thing you can do is fight. Lie back, don't enjoy but at least try to relax because it'll be less painful. Her mind momentarily touched the horror, would they make her pregnant, or pass on a disease.

They stripped her naked, held her down on the rough carpet and raped her one at a time, hard and brutal so that she tried to divorce herself from the tearing, the violent thrusting and the pain.

She didn't think of England to get her mind away from what was happening. Instead she tried to listen to popular songs in her head. Before the first man had finished with her she had gone through *It's a lovely day tomorrow, Tomorrow is a lovely day*, and *I've got my eyes on you, I'm checking on all you do from A to Zee.*

The second man now started and she had to try to break through the pain, not just the obvious hurt, but the bruising to her arms and legs where they held her. The second one had problems and, she thanked heaven, it was over before it had hardly begun. She only got through one verse of 'The Quartermaster's Stores' –

> *There were rats, rats, big as blooming cats*
> *In the stores, in the stores.*
> *There was ham, ham mixed up with the jam*
> *In the Quartermaster's Stores.*
> *My eyes are dim, I cannot see,*
> *I have not brought my specks with me.*

Finished. Off. Momentary relief, then pain again and the sense of being violated, of having been made filthy, and it was difficult now to get her mind off what was happening. The third one tried to kiss her and she spat, twisted her head and tried to bite him, but this made him more ferocious.

It's not happening. Get your head out of this. Listen to the music and hear the voices singing:

I know we stood and talked like this before
Looked at each other in the same way then
But I can't remember where or when.
Things that have happened for the first time,
seem to be happening again . . .

He was thrusting angrily, breath above her, rasping, then he sagged, heavy on her body.

Another? She had thought three would be all, but no, either they were having seconds or . . . Pull away, get your brain somewhere else, Suzie or you'll go mad. She now felt totally filthy. Already started to hate her own body. Get off . . .

You smile, and the angels sing.

What's this? She knew him, but didn't understand why . . . Knew this bastard. Why, though? How?

An apple for the teacher, will always do the trick

Teacher? Why? She could smell him. Peppermint. Peppermint not quite blotting out the whisky . . .

Any time you're Lambeth way
Any evening any day
You'll find them all . . .

Far away, an engine, car doors slamming, a crash and the sound of footsteps nearby. Sudden panic. Hands releasing her. A shout. The weight on her violently come away as though her tormentor had been dragged off her.

'Stand just where you are.' She had heard the voice before. Recently. Topping, the DCS from the rubber heels. 'Get me a WDC or a uniformed girl.' She could tell that he'd turned his head away, 'And ring for an ambulance. Now, you idiot. This minute.' Shouting.

She began to drag the piece of sacking from her head as someone dropped her trench coat over her, dazzled by the lights, screwing up her eyes, able to see, she heard Topping speak again.

297

'Anthony James Harvey, I am arresting you for common assault, and for attempting to pervert the course of justice. Get some cuffs on him, Sergeant Argyle.'

'Big Toe' Harvey stood near enough for her to touch, fumbling with the front of his trousers, his face drained, a yellowish white. There were other people in the room looking in every direction except towards her: Cheesy Fowles, Bob Paine, two uniformed men she only knew by sight. And there were noises off, shufflings out of sight.

Raising his voice, calling to people in the next room, Topping asked, 'What you found out there, Rufus?'

'We've got three, sir. I think one's already legged it. Big bloke.'

'Porky Pine,' Cheesy said. 'Local villain. Knew him well, sir. He's on our books and I saw him running fit to bust, sir.'

Suzie grasped the edge of her coat, pulled it up to her throat and threw up, vomited over the carpet. Ashamed and miserable she stayed there, not looking up, for hours it seemed, the men not really knowing what to say. Then somebody shepherded WPC Ruby Newman, Night Duty Clerk at West End Central, into the room.

'Sarge,' she came and held Suzie's head, wiped her mouth, cradled her. 'Sarge. It'll be okay, Sarge. Don't worry, it'll be okay.'

Suzie said, 'I want my Mum.'

They wouldn't let her walk to the ambulance, though she was quite capable of doing so, argued with them, kept saying, 'I'm okay.'

'Never walk if you can ride,' one of the ambulance men said.

'Or stand when you can sit,' she tried to smile but it was difficult. The air outside was good. What I needed, she thought. Nice lungful of fresh air, but I'd also like a fag, asked Ruby to get hers in her shoulderbag, and the ambulance men didn't mind.

She turned her head, as they were carrying her to the ambulance, and through the light mist she saw a grey-white van, creeping along, trying to find the turning, it would be Greek Street. She thought nothing of it.

In the front of his van, with the big fitted cushion that allowed him to see out of the windscreen, Little Nell thought: Hello, what's going on here? Something's up. Something's happened to that tart of a Woman Detective Sergeant always wanted to cause grief to Porky Pine and the others, bloody Balvaks. What's happened to her then? Drive around a bit, they'll take her to the Middlesex. That'd be handy. He was looking for a body. It was late now and he was out. The Ghoul was out and about. The Ghoul smiled his wicked smile, and used the clutch and accelerator that were lengthened specially for him, drove off, knew what he'd do.

Twenty-Four

They were kind to her, the ambulance men and the nurses, when they got her into the Middlesex Hospital.

'I'm okay,' she said. 'Really okay. I can walk. I want to go home.'

'You need cleaning up a bit and you'll need to rest,' a female doctor told her, looked younger than Suzie, the medical profession had taken to cradle-snatching. 'What I need is a nice warm bath.'

'You'll get one, and if you're certain and we're certain we'll let you go home, but they're sending someone over to take a statement.'

The child doctor went to work and fiddled about, a nurse helping her, Suzie's feet in the stirrups. Some of it the doctor told her would 'cause a little discomfort'. That was medical code meaning it was going to hurt. The doctor was called Plumb. 'Felicity Plumb, isn't it ghastly?' she said.

'What happens if the bastards've made me pregnant?'

'Come and see me,' Dr Plumb whispered, the nurse had gone. 'We've washed you out pretty thoroughly, but come here and ask for me. I'll suggest a decoke in any case, D & C but not tonight. If there's a problem that should fix it, I'll make an appointment for you in about two or three weeks. How're you really feeling? In yourself I mean.'

'Pretty bloody.'

The doc muttered some platitudes about her probably being in shock at the moment, but things would improve. 'You're a sensible enough girl.'

'What's sensible got to do with it? Three men I've never seen have schtuped me, then one I loathed did it the fourth time. I'd like to castrate the bastard.'

300

'Know what you mean. Can't be done legally, more's the pity because that's the sentence I'd chose for any rapist.' She paused and then said something about rape not being easy to prove, and that the police appeared to discourage victims. 'That's got to change.'

'And what if it's the other thing?'

'What other thing?'

'What if one of them's got the clap?'

'Thank heaven for penicillin.'

'You know what he said, the DCI whom I loathed? When the arresting officer asked him if he had anything to say? He said, "It was only a bit of fun." Then he told them he thought I'd probably enjoyed it.'

'You seeing anyone? I mean have you got a sex life? I know you weren't a virgin before this.'

Suzie said yes. Yes, she had a regular sex life. She thought people like the doctor may be shocked when she told her.

'You know what?' Felicity Plumb said. 'There are an awful lot of unmarried people out there with regular sex lives. The public moralists would be horrified if they had the true figures. Sometime in the future the historians're going to say there was little sex in the first half of the twentieth century because of the strong moral tone of the time and because girls were afraid of getting pregnant. Rubbish. Everyone's at it like stoats. They just don't talk about it that much.' She added that, to help matters, the VD figures were going through the roof. 'Up one hundred and thirteen per cent this year. Gloomy thought.'

'Will you come and cut that bastard's balls off for me? The one that did this.'

The doctor nodded and made a chopping motion with her hand, and Suzie went off to have a long hot bath, told herself she'd have another when she got home. If they let her home.

The officer who came to take her statement was Shirley Cox, her old mate from Camford days, now with the Reserve Squad under Tommy Livermore. Her first words were: 'Tommy's doing his nut. Says he'll be over as soon as he can. Really, Suzie, he's distraught . . .'

'Tell him I'm going home soon.'

'He's in a bad way, I mean it. Very worried about you.'

She gave a little laugh. 'I gather you've been spying for us. Tommy's talking commendations and stuff like that. Are you really okay, Suzie?'

'Yeah, it's a bugger,' Suzie said, then, with a hint of her old self, 'Worse things happen at sea, though. I can't think what, but that's what my mum'll probably say.'

'How are you really, Suzie?'

'That's what everyone wants to know. How do you think I feel? I feel like shit – literally. I don't ever want to see a man again and I'm not terribly impressed with my own body.' She knew there were tears just below the surface. 'Come on, Shirl, let's get the paperwork done.'

Shirley asked all the right questions, did the job, got Suzie to sign the statement. 'The bastard,' was her comment about Big Toe Harvey: another member for the anti-Harvey fan club.

'I've got to get back,' Shirley said. They needed every spare hand in the Squad to deal with what she called 'severe overcrowding in the cells at Vine Street'.

What should she tell the Chief? That I'll be out of here tonight with luck. Shirley told her again what a state Tommy was in. 'Oh, yes, they've caught up with some of the missing blokes: the Geordie Matt Brown, Porky Pine and the other lad who was mixed up with you.'

The name Moke meant nothing to her and she reckoned he was just a hired cock, even managed a smile at that, but things were dark and unpleasant under the surface.

They hadn't got the dwarf, Little Nell.

'Tell Tommy congratulations and I'll probably see him later.' She could trust Shirley.

Ten minutes after Shirley Cox left, Felicity Plumb came in, interrogated her about whether she really felt well enough to go home. 'If I don't let you, I suppose I'll never hear the end of it. We'll take you in an ambulance.'

Suzie said no, she'd ring West End Central and get them to pick her up. She was actually going to ring Vine Street nick and see if Brian would take her. Safer that way.

Couldn't get through to Tommy, but she finally asked for Brian and he came on straightaway.

'I'm just sitting here cooling my heels,' he told her. 'Yes, I'll come straight up for you. Ten minutes.'

'I'll be outside waiting.' She checked herself out with the nurse, then went to stand directly in front on the main doors, where a lot of cars were already parked right across the wide courtyard. She lit a cigarette and saw a pair of hooded headlights coming from near the entrance that led in from Mortimer Street. It wasn't Brian, it was a grey-white van, like a GPO van but sprayed a lighter colour. She couldn't see anyone driving, even moved a couple of paces towards it, looking over into dark Mortimer Street watching for Brian in the Wolseley.

Nell revelled in his own cleverness, letting the van coast to a halt, everything ready, him lying almost flat in his seat, easing the door open and sliding out, couldn't be seen.

He pranced around the van, silent as a worm, slipped the rear doors open and got the pad of gauze, crossed his fingers that his luck would hold. Now, get the body, he picked up his long piece of four by two and pulled it out of the van.

Suzie took a long drag on the cigarette and turned, walking two paces then turning again, thought she saw something move deep in the dark, then something hit her hard behind the knees. Then again and she went sprawling. A strong arm came round her throat and there was something over her nose and mouth. She reached up and tried to grab whatever it was because she couldn't breath and there was a terrible burning around her lips and nose. Then the world went away and she fell into darkness.

Little Nell was exceptionally strong, exercised every day, used the horizontal and parallel bars when he could and his tumbling routines kept him strong in the shoulders. He got his hands under Suzie's arms and heaved her the four feet or so to the back of the van, then hoiked her inside, had the handcuffs ready for her and drove away with her rolling around in the back of the van, drove to the far end of the courtyard in front of the hospital. Stopped there, got out, went round to the rear of the van again, got in, lifted Suzie by her shoulders and started to feed her the special drink he kept in a lemonade bottle all ready in the back. 'There, there,' he crooned. 'You had a nasty

303

fall. Soon be better. Drink this. Make you feel all better.' Never failed. After the chloroform they felt like a clean drink and he had it all ready, complete with the sleeping powder that he bought from a bent nurse at St Mary's, Paddington. Soon she was sleeping like a baby and he was able to tie her ankles together and secure her with soft rope so that she wouldn't roll around: the soft rope he bought from the magic shop, Davenports in New Oxford Street. Used to go in there, watch Gilly Davenport make all manner of things vanish behind the counter.

Nell got in the front and drove off into Mortimer Street, kept a steady pace all the way, drove with great care, didn't want an accident with a body on board. Neville Bellman. Little Nell. Now the Ghoul out doing his ghoulish work, feeding on bodies, getting strength from them.

When Suzie woke she was lying on a stone floor in the dark. There was a light showing some stone steps into the place where she lay and it was very cold and someone was banging with a steady rhythm. There seemed to be moving light as well. She turned her head and it hurt, her neck was on fire she thought and she saw two lanterns nearby, on the floor. They were the cause of the flickering light that threw odd moving shadows across the chamber or whatever it was. Against one rough wall she saw a huge shadow moving, a misshapen little man, big in the shadow, wielding a pick axe. Clong-clong-clong, went right through her head. She knew who it was and couldn't stop the song turning in her head. *We dig-dig-dig-dig-dig-dig-dig – In a mine, where a million diamonds shine.*

Tommy Livermore was doing an initial interview with Connie Balvak in an interview room at Vine Street nick when the telephone rang for the umpteenth time. He had a constable in the room and another just outside the door.

'I am not to be disturbed, even if you're the king. Go away,' he barked into the phone. Brian, at the other end said, 'Sir, I think you'll want to hear this. It's about Suzie Mountford. Very serious, sir.' He was outside with Molly Abelard in tow.

Brian had never known Mr Livermore so quiet, listening

304

with such a serious concentration, listened carefully about Suzie disappearing, not being at the Middlesex when Brian went to pick her up, and the possibilities of Little Nell making off with her. 'Some of the lads up West End Central went to the house in Lexington Street, where the murder took place, the head on the assegai, all the papers full of it. No dice, Chief. Place is empty from attic to cellars. Nobody has a clue.'

Tommy frowned, asked himself who'd know. What sort of place would Little Nell go to? Relatives? Friends?

Molly looked up. 'Connie,' she said. 'Isn't Nell supposed to have had a relationship with Connie Balvak?'

'I'm just getting to know him,' Dandy Tom's eyebrows went up and Molly asked if he would like her assistance. 'If anyone would know he would,' Molly said. Privately she was thinking that she would beat it out of him if she had to.

'Connie?' Tommy sat opposite the little thug, knowing he had killed at least one person, and could prove it. 'Connie, we need your help. It's important.'

A worm of cunning moved in Connie Balvak's eyes. 'Important? Important enough for you to help me if I help you?'

'Quite possibly,' lied DCS Livermore.

Molly said, 'I'm sure Mr Livermore'll be very understanding if you can help.'

'Ah.' He nodded, big slow movements of the head. 'My brother says they'll hang me,' his eyes locked on to Tommy as though pleading. 'Says my only chance is insanity. You think I'm an insanity, Mr Livermore?'

'If you help me, Connie all things are possible.'

'I have a wireless set in my cell?'

'Anything within reason, Conrad.'

'What you want to know?'

'Connie, you know Neville Bellman very well, don't you?'

'Little Nell? I know him better'n anyone. Little Nell liked me a lot. Tell you the truth, Little Nell was like you might say, the brains of our business. He had business vacuum.'

'Acumen?' Tommy tried.

'That's the one,' Connie nodded.

Molly stepped in. 'Little Nell had a house in Lexington Street, didn't he?'

'Yeah, of course, Nell had two houses, the one in Lexington Street, then the one . . . Now where was that? He never got rid of it. Big old place, yes. Out the other side of King's Cross, off the Caledonian Road. Big place, near your Blessed Sacrament Primary, your Roaming Catholic place; use to belong to them. Near Copenhagen Street, big place, had it's own lawn. The lot. We used to have larks there, I remember once . . .'

'What was it called, Connie?'

'What, Nell's house? Called a funny name. Host Hall, that was the name . . .'

Molly slipped from the room.

'Yeah, Host Hall. Once we was playing a game of hide and seek there, big old rambling house it was. Got attics and a big old cellar: creepy down there, I got lost in it playing hide and seek. Fell asleep. Lost for nearly two days.'

'Really, Connie. How interesting.'

Then Molly came back, signalled Tommy, who courteously told Connie he'd see him again tomorrow and followed Molly out of the room.

'We ride the bell, Chief?' Brian asked. He meant could they go full out through the blackout with the bell ringing and the blue lights flashing.

'You can fire broadsides as long as we find Suzie. You know where this place is?'

'Used to belong to the RCs, a kind of parish house, yes. Host House. I've been on the blower to the local nick. They offered help. Said they'd send someone round. They knew Nell owned it. Quite a favourite round there is Nell. Doesn't have form there according to the bloke I spoke with.'

'Really?' Tommy was running to keep up with Brian, 'Little Nell: whiter than the whitewash on the wall, eh?' he said.

The clang of the pick on stony ground stopped suddenly and the shadow moved, saw Suzie turn her head. 'Awake are you,' his voice high, squeaky. 'Not long now. I've got the paving stone up. Now I've got to dig. Hard work, but I'll have it done in an hour or so.' A little echoing laugh. Creepy. 'Then there'll

306

be a nice place for you to rest. You'll be very comfortable. I've never had any complaints and you're in good company. Not long.' He had started to dig with a big shovel.

Little Nell, she thought. But Little Nell's dead. Am I dead? Then she heard the noise from far off. A ringing.

'Who the hell's that, this time in the morning?' Nell sounding aggravated, irritated.

As well as the bell there was knocking now. Nell threw the shovel back on to the rectangle of earth from where he'd pried off a stone slab, and he hurried to the steps. 'Knock, knock, knock,' he said. 'Here's a knocking indeed,' as he went up the twisting stone steps.

Suzie tried to turn. She was bound fast, trussed like a turkey and it would soon be Christmas. Her head was like a balloon filled with angry wasps and she felt sick again. She vaguely remembered the van and someone making her drink. She remembered the rape and wanted to scream.

There were sounds from above and Nell came clattering down the steps again. 'Bloody cheek! Bloody cheek! Sending a copper out to see if I was okay. Well, he'll rest in peace now. You'll have a mate in the ground with you, Sergeant M. Another copper. Two peas in a pod.' He picked up the shovel again and started to dig.

Brian turned the bell off when they reached the Caledonian Road. 'It's on the left here, that's where we turn. On the left before we get to Copenhagen Street.' Molly was navigating. 'Shouldn't be much further. Here. Here, Brian, go left now and it should be a hundred yards or so down on the right. There.'

There were old stone gateposts, incongruous in this area, pineapples on top of them, and an overgrown path that led between buildings then out to run beside a stretch of lawn, the house looming ahead.

'Big old place,' Tommy whispered.

'There's a light in the hall,' Molly had braced her feet against the floor, hand on the door ready to leap out.

Dawn was not far off, a grey wash in the sky, the house sinister in silhouette. Brain braked, cut the engine and they were out on to old gravel and weeds, closing the doors quietly.

The front door was half open, old green flaking paint and dirty stained glass.

'Jesus,' said Brian as he saw the body.

'The local gendarme,' Tommy said. 'Poor devil.'

The uniformed constable lay on his face, the blood pooling out from his neck, the instrument of his death – a thing that looked like a cutlass – thrown to one side. There were similar weapons; axes, swords, daggers and shields on the walls of the hall, stretching away past the stairs to an open door. Flames seemed to dance on the other side of the door as though an evil tribe of spirits were cavorting below, down the steps, and echoing up was the harsh sound of metal on earth and stone: regular and steady. Above that a thin, reedy voice singing –

> *'There'll always be an England*
> *And England shall be free*
> *If England means as much to you*
> *As England means to me.'*

Molly went forward, then Tommy Livermore touched her shoulder. 'I should go down first,' he whispered.

'You carrying, Chief?'

He shook his head and stepped back. Molly was a marksman and licensed to carry a weapon on Tommy's say so. She carried most of the time: no one had the heart to stop her. She still had the weapon Tommy had authorized when they took Sybil down to Newbury.

They began their descent, hugging the cold damp wall, the singing growing louder and turning into a strange dirge –

> *'Red, white and blue*
> *If England shall be free*
> *Means to me –'*

And they saw the shadow of Little Nell, grotesque against the stone wall, bending, digging, throwing the earth and stones into a pile, breathing heavily and working away with a manic energy, digging an obvious grave in front of which Suzie lay, so still that she could be dead.

'Christ Almighty!' Tommy said, loud enough to be heard.

Little Nell straightened up, 'What you doing here?' He sounded calm, piping voice, aggressive.

'We've come to take you home, Nell,' Molly called, slipping her pistol from its holster. 'You're to stop what you're doing, put down that spade and come over here.'

'Not on your Nellie,' he laughed, the peculiar high-pitched laugh, a squeak. 'You're on private property here. You're on holy ground as well. I care for these people and I do them great honour.'

'Molly! Tommy!' Suzie called weakly, and Tommy let out a sigh of relief.

'Come on, Nell, don't mess me about,' Molly levelled the revolver, and Little Nell jumped forward, standing over Suzie's prostrate form.

'And don't mess me around either whoever you are. This one has to join the others,' and he raised the heavy spade, lifted it up and started to bring it down in a great sweep . . .'

Molly fired, two shots, the noise huge in the ears, as Nell brought down the spade and Suzie summoned enough strength to roll away from the blow.

Nell shrieked a great cry of frustration and fury as the blood bloomed from his chest, then toppled back into the grave he had been making: a tangle of little arms and legs.

They sent for an ambulance and she was taken to the London Clinic. 'My treat, heart,' Tommy said.

Once more they cleaned her up, wrapped her in blankets, put her to bed and gave her a warm sweet drink and something else, an injection.

'You don't get out of here until I say so.' Tommy Livermore laying down the law.

'I feel like shit,' she said. Then, 'Tommy, we have to talk. I have to tell you . . .'

'Of course you do, heart. Yes, we'll have a good talk when you're feeling better.'

She thought, yes, that would be best. Deep down she was still confused, didn't know what to do about Fordy or Tommy. Didn't want to know. Have to talk to Fordy as well. Not today though. Later. What was it Daddy used to say? Joking? Always put off today what you can leave until tomorrow.

Sounded good to her.